"*I* need your brightness, your laughter. I need to feel you wrapped around me. I need you."

That bewitching voice vibrated against her skin as his lips nuzzled the sensitive area just behind her ear. "You will be my salvation."

Blaise's breath locked in her throat as his mouth skimmed hot and open along her neck. She wanted his kisses; her body wanted the pleasure of his touch. The sensual assault of his lips made her feel wanton, made her skin tingle with the hot flush of desire. She closed her eyes helpelssly, her body trembling.

"Are you cold?" he asked. "Let me warm you, my love."

"No," she whispered, "this is madness. We are . . . too different."

"Yes. Sweet madness . . . "

D1023775

By Nicole Jordan

Paradise Series
MASTER OF TEMPTATION
LORD OF SEDUCTION
WICKED FANTASY
FEVER DREAMS

Notorious Series
THE SEDUCTION
THE PASSION
DESIRE
ECSTASY
THE PRINCE OF PLEASURE

Other Novels
THE LOVER
THE WARRIOR
TOUCH ME WITH FIRE

TOUCH ME WITH FIRE

A Novel

NICOLE JORDAN

BALLANTINE BOOKS • NEW YORK

2006 Ivy Books Mass Market Edition

Published in the United States by Ivy Books, an imprint of The Random House Publishing Group, a division of Random House, Inc., New York.

Ivy Books and colophon are trademarks of Random House, Inc.

Originally published in mass market in the United States by Avon Books, a division of the Hearst Corporation, New York, in 1993.

ISBN-10 0-8041-1987-2
ISBN-13 978-0-8041-1987-0

Cover illustration: Aleta Rafton

Printed in the United States of America

www.ballantinebooks.com

OPM 9 8 7 6 5 4 3 2 1

To those not-so-Turkish Delights, Jennara and eluki,
with heartfelt thanks for all the years of
commiseration, hand-holding, and worldly advice.

> . . . his form had yet not lost
> All her original brightness, nor appeared
> Less than Archangel ruined . . .
>
> JOHN MILTON
> *Paradise Lost*

Prologue

Through hooded eyes he watched the woman undress in the moonlight, his carnal hunger tempered by pain. His right thigh, mauled by a volley of cannonshot six weeks before, ached dully, although not enough to make him refuse his hostess's late-night visit to his bedside. He would not ask her to leave. It would be rude and pointlessly cruel to reject her after all she had done for him these past weeks.

Naked except for the heavy bandage on his thigh and the cool sheet drawn up to his waist, Julian, Lord Lynden reclined against the pillows. Waiting.

With a whisper of black silk, she let the dressing gown fall to the floor, revealing lush, full breasts, with nipples peaked in anticipation. "Do I please you, *señor*?" Pilar asked in soft, throaty Spanish. She moved toward him slowly, her dark eyes shimmering with sexual awareness.

Although not fluent in her language, he comprehended her meaning and replied politely, "Very much so, *querida*. You are exquisite."

He did not greatly exaggerate. The silver light flooding through the open patio doors spilled over her nude body, turning it mysterious and pale. He knew that voluptuous body with a fair measure of intimacy now. This was not the first time Pilar had played the ministering angel, slipping secretly into his bedchamber at night to comfort

1

and soothe him—and to indulge in a few stolen hours of forbidden passion.

The first time had been a surprise. She was a highborn Spanish lady, older than he by several years—a beautiful widow, lonely and hot-blooded. This *hacienda* was her home. Despite the fact that he had helped drive the conquering French troops from her country, she hadn't been eager to let a wounded British cavalry officer billet there, not until she'd learned he was a war hero and an *aristocratico* as well. Even then she'd demanded an extravagant sum for his accommodation.

The cost had been worth it. The opportunity to recover from his injuries here rather than in a wretched field hospital had undoubtedly saved his life. And the attentive personal care he had received from the lovely widow had been an unexpected bonus.

Demonstrating that same attentiveness now, she climbed into his bed to kneel naked on the mattress at his uninjured side. Her gaze was fixed on his lower body, on his arousal rigidly defined by the pale linen sheet.

"You please me also," she murmured with a seductive smile.

Reaching for her hand, he kissed her fingertips lingeringly, one by one, while he held her heated gaze. "I fear the honors must again fall to you," he apologized. Before his wounding, he could claim an advanced degree of sexual prowess, but although his body was mending, he was not in the best condition to perform any demanding feats of athleticism.

His hostess responded by reaching up to touch tenderly the savage wound that slashed across his right cheekbone all the way to his temple. "Leave everything to me, *vida mía*." Her throaty whisper resonated with promise as she brushed back a tousled lock of his pale golden hair. "I will help you to forget your dark dreams."

Doubting, he remained silent.

The warm, moon-splashed room grew hushed. The woman bent over him, scattering kisses along his throat, his collarbone, his bare shoulder, while her hands traced the smooth contours of his naked chest. Before his injuries had weakened and scarred him, he had been endowed with a beautiful male body, graceful and tautly muscled, well-toned by years of sporting endeavors, honed to steel by the rigors of a military campaign. His lover's roving, slowly gliding hands expressed her appreciation now, lingering on his belly, flat and hard, circling his lean hips, drawing down the sheet that covered him.

She drew a sharp breath as she boldly revealed his rigid manhood, her gaze riveted by the sight. In the pale light his erection stood blatant, powerfully formed.

"*Magnífico.*" Almost reverently, she took his hard, straining arousal into her hand and caressed it with long, lingering strokes.

Shuddering, he closed his eyes. His desire was insistent and sharp now, dominating the diminishing ache in his thigh.

She continued to tease him, moving her hand slowly up . . . then down. At length, she lowered her mouth to his chest, arousing him further with tongue and lips. When she encountered a hard male nipple, she bit lightly with her teeth.

Reaching up, he closed his fingers urgently on her shoulders, drawing her against him in a wordless command.

She mounted him then. With careful regard for his bandaged thigh, she settled one leg over his hips and lowered herself onto his pulsing arousal, her gasp of pleasure loud in the heated quiet of the room as he penetrated her moist entrance.

"Slowly . . ." he murmured. His hands moved to cup her full white breasts with their tight brown nipples. Restraining her momentarily, he raised his good left knee and braced it against her back to keep her from sliding onto his wounded thigh. "Now," he ordered as he surged deeper into her sleek, hot passage.

Her dark, passion-hazed glance locking with his, she obeyed, riding him slowly, clenching her inner muscles

with practiced expertise, her honeyed silkiness holding
him tight.

He tensed with mingled pleasure and pain. Shifting his
hands, he grasped the smooth mounds of her buttocks
and hauled her closer; at the same time he arched his
hips upward, swelling and probing deep within her.

Her eyes shut. Her mouth went slack. Soon she threw
her head back, and the room grew loud with the ragged
moans that tore from her throat. As he rhythmically thrust
into her, she dug her nails into his shoulders, whimpering
and writhing and grinding her hips against his.

A few moments later, the flame-hot woman above him
cried out and her body jerked in a wrenching shudder.
Closing his eyes, Julian let the searing release flood
through him in a rush of sensation.

Eventually he regained awareness and found her lying
limply on his chest. A thin sheen of perspiration covered
his body, while pain throbbed in his right thigh. With
care, he rolled onto his uninjured side, easing her onto
the mattress.

In the dim light her eyes were half-lidded in languorous
contentment, her pale flesh suffused with the afterglow of
passion.

Solicitously he brushed his lips against her damp temple. "Forgive me, *querida*, for being unable to pleasure
you as you deserve."

She opened her heavy lids, her slow smile sated and
amused. "I doubt that I could bear any more pleasure,"
she replied in thickly accented English. Her glance
dropped below his waist. "A wound could not slow
a magnificent man like you. It is fortunate, however, that the injury was not slightly higher and to
the left."

He laughed, a pained sound as the ravaged muscles
in his thigh cramped in protest. With clenched teeth he
waited until the spasm passed. Then he kissed Pilar's
fingers once more and shut his eyes, wondering if he
would be able to sleep without the drugging effects of
laudanum.

He forced himself to think of something other than his injury. Home. His family seat in England. Lush pastures, ripe fields, thick woodlands teeming with game. His longing to see the cool green country of his birth was like a physical ache inside him . . . an ache that turned to fire as he drifted into a doze . . .

The searing heat originated in his right thigh and speared throughout his body, echoing sharply in his right temple and cheekbone. Half blinded by the blood streaming from his brow, he tried to lift himself from the rocky ground and nearly screamed in agony.

Where in God's name was he? Who was he?

Recognition of the tumult came slowly . . . the explosive booms of cannon, the crackle of musket fire, the moans of dying men, the screams of horses. An acrid black smoke obscured his vision, but through the haze he caught glimpses of devastation. The hillside was dark with dust and blood, splashed with the scarlet and blue of shredded uniforms.

Ah, yes. This hell was Spain. Vitoria, he remembered. A battlefield . . . one of many he'd seen during the four years since he'd condemned himself to this war. He was Julian Morrow, Sixth Viscount Lynden. Lieutenant Colonel Lord Lynden, second-in-command of the Fifteenth Hussars. His wife was Caroline . . . No . . . Caroline was dead. He had killed her. This hell was his penance for causing her death.

His mission . . . to lead a cavalry charge against a French divisional battery. He remembered succeeding, and yet he must have taken a volley of cannonfire at close range.

He lay where he'd fallen, on a rocky hillside, surrounded by the piteous moans of wounded men and horses. The battle still raged around him. Mortar shells shrieked overhead and burst, the thunder of artillery fire rolling and echoing around the hilltops. The suffocating stench of powder smoke burned his nostrils and throat, while his mouth filled with the coppery tang of blood . . . the acid taste of fear.

Fear. He was afraid to die.

No, not afraid. Simply not eager. He wanted to live after all. Surprising, considering how zealously he had courted Death for the past four years. He truly wanted to live. Ironic to discover it only now, when Death stared him in the face. His right thigh was a mangled, bloody mass of torn flesh.

He knew he should try to stanch the flow of blood, but the effort was too overwhelming. Abandoning the struggle, he slipped back into oblivion . . .

Voices, snatches of conversation drifted toward him in the darkness. Something about his leg. He tried to open his eyes, but he couldn't manage to weave his way through the labyrinth of pain and fever fogging his mind. The harsh pain dulled his senses, weighted his eyelids . . . while images floated in the fuzzy corridors of his mind . . . haunting images of Caroline . . . her lifeless body lying amid the stone ruins. He let himself slip back into the dark world where the pain was not so fierce.

"Please, *señor,* lie still. You will hurt yourself."

He came awake with a start. At first he didn't recognize the darkened room, but the dense night air was warm with the musky scent of lovemaking, and the cool hand on his brow was one he remembered from his weeks of convalescence. The Spanish widow. His hostess.

"You had the dream again, no?"

He closed his eyes, trying to ignore the question, trying to shut out the haunting memories.

"What are these dreams, *vida mía,* that torment you so? Who is this Caroline? You cry her name in your sleep."

He didn't answer, yet his thoughts would not be silent. *Young, beautiful, unfaithful Caroline. As blond and blue-eyed as he was himself. A member of the nobility as he was, raised to wealth and privilege, indulged and fawned over. They made the ideal couple, until their last fierce argument had ended in her death . . .*

The woman beside him ran her tongue lightly, provocatively, along his naked shoulder, and slid her arm around his lean waist. Pouting as if jealous, she glanced up at him, her dark eyes flaring hot with a familiar emotion.

"I shall drive away your nightmares," she murmured, pressing her nude, voluptuous body against his in an unmistakable invitation.

He had not planned on taking her again tonight. Certainly not with such force. Definitely not with her beneath him, a position which placed a severe strain on his healing thigh. But she was a willing body. And she had black hair, not blond like Caroline's. She could help him forget, at least momentarily.

Her gasp was loud and startled when he rolled over her and plunged his rising maleness between her open legs, but then her eyes widened in pleasure as she caught his savage rhythm.

Roughly he buried his hands in her hair and drove into her, slamming his body against hers, thrusting hard, over and over again, as if he could exorcise the devils in his soul. In response she clung to him, whimpering raggedly, her climax coming swiftly, with racking power.

His own violent release followed shortly. His breathing was harsh, his body glistening with sweat when he gave a final shudder and collapsed against her, his leg wound throbbing like fire.

Far from being offended by his fierceness, though, she stroked his spine soothingly, offering comfort, whispering endearments in soft Spanish, until he eased his body away and rolled onto his back with a groan. "Forgive me, *querida*."

"There is nothing to forgive." But instead of drifting back to sleep, she kissed the damp skin of his shoulder and slid out of bed in order to dress. "I must go. It will not do to have the servants find me in your bed."

Julian made no protest.

When he was alone once more, he lay there and stared at the ceiling, remembering the past, thinking of the events four years ago that had brought him here.

Murder. That was the allegation whispered behind his back.

He was never officially charged, of course, since there was no proof. He was too wealthy, too wellborn, and too high-ranking to be arrested for murder on only circumstantial evidence. Lady Lynden's death was ruled the result of a riding accident. Yet the rumors, fanned by her lover's grief, persisted.

The rumors were not unfounded; Julian had been unable to refute them with any degree of honesty. He was to blame. He had killed his wife.

In the end it was his own guilt that had decided him. To punish himself, he had gone off to war—bought a commission in the cavalry and joined the Peninsular Campaign in Portugal and Spain against Napoleon's invading forces.

Not caring whether he lived or died was a decided asset in war. Ironically, his indifference had often been mistaken for courage, his reckless deeds hailed as heroic. He had driven himself relentlessly, desperately, only to discover he could never toil hard enough, never ride swiftly enough to escape his guilt and self-recrimination. He couldn't fill the aching void in his soul. There was nothing left in his life. No joy, no passion, no fire. Nothing but dreams of his late wife. Nothing but his guilt . . .

The sunlight streaming into the room made him wince as he slowly came awake. He was lying in bed, naked except for the bandage that wrapped his injured thigh. Feeling a familiar touch on his leg, he groaned softly and squinted against the bright light.

Will Terral, his batman and personal servant, was leaning over him, scowling as he probed the bloody bandage.

"I never would have taken you for a fool, m'lord, but you've proved me wrong. The scab has broken open."

Julian bit back a savage retort. His exploits last night *had* been imbecilic. And his batman had a right to criticize. Will had saved his leg from the "butcher" field surgeons, later nursing him through the worst dangers and the long bouts of agony that followed his injury . . . feeding him, changing his bandages, forcing him to drink bitter-tasting nostrums. Once, the terrible wound had putrefied and had to be drained, the mortified flesh cut away. But Will eventually had triumphed with his simple home remedies and the same poultices he used for his master's horses. Julian had emerged from the ordeal a gaunt, pain-racked ghost of his former self.

And now, just when he was beginning to recover his health, he had set back his progress in exchange for only a transient moment of forgetfulness.

Still grumbling, Will changed the bandage, then brought water, razor, and soap in order to shave his patient. Looking in the hand mirror afterward, Julian hardly recognized the man he had once been. His skin was tanned from the summer months he'd spent fighting, but beneath the tan waxed an unhealthy pallor. Worse, his once-handsome face was disfigured by the savage puckering scar that slashed across his right cheekbone, upward toward his temple. It was probable, as well, that he would always limp. And yet he was grateful to still have the leg. He had survived, thanks to Will, and with that he would have to be content.

His batman was not so content. As Will gathered up the shaving equipment, he muttered for perhaps the hundredth time, "I'll be right glad to see the last of this Papist country," before he stalked from the room.

Julian lay back wearily, contemplating his future as he had frequently during the past weeks. He would be invalided home to England unless he asked to remain here in Spain. Did he want to make such a request?

He knew Will's feelings on the subject. Not only did his faithful servant wish to return home, but Will didn't mind saying, regularly and frankly, that his lordship had wallowed in guilt long enough.

Perhaps his batman was right, Julian reflected. Perhaps it *was* time to end his self-banishment and go home. Perhaps he had suffered enough. He had lost his wife, his friends, his good name, the life he once knew . . . In four years he hadn't found the redemption he'd sought. And he was so weary of war, of death, of pain.

Gritting his teeth, he slowly sat up and swung his legs to the floor, then reached for the crutches that stood beside the bed, prepared to endure once more the torture of forcing the knotting muscles of his thigh to function.

But he was girding himself mentally, as well. He had finally come to a decision.

He had punished himself long enough. His penance had been served.

It was time that he returned home and faced the ghosts of his past.

Chapter 1

I n the ordinary course of events, Blaise St. James would never have contemplated anything so drastic as running off with a tribe of Gypsies. But these were not ordinary circumstances. She was *desperate.* Her stepfather had banished her to England with orders to acquire a husband.

Not that she objected strongly to marriage. She gladly would have returned home to Philadelphia to conduct the search if given the choice. But America was currently at war with Britain, making ocean travel exceedingly dangerous. And her English relatives had banded against her, determined to bring her to heel.

Blaise was just as resolved to foil their plans. She absolutely did not want a stuffy, stiff-necked husband from the British upper class like her stepfather or her English cousins, or the stodgy gentleman farmer her aunt had chosen for her. Squire Digby Featherstonehaugh was *not* the pinnacle of a young girl's dreams—especially Blaise's dreams. Merely the idea of being wed to him for life made her shudder.

"Englishmen are cold fish," Blaise muttered as she struggled into the borrowed gown of drab brown broadcloth. "And no one will ever convince me otherwise."

"Beg pardon, miss?" The chambermaid at the Bell & Thistle, at a loss to explain the strange doings of the Quality, watched with wide eyes as the raven-haired lady disappeared beneath the folds of her best dress.

"Nothing, never mind." Blaise's dark head emerged from the plain, ill-tailored garment. "But take my word for it. I've lived in a dozen countries and there is nothing so cold and unfeeling as an Englishman. A trout has more passion." She finished buttoning the high-waisted bodice of the dress and straightened the long sleeves. "There now, how do I look?"

The chambermaid blinked. "Ah . . . well, miss . . . the fit is well enough, but 'tisn't likely that you'll pass for me."

"Whyever not?"

"Well . . . you still seem too fancy. Your 'air and face . . ."

"I don't suppose you have a mirror?" Blaise glanced around the tiny garret room and realized the foolishness of the question. Except for a lumpy pallet and a small clothes chest, the room was starkly bare of the simplest amenities, attesting to the vast differences between the servant class and the gentry in England. "I shall just have to make do, then. I can darken my face a bit with soot and cover my hair . . . Do you have a kerchief? I'll pay you an extra guinea."

"Oh, miss . . . you've already offered me too much. I'll be taken for a thief if I turn rich of a sudden. But I do 'ave a kerchief."

When the girl turned to rummage through the meager belongings in the chest, Blaise knelt at the small window under the eaves. Her aunt's traveling chaise still stood below in the bustling yard of the posting inn.

Blaise frowned. Lady Agnes would never leave as long as her errant niece could not be found.

The shrill blare of the Royal Mail Coach announcing its departure, however, gave her an idea.

Quickly she pulled the pins out of her elaborate coiffure and shook her head, letting the ebony tresses fall to her waist in a thick cloud. Accepting the kerchief she was handed, Blaise covered the silken mass of her hair and tied the cloth ends at the nape of her neck. Then standing, she withdrew a double handful of silver shillings from her reticule and dropped what was no doubt a half year's wages into the palm of the wide-eyed servant. Finally Blaise pinned her purse beneath her skirt and drew the girl's plain brown cloak around her own shoulders.

"Now," she announced, smoothing the woolen folds of the well-worn garment. "The lady who accompanied me will be searching for me any moment now. You must tell her that I left on the Mail. She is sure to give chase in her carriage, and then I shall slip away with no one the wiser."

Looking doubtful, the maid nodded.

Blaise flashed a brilliant smile. "I can never thank you enough for lending me your clothes and coming to my rescue. Now go, please—and don't forget, you saw me leave on the Mail Coach."

The girl, after bobbing a curtsy, scurried from the room. Blaise counted to one hundred, then went to the door and pressed her ear to the panel. Her Aunt Agnes had the voice of a shrew and a temperament to match, and Blaise was certain she would hear the commotion when her ladyship discovered her niece missing.

It came almost immediately: a shriek and a thump, as if an outraged female had stomped her foot in fury. Blaise could indeed hear the tirade that followed, albeit not too clearly, since it issued from the floor below.

"The Mail Coach? That wicked girl! I vow she'll be the death of me. I *warned* Sir Edmund I could never handle her, but would he listen? No, he had to saddle me with that shameless wretch for the entire season!"

The soft murmurs that succeeded this outburst, Blaise knew, came from her own abigail, Sarah Garvey. Garvey had accompanied her all the way from Vienna in order to attend her during the London Little Season—the winter months when the fashionable upper crust of British society gathered in the Metropolis to see and be seen, when young ladies of quality were sold to the highest bidder on the marriage mart.

Blaise wrinkled her nose at the mere notion. It would be so humiliating to be paraded like a filly at a horse fair and then purchased for the dubious privilege of breeding some stuffy Englishman's heirs ... principally Squire Digby Featherstonehaugh's heirs. Well, she wouldn't surrender meekly! She would marry for love, if she had any say in the matter just as her parents had done. And if she were extremely lucky, her love would be an American, as her father had been.

Passing the cavalcade of traveling Gypsies upon the road a short while ago had been the greatest stroke of good fortune. She knew that particular tribe; Miklos's little band was as familiar to her as her own English cousins—and far more dear. Indeed, some of the happiest hours of her happy childhood had been spent in Miklos's camp, in the company of her adored father. And after her father's death ... well, she might have died of grief herself if not for Miklos.

She would be entirely safe with his tribe. Contrary to ignorant popular belief, Gypsies were not the licentious degenerates purported in old wives' tales. Where females were concerned, their morals were as prudish and proper as the highest stickler's. Miklos would be as protective of her as he would his own daughters, Blaise knew. Almost certainly he would offer her refuge if she asked. And if she was ever to escape the vigilant chaperonage of her aunt, her best chance was now, before she was incarcerated in the country, at Lady Agnes's mercy, for the months prior to the beginning of the social season.

For that interim Lady Agnes had arranged to hold a house party, specifically so Blaise could become better acquainted with her prospective suitor. Squire Featherstonehaugh was a wealthy farmer and a neighbor of her aunt's, and Blaise had met him on several occasions in past years. He wasn't quite as cold or formal or distant as her English stepfather, yet he was more than twice her age—stodgy, stiff-necked, and just plain dull. Perhaps she was unrealistic in her dreams, but she wanted more passion, more spirit, from the man with whom she would spend the rest of her life. She was not even nineteen yet, and she wasn't ready to give up those dreams, or to be coerced into a marriage of convenience—which was precisely what her aunt intended.

Lady Agnes hadn't wanted the responsibility thrust upon her, but she was determined to do her duty by her sister's child, which included arranging a suitable marriage. More impossibly, she'd sworn to turn Blaise into a proper English lady if it killed them both—which it very well might, if the past two days were any indication. Blaise had spent the excruciating journey from Dover to London to Ware confined in the traveling chaise with her shrewish aunt, who alternatingly scolded her for her latest disgraceful conduct and sang the squire's praises. Blaise's ears were still ringing from the tirades. She didn't think she could bear another hour of that constant haranguing, much less an entire season.

When the chaise had stopped to change teams at the posting inn at Ware, Blaise had partaken of luncheon—an escape would be better executed on a full stomach, she prudently decided—and then left the private parlor with the stated intent of visiting the ladies' necessary. It had been the work of a moment to find a chambermaid and bribe her to provide a change of clothing.

With a feeling of triumph, Blaise listened now as her aunt's angry voice faded away. She waited until she heard it again in the yard below, calling impatiently for the coachman to hurry if they expected to catch the Mail. Then she slipped quietly from the attic room.

Her jean half boots made little sound as she crept down the narrow servants' stairs to the floor below. On either side of the corridor stood some dozen doors, most of which led to bedchambers, according to the maidservant. The two last were private parlors.

Not wanting to use the same parlor her aunt had hired for their luncheon, Blaise glanced inside the opposite one and found it unoccupied, although a fire burned merrily in the grate. After shutting the door softly behind her, she crossed the room and bent down to carefully scoop up a handful of warm ashes from the hearth.

It made her grimace to think of smearing them on her fine complexion. "But it's for a good cause," Blaise reminded herself aloud as she patted her cheeks and brow. And so was her latest scheme. What she was about to do might put her beyond the pale, but she considered the risk worth it. Ruining her good name permanently was *not* her goal. With her reputation in tatters, no gentleman of consequence, including Squire Featherstonehaugh, would have her to wife, and thus she could evade an unwanted marriage. But she might eventually want to wed someday, and she would be foolish to destroy her chances forever.

She didn't think it would come to that, though. Aunt Agnes would hardly wish to risk a public scandal by advertising her niece's disappearance. And Blaise didn't really want to expose her aunt to such ridicule, in any case. No, all she wanted was to show Aunt Agnes she was serious about not wishing to marry Squire Featherstonehaugh— and to have at least a small say in who her future husband would be.

Absconding with her Gypsy friends should accomplish those goals. Now all she must do was catch up with Miklos's tribe. They shouldn't be too difficult to follow. When she'd passed them earlier, they had been heading south, although they might have turned off before reaching London. Like most Gypsies, they traveled the same roads each year in search of work and opportunities to trade. She would hide herself with Miklos's tribe for a week or two. Then, when the dust settled, she would present herself at her aunt's doorstep and—

A crackling sound behind her made Blaise jump. Abruptly she spun around.

A gentleman, dressed in the height of elegance, reclined on the settle before the fireplace, a cushion supporting his shoulders, a sheet of newsprint in his hands. She had failed to see him over the bench's high back when she'd entered.

He was watching her curiously over his paper, with eyes as deep and rich a blue as sapphires.

Blaise stared back at him in shock. He had the features of an Adonis, while his thick, softly curling hair shone a pale burnished gold, the color of winter sunlight. What startled her, though, more than his presence or his aristocratic good looks, was the long, savage scar that slashed across his high-boned cheek to his right temple.

He must have been a beautiful man once, she thought with sympathy.

He noted her reaction, saw the fleeting look of horror and pity race across her expression, and his mouth curled briefly at the corner. "A souvenir of the Peninsular Campaign, nothing more," he asserted. "I'm no monster to harm you. What is 'for a good cause'?"

The voice was low and resonant, and would have been quite appealing if not for the note of cynicism underlying it. Blaise eyed him blankly, not comprehending his question.

"A moment ago you said, 'It's for a good cause.' What did you mean?"

Belatedly, she recalled the role she was supposed to be playing and bobbed a quick curtsy. "Er . . . nothing, sir. Forgive me, I wasn't aware the room was occupied. I shall leave you now."

Dropping her gaze, she edged her way past the end of the settle and made for the door.

"One moment, if you please."

The authority in his calm tone brought her up short. Feeling like a child who had been caught misbehaving—a common occurrence for her—Blaise slowly glanced over her shoulder.

"Would you care to explain why you found it necessary to blacken your cheeks with ashes?"

No, she didn't care to explain, but neither did he appear to be the type of man to be fobbed off, especially by a servant. Quite without meaning to, Blaise found her attention caught again. Even lounging as he was, he commanded interest. Lithe and broad of shoulder, he had a refinement that bespoke money and breeding. He wore buckskin breeches encased to the knee in gleaming Hessian boots, a high starched shirt collar, a pristine-white cravat, and a superbly tailored coat of blue superfine that could only have come from London. It was his aristocratic bearing, though, even more than his attire, that lent him an unmistakable elegance.

Only then did she notice the cane propped beside him. While his left foot rested on the floor, his right leg was stretched out carefully on the bench. Another war wound? she wondered.

Lifting a searching gaze to his face, she detected a pallor to his complexion that she had missed before, as well as lines of pain fanning out from his blue eyes. His indolent position had nothing to do with laziness, she apprehended. The realization aroused the most absurd desire in her; she wanted to go to him and offer him comfort.

Blaise shook herself mentally at the inappropriate impulse. Finding him watching her with an unsettlingly candid blue gaze, she suddenly remembered that he had asked her a question. She was pondering a reply that might be even half credible when a shrill female voice sounded from outside the parlor.

Blaise took an involuntary step backward. Her aunt had returned, no doubt searching for her.

Glancing about the parlor, she realized with dismay that there was absolutely no place in the room to conceal herself, not unless she crouched behind the settle and pleaded with the golden stranger not to give her away. In fact, that seemed her best option. She could throw herself on his mercy and hope.

"Well, you see," Blaise began, "I am in dire need of rescue, sir. That female dragon out in the corridor is pursuing me."

His eyebrow rose. "Indeed?"

Just then a slamming door could be heard, followed by her aunt's strident voice. "She might still be here, I tell you! I wouldn't put it past that wretched girl to try and trick me."

"But, madam, I assure you," the innkeeper implored in a low tone. "She is no longer here! Please, I have guests . . ."

"I have to hide!" Blaise whispered frantically, retreating to kneel beside the settle and the golden-haired gentleman. "Oh, there is no time to explain!"

He stared at her measuringly another moment before apparently coming to a decision. Tossing his newspaper on the floor, he raised himself to a sitting position and held out his hand imperiously. "Come here."

"Wh-what?"

"You heard me. Don't argue."

Blaise had no idea what he intended, but compared to her Aunt Agnes, he was by far the lesser evil. If her aunt caught her, she would spend the rest of the season being browbeaten into a loveless marriage with that cold fish, Squire Digby Featherstonehaugh.

Taking the stranger's hand, Blaise allowed him to pull her up to sit beside him on the bench. She couldn't help but gasp, though, when he grasped her shoulders and pushed her back to lie against the cushion, in the position he had vacated. It was a greater shock, still, to feel the weight of his hard body pressing her down, his groin fitting the curve of her hip, his chest brushing against her breasts, his palm cupping her cheek, and finally the warmth of his lips as they covered hers.

His startling kiss would have silenced any protest, had Blaise wanted to make one . . . and yet she didn't. She *couldn't.* A tentative knock sounded at the door, but she was only vaguely aware of it. She was too intent on the compelling sensations besieging her as his lips moved softly over hers. Her body had grown suddenly warm, her skin flushed as with fever, and yet oddly she wanted to shiver. Her breasts felt heavy and full, while tingling waves of heat fluttered and curled in her belly, and lower, between her thighs. Her breath seemed to be suspended, even as it mingled with his.

She had been kissed before, but never like this . . . as if he were intent on conducting an exercise in sensual pleasure. His warm mouth languidly molded hers, his tongue penetrating and exploring her moist interior, executing a slow, erotic dance as it dipped and surged and swirled. Of their own accord, her fingers tangled in the gilded hair that curled at his nape.

She dimly heard the door opening behind her, followed by hesitant footsteps and a disembodied male voice. "Begging your indulgence, m'lord, but—oh! I had no notion you were engaged. I'm right sorry, pardon me, forgive me, your lordship."

Viscount Lynden raised his head and narrowed his gaze on the hapless proprietor. "Get out."

"Aye, m'lord, certainly, of course . . ."

Lady Agnes's sniffed exclamation, "How rude!" was cut off as the door slammed shut, but her shrill voice could still be heard castigating the innkeeper. Finally, though, she concluded with a frustrated huff. "Oh, never mind! That ungrateful chit has gone haring off on some mad scheme, and I refuse to be dragged into it. I don't have the constitution to go chasing over the countryside after her, and I have a houseful of guests, besides—dear heaven, the squire! What shall I tell him? I vow I'll wring that girl's neck when I find her . . ."

The commotion at last trailed off to leave a blessed silence in the private parlor.

Alone again with the stranger, Blaise knew she should do something, say something, if only to express her gratitude for his quick action in rescuing her, but all she could do was stare at the man whose beautiful, scarred face was so close to hers, whose lips were moist and glistening with her kiss.

A curling lock of gleaming blond hair had tumbled over his high brow, and she found herself wanting to smooth it back into place. More urgently, she wanted to reach up and trace with her fingers the savage purple scar that puckered the flesh of his right cheekbone, to soothe the hurt.

"You," Blaise murmured finally, her voice unexpectedly breathless, as if she had run a great distance, "do
that quite well."

"Order away intrusive innkeepers and tiresome harri-
dans?"

"No . . . kiss."

The ingenuousness of the comment caught Julian off-
guard, and he didn't know quite how to reply. He could
have told her that he'd had a good deal of practice. In his
earlier life, he had kissed so many females he thought he
knew every nuance of sensation a man could experience.
And yet this fetching, unpredictable wench had surprised
him. He felt bemused, intrigued as he hadn't been in a
long while.

His smile, slow and sensual, held the brilliance of his
sun-gilded hair. "I'm gratified that you think so."

She blinked, watching him as if fascinated by his
mouth. His own attention caught, he moved his hand
slightly and tilted her chin up. "I'll be damned," he said
softly. "Your eyes truly are purple. I thought it must be
a trick of the light."

Unexpectedly she wrinkled her nose and gave a throaty
chuckle that was infectious. "Not purple, *violet*. It's a
more flattering term, sir."

"Violet, then." They were indeed a deep, dark violet, and contrasted richly with her white skin, despite
the incongruous streaks of ash that marred her flaw-
less complexion. She was not a *beautiful* girl, precisely. At least not in the common way. Eye-catching was
perhaps a more appropriate description for the heart-
shaped face and regular features. And yet the laughing
mischief in her bright eyes enlivened her entire expression, giving her an uncommon appeal and filling him
with the desire to know her more intimately. *Far* more
intimately.

The primal rush of attraction he felt for her surprised
him. Surveying her silently, Julian followed the arc of
her cheek, ever so gently, with his fingertips, upward to
her temple, then brushed back the kerchief that covered

her gleaming tresses. Her raven hair was so black, the highlights that shone off it were almost blue.

Blaise, recognizing the obvious admiration she read in his eyes, suddenly became aware of the boldness of his body, his maleness, and the impropriety of being in this strange man's arms. Even for her, such behavior was scandalous. "You . . . may let me up now," she murmured, her tone more breathless, less commanding, than she'd intended.

The husky catch in her voice raked across Julian's sensitive auditory nerves like a caress, making him wonder about the drawling softness he heard in her accent. Her voice was, he decided, appraising her with absorbed interest, as tempting and appealing as the laughter that had danced in her lustrous eyes a moment before. Both aroused him in an elemental—and yet unexpected—way. He wanted her. With a kind of hunger he hadn't known in a long, long time.

The feeling was not purely sexual, although that was a good deal of it; his lips curled wryly at the swelling ache in his groin, where sensation had collected heavy and thick. But his desire went deeper than mere lust. He *needed* her. He sensed she could fulfill him in some unimagined way, could bring laughter and brightness to his life, which had been barren of both for so long.

The conviction, as inexplicable as it was profound, kept him silent and thoughtful as he contemplated the young woman sprawled gracefully beneath him. His fingertips brushed her lips, skeptically, wonderingly, exploring the texture and shape. Drawn by an urge more powerful than reason, he bent his head again.

Her amethyst eyes widened fractionally in surprise as she realized his intent, but she didn't pull away. She couldn't. Not if her life had been at stake, could Blaise have managed it. She was caught once more by the spell of his gentle lips, the sensual pleasure that spiraled through her, making her breasts swell painfully and her body ache with a need she had never before experienced.

His mouth stroked hers, playing, seducing with heart-stopping tenderness, while his hot, thrusting tongue expertly enticed. His hands—his long-fingered, elegant hands—slipped beneath the folds of her cloak and gently held her prisoner, kneading and plying the soft flesh of her shoulders.

When finally he drew back and allowed her up for air, her heart seemed to be lodged in her throat. His blue eyes were searching her face intently, a question in their luminous depths, a question she could not have answered, even if she'd understood it. Unable to speak, Blaise licked her lips and found the warm taste of him still on her mouth.

His gaze dropped, and lingered there, on her mouth.

Then he smiled, that slow, sensual, brilliant smile that made her feel as if she'd stared at the sun too long.

"I am more than willing," he said finally, in a voice that was sultry and low, "to take you under my protection, my sweet, but I'd rather that you clean your face first. Making love to a chimney sweep is not my ideal notion of pleasure."

Chapter 2

"**Y**ou are offering to make me your *mistress*?" Blaise asked, frankly shocked by his temerity.

His mobile eyebrow rose. "I would not have put it quite so indelicately . . . Nor was I considering anything quite so permanent just yet. I rather had in mind an evening's pleasure."

"Oh."

"Does that disappoint you?" He sounded thoughtful. "A trial engagement is the usual course before discussing terms, but I imagine I could be persuaded to make the arrangement more permanent."

Blaise drew a deep breath, aware of the slight trembling of her body. She should not have been so surprised by his indecent proposal, given the inferior social status of the role she'd assumed—a role she'd momentarily forgotten. He was obviously a wealthy nobleman, and serving wenches were fair game for his sort. Really, it was appalling how the Quality in England often treated the lower classes. She was almost certain that in America, the difference in their apparent stations would not have been an open invitation for her seduction.

But this was not America, much to her everlasting regret, nor had she even set foot there since she was ten, so her view *might* be a trifle shaded; the land of her birth might not be quite the idyllic paradise she remembered. And dressed as she was, this handsome lord could not be faulted for mistaking her gentility. Ladies did not frequent public inns attired as serving maids. Besides, she hadn't put up the slightest resistance

24

when he'd kissed her . . . twice. She could still feel the
burning brand he had left upon her mouth.

All in all, she ought to be delighted her disguise was
working so well that he wished to share "an evening's
pleasure" with her.

"I assure you," he commented as he retrieved a snowy-
white handkerchief from within his coat and began to
wipe the ash off her face, "you will find me quite generous."

"But . . . you don't even know me."

"At present, no." His eyes were amused, his voice
like velvet. "But I'm eager to remedy that situation, my
sweet . . . What is your name, by the way?"

Her mind still tangled with the predicament she'd
landed herself in, Blaise nearly replied, "Miss St. James,"
as she would in normal social situations. But identifying
herself as "Miss" anything would be pretentious for a
servant, and hardly in keeping with her role. Nor did
she think it wise to bruit about her family name.

"Blaise." She murmured her given name instead.

"Blaze, as in fire?"

"Blaise, as in my great-grandfather. My father admired
him exceedingly and wished someone to carry on his
name, so I was elected. The spelling is different—"

She bit her lip, suddenly realizing the imprudence of
letting her tongue run away with her. There was no reason to share the intimate details of her life with this man,
a perfect stranger. She would be better employed figuring
out how to extricate herself from his unwanted attentions.
Judging by the warmth and interest in his eyes, though, it
appeared that might be a rather difficult task. He would
not give up easily, Blaise was certain. She considered a
dramatic swoon, but decided that would only put her at
a further disadvantage.

"And I don't know you," she finished weakly.

Concluding the task of cleaning her face, he returned the
handkerchief to his pocket, then made a slight bow from
the waist, a graceful gesture despite the awkwardness of
leaning over her. "Julian Morrow, Viscount Lynden, at

your service. The title is rather tarnished at the moment, I'm afraid, but I imagine I still have a few friends among the peerage who will vouch for me. And I served as a soldier until recently. General Wellington can supply references if you require them."

His smile was disarming, taking the sting from what might have been sarcasm. Yet Blaise wasn't certain how to receive his puzzling comments. In fact, he seemed a very contradictory man. He was no ordinary frivolous nobleman, evidently. His hands were long-fingered and elegant, yet there were calluses on his palms. She'd felt them when he'd caressed her cheek moments ago. He must have taken his military duty more seriously than the typical British officers of her acquaintance. Usually play and the pursuit of pleasure were their prime, if not sole, concerns.

Realizing those elegant hands were again resting intimately on her shoulders, Blaise struggled to sit up. He let her go at once, somewhat to her surprise, and drew back, giving her space on the bench.

Feeling somewhat light-headed—and unaccustomedly nonplussed—Blaise fumbled for the head kerchief that had slipped from its moorings, and busied herself rearranging it over her hair while she considered her reply.

Julian leaned back casually, watching. A vision of her with that black witch's mane tumbling about her bare breasts as she arched in passion against him caught hold of his imagination and refused to let go. She was right; he knew nothing about her. Yet he wanted her. In his bed, in his life.

The strength of his desire was unexpected. How, in a matter of moments, had he gone from contemplating an evening's wanton revelry to seriously considering offering her a position as his *chère amie*? The volley that had nearly taken his leg must have addled his wits. He had not mounted a mistress in years, not since before the disintegration of his marriage, not even after his wife's death. Nor had he wished to. All his carnal relationships since had been much less permanent, due partly to the transient nature of a soldier's life in a foreign land, but primarily because he'd wanted none of the emotional intimacy or entanglements that keeping a mistress would have entailed.

He still didn't want that kind of burden. But he had just effected a drastic change in his life, returning home after an absence of four years. If he was to deal with his ghosts, how much easier would he find it with this live-ly, unpredictable wench to turn to in the night, to offer the refuge of her sweet flesh? She could be precisely the balm he needed to comfort him while he sought to become whole again. There was an open, forthright quality about her manner, with perhaps a hint of the coquette in her remarkable eyes, and yet he sensed a wholesomeness of spirit that drew him like a beacon . . . or a flame.

Blaise, she had said was her name. Rather appropriate.

His mind persisted in seeing a blaze of fire. A healing fire. A cleansing one. And when it came to holding the nightmares at bay, he would take his diversions where he could find them.

"Well?" Julian urged, aware that she hadn't yet given him a reply about the evening. "What is your answer?"

Those lovely amethyst eyes turned his way. "I'm thinking."

It was another surprising response, but he thought he understood her game. She was holding out for bet-ter terms, intending her hesitation to pique his interest further. Well, he would be willing to accommodate her within reason . . . and perhaps beyond.

He regarded her with a critical masculine eye, trying to divorce himself from his blind feelings of attraction. She could hardly be twenty years of age—perhaps a dozen years his junior. He wondered who, and what, she was. For a brief moment he had thought her an innocent runaway, in which case he should have handed her over to that shrill-voiced harridan rampaging out in the hallway. But her bold query about becoming his mistress had been anything but respectable. Indeed, it could very well have been the opening line of an artful negotiation.

When she'd first entered the room, he had taken her for one of the maidservants, but he'd seen little indication of servility in her behavior. And her well-bred accents were unmistakably not those of a menial at a country posting inn. Her speech was too refined . . . with a slight, drawling flatness to it that he couldn't place. Perhaps American or Continental.

She might be an actress who had learned to emulate her betters. If this were London, he would have thought her a courtesan. She had enough feminine graces for one, certainly. The slender hands and fine porcelain skin suggested good bloodlines. She might be a gentleman's by-blow who had been forced to earn her living as best she could.

In any case, she almost certainly had lost her innocence long ago. Any unprotected female that fetching would be too great a temptation for a warm-blooded male to resist. He doubtless was not the first man to offer her payment in exchange for her favors.

She might possibly even be in keeping now—which also could explain her hesitation, Julian reflected. She might be comparing his probable net worth with her current protector's, debating the chances of improving her lot. If so, then he was willing to negotiate. Poaching on another man's preserve was not considered the act of a gentleman, but he already bore the label of murderer. The lesser offense of trespass could hardly tarnish his reputation further.

He didn't think, however, that she was a seasoned courtesan. Her kisses had not seemed practiced enough. A talented amateur, perhaps. Certainly he had felt passion in her response. But an entirely natural passion that was unfeigned. An eminently agreeable quality in a mistress. He would not mind if she lacked skill. Indeed, it would be refreshing to make love to a desirable woman who had not yet been hardened, as his former mistresses had been, by a career of bartering her body.

No, Julian thought, surveying Blaise speculatively. He would not object in the least if she had little in common with his previous women. Her instincts seemed good. Everything else he wanted her to know, he could teach her.

"Very well," he said, coming to a decision. "You appear in need of protection, and I am in a position to oblige. I'm willing to offer you a permanent arrangement. Naturally, I shall furnish you with a house and an allowance adequate to keep you in style."

Still she remained silent, a silence that only served to increase his desire and impatience—as perhaps she intended it to.

He was about to assure her of his willingness to meet her monetary demands when she primly folded her hands in her lap and spoke, not meeting his gaze.

"I am highly flattered by your generous offer, my lord, but I must regretfully decline. I fear we wouldn't suit."

The prepared little speech sounded absurdly like the catechism young ladies recited when refusing a proposal of marriage. Julian might have found it humorous had his vanity not been pricked. Accustomed once to being pursued by women of every station and class, he had limited experience with rejection in this situation. Then he suddenly recalled another possible explanation for her refusal.

"Is it the scar that offends you?" Julian inquired in a tone curiously devoid of emotion. "Does this disfigured face repulse you?"

Blaise dragged her thoughts from her own concerns and gave him a startled look. No, his face didn't repulse her. Her chief response when she regarded the savage scar was compassion for his suffering, and regret that something so aesthetically beautiful should have been marred so terribly. Her prime instinct was to touch that ravaged cheek, to soothe it.

"To be truthful, I find your scar more interesting than offensive. And if you attained it honorably, in defense of your country, it would hardly be very sporting of me to turn you down because of it. No, that didn't even enter into my reasoning."

Julian probed her face for a sign of prevarication. Not one woman in a hundred would have replied in such a way. But then he was beginning to realize how uncommon this intriguing female was. He had been prepared to compensate her for his physical inadequacies; jewels usually made up for the most glaring of faults. But he was beginning to suspect that the normal methods of persuasion might not work with this young woman. It only made him more determined to have her.

"I expect you could call it honorable," he replied, relaxing against the settle. "I was wounded in battle a few months ago. I've been sent home to recover."

Her eyes searched his with apparent concern. "You don't sound particularly elated at the prospect. Do you miss the war?"

Julian shrugged his elegant shoulders. "Most of the fighting in Spain is over for the moment. I would not be of much use to the cavalry in any case, since I cannot even sit a horse for long—"

He stopped, realizing that she had somehow managed to turn the subject. "Would you care to give me an explanation for your refusal?"

Blaise hesitated, wondering how much she should say. Should she reveal, for instance, that she hadn't dismissed his proposal out of hand? For a moment she had actually considered the ramifications of accepting. There would be no surer way of ruining herself in the eyes of society than joining the muslin company and taking up with a profligate nobleman. Squire Featherstonehaugh would certainly not wish to marry her then.

And if she were honest with herself, she would admit to feeling a measure of curiosity about what such a scandalous life would be like. She couldn't deny, either, the illicit appeal this golden stranger held for her. A faint flush of color stained Blaise's cheeks as she remembered the forbidden excitement that had coursed through her when he'd kissed her in that possessive, intimate way.

But she needed only a *temporary* ruination. And if Lord Lynden's kisses were anything to judge by, he would expect far more of his paramour than she was willing to give, her virtue first and foremost.

"Well, it isn't," Blaise said regretfully, "that I am ungrateful, truly. It's just that . . . I have other plans."

"Plans?"

"Well . . . yes."

When he saw she didn't mean to be forthcoming with her confidences, Julian reluctantly decided to abandon his line of questioning. He wouldn't press her further. He had not earned the reputation of being a brilliant military tactician by always relying on a frontal assault. Often there were more effective ways to achieve an objective.

"The dragon lady," he mused instead. "Why were you hiding from her? I trust she didn't catch you engaged in something unlawful, like making off with her jewels or the family silver?"

Laughter crept back into her eyes. "I am certainly not a thief, my lord."

"What are you, then? Come now," Julian said when she hesitated. "After conspiring to rescue you, I think I have at least earned an explanation."

Blaise had to agree. By helping her avoid the detection of her aunt, he had saved her from a disagreeable fate. His chivalry deserved to be rewarded. Besides, she couldn't see what harm it would do to give him some partially amended version of the truth. Judging from the intelligence in his blue eyes, however, coming up with a version Lord Lynden would believe might be rather difficult.

"Well, if you must know, the dragon is . . . was my employer."

"You are no servant," he observed levelly. "And no country maid, either."

"Actually, I was engaged as a companion. Do you doubt me?" Blaise asked when his lordship's eyebrow rose skeptically. "Have you no poor female relations who depend upon you for support?"

"One or two. Are you claiming to be the dragon's poor relation?"

"Distant relation," she replied vaguely. "And I am indeed poor," she insisted with a measure of truth. "You find me in *very* straitened circumstances."

"But why the disguise?" He indicated her shabby garments with a gesture of his elegant hand. "And why did you leave the lady's employ?"

"I thought I could escape her notice more easily if she couldn't recognize my appearance." That certainly was no falsehood. "And if you knew how cruelly she mistreated me, you would not ask why I left."

"She was cruel to you?"

"Oh, yes, very."

"She beat you, perhaps?"

"Regularly."

"I suppose you have black and blue marks to prove it?"

"Dozens and dozens."

His shimmering blue gaze held humor and a hint of challenge as it traveled down her body to rest on her breasts. "Of course you would be willing to show me these terrible bruises."

That gave Blaise pause. Perhaps she had embellished her tale a bit too much. "I . . . fear I am not an accomplished liar."

"It would seem not," he agreed pleasantly.

She laughed, conceding this round to him.

The husky-honey sound of her laugh made Julian, strangely, want to join in. It had been so long since he'd felt something so blithe as laughter; Caroline's death had destroyed the laughter in him. Yet in the space of ten minutes, this enchanting girl had made him feel more lighthearted than at any time in the last four years. Her banter was not flirtatious, precisely, but rather, he suspected, the result of naturally high spirits. Her eyes sparkled with mischief and a joie de vivre that was contagious. She fascinated him. In fact he couldn't remember ever being so intrigued by a woman.

That was not to say he believed the tale she was spinning. But he couldn't yet tell which part of it was false. She might possibly be a poor relation. And if she was a hired companion, she would indeed have found it difficult to live with that sharp-tongued biddy he'd heard screeching out in the corridor.

"Why don't you tell me what truly happened?" he said finally.

Blaise knew very well she ought to end this conversation at once and be on her way. But the truth was, she was enjoying herself shamelessly. So rarely was she ever permitted the freedom her current guise afforded her. As a servant, she could abandon the restrictive codes of behavior that governed the conduct of young unmarried ladies of quality without fear of censure.

"Oh, very well, I did exaggerate a bit," Blaise admitted ruefully. "The dragon never actually raised a hand to me. But she expected perfection, and I couldn't manage it." That was also true. Aunt Agnes had demanded a standard of conduct not even a saint could live up to. "I couldn't bear another moment of her scolding."

He seemed to consider that. Instead of replying, though, he reached out to stroke her arm lightly with the backs of his knuckles.

It was, Blaise realized with a sudden return of feminine awareness, the kind of caress a man might use to seduce a woman. "Ah . . . I am exceedingly grateful to you for rescuing me, my lord, but I really must go."

She started to rise, but he caught her wrist in a gentle grip, staying her. "Must you?"

Those alarmingly blue eyes held hers, making Blaise temporarily forget what she'd meant to do. "Ah . . . yes."

"Where will you go? I don't like the idea of you having to fend for yourself."

"I have friends who will aid me." She saw his slight frown. "Really, you needn't concern yourself with me."

"But I wish to, sweeting."

She drew in a breath at the husky half-whisper. How did he do it—make her feel as if she were the only woman in the world? As if she were the sole focus of his every intimate thought? Was it due more to his intent, admiring gaze, or to his caressing touch? He was still holding her wrist with one hand, gently, possessively, as if he didn't mean to let her go. Yet Blaise didn't think that she was in any real danger, that he would force his attentions on her. There was something honorable about him, a nobility that went deeper than his patrician appearance. It was obvious, though, that he did not intend to give up easily.

"I think you should reconsider my offer," he murmured. "I am very generous with my mistresses."

"Perhaps so," Blaise said a bit breathlessly, "but I really must decline."

Julian's golden eyebrows drew together as he pondered how he might persuade her to change her mind. Dealing with a reluctant lover was one area in which he lacked expertise. He could not recall ever having had to actively court a woman in his life. Normally they sought *his* patronage. "If you were employed by the dragon, then you have no protector currently."

"No . . . not precisely."

"Then what, *precisely*?"

"I am . . . spoken for."

He waited politely, while she apparently debated with herself what more to say.

"If you must know, I am a Gypsy. I am on my way to rejoin my tribe."

"Indeed?" His smile held total disbelief. "A Gypsy would not have such soft white skin as you have," he pointed out, "or smell so sweet. And I've never seen one yet with violet eyes."

"I was adopted by the tribe. That primarily is the reason the dragon held me in such low esteem."

Julian's chuckle was rusty, but he was surprised how good it felt to exercise it. "Dragons and Gypsies ... why do I feel like you're spinning me another Banbury tale?"

"But I'm not! I *am* a Gypsy. And I'm engaged to marry the chief's eldest son. The wedding will be held shortly after I return. In fact, I only sought employment with Lady Agnes to earn money for my dowry."

Julian's thumb moved slowly, absently, over the pulse of Blaise's wrist. He had no idea how much of her wild tale was dissimulation. He was only certain of one thing: he did not intend to let her out of his life.

His slow smile held the charm that, before his marriage, had never left his bed empty. "Very well," he agreed, intending to call her bluff, "you are a Gypsy who plans to marry the chief's son. I won't press you further with my unwanted attentions. But I should like to be certain you arrive safely at your destination. This Gypsy tribe, where will we find it?"

"We?" Blaise asked guardedly.

"Yes, we. I intend to accompany you."

"But you can't!" Pulling her wrist from his grasp, she sprang to her feet and stood staring down at him.

"Yes, I can, sweeting. Indeed, I insist. As a gentleman I could do no less than to aid a lovely young woman in returning to the bosom of her family."

She was about to protest further when Lord Lynden reached for his cane and tried to rise. With a grimace, he fell back on the settle, biting back a curse.

He had turned white around the mouth, Blaise noted in dismay, while his hand rubbed his right thigh. The gesture was so weary and unconscious it pulled at her heart.

Forgetting that she wanted to elude this man, she watched him in concern. "Are you in great pain? Should I summon a servant?"

"No ... it will pass. I took a round at Vitoria, and while the wound has healed, the muscles of my thigh tighten like wet rawhide when I remain immobile too

long." He looked up at her with those somber blue eyes.
"Fetch my coat and hat, if you would, please? There, by
the door."

Blaise stood motionless for a moment, debating whether she should obey. This was her chance to escape him;
she could easily outrun a crippled man. Yet she knew
guilt would haunt her if she abandoned him in this condition.

She did as she was bid, going to the wall hook by the
door and returning with a double-breasted, knee-length
redingote and a tall crowned beaver hat with a curled
brim. Lord Lynden had managed to stand in the meantime, and as he donned the garments, he smiled down
at her, a pained smile that betrayed the effect of his
exertions. "I would be infinitely obliged if you would
lend me your support."

It was not a request she could easily refuse. Reluctantly, Blaise moved closer, offering her right shoulder
for him to lean on. The least she could do was help his
lordship down the stairs and find one of his servants
before she left him. There was something unsettling,
though, about having the length of that hard male body
pressed against her side.

The going was slow, with Lord Lynden heavily favoring his lame leg. His uneven gait sat oddly on a man of
such elegance, Blaise thought in distress as they negotiated the steep wooden stairway.

Rather than leaving through the front entrance, though,
he guided her to the doorway of the busy taproom and
glanced inside. A dark-haired, burly fellow immediately
jumped up from the pine-board table where he had been
enjoying a tankard of ale and came forward.

"M'lord, is somethin' amiss?"

"We are leaving, Will. Have Grimes ready the carriage."

"Aye, m'lord, as you say."

The manservant gave Blaise a brief glance that was
more disapproving than curious, but held his tongue as
he turned away.

The landlord came scurrying forward then. Blaise had pulled the hood of her cloak up to cover her hair, but she hid her face in Lord Lynden's shoulder while the obsequious man bowed and scraped to his noble guest. His lordship's servant must have already settled the bill, Blaise realized, for soon they were left alone again.

"You can come out now," Lynden remarked, amusement softening his voice.

Blaise felt warm color rising to her cheeks, and was grateful when he released her to draw on his gloves.

When the task was done, she lent her shoulder again, helping his lordship the final steps to the door and then outside into the bustling innyard. Her Aunt Agnes's coach was nowhere in sight, Blaise noted with relief. She had made good her escape. Her abigail, Garvey, would be wringing her hands with worry by now, Blaise realized guiltily, but Lady Agnes would doubtless be only too glad to be rid of her troublesome charge.

An impressive black traveling chaise which boasted a crest on the door panel stood to one side of the yard. While ostlers scurried to secure the harnesses of the four sleek bay horses, a postboy prepared to mount the left leader.

Lord Lynden made for the crested equipage, but when she realized his intention, Blaise stopped cold. "I cannot ride in a closed carriage with you."

"Whyever not?"

She hesitated, remembering that she wasn't supposed to have a reputation to lose. "My betrothed would not like me to be so intimate with a strange gentleman," she said finally, rather weakly.

"I doubt he would have cared to have me kissing you earlier, either, but I don't remember you protesting then."

She glanced up to find those blue eyes watching her, a gleam that looked suspiciously like smugness dancing in their depths. He knew she was fibbing. "That was different. I was desperate."

"I won't accost your virtue, upon my honor," he murmured in a voice that felt strangely like warm hands on her skin. "I promise I won't even try to steal a kiss."

Blaise did her best to ignore his provocative comment. "You really don't have to accompany me, you know."

"I thought we had already settled that issue. I don't intend to abandon you." He must have understood her genuine reluctance, however, for he shifted his gaze to his chaise. "But it would seem we have a dilemma. You cannot ride and I cannot walk." He looked up at his coachman, who occupied the driver's box. "Grimes?"

"Aye, m'lord?"

"Be so kind as to step down and ride inside the carriage."

"*Inside*, m'lord?"

"I shall take the reins. The lady wishes to ride on the box."

Blaise muttered a mental oath. It didn't seem as if Lord Lynden would take no for an answer. And yet his offer *did* have something to recommend it. If she accepted his escort, it would save her a good deal of walking. It would also increase the likelihood that she would catch up with Miklos today, before it grew dark; the Gypsies already had a full two hours' head start. Besides, Lynden's protection might be welcome. A lone female on the English roads would be prey to all sorts of dangers.

With a sigh, Blaise capitulated. She would be rid of this persistent nobleman, though, as soon as she reached Miklos's camp. "Very well, my lord. I thank you for your kindness."

She was helped onto the driver's box by the frowning manservant named Will, whose scowl only deepened when he next aided his master. Blaise saw Lord Lynden wince in pain as he climbed onto the seat to her right, but she didn't know quite what to say.

He settled himself, took up the reins and the carriage whip, then sat waiting. When the ostlers finished harnessing the team and the two liveried grooms had climbed into place at the back of the coach, Lynden turned to look at her. "Which way?"

"The London road, I think."

"You don't know?"

"My aun—" Blaise broke off, realizing her near slip; she had started to say that her aunt's carriage had passed Miklos's little band that morning, heading in the opposite direction. "I saw my tribe this morning traveling toward London, but they may have turned off the road. I'll have to stop at all the junctions to discover their direction."

Lord Lynden raised a skeptical eyebrow, but all he said was "Good enough." Releasing the brake, he snapped the reins and swung the team out of the yard.

There was not much opportunity for conversation after that. With such fresh horses, they rapidly left the village of Ware behind and sped south toward London, through the green English countryside with its splashes of autumn color. For the first few moments, Blaise clung tightly to the side of the box. But then, recognizing Lord Lynden's skill, she settled back to enjoy the drive. The brisk September wind buffeted her face and tugged at the hood of her cloak, and the sky was somewhat overcast, but the sun occasionally broke through the scudding gray clouds to warm her.

It was not long, however, before the man beside her slowed the chaise.

"You wished to stop at all the crossroads. This road leads to Hertford and then St. Albans, if I'm not mistaken."

"No, they didn't go that way," Blaise replied. "They were already a half-dozen miles south of here when I saw them."

Lynden gave a nod and prompted the horses into an easy gallop again.

He was an excellent whip, Blaise noted with admiration, handling the powerful team with a dexterity that she envied. Really, it was the height of unfairness that females were never allowed to drive more than a plodding pair without raising a scandal.

That long-held grievance reminded Blaise of why she had been exiled to England in the first place. Scarcely in Vienna a month and she had challenged an Austrian count to a curricle race—and won. The count had taken the loss in very poor grace, though, and barely a week later, when she'd slipped out of the house to attend a midnight masquerade, he'd reported her scandalous behavior to her stepfather. Sir Edmund, exasperated to the point of apoplexy, had finally washed his hands of her and, as punishment for her sins, had turned her over to her English mother's sister, Lady Agnes.

Blaise supposed she could not really blame him. It could not have been easy being burdened with her for the past five years since Mama's passing. She had a knack for landing herself into scrapes and offending Sir Edmund's highly developed sense of propriety.

He was not a cruel man. In fact, he took his responsibility in raising his adopted stepdaughter quite seriously. He simply had no imagination, practically no soul, and even less idea how to rear a spirited, motherless, adolescent girl who had been nurtured on democracy and American independence.

It wasn't his fault that he was so unlike her late father, Blaise knew, although he *was* to blame for adopting her and depriving her of her adored papa's name by forcing her to become a St. James. She couldn't forgive him, either, for marrying Mama so soon after Papa died—scarcely a year later—even if he *had* been a good husband to Mama. Even if he *had* provided them a home away from Mama's shrewish sister, Lady Agnes. Blaise had bitterly resented Sir Edmund for trying to take her father's place.

From the beginning, she'd been at odds with him. They had absolutely nothing in common. Sir Edmund St. James was an aloof, dignified British diplomat, while she was a complete hoyden, entirely deserving of the name. And then Mama had died, leaving her alone in Sir Edmund's care. The unconventional, rootless, lonely existence she'd led for the past five years, being dragged from country to country while he fulfilled his prestigious diplomatic posts, had done little to moderate her conduct.

She was never *deliberately* bad. Impulsive, perhaps. Mischievous, certainly. Adventuresome, definitely. But not *wicked*. If anyone had accused her of hatching her escapades in order to gain her stepfather's attention, Blaise probably would have denied it, and yet she knew that if just once Sir Edmund had ever smiled at her with genuine affection, or treated her as a cherished daughter instead of a troublesome nuisance, she would have forgiven him his cold nature and done her best to act with circumspection and decorum.

It was his coldness she resented, not his control. She even saw the necessity of discipline when she misbehaved. Indeed, she usually suffered her punishment cheerfully. But *this* was too much to bear—being ordered to acquire herself a husband who would take her off Sir Edmund's hands. Blaise couldn't comply. When she married—*if* she married—it would *not* be to a stuffy, unfeeling Englishman like her stepfather or Squire Digby Featherstonehaugh, or any of the countless other spiritless, cold-fish gentlemen of her acquaintance.

Seeing the band of Gypsies on the road that morning had decided her. Miklos would be her salvation. He would offer her refuge until she managed to foil her aunt's hard-hearted schemes of marrying her to the squire.

From her high perch, Blaise watched fields and forests and hedgerows flash by, her spirits rising with every mile. It was glorious to be out from under her relatives' oppressive thumbs, and even more wonderful to be without the immediate threat of marriage hanging over her head. She intended to make the most of her freedom—once she disentangled herself from this latest predicament, a wounded nobleman whose kisses turned her limbs to jelly and whose perseverance had proved a redoubtable force, even for her. She wasn't yet certain whether meeting Lynden was a stroke of luck or of misfortune.

Covertly Blaise studied him as he drove. He was frowning in concentration at the road, but still he was a devastatingly attractive man. The sunlight made the curling strands of his hair glint flaxen and gold and accentuated the nobility of his features. If not for the savage scar that slashed across his cheek and the shadow of pain in his eyes that lent him an air of haunted vulnerability, she might actually have been intimidated. Those keen blue eyes seemed to see much more than she wished him to see.

Moments later, at a new junction, he slowed the carriage again and turned those intense blue eyes on her, making her feel unaccountably breathless all of a sudden. "Well?" he said.

"I need to get down and look."

Julian brought the team to a halt and motioned for one of the grooms to help her down. Then he watched curiously as she paced the side of the road, eyeing the dirt. At one corner of the intersection, she bent down to inspect what looked to be a small jumble of twigs and bits of rag. The satisfied smile that curved her mouth told him she had discovered something of importance.

"They went this way, along this lane," she said as she climbed back up beside him.

"How can you tell?"

"Every tribe has its own badge to identify it. Miklos's badge was there, along with a sign to let all the other Gypsies know where he can be found."

"You can read these signs?"

"Oh, yes. All Gypsies can."

Julian shook his head. Why she persisted in this fanciful tale of belonging to a tribe of Gypsies, he wasn't certain, but he was willing to play along . . . for a time.

He took up the reins again and set the team in motion, wincing at the jolt of fire that stabbed his thigh as the carriage hit a rut in the road. He ought not put his leg through such physical strain, he knew. Even though he'd recovered his health enough to travel, he was in no condition to go gallivanting around the countryside, chasing phantom Gypsies.

And yet he wasn't about to give up this bright-eyed enchantress without a fight. He'd even dusted off the legendary Lynden charm in an effort to persuade her to accept his patronage. But she was either immune to his appeal—a first for him—or she was the most accomplished actress he'd seen outside of London.

He was not unaware, however, of another reason he'd so willingly allowed this interruption of his plans: it gave him an excuse to delay his return home. He was close to his own shire of Huntingdon now, merely a half day's drive, but the nearer he'd come, the stronger his dread had grown. He had tarried at the Bell & Thistle as long as possible, postponing his departure the way a child would avoid punishment. The appearance of this spirited lass had been a welcome reprieve, like a breath of fresh air in a dark room shrouded with cobwebs. No, he wasn't about to let her go, Julian thought with renewed determination.

It was only a short time later, though, that his determination received a blow. Feeling her hand touch his arm, Julian followed with his gaze to where his lovely companion was pointing.

Some distance off the lane, beyond a gentle rise, stretched a meadow that bordered on a beechwood. There, a dozen or so canvas-covered carts stood arrayed in a semicircle, while twice that number of low tents had been erected along the edge of the wood.

A Gypsy camp, Julian realized with a sense of dismay. He had seen such tribes often enough before, traveling about the English countryside and at local fairs, and more recently in Spain. Absently he slowed his team, bringing the coach to a standstill.

His companion turned her lively eyes on him and flashed him a smile of incredible brilliance. "I thank you, my lord, for going to such trouble on my account and delivering me safely to my friends. I don't know how I will ever repay you."

Even as she spoke, she began climbing down from the box. "You needn't accompany me," she added when he reached out his hand—whether to detain her or aid her, even Julian wasn't certain. "I know you are eager to be on your way. And my friends are wary of *gorgios*."

The term *gorgio*, Julian vaguely remembered learning somewhere, meant non-Gypsy. And Blaise's politely phrased comment held a sincerity he couldn't mistake. He had just been dismissed.

He was still recovering from the novelty of it when he realized that a crowd of colorfully garbed Gypsies had begun to gather at the edge of the camp. Blaise waved at them, then dipped a brief curtsy to Julian, giving him another of her bright smiles. Then, turning, she slipped through an opening in the hedgerow and ran lightly across the meadow, dodging the hobbled horses that had been turned loose to graze.

Julian watched her go, absently kneading his aching thigh, conscious of an unjustified feeling of betrayal. She had actually been telling the truth about the Gypsies. And she had dismissed him!

Just then, a swarthy, lithe-limbed figure of a man separated himself from the crowd and moved toward her. Julian couldn't tell what was being said, but he could see Blaise's excitement as she offered her hands to the fellow, could hear the husky trill of her laughter as she was spun around in a dance of welcome.

A frown darkened Julian's scarred face. He had no trouble recognizing the hot, primitive emotion surging through him. It was jealousy, pure and simple. More than that, it was regret. It was like unexpectedly finding a hidden treasure, only to have it suddenly snatched from him.

"M'lord?" His coachman had stepped out of the carriage and stood looking up at him quizzically. "Will ye be wantin' me to take over now?"

Julian recollected himself. "Yes, Grimes . . . and walk the horses along the road for a time, if you please. I have some business with these people."

He ignored the startled look his coachman gave him, as well as Will's disapproving frown, and climbed painfully down from the box, intent on recovering his treasure.

Chapter 3

"**M**iklos, you can't know how wonderful it is to see you again!" exclaimed Blaise when he ceased spinning her around.

"Aye, my little lady o' fire, 'tis a true delight to see you, too. You've grown up these past—'ow long has it been? Three years?"

The Gypsy's musical voice was deep and laughing, with an accent that, despite his foreign appearance, sounded as British as any yeoman farmer's. Miklos Smith had been born in nearby Essex, and bred along the roads and byways of the Home Counties.

He was dressed much like the lower classes as well, except a good deal more colorfully. His saffron frieze shirt, red waistcoat, yellow neckerchief, and green woolen cap brightly embellished his otherwise plain costume of loose broadcloth breeches and heavy shoes. No one would mistake Miklos for anything other than a Gypsy, however; not with his coarse blue-black hair and swarthy complexion. His teeth flashed white in his face as he beamed at Blaise.

"What brings you 'ere?" His black eyes swept her figure in puzzlement, taking in the drab woolen cloak and servant's garb. "An' what are you doin' in that twig? You're a fine *rauni* now, a lady."

"Oh, Miklos, I am in a terrible coil. I've run away from my Aunt Agnes. Will you allow me to stay with you? Just for a few days? A fortnight at most. It shouldn't take any longer than that to prove my point and make her see reason."

His hesitation was obvious, giving Blaise a moment's worry. He was concerned about the authorities, she knew. Local magistrates often used even the flimsiest evidence as an excuse to drive the Gypsies from a territory. They would be quick to accuse Miklos's tribe of abduction if she were found in his company.

But then Miklos patted her hand with fraternal affection. "For you, the beloved daughter o' my *pal,* I will do anything," he announced gallantly.

"Oh, *thank* you, Miklos." Blaise smiled in relief, grateful that Miklos hadn't forgotten his friendship with her father. Years ago, before she was born, her American father had come to England to tour and to study the Romany culture. Drew Montgomery had spent much of that summer traveling with Miklos's tribe, later wintering near their camp in Hertfordshire, where he'd met and fallen in love with Blaise's mother, an English gentlewoman of good family. Mama's relatives hadn't relished her choosing an American suitor, but resigned themselves since it was a love match. The couple had married the following spring, but although Drew took his new bride home to Philadelphia, they'd returned to England every few years to visit Frances's family and show off their new daughter. Each time, Drew had sought out Miklos wherever his camp might be, and their friendship had only deepened over the years.

Blaise had delightful memories of being dandled on Miklos's knee as a child as she shrieked with laughter, of being showered with the unstinting love all Gypsies showed their children, of being spoiled entirely rotten by the entire clan. Yet she also had more painful memories. After her adored father's death when she was ten, she and her mother returned permanently to England, to live with Frances's widowed sister, Lady Agnes. Blaise had thought she would die that winter. She'd lost her father, her home, and her country, all in one fell swoop. But Miklos and the tribal mother, Panna, had made her grief more bearable.

The miracle was that Blaise's own mother had permitted her to run tame in the Gypsy camp all during that terrible winter, against every dire prediction of scandal and disaster that Lady Agnes could conceive; even at the tender age of ten, a young girl's reputation was a fragile possession. It was only later that Blaise came to understand why her mother had allowed such risk. She'd known how much Blaise *needed* that tenuous connection with her father's memory.

Blaise was no longer a child now, but the effect was still the same. When she was with the Gypsies, her father was always with her, surrounding her with his laughter and love, his zest for life. No one had ever found more joy in living than Drew Montgomery. For his sake, if nothing else, Miklos would welcome her as a daughter.

Even as Blaise had the thought, Miklos suddenly tensed, the grin fading from his face as he stared over her shoulder. "And who is the fancy *rye* ye've brought with you?"

Recalling that *rye* was the Romany word for gentleman, Blaise turned to look.

"Oh, mercy," she muttered under her breath. Lord Lynden was walking slowly across the meadow toward them, aided by his gold-handled cane. "I didn't bring him here, Miklos. He brought me . . . He insisted on escorting me."

" 'E's not a *thomyok* come to send us packin'?" Miklos asked worriedly.

"No, I don't think he's a magistrate. But I haven't a clue why he's still here. He doesn't even know who I am. In fact, he thinks I'm an adopted Gypsy."

Miklos sent her a curious look. "Why would 'e think that?"

"Because I told him so. Please, don't give me away?" She didn't want Lord Lynden finding out who she truly was and somehow divulging her whereabouts to her Aunt Agnes, not until she was certain her reputation was thoroughly—and safely—compromised. "I'll pretend to be . . . Blaise *Smith* instead of Miss St. James."

"Aye," Miklos agreed, "but I'll want you to empty the bag and tell me all as soon as 'e's gone."

Blaise nodded. She would explain how she'd come to be with Lord Lynden, but it would be an abbreviated version of the truth. She wasn't about to let Miklos know that this fancy lord had offered to make her his mistress. Miklos was as protective as a father, and with his hot Gypsy temper, he had been known to shed blood over lesser insults. And, really, it had been her fault. Lord Lynden would never have attempted to seduce her if he'd known she was a lady . . . Would he?

Blaise watched with wary regard as Lynden closed the final distance between them. Despite his definite limp, his movements were graceful, his bearing elegant and commanding.

"My lord, you surprise me," she said when he stood before her. "I thought you would be well on your way by now."

"I wished to make certain you arrived safely."

"There really was no need—"

"I know." He smiled charmingly and glanced at the Gypsy, who had tugged off his cap out of respect. "Do you intend to introduce me?"

"Well . . ." Having little choice, Blaise complied. "My lord, may I present my good friend, Mr. Miklos Smith. Miklos, this is Viscount Lynden."

To her surprise his lordship made the Gypsy a polite bow, just as he would to any gentleman, before cutting his blue eyes back to her. "Friend?" The inflection in Lynden's voice was shaded with meaning. "Not your betrothed?"

"N-no," Blaise said, caught off-guard. "Miklos is chief of the Smith clan."

"Ah, the *father* of your betrothed."

To her chagrin, Blaise felt herself blushing. She'd lied to Lynden and told him she planned to marry the chief's eldest son. Well, there was nothing for her to do now but brazen it out. "Yes," she murmured. "My betrothed's father."

Miklos, to his credit, did not twitch a muscle, although he must have been puzzled by the conversation. "I'm that grateful to you for comin' to her aid, your honor. Miss . . . Mistress Blaise is like a daughter to me."

"Indeed?" Lynden's caressing blue gaze swept her briefly. "I can understand how you would wish to protect so lovely a daughter."

"Aye."

From the awe in his tone Blaise perceived that Miklos was impressed by the stranger's consequence and civil, polished address. Most likely the Gypsy hadn't been this close to a highborn lord except for the times he'd been hauled before a magistrate.

She, however, was not impressed. Traveling with her diplomat stepfather, Blaise had known scores of British aristocrats, and not a one had changed her conviction that Englishmen—especially blue-blooded Englishmen—were very cold fish.

An awkward silence ensued. Miklos glanced behind him to where most of his tribe waited in wary silence, then finally said to the viscount, "Might I offer ye a drop of ale, your lordship?"

That charming smile flashed again. "I would be exceedingly grateful. I'd count it an even greater kindness if you would allow me to sit down. My leg is paining me terribly . . . a war wound, you understand."

Miklos hastened to shout a series of orders to his clan, while Blaise glanced at Lynden in suspicion. He did not look to be in any great pain, at least not as severe as what he'd suffered at the inn. It seemed he was not above using his infirmity to garner sympathy and achieve his own aims—whatever they might be.

"Would you not find a seat in your own carriage more comfortable than an open field?" Blaise asked sweetly but pointedly.

Lynden was not a slow man. "Perhaps. But then"— he bent that disarming grin on her—"I would lose the opportunity to persuade you to change your mind about our relationship."

Blaise stared at him blankly, one of the rare times in her life she was unable to think of a reply. She wished he would give up the absurd notion that she might actually consent to becoming his mistress. It had been thrilling for a moment to pretend that she could possibly attract a man like Lord Lynden—what feminine heart wouldn't be flattered?—but his persistence could get to be a definite nuisance.

She was spared the necessity of a reply, though, when Miklos returned. He had evidently decided to show their noble guest the kind of hospitality Gypsies were famed for. A keg of ale had been broken out, a quilt spread on the ground, and the men of the tribe summoned forward to meet his lordship.

As if realizing he was to hold court on the quilt, Lord Lynden gave a wry twist to his mouth and contemplated Blaise. "You will join me, I trust."

"Oh, no, my lord, I couldn't." She shook her head. "Women are not welcome in men's business. That is not the Gypsy way."

"You mean to abandon me?" His eyebrows shot up. "And after I rescued you so gallantly at the inn today? Such gratitude."

Blaise took a step back, repressing an arch grin; no doubt it was rare that his lordship found his plans thwarted. "Surely a gentleman with your resources does not need rescuing, my lord. And I must greet the rest of my family. I wish you good day . . . and Godspeed."

With a saucy chuckle and an equally bold curtsy, Blaise turned and made her escape. Very likely he would grow bored with the company and leave. She almost regretted that she would never see him again.

She could feel his blue eyes following her as she walked away, but shortly she was swallowed up by the crowd of Gypsy women and ragged, half-dressed children, who all began laughing and questioning her and tugging on her hands at once.

Isadore, Miklos's wife, thankfully took charge and established some sense of order. They bore Blaise away to the opposite edge of the camp, where she spent a delightful hour renewing old acquaintances and learning about the children who had grown almost beyond recognition during the three years since her last visit. It was Panna, however, whom she longed most to see . . . Panna, the tribal mother, and the one person in the world besides Miklos who had Blaise's total devotion and respect. Yet Panna would bide her time until the worst of the commotion was over, Blaise knew.

It happened just as she predicted, some ten minutes later. Through the audience seated around Blaise came hobbling an old woman—gray-haired, leather-skinned, and nearly toothless, but with sharp black eyes that missed little. Panna resembled a witch more than a Gypsy, and cackled like one, as well.

She let out a raucous chortle as Blaise surged to her feet and with a glad cry launched herself into the old woman's bony arms.

Panna's embrace was surprisingly strong, and Blaise was a bit breathless when she emerged.

"I was worried about you growing old, Mother," she said with playful formality, "but you still have the strength of an ox."

"And ye still have the cheek of a magpie, child."

Blaise dimpled. "I'll turn nineteen next month, Panna. I'm not a child any longer."

"Aye, that you aren't. You've grown into a fine lady."

"Alas, I fear I'm not that, either. Sir Edmund thinks I'm a hopeless hoyden, and Aunt Agnes says I'm a disgrace—and I'm sure they are both right."

Panna's lined face grew suddenly sober. "I knew ye would come to us."

Blaise didn't need to question that pronouncement. Panna claimed to have the Sight, and often her predictions were uncannily accurate. But her greatest skill lay in her knowledge of people rather than events. Panna could ferret out secrets of the heart even the owner had no notion of.

She did it now as she searched Blaise's face. "Ye've been unhappy."

"Miserable is more exact. Oh, Panna, they mean to marry me off," Blaise lamented.

"Come wi' me to my tent and you can tell me all about it."

Panna's tent at the edge of the camp was an oblong affair, constructed of worn strips of brown canvas and green branches, with rush matting and carpets serving for a floor, and a few scattered cushions for seats. She led Blaise inside, folded away her guest's cloak, fed her a cup of lukewarm tea, and listened wisely and silently as Blaise poured out her tale of woe.

It was wonderful, thought Blaise, to be able tell someone who would understand and not judge.

" . . . and all Aunt Agnes would talk about the entire way from Dover," she finished up, "was what a disgrace I was to the family, and how vulgar my manners were, and what an admirable husband Squire Featherstonehaugh would make me, and how he wouldn't put up with any scandals in his wife—" Blaise ran out of breath. "I just couldn't bear it any longer."

"Does yer aunt have the power to force you to wed?" Panna asked thoughtfully.

"Well, no, not really. But Sir Edmund holds the purse strings. Until I reach my majority, I won't be able to touch the portion Mama left me, and that's more than two years away. I'll have to live with Aunt Agnes till then—none of my other relatives would want me—and I know what *that* would be like. I'd never have a moment's peace. She'd keep harping and harping until I went mad or gave in. I had to do *something*, Panna. When I passed you on the road this morning, it seemed like providence."

"Aye, 'twas fate," the old woman declared.

"Well, I wasn't completely sure you would take me in."

Panna cackled. "You're always welcome 'ere, as you well know, Mistress Minx. 'Tis not likely we'd forget what you did for us all those years past."

Blaise shook her head, remembering the incident six

years before, when she was thirteen. One of Aunt Agnes's noble cronies had had a diamond necklace turn up missing while Miklos's tribe was camped in the neighborhood. Miklos and a half-dozen other Rom had been arrested for the theft, and probably would have been hanged and the entire tribe transported had not Blaise come forward and confessed to the crime.

"What I did wasn't so special," she murmured.

"Hah! No *gorgio* ever born would raise a pretty finger for a Rom. But you took the peril on yourself—and you just a child!"

"Well, Miklos was innocent. I couldn't let him die for something he didn't do." She *knew* Miklos. He wasn't above lifting a chicken or two from a henhouse, or illegally scouring a farmer's orchard for fallen apples, but he wasn't stupid enough to take something so valuable as a diamond necklace and risk his fairly lucrative horse trade and the welfare of his tribe. His innocence would have made no difference in that case, though; in England, as in most parts of the civilized world, a Gypsy was considered guilty by mere reason of being a Gypsy.

When she'd learned of the false charges, Blaise had intervened and assumed the blame; she could do nothing less. Spending two weeks locked in her room on bread and water had not been too great a price to pay for saving the life of one of her father's friends, a man who had comforted her and brought her joy.

Actually, though, the two weeks were her punishment not for the theft, but for lying. Blaise had been cleared of the charges when the dowager had miraculously "discovered" her missing necklace, but Aunt Agnes had flown into a second rage upon realizing her niece had sacrificed her dignity and honor in order to protect those "filthy heathens." Blaise had felt no remorse; Papa would have understood her actions and approved.

Mama, of course, had been disappointed, but she hadn't scolded the way Aunt Agnes had. No one scolded the way Aunt Agnes did. The two sisters could scarcely have been more different. Mama had been elegant, charming, soft-spoken—everything a lady should be—while her sister was a veritable shrew. Like most people, Mama often hadn't possessed the backbone to stand up to Lady Agnes. Still, Blaise had loved and respected her mother, and missed her dreadfully after she was gone. Almost as much as she missed her father.

" 'Twas right for you t' come to us, your family," Panna said now. " 'Twill all work out, you'll see. You may stay as long as you have need to, o' course, and you'll sleep 'ere in my tent wi' me."

"Thank you, Panna."

"And Isadore'll find you some pretty clothes to wear."

By "pretty" she meant colorful, Blaise knew. A Gypsy loved gay colors.

"But tomorrow you'll help wi' the chores, like always. You may be a fancy lady, but you'll be a Romany *chi* 'ere and earn yer keep."

Blaise smiled, completely satisfied. She could think of no greater honor than being considered an equal among these people.

"Now, off wi' you," Panna added with a shooing gesture. "Go an' dance an' put some bloom in those pale cheeks."

Laughing at her abrupt dismissal, Blaise did as she was bid and left the tent, intending to seek out Miklos's wife and offer to help with supper. She gave a skip of joy as she crossed the camp toward his tent, relishing her freedom. After her despair of this morning, she could scarcely believe her sudden reversal of fortune.

The scores of Gypsy children had been sent off into the woods to gather faggots for the cooking fires, while the women had begun making preparations for supper. There was no immediate sign of Miklos, however, or of his wife, Isadore.

Letting her gaze search the edge of the meadow where she'd last seen him, Blaise was surprised to discover that the crowd of Rom had vanished, leaving a single fair-haired man in sole possession of the quilt.

Lord Lynden, she realized with a jolt of remembered

awareness. He lay on his back, one hand behind his head, his right leg stretched out carefully.

Blaise told herself it was merely curiosity and concern that lured her, almost against her will, to his side, and yet she knew her attraction was more elemental and less altruistic than she would admit. He had discarded his outer garments and his frock coat. In his waistcoat and shirtsleeves, he looked a superb figure of a man ... strong athletic shoulders, narrow masculine hips, the long muscular legs of a horseman.

Her footsteps slowed as she approached. He lay so still and quiet that she thought he might be asleep. His eyes were closed, and the sharp lines of pain that had marred the stark beauty of his face had relaxed somewhat. Just then, for a brief moment, the scudding clouds in the sky parted and a ray of late-afternoon sun shafted off his curling, pale gold hair, giving him an almost heavenly aura.

Blaise couldn't help but catch her breath. He was no angel, she reminded herself, recalling the very earthy kisses he'd given her in the inn. A fallen one, perhaps ... but no one a young lady of repute would become entangled with, certainly not if she had a care for her virtue. And yet drawn as if by a hidden force, Blaise slowly knelt beside him and bent closer, her hand stretching out of its own accord as if to touch his ravaged cheek.

He must have felt her shadow or sensed her presence, though; before she could achieve her aim, his eyes suddenly opened. Drawing her hand back swiftly, Blaise sank onto her heels and blushed, feeling absurdly like a child caught acting out some forbidden desire.

He blinked—sleepily, she thought—and shielded his gaze from the sunlight, his blue eyes suddenly becoming alert and fixed intently upon her face.

"Are you ill?" she asked, relieved to have thought of an adequate excuse for her attentiveness.

Lynden sat up politely and ran a distracted hand through his hair, disheveling it attractively. "No, just weary. I haven't been sleeping well at night."

It was an honest reply, she decided, not an attempt to garner sympathy. And yet his very simplicity touched her heart. "Your wound troubles you?"

"In part." Lynden's tone was suddenly terse, his brow furrowed in a dark scowl, as if he remembered something exceedingly unpleasant. But then he seemed suddenly to relax as he leveled a measuring look at Blaise. "I should be angry at you for deserting me, sweeting."

"Deserting you, my lord? I don't believe that was the case at all. I warned you I didn't need your escort."

"Craven."

The soft accusation was murmured in a teasing undertone that held both challenge and unnerving sensuality. Blaise couldn't help the shiver of awareness that it aroused in her—or think of a rejoinder. It *had* been cowardly of her to leave him to his own devices with the Gypsy tribe. She hadn't wanted to give him any further opportunity to work his practiced charm on her.

"Shouldn't you be leaving now? You won't want to keep your horses standing."

"Are you trying to hint me away?"

"Without much success, evidently. You don't seem inclined to take hints, my lord."

He laughed, a husky, friendly sound that made a responsive smile tug at her mouth. "You'll find me rather stubborn in that respect. And I fear you won't be rid of me anytime soon, sweeting. I've accepted your friend Miklos's invitation to supper."

"Supper?" Her smile faded as she stared at him blankly.

"Surely you're acquainted with the term . . . evening meal, food, dine?" When she remained wordless, he leaned back lazily, resting his weight on his elbows. "I've already seen to my horses, thank you for your concern. I sent them with my servants to the nearest village to spend the night. So, you see, sweeting, my evening—and night, as well, if I can interest you—is entirely free. You have me all to yourself."

Trying to ignore his suggestive remark, Blaise lifted

her gaze beyond Lynden to the distant road, understanding now why she had seen no sign of his carriage. He had dismissed it. What made less sense, though, was Miklos inviting this highborn lord to supper. She knew Miklos had been relieved to learn the *gorgio rye* was not a local magistrate intent on chasing them out of the district. But to extend the hospitality of the camp to this stranger so easily, to have lost all wariness in so short a time . . .

"However did you manage an invitation to supper?" she wondered aloud.

"Is that so unusual?"

"For a *gorgio*, yes. Ordinarily a Gypsy wouldn't invite a *gorgio* to share a meal except to seal friendship."

"No doubt your Mr. Smith was dazzled by my famous charm and address."

Lynden's disarming tone was light, teasing, but Blaise suspected there was more than a grain of truth in his remark. He must have used his potent charm to lethal effect to have convinced Miklos to let down his guard so readily.

"No doubt you pulled the wool over his eyes, you mean," she replied pertly. "But there must be more to it than that. Miklos does not fool easily."

Lynden feigned a wince. "You wound me, sweeting. But in this case, you're on the mark. I suspect my interest in his horses turned the trick. I'm still in the process of setting up my stables, and as a horse trader, Mr. Smith could hardly pass up the opportunity to show off his wares. I pleaded fatigue, however, and asked if we might conduct our business on the morrow."

That explanation made more sense; Lord Lynden had bribed Miklos with the lure of a sale. Yet Blaise could only view Miklos's invitation with dismay—and, if she were honest, an uncontrollable quiver of excitement. Lynden's presence here at the camp would only complicate her life, and yet the thought of matching wits with this elegant, wounded nobleman made her pulse beat faster. She *wanted* him to stay. Besides, it was only for one night. Surely she could manage to evade his persistent attentions for one night.

"I won't change my mind," she said finally, searching his face.

His smile was lazy, masculine . . . supremely confident. "I'll take my chances on my powers of persuasion."

The gentle promise in his expression, in the flickering depths of his eyes, held her spellbound for the longest moment. She was conscious of the sun-warmed scent of ripened grass rising up to surround them, of the muted distant sound of activity in the Gypsy camp behind her. Then Lynden's gaze dropped to her lips, and Blaise felt the oddest sensation, as if he had kissed her with his gaze, caressed her mouth without touching. Falteringly she swallowed.

To break the spell, she finally averted her gaze and looked about her. "Where is Miklos?" she murmured, intent on changing the subject.

"Rabbit hunting with Bruno, I believe."

"Bruno?"

"The four-legged black beast who was barking his head off a while ago. A lurcher, I think. You aren't acquainted with Bruno?"

"I've been away for a time," Blaise said, hoping to excuse her ignorance. "I don't know everyone in the camp."

"I imagine Bruno is a fine poacher."

Blaise stiffened warily. "The law doesn't consider it poaching if a dog makes the catch."

"I know, sweeting. Don't get alarmed. Your Gypsies have nothing to fear from me, as I told them. I don't begrudge them a few rabbits for the cooking pot. Especially since I plan to partake of the bounty."

Lynden's easy reply made her defensiveness seem an overreaction, and Blaise made herself relax. His next casual words, however, did not strike her as particularly soothing.

"Miklos introduced me to his eldest son, by the way."

"Yes?"

"A fine lad, Tommy." Lynden reached out beside her to pluck a blade of grass and brought it to his lips, chewing on it thoughtfully. "How old would you say he is? Thirteen? Fourteen?"

Blaise felt her blush rising again as she realized where the conversation was leading.

"Your betrothed—you do remember *him*, I trust?"

She'd planned to brazen out the lie, yet her sense of humor got the better of her and she spoiled the effort by laughing. "Yes, of course I remember him."

"Isn't he rather young to be your intended husband?"

"Tom looks young for his age. And Gypsies marry young in any case."

"Yet you apparently managed to escape matrimony until now."

"I told you, I am adopted."

"So you did." He slanted her a curious glance. "I wonder how much of your tale I should believe."

Blaise tossed her head mischievously. "All or none, my lord, it matters little to me." Which was true. It only mattered that he not learn her identity. And as long as she didn't sway from her story, she would be safe. She knew she didn't have to fear exposure by Miklos's tribe. With their childish love of games, the Gypsies would be more than willing to play a trick on the *gorgio rye* and help her pretend to be one of the Smith brood instead of Miss St. James. And yet it probably was not wise to tempt fate and Lord Lynden by continuing to remain in his company.

"I had best be going if I mean to help with supper." She rose to her feet and dusted off her grass-stained skirt.

Lynden sat up. "Forgive me for not rising. My leg . . ."

"Certainly, I understand." Her own legs were a bit numb from having knelt there so long. "Please, I don't wish you to trouble yourself on my account. And that, my lord," Blaise added with a smile, "you may believe."

Julian followed her with his gaze as she walked back to the camp, unable to tear his eyes away. From beneath the confining head kerchief, her glorious cloud of ebony hair fell nearly to her slender, swaying hips . . . but there his mind rebelled. The drab, ill-tailored dress she wore was a blatant insult to her grace and femininity. He narrowed his eyes, mentally stripping her of the atrocious garments and redressing her . . . undressing her. A diaphanous negligee draping her lovely body, open to his gaze . . . rubies at her throat, bloodred against her snow-white skin . . . breasts full and pink-nippled, pleading for his touch . . . a raven triangle of down that hid the portal to an earthly heaven.

The image was enough to arouse his loins uncomfortably. Setting his jaw, Julian lay back on the quilt and stretched his legs out carefully, welcoming the last rays of rare afternoon sunlight. They warmed his body and soothed his aching thigh muscles, but did little to cool his overheated blood or subdue his erotic thoughts. He wanted that bewitching wench. And he would have her. He intended to do everything in his power—short of abduction or rape—to make her his.

He did not consider his competition formidable. Relying on well-honed masculine instincts, Julian sensed he had little reason to be jealous of Miklos. The Gypsy chief was a handsome, swarthy devil, to be sure, but he was more than twice Blaise's age—and a married man with a large family, besides. Moreover, Miklos had treated Blaise much like a younger sister. The boy Tommy was no threat, either. She had claimed the lad was her betrothed, but her bright eyes had brimmed with secret mirth when she'd said it, while her saucy laughter had challenged Julian to prove otherwise.

He didn't see the need to take up the challenge, though. Whatever her relationship with the Gypsies—and he was rabidly curious about it, no mistake—it made little difference to his determination. He had methods of pursuit he hadn't yet employed, powers of seduction he hadn't yet called upon.

His violet-eyed minx would soon discover how meager her defenses were when Julian Morrow, Sixth Viscount Lynden, late of His Majesty's Cavalry, decided a breach was in order.

Chapter 4

The crackling flames of a Gypsy campfire . . . the pungent scent of woodsmoke mingling with the fragrance of simmering stew . . . the jovial sound of male laughter as his hosts gathered for the evening meal.

Julian found himself caught up in the spell the Gypsies weaved, yet he was aware of a keen sense of disappointment. The Gypsy women ate apart from the men, and would join them only after the dishes were washed and the youngest children tucked into bed within their tents. He had a while longer before he could see his bewitching minx.

" 'Tis simple fare, m'lord," Miklos apologized as his wife, Isadore, served the lord a wooden bowl and spoon.

Resigning himself to the wait, Julian smiled easily and bent himself toward making himself agreeable. "I'm accustomed to simple fare," he lied. "I was a soldier, you see." He didn't add that rations for cavalry officers were often elaborate feasts. He tasted the food in his bowl and closed his eyes in appreciation. "Excellent," he pronounced quite truthfully. The dog Bruno had flushed out a half-dozen hares for the cooking pot, and the stew made with wild onions and potatoes held a mouth-watering flavor.

The conversation turned general as the meal progressed. Julian pretended attentiveness and tried to discipline his impatience, but his thoughts centered around a laughing enchantress with flashing violet eyes and gleaming midnight hair.

As evening fell, the women began to join the group

around the campfire. Only when Julian's anticipation was at a fever pitch, though, did Blaise finally appear.

She met his eyes briefly, through the crowd, her long-lashed gaze seeking him out, as if drawn against her will.

It hit him then—desire like a hunger in his belly, a gnawing, twisting hunger that made him ache as fiercely as his wound had ever done. For a dozen heartbeats the force took his breath away.

She wore the clothes of a Gypsy: a bright yellow blouse, lavishly embroidered along the full sleeves and drawstring neckline that was far too high and modest, in his opinion; a blue velvet corselet that hugged her slender waist; a bottle-green shawl that protected her graceful shoulders from the chill night air; a vivid scarlet skirt that swirled about her ankles; a beaded necklace of red and black that hung between her high, firm breasts; and gold earrings that caressed her cheeks whenever she turned her head. Her long jet hair had been intricately plaited and dressed in fanciful loops and knots in the Gypsy fashion, although Julian would have preferred to see it unbound.

But it was the woman herself, not her clothing or hairstyle, that affected him so powerfully. Her creamy skin glowed in the firelight, while her bright eyes took on the deep luster of amethysts. With the fall of darkness she had become a sultry, sensuous creature of the night.

Julian felt himself harden abruptly with arousal, and it was all he could do to clamp down on the savage, primitive urge to sweep his enticing Gypsy up in his arms and carry her away from here, far from the crowd and the light and the noise, into the darkness of night, where he could be totally alone with her, where he could slowly remove her garments one by one and explore the luscious, delicate body beneath, where he could wrap himself in that rippling ebony hair, where they could give themselves to each other, and take comfort from the giving.

It was impossible, of course. They were surrounded by

a jovial but protective throng who would certainly object if a strange Englishman, no matter how lordly, were to carry off one of their number.

He hoped Blaise would come to him, merely to sit beside him and allow him to share her closeness, yet she seemed intent on avoiding him. She took a seat quite some distance from him, halfway around the campfire, drawing her knees up and demurely arranging her skirts as the other women were doing.

"Now," Miklos announced for the benefit of his aristocratic guest, "we will 'ave stories. I'll wager ye never 'eard the like, m'lord."

Julian dragged his gaze away from Blaise and smiled politely as one of the older Rom stepped forward.

The storytelling turned out to be quite entertaining, fanciful tales of derring-do, embellished with unbelievable avowals of incredible feats, punctuated with expansive gestures, and underscored by simple morals. With effort Julian kept his attention on the speakers and away from the young woman across the campfire. Yet he couldn't keep the smoky images of her from his mind, fantasies that heated his blood and made the muscles of his body taut with anticipation and tension.

"So, what think you, m'lord?" Miklos asked at the conclusion.

"Enchanting," Julian replied without hesitation, his eyes on Blaise.

Miklos had obviously wanted his opinion of the stories, but the answer must have been satisfactory, for the Gypsy chief beamed. "I'll wager you yerself 'ave a tale or two worth 'earing," Miklos prodded.

"Nothing that could compare to yours."

"Mayhap you're too modest, m'lord."

"Well, I suppose I could tell you about the time I managed to trick my father's gamekeepers when I was a lad."

Immediately two dozen pairs of dark eyes brightened, and Julian knew he had hit on a topic dear to the hearts of the Gypsies.

"Aye, that would be capital," Miklos agreed.

With a wry, self-deprecating smile, Julian launched into a tale about poaching his own father's game and escaping punishment by the skin of his teeth. He created much of the story as he went, but he shortly had the Gypsies exclaiming at his bravado and laughing at the fate of the wicked gamekeepers, one of whom wound up flailing in a fishpond, the other hanging by his heels from a tree limb, caught in the snare Julian had fashioned.

From across the way, Blaise watched the exchange with growing fascination and no little dismay at Lord Lynden's success with his rapt audience. She could see now how he had managed to charm Miklos into inviting him for supper. He had the knack of disarming the simple Gypsies with his genuine interest and sincere flattery. The kindhearted Rom were much more accustomed to shouted insults and invectives from *gorgios*, but Lynden's appreciative laughter when they told a jest, his evident fascination at their tales, and his obvious admiration for their athletic feats served to win them over. Indeed, he fit in remarkably, despite his fair coloring and elevated station. The Gypsies were obviously eager to impress the highborn lord, but he was clearly willing to be impressed, never once looking down his aristocratic nose at them or treating them as less than equals. Blaise found herself enchanted against her will. She was almost disappointed when the violins and tambourines were broken out—and the dancing was usually her favorite entertainment.

Julian, too, felt disappointed—to be denied the opportunity to pursue his aims concerning the young woman sitting so far from him. Chafing at his inaction, he watched with assumed enthusiasm as the stage was set for the performance. The leaping flames of a Gypsy campfire . . . the plaintive, throbbing melody of a violin . . . silhouettes outlined by firelight as the musicians and dancers took their places.

But then the incredible music began in earnest. Wild, soaring, ecstatic notes that trailed into long, drawn-out

sobbing chords, a lamentation of death and grief. Slow,
heavy rhythms that grew and swelled and tumbled about,
faster and faster, racing with gaiety and joie de vivre,
a celebration of untamed passions and free spirits, a
triumph of life over tragedy.

Julian had heard such crescendos of sound only a few
times before, in Spain, when the local Andalusian dancers of the famed flamenco had been hired to entertain
the regimental officers. Now, as then, the music was like
balm to his wounded soul . . . yet at the same time, it also
acted as a painful prod, arousing emotions he thought
long buried, those deadened by his own personal nightmare and four hellish years of war . . . eagerness, hope,
joy in simply being alive.

He thought he'd lost the ability to feel joy, but he
could feel it now, in the stirring music, in the leaps
and whirls of the Gypsy dancers who accompanied the
instruments, in the sight of the raven-haired girl across
the way. Julian was outwardly aware of the dancers'
expressive movements, but he had eyes only for Blaise.
She sat surprisingly still, watching the performance, her
arms wrapped about her knees, a look of longing on her
face, as if she yearned to join in. Why she did not was
a mystery to him, but then much about her was still a
mystery—which he hoped to soon unravel.

His chance came when the last throbbing chord had died
away. Julian applauded enthusiastically and expressed his
compliments to the entire tribe. "Remarkable. I've never
seen such skill. I could never dance half so well, even
before my injury."

The Gypsies preened proudly.

Then Miklos announced that it was time to retire and
opened a discussion on the sleeping arrangements for
the night. Julian offered to camp out in the open, to
make do with a blanket, but his suggestion was met
with vociferous protests. When a lively argument ensued
as to who would have the honor of loaning his tent to
the *gorgio rye*, Julian was momentarily left alone.

He rose, absently kneading his lame leg to take the

stiffness from it, and with the help of his cane, crossed the short distance to stand before a silent Blaise, offering his hand to help her rise. She looked up with a start, which made Julian experience an absurd surge of jealousy that her thoughts should have been so far from him.

"Where has your attention been, sweeting?" he probed as she accepted his aid in standing. Her action brought her face close to his, and he was startled by the sadness he glimpsed in her eyes and the tears that shimmered there.

Julian's tone was sharper than he intended when he demanded, "What troubles you?"

She averted her face, wiping her cheek with the back of her hand. "Nothing . . . only memories."

He knew all there was to know about unpleasant memories, but it disturbed him that his laughing minx should have any such troubling remembrances in her past. Unreasonably he'd assumed her incapable of dark thoughts. Reaching up, he touched a finger to her chin, turning her face back to his. "It distresses me that anything should be so painful as to make you cry."

The tenderness in his tone, in his sapphire eyes, shook Blaise out of her melancholy and held her immobile. She had been remembering her father the last time they'd visited the Gypsy camp together, how funny it had been to watch him try breathlessly to outdance Miklos—an impossible feat, since Miklos was a champion dancer.

But she'd never been one to dwell on the past, nor would her father have wished her to. Scolding herself silently, Blaise swallowed her tears, yet she couldn't manage to look away from the golden-haired lord who had taken her chin in a gentle grip.

He was searching her face intently, a faint scowl between his brows, as if he might by sheer force of will drive away her unhappiness.

"I'm all right, truly."

His scowl relaxed; his hold did not. His thumb began to move, stroking the delicate line of her jaw. Blaise felt her pulse escalate at the gesture, at his nearness. She was uncomfortably aware of his attractiveness, of how the gilded strands of his hair gleamed like minted gold in the firelight, the gentle way his thumb shifted to caress her lower lip.

Suddenly recalling their circumstances, she attempted to draw away, taking a step back to break the intimate contact.

He let her go with obvious reluctance.

"You did not dance tonight." His beautiful voice held a seductive quality; she felt his words touch her like caressing fingers. "I confess to disappointment."

Blaise forced a smile. "You didn't miss much. I'm not at all proficient."

Whatever Lord Lynden might have said was lost when Miklos suddenly appeared. "There's no call for misplaced modesty, Rauniyog. You are indeed proficient. She's a fine dancer, m'lord. I taught 'er the way of it myself."

Julian looked from one to the other of them. "Rauniyog?"

" 'Tis only a pet name for Miss—Mistress Blaise," Miklos explained. "It means lady o' fire in Romany. Her papa was always one for using 'andles."

An appealing flush had crept over Blaise's cheeks, Julian noted, but it was more than just the intriguing nickname that caught his curiosity. "You knew her father?"

"Aye, 'e was a good friend to the Rom. Well, now, your tent awaits you, m'lord. If you'll please to come wi' me?"

"Yes, thank you. But perhaps you'll allow me a moment to say good night to Mistress Blaise."

Miklos looked taken aback by the request, but he tugged on his forelock respectfully and moved a short distance away, giving them privacy.

A bit annoyed by Lynden's ease in commanding obedience, Blaise eyed him warily. She was surprised, though, by what he said.

"I thought you might instruct me as to the proper etiquette under the circumstances. I shouldn't like to think I'm evicting someone from his bed, but I imagine it would be impolite for me to refuse."

Blaise had to admire his consideration. "Yes, it would. They would be hurt if you refused their hospitality. But," she gibed, "I doubt the accommodations are what you are accustomed to, my lord. It will be cold tonight."

At her subtle emphasis on his rank, his lips curved in a wry smile. "On the contrary. I've suffered far worse upon occasion as a soldier—bivouacking in an open field in a freezing rain, with only my cloak for shelter."

In contrition, she fell silent. Lynden *had* suffered much worse than spending the night in a Gypsy tent; his war wounds attested to that fact.

"Where will you sleep tonight?" he asked when she didn't respond.

There was a suggestiveness, an intimacy, in the question that no gently reared young lady would allow from a strange man. Blaise opened her mouth to give him a setdown for his boldness, then remembered that she was not supposed to be a lady.

She managed an arch smile. "I shall be well-chaperoned, my lord, you may be certain. You *gorgios* have some vast misconceptions about Gypsy women. You consider us shameless and abandoned, but I assure you we are as chaste and protected as any novitiates in a convent."

He didn't look as if he believed her. "A pity" was all he said. Then he lightly touched a finger to her nose and stepped back. "Think of me when your head touches the pillow."

He left her standing there, staring after him, and followed Miklos through the camp, to the tent he had been loaned for the night.

"I fear there's no chamber pot," the Gypsy chief apologized. "We use the woods. But I'll 'ave Tommy fetch ye some 'ot water to shave with on the morrow."

"I'm much obliged."

"Will you be needin' anything else then, your lordship?"

Julian paused. "I hesitate to ask."

"Nay, you go right ahead. Whatever we 'ave is yours."

"Would it be an affront to request assistance in removing my boots? I'll be required to sleep in them otherwise."

Miklos's teeth flashed white in his swarthy face. "I'm your man, yer honor."

The burly Gypsy good-naturedly made short work of tugging off Julian's form-fitting boots, saying not a word about how helpless fancy coves were without their servants to do for them—although he must be thinking it, Julian suspected wryly. Yet the aid was worth the blow to his pride. He might have managed his boots on his own, but it would have proved a strain to his wound. As it was, Miklos's efforts left him a bit white around the mouth.

He denied being in any discomfort when the Gypsy chief asked, however. Thanking Miklos for his generosity, Julian crawled inside his night's lodging, where a little candle lamp had been left burning, suspended from the roof rods overhead.

The tent was small and primitive but amazingly clean, he discovered. At the farthest end, a curtain hung before the bed, which was little more than a pile of straw covered with sacking, raised several inches off the earthen floor by leafy branches—to keep rain from drowning the sleeper, Julian assumed. The blankets he found to be fresh and sweet-smelling. It was a pleasant relief to know he wouldn't be chewed alive by bedbugs. He'd had his fill of sleeping with vermin in the Peninsula.

After dropping the tent flap which served as a door, he took off his redingote and coat, his cravat and shirt collar, and set his pocket watch aside. Then he snuffed the candle wick, lay down, and drew the blankets over him. He was weary from the day's exertions, but there was a lightness in his heart that he hadn't felt in a long while.

The reflection took him by surprise. Not once tonight had he thought of Caroline or her untimely death, or his guilt. His thoughts had all been taken up by a bright-eyed witch who delighted in keeping him guessing.

Softly Julian chuckled in the darkness, thinking of the sobriquet Blaise had been called by the Gypsies. Lady of fire. Perfect.

He closed his eyes, letting himself recall that afternoon, the sensations of having her lying beneath him as he kissed her, of feeling her sweet response. His body tightened in remembrance.

Yet what he felt for her was somehow more than lust, more than desire. Strangely, it could almost be called gratitude. However unwittingly, his minx had given him a goal, a challenge. Pursuing her had provided a focus for his dark thoughts, an escape from his ghosts. For the first time in years he could look forward to the future with something other than anguish or apathy.

And he knew somehow, as he wrapped the covers more closely about him, that despite his aching thigh, he was about to enjoy his first peaceful sleep in years.

Chapter 5

The nightmares stayed away that night. Instead, he dreamed of holding a raven-haired enchantress in his arms, of having her soft, silky body arching in passion beneath him, of drinking from her sweet, warm lips.

He woke to a cold, unfamiliar wetness prodding his nose.

Startled by the sensation, Julian sat up abruptly, and in the dim morning light, he found himself staring at a beastly black visage with a lolling tongue. It was the sudden spasm in his thigh, however, more than the shock, that made him groan.

Unrepentant, Bruno the dog shrank back beyond the tent flap that he'd managed to open and sat on his haunches, grinning at the gentleman.

"You, sir, were not invited into my humble abode," Julian said through clenched teeth. "Now take yourself off."

He wasn't to discover the effect of his command, for just then a gruff shout sounded from nearby. The Gypsy youth Tommy came running up to drive the dog away with a kick to the ribs. Then the boy dropped to his knees at the tent entrance, spilling half the contents of the water basin he carried.

"Oh, m'lord, beg pardon! It won't 'appen again, I swear."

Julian managed to murmur, "No harm was done," even as he broke out in a sweat at the sharp pain coursing through his leg.

"But the *jook,* 'tis unclean."

Julian suspected the lad was speaking of the dog, but he was in no position to discuss Gypsy vocabulary at the moment, or to argue the beast's shortcomings. Gritting his teeth, he rubbed the muscles of his thigh savagely until the spasm at last subsided. Then he looked up and forced a smile.

"If that is hot water you've brought me, then I can forgive anything."

"Aye, m'lord—but I'm right sorry. Bruno 'as been trained better, 'e 'as. 'E didn't ken that ye're not a *gorgio* for plucking. Most *gorgios* are all alike to 'im."

Subjected to another spate of profuse apologies, Julian listened politely while studying the boy. A handsome lad with dark, passionate eyes and a flush of youth on his dusky features, Tommy was quite definitely far too young for the woman Julian had spent the night dreaming about, not only in age but in experience. His minx would run circles around a lad like that, and leave his head whirling.

He managed to send Tommy on his way after giving assurances that he'd survived the terrible ordeal of having a dog lick his face and was not in the least overset.

In the blessed silence that followed, he could hear the bustling activity of the camp as it began the day. When he looked out, he saw the blue smoke of the cooking fires spiraling upward, mingling with the chill, early-morning mist that hung over the meadow.

Suddenly shivering at the damp cold seeping into his tent, Julian hastened to shrug into his coat. He was girding himself for the ordeal of pulling on his boots when he heard footsteps through the open flap. Looking out, he spied Blaise coming toward him, with Miklos trailing hesitantly behind.

When she reached his tent, she sank to her knees, so that her eyes were generally on his level. Julian's first thought was how fresh and lovely she looked in her colorful Gypsy garb when he had yet to shave or wash. His second was how uncharacteristically subdued her expression was.

Hesitantly, she cleared her throat and held out a gold watch. "Does this, by any chance, belong to you, my lord?"

Julian's hand automatically went to his coat pocket, before he remembered he had laid his watch beside his blankets. A quick search told him it was gone. "I suppose it must belong to me. Mine seems to be missing. I take it I have Bruno to thank for its disappearance?"

A soft flush crept over her cheeks. "He didn't *steal* it, exactly. It's just that . . ."

"He borrowed it in order to tell the time. Such a clever dog." Julian smiled wryly and took the proffered watch, tucking it safely in his pocket.

Blaise knew Lord Lynden was not gullible enough to believe *that* interpretation of events. Besides being a great rabbiter, Bruno was a model Gypsy dog, trained to lift watches, spoons, money, anything small and valuable from unsuspecting *gorgios*. He merely had chosen the wrong target this morning. Stealing from a guest violated every law of Gypsy hospitality. Miklos had been mortified to learn of it and had asked Blaise to intervene with his lordship.

"I'm truly sorry, my lord—"

Julian shrugged easily. "Don't regard it. It really is no great matter. Indeed, it has made my introduction to Gypsy life a memorable experience."

Miklos stepped forward then to express his sincere regrets, and proceeded to become so grovelingly apologetic that Lord Lynden looked uncomfortable. Observing him, Blaise was grateful he was taking the theft of his watch by the tribe's dog with such good grace. Many noblemen would have been outraged enough to destroy the animal and have its owner tossed in jail. But then Viscount Lynden was not the typical nobleman, she was beginning to realize.

His frankly admiring stare a moment earlier had unaccountably flustered her, something that no man had ever managed to do before. That look she'd seen in his blue, blue eyes had almost made her forget her

purpose for coming. Even in his stocking feet, with his
lawn shirt open at the neck without shirt collar or cravat,
with a day's growth of dark golden stubble marring the
aristocratic line of his jaw, and with the scar on his cheek
gleaming a savage red, he still was the most aesthetically
attractive man she had ever met.

It was only when he edged his way out the entrance
and tried to stand that he appeared at a disadvantage.
Grimacing in pain, Lynden clutched at his thigh, while
beads of perspiration broke out on his forehead.

Miklos looked alarmed, but Blaise jumped to her feet
to assist him, supporting his arm until he could manage
to stand on his own. "Shouldn't you lie down?" she asked
anxiously.

"No," Julian said in a hoarse voice. "The spasm . . .
will pass."

She wished there was something she could do to ease
his suffering. She'd seen him rubbing the muscles of
his bad leg yesterday, and knew his wound still caused
him great pain. "Our tribal mother, Panna, is extremely
skilled with herbs and medical remedies," Blaise offered.
"Perhaps she can help."

"Aye," Miklos agreed. "Panna will surely ken what to
do. We can fetch 'er right away."

"I wouldn't . . . want to put her to any trouble."

" 'Twon't be any trouble. And mayhap 'twill make up
for Bruno's mischief."

"I should be grateful, then," Julian admitted, glancing
down at Blaise, who was still holding his arm.

Quite improperly, she felt an urge to touch his face,
just to smooth away those strain lines around his mouth
and eyes. It was a moment before she realized Miklos
had spoken to her, suggesting that she go and find Panna.

"Yes, of course," Blaise said quickly. Releasing Lord
Lynden's arm, she hurried to do the Gypsy chief's bidding.

Panna Smith might have the haggish looks and cack-
ling laugh of a witch, Julian thought an hour later, but

the sorcery in her age-spotted, gnarled hands relied more on gentleness and skill than on black art.

He'd first found it embarrassing to be required to undress and have his ravaged thigh examined and probed by Panna—and by a curious Miklos, as well—but after the ordeal was over, he could not doubt the old crone's claim that she was a healer.

Panna had prescribed a liniment made from her own secret Romany recipe, which she rubbed on the wound, massaging the ropes of scar tissue on his thigh and working it deep into the knotted muscles. The liniment smelled not unpleasantly of mint, and Panna vowed it would help control the spasms that usually left him stiff and sometimes half sick with pain.

"Now ye'll be quicker on yer feet," the old woman pronounced after she finished wrapping the leg with a length of muslin and wiped her hands clean.

"Amazing," Julian said thoughtfully. "It feels a good deal better already. I'm more grateful than you know."

The Gypsy gave a raucous chortle. "I *know* how grateful ye are, me fine lord. It don't take a seer to ken a recipe of the Rom is worth ten of yer *gorgio* cures. But if you'd care to be truly amazed, then come to me wagon, by and by. I'll tell you yer fortune."

He agreed politely, not because he believed in such flummery, but because he was indebted to her for her help, and because she hadn't condemned him to his bed for rest and recuperation. Not only was he weary of such confinement, but bedrest seemed to make little difference to his spasming muscles.

Julian tested the leg when his visitors had left, letting it bear his full weight for upward of a minute at a time. The strength was still impaired but the ache had diminished significantly. Will Terral was going to be envious.

His spirits lighter than they had been in four years, Julian finished shaving and dressing and making himself presentable. He decided against the cravat as too formal for the simply garbed company he was keeping, so he merely buttoned on his shirt collar and made a mental

note to have Will bring him a change of linen for the
morrow. If he planned to remain here for any length
of time—and it looked as if it would take longer than
he hoped to achieve his goal—then he would prefer to
maximize his comfort. With a wry glance at his primitive surroundings, Julian picked up his cane and went in
search of his lady of fire.

He found her racing across the meadow with a band
of raggle-taggle Gypsy children, their shouts and shrieks
of laughter loud enough to startle the horses that grazed
nearby. Blaise looked like the ringleader of their play,
although she had to be at least five years older than the
oldest child.

Julian wondered how he had ever disbelieved her story
about living with the Gypsy tribe. Her skin might not be
the same dusky color, and her speech might be more
refined, but she was every bit as high-spirited and wild
as they. She looked as if she truly belonged here.

He watched her scampering merrily across the damp
grass, occasionally hiding behind a horse and leaping out
to tag a giggling child. How long had it been since he had
enjoyed such simple, uninhibited pleasure? Had he ever
felt that free?

She saw him eventually and gave a guilty start, then
made a visible effort at decorum: ceasing her play,
holding her shoulders erect, smoothing her skirts, and
brushing back the wisps of raven hair that had escaped
their intricate plaits. Julian regretted that he had intruded
on her joy.

Her pace was modest as she came up to him, but she
was still panting for breath and her eyes sparkled with
laughter. Not even the vivid colors she wore could match
the brightness of her eyes. Julian found himself feeling a
fierce desire to lift her by the waist and whirl her around.

She dropped him a saucy curtsy when she reached him,
but her expression became more sober as she searched
his face. "Are you still in pain, my lord?"

He smiled wryly. "Remarkably, no. I'm not yet able
to engage in such abandoned sport as occupied you

just now, but the pain has diminished significantly." He flexed his right leg to show his newfound
mobility.

"I'm glad Panna was able to help. She usually does."

"She worked a miracle in my case. How did she manage it? I was afraid to inquire too closely into the ingredi-
ents of her secret recipe for fear I'd learn she uses ground
snails or frogs eyes or bat's blood."

Blaise gave a husky chuckle. "Nothing so sinister!
She relies on yarrow and St. John's wort and comfrey
for her poultices, I believe. They are all highly effective
on horses, at least."

"I don't suppose it would be in order for me to offer
her payment?"

"Oh, no, absolutely not. You are a guest. Any Gypsy
would be gravely insulted if you were to try to pay for
simple hospitality."

"But surely there must be something I may do to ease
my conscience and express my gratitude."

"You might give the tribe a gift of some sort . . . a cask
of wine, perhaps. Panna might like a length of material
to make a scarf, or a string of beads. Gypsy women have
a great fondness for beads. And"—a mischievous gleam
lit Blaise's eyes—"if your conscience truly troubles you,
you could always buy a horse from Miklos and let him
overcharge you. The men of this tribe pride themselves
on driving a hard bargain."

Julian winced at the suggestion. "The price is not an
issue, but I don't relish the thought of adding a nag to
my stables."

"Oh, you wouldn't get a nag. Miklos is a skilled breed-
er, and most of the horses he deals with are excellent
animals. Besides, he wouldn't try to hoodwink *you*."

"Meaning he would do so with others who were not
his guests."

Blaise laughed outright. "Well, they do have to make a
living. And outwitting gullible *gorgios* is a time-honored
custom among Gypsies."

"Is that how you view me? As someone to outwit?"

He saw the subtle flush of response in her heightened color and knew he had guessed correctly; she saw him as an adversary. She had dropped her lashes to veil her eyes, but although the gesture was incredibly seductive, it was not coy or flirtatious—not the kind of practiced art women usually employed to arouse a man's interest. In fact, his lady of fire seemed to have no idea of her enchantingly feminine charms and how effective they were against him. He would have to be on his guard if he meant to succeed in his pursuit of her.

When she remained silent, Julian decided it was high time he went on the offensive and employed his own methods of attaching a woman's interest. Placing a finger under her chin, he captured her gaze. "Very well, but if we are to engage in a game of wits, I think it only sporting that you give me a fair chance to win."

"What . . . what do you mean?"

He favored Blaise with a slow smile, irresistible in its blatant male charm. "Allow me to spend time in your company while I am here in your camp. That is all I ask."

"That's all?"

"Yes." His eyebrow rose innocently. "Can you in good conscience refuse such a simple request? If your people hold hospitality in such high regard, then as your guest, would I be remiss in claiming your companionship as my due?"

"Might I remind you, my lord, that you are Miklos's guest, not mine?"

He drew a finger slowly along her lower lip. "Miklos is not the reason I am here, sweeting, as you well know."

Blaise swallowed. Those clear, dazzlingly blue eyes of Lynden's were warning her quite brazenly that he hadn't given up his determination to persuade her to become his mistress.

"Are you afraid of me?" he asked softly when she didn't reply.

No, Blaise thought with certainty. He aroused a dozen disturbing feelings in her, but fear was not chief among them—unless it was fear for him. Earlier this morning, when he'd been in such pain, her heart had gone out to him. But she shouldn't let compassion for his suffering blind her to his true aims.

"What . . . would you require me to do?" she said finally, warily.

"Nothing too onerous. I merely hoped you would show me about the camp and perhaps conduct me to Panna's tent. She bade me call on her to have my fortune read."

"She did?"

"You sound surprised. Is her request so unusual?"

"I suppose not. Like most Gypsy women, Panna earns her living by telling fortunes."

"Promising riches and happiness to gullible *gorgios*?"

That brought a rueful smile to Blaise's lips. "Not always. Panna truly has the gift of Sight. If she sees you in a vision, she's likely to tell you the truth, even if it isn't something you would wish to hear."

Lynden's eyebrow rose skeptically.

"Honestly! Panna knows things that have no rational explanation. She knew I would return to the tribe yesterday, even before I myself did."

"Indeed?"

Blaise looked intently at him, a worried frown shadowing her eyes. "If you hold that attitude, my lord, it would be better if you declined to have Panna tell your fortune. You would disappoint her if you didn't appear to believe her."

He smiled suddenly, a seductive smile that made her think of the sun breaking out from behind a cloud. "I shall certainly make the effort, then. If, that is, you will agree to keep me company while I am here."

Blaise hesitated. Lynden was right about having a reasonable claim on her time; it was the Gypsy way. She owed him the simple courtesy she would afford any guest, even if he meant to use her politeness to achieve her downfall. Surely, though, she would be able to withstand his attempts at seduction. She had never been the kind of female to be swayed by a man's blandishments.

She ought to be able to resist even so charming and attractive a nobleman as Lord Lynden.

"Very well," Blaise replied, wondering if perhaps she *should* be afraid.

As if the outcome had never been in doubt, he nodded. "Are you free now, or do you wish to return to your games?"

Blaise glanced behind her at the meadow where she had romped with the Gypsy children. Her young playmates had run off to one end and did not appear to be missing her. She could not look to them for protection.

Realizing Lord Lynden was offering his arm, Blaise couldn't quell a shiver. With a feeling of forbidden anticipation and excitement, she placed her hand on his sleeve and accepted his escort.

Chapter 6

Blaise clung to the seat of the rumbling cart as it rocked through a muddy pothole, her thoughts far away from the deplorable condition of the English country roads. Three full days, and she was no closer to being rid of Viscount Lynden. He seemed intent on becoming a permanent fixture at the Gypsy camp.

She glanced behind her, where his elegant traveling chaise held the rear position in the procession of bow-topped canvas wagons. The crested carriage drawn by the team of sleek matched bays looked absurdly out of place amid the rickety and patched carts belonging to the Gypsies. And its presence made her feel *hunted*.

It was annoying, how trapped she had begun to feel. Her first real freedom in years, and it was being ruined by a gilt-haired nobleman determined on her seduction. Not even the most blatant hints had driven him away. He was all politeness, but he simply refused to accept defeat. Instead he had put himself out to be agreeable to the entire tribe, not only exercising a subtle charm that masterfully overwhelmed the humble Gypsies, but bribing them daily with gifts of the sort she had suggested, as well as supplying additional provisions for the cooking pots. Many of the Rom had even begun to feel easy with the *gorgio rye*, despite his effortless elegance and sophisticated manners and quietly commanding air of authority. Miklos, who normally was as suspicious of *gorgios* as of the plague, actually *liked* him. And Panna was oddly silent on the subject.

Blaise shook her head at Lynden's bewildering success. He was unlike any man she had ever met, English or otherwise. Once or twice she'd even wondered if he might not have Gypsy blood flowing in his veins. She'd watched Lynden's beautiful, scarred features as he listened to the wild violin concertos around the campfire. His keen enjoyment of the music was unfeigned—and vastly different from the superior ennui affected by the blue-blooded gentlemen in her stepfather's elite circle.

Perhaps Lynden had hidden depths of passion that most Englishmen lacked. Certainly he possessed a sensuality that was uncommon in the phlegmatic British temperament. Sometimes when he looked at her, the blatant masculine desire in his blue eyes, in his golden smile, made her limbs grow weak and her heartbeat quicken. It was as if he already had carnal knowledge of her.

Then again, his passion could be no more substantive than that of other wealthy, depraved young bucks of the nobility who were merely concerned with gratification of the senses, indulgence of physical appetites. Lynden had adapted with amazing ease to the simple life of the Gypsies, but he had a sinister reason for appearing to fit in, Blaise remembered: his determined pursuit of her. Her complete seduction was his stated goal. She'd been certain he would grow bored with his little game, but instead he had settled in for a long siege, like the cavalry officer he was. And she resented it.

She had so looked forward to enjoying this brief interlude in her otherwise stifling existence. Up ahead, the road stretched out before the wagons, beckoning to the adventuresome with the alluring illusion of freedom. Generations of Smiths had traveled these same routes for centuries—except for the lengthy interval when the Romany people were outlawed entirely. Several hundred years ago, Queen Elizabeth had decreed death to all Gypsies in England. The ones who escaped hanging or transportation survived as slaves or hunted criminals, or else as beggars hiding their Gypsy heritage. Only during the last several decades had they been allowed to live openly and practice their age-old customs.

Miklos's tribe moved camp every day or two, hunting for work, calling at farms and villages along the way, the women telling fortunes and selling baskets, the men doing odd jobs and dealing in horses.

At the moment Blaise rode in Panna's wagon. Tommy drove, while the old woman rested in the back.

"Is it much farther till we set up camp?" Blaise asked the lad eventually.

"Nay . . . 'tis but a league or so, Mistress St.—"

"You must remember to call me Blaise, Tom. We are supposed to be promised. And an occasional endearment in front of Lord Lynden would not be amiss, either."

"A-aye, I forgot," Tommy stammered, flushing beneath his swarthy complexion. He had been coloring up like that for three days, obviously uncomfortable with the role Blaise had assigned to him—that of lover and affianced husband.

She fell silent again, regretting that she had dragged the Gypsy youth into her schemes. She had thought it wise to keep up the appearance of her "betrothal"—not that Lord Lynden believed her. In fact, she had found it frustratingly difficult to maintain her role of Gypsy while subjected to Lynden's constant scrutiny.

It had rained much of the past two days, a chill, blustery rain that drove even the Gypsies to take refuge in their wagons. Blaise had shared Panna's, and much to her annoyance, so had Lord Lynden.

Bewilderingly, Panna had invited the viscount to make himself at home in her wagon, displaying a generosity that went far beyond simple hospitality, a generosity that had left Blaise feeling somehow betrayed. She couldn't understand it. Nor had she comprehended Panna's cryptic remarks concerning Lord Lynden's future.

Blaise frowned at the memory of that gray afternoon. She had been present when he'd had his fortune told, an unusual occurrence, since Panna never liked to have an audience when she read the tarot cards. The old Gypsy possibly had her reasons, but Blaise couldn't fathom them.

"So, me fine lord," Panna said with deliberate provocation, "are ye brave enough to dare learn what fate has in store for you?"

Lynden smiled charmingly, though his eyes remained somewhat shuttered. "Given that you've challenged my courage with your offer, how do I dare refuse?"

The Gypsy cackled with glee. " 'Tis not yer courage I question. 'Tis yer closed mind and 'eart. Aye, ye put no trust in the truth of the cards. But mayhap ye will a'ter this."

"I find the possibility . . . intriguing. Do your worst, Mother," he said, addressing her by the term of respect the other members of her clan used.

The wagon was crowded with all Panna's worldly possessions, the breakable items carefully stowed for travel in a gaily carved chest built for the purpose of storing china and food. Not wanting to intrude, Blaise settled at the rear of the wagon, while the fortune-teller and the golden lord sat on carpets in the center, a short table between them. On the table's surface, special pictorial cards numbered 0 through XX were laid out in a triangle, then surrounded by the rest of the pack, which formed a square.

The scene itself held a hint of the mystical, Blaise thought. A handmade oil lamp hung overhead from a hook, washing the wagon's interior with a golden light, while the rain drummed down on the canvas roof, creating a hollow sound that shut out the rest of the world.

Panna took a very long time, studying the sequence of each bit of pasteboard to determine its numerical and symbolic meaning. She frowned particularly over the cards representing the High Priestess, Judgment, and the Devil, but nodded sagely over Strength and the Lovers.

Blaise didn't pretend to follow her progress. Instead she found herself helplessly watching Lord Lynden. In the lantern light his hair glimmered, its soft curls threaded riotously with flaxen and gold, while the harshness of the scar on his cheek faded. Lynden did not appear antagonistic toward the fortune-telling exercise. Merely resigned. His gratitude toward Panna for easing the pain of his wounded leg was entirely genuine, Blaise was certain, but it did not extend to believing in the rest of the old Gypsy's skills.

"You've known great sorrow," Panna declared in a subdued voice as she came to the last of the cards.

Lynden's mouth twisted wryly. "An astute observation. Four years of negotiating battlefields might qualify as sorrow, I would imagine."

Blaise had to agree that Panna's deduction was not overly impressive. His war wounds alone were enough to justify her prediction.

"Ye willfully misunderstand me," Panna grunted. " 'Tis not war I speak of."

She hesitated, then nodded slowly. "You've yet to know love. But you will find it. Aye, ye will."

Something dark and bitter flickered in his expression, but he remained silent; the rain slashing against the canvas overhead was the only sound.

The Gypsy suddenly stiffened as she stared down at the cards. "I see a dark place, with stones and crumbling walls. I see death."

Lord Lynden suddenly did not look quite so stoical; Blaise saw him turn pale, while his fingers clenched into fists.

"I see shadows," Panna murmured finally, before shaking herself and coming out of whatever momentary trance she had been locked in. She raised her gaze to his, not in triumph but in sadness, her lined face old and haggard. "Do I speak the truth?"

He collected himself visibly. "My favorite nightmare," he said lightly, but the haunting look of desolation in his eyes made Blaise want to shiver. "I congratulate you on your perceptiveness, Mother. Can your cards predict how the nightmare ends? I usually awaken at that point."

Panna looked troubled. " 'Tis only shadows I see. Mayhap they will become clearer in time."

Remembering that cryptic remark now, Blaise shivered as Tommy drove the wagon around a bend in the lane and headed into the wind. There had to be some truth to Panna's interpretation of the tarot cards. Lord Lynden certainly hadn't denied it. Blaise wondered what great sorrow he had endured, and what dark events shadowed his future. But it was Panna's next prediction, after the rain had stopped and Lord Lynden had left, that actually worried Blaise more.

The Gypsy fortune-teller still had that troubled look in her black eyes when she turned to her young guest. "The *rye*'s future is knotted with yer own, I'll say that much."

It was Blaise's turn to be skeptical. Panna had to be mistaken—at least she hoped so. She didn't want her future to be linked to Lord Lynden's. She scarcely knew the man, but she doubted he would measure up to her ideal. Simply because he had put himself out to be charming and amiable during the past few days didn't mean he would always do so. Here in the Gypsy camp he was out of his element. And he had a definite purpose for making himself so agreeable: his pursuit of her. Once he regained his own surroundings, his own upper-class society, once he achieved his stated goal, Lynden might very well revert to the bloodless British aristocrat she was accustomed to knowing—cool, distant, dispassionate, the very sort of man she had done her utmost to avoid marrying.

Blaise shook her head as the wagons in front of her turned off the lane onto a roadside verge. Perhaps she should run away to America after all. She still had friends in Philadelphia who might take her in merely for the sake of her late father's memory. It might be worth risking getting caught in the conflict between America and England—

The wagon lurched over a rut as Tommy drove the lumbersome vehicle beyond a copse of trees, toward an open meadow where the Gypsies would set up camp. Blaise held on tightly to the seat, but the unladylike oath that sprang to her lips had less to do with the jostling than with the helplessness of her circumstances. How she wished she'd never encountered Lord Lynden at the posting house in Ware, or accepted his escort to find her friends.

It was still early afternoon when the Gypsies finished setting up camp and ate a cold lunch of bread and cheese and sausage. Afterward, most of the Rom, including the older children, left for the nearby village to ply their various trades and bring home much-needed wages.

Blaise didn't dare go with them. If her Aunt Agnes was indeed looking for her, she would be wise to keep out of sight. Certainly she didn't dare show her face dressed as a Gypsy. Even if she could have read palms and told fortunes, the *gorgio* villagers would be suspicious of her ivory skin and polished speech and perhaps leap to absurd conclusions. Most people were terrified by the old wives' tale that labeled Gypsies child-stealers, and her presence might be misinterpreted. At the very least her unusual appearance would be remarked. Blaise wanted nothing to connect her to Miklos's tribe, both because she couldn't bear to cause him unnecessary trouble and because she preferred not to give her aunt any help in locating her.

Still, there was something she could do to be useful. Remembering having passed a farm along the road a short distance back, Blaise decided to call there and buy some chickens, and thus make a contribution to the cooking pot. It was high time that she aided the tribe and ceased being quite such a burden to her Gypsy friends.

In the privacy of Panna's wagon, she let down the numerous loops and plaits which Miklos's wife, Isadore, had painstakingly arranged in her hair, and worked out the kinks.

Blaise was engaged in brushing her long hair when she heard a rap at the front of the wagon, then Lynden calling her name. For a brief instant she thought about not answering and pretending to be absent, but he might simply wait for her rather than go away. He was certainly determined enough. And if he did catch her hiding from him, she would never live it down. Such evasion smacked of cowardice, pure and simple.

Lifting her chin, Blaise raised the front canvas flap and secured the tie.

The sun had finally come out and its rays struck her full on the face, making her shield her eyes against the sudden brilliance. When her vision adjusted, she could see Lynden staring up at her, an arrested expression on his face.

"I wish," he said, his voice oddly husky, "I had just that portrait."

Blaise glanced down at herself. Except for the vest, she still wore her colorful Gypsy garb, but the neckline of the embroidered yellow blouse had slipped down over one shoulder, baring far more skin than was proper. Flushing, Blaise hastened to tug the blouse up.

Lynden watched her intently, his sapphire gaze traveling over her body, lingering on her full breasts, her waist, her hips, then back up to her face and hair. She felt his gaze like a physical touch—shockingly intimate and highly disconcerting.

"You have beautiful hair," he murmured in that same warm tone. "Why do you insist on pinning it up?"

Distracted by the way he was looking at her, Blaise had difficulty finding her own voice, and then in keeping herself from stammering. "You forget . . . I am a Gypsy. It is considered immodest for females my age to wear their hair down. A Gypsy would never do so in public."

"A great pity," Julian said fervently, and meant it. Her glossy black mane gleamed like watered silk, while the sunlight shone down, creating rays of deep violet streaks amid the waves of jet. It was all he could do to prevent himself from reaching out and tangling his fingers in the silky strands.

"Is there something you wanted, my lord?" she said warily.

"I came to invite you for a stroll in the meadow."

Blaise glanced down at his legs encased in biscuit-colored trousers and gleaming boots, realizing he had discarded his cane. "Is that advisable with your wound?"

"My leg is much improved, thanks to Panna's liniment. And exercise helps, I've found. It must be a *slow* stroll, naturally," he added with a charming, self-deprecating smile.

"Well . . . I regret I cannot this afternoon. I . . . have an errand to perform."

"Oh?" When no explanation was forthcoming, he added, "May I assist you in your errand?"

"Thank you, but no." She didn't think it would be wise to tell him about her plan to purchase chickens from the neighboring farm. He would wonder where she had gotten the money, and he was already suspicious enough. She still sometimes had the feeling he didn't believe she was a real Gypsy. Like now.

Lynden eyed her curiously as he said, "Why did you not accompany the others to the village?"

"I . . . they didn't need me."

"Aren't you skilled in telling fortunes?"

"Not really."

"I thought all Gypsy women professed to have the talent."

"I told you, I was *adopted* by the tribe. I cannot do everything as well as other Romi. And I am rather busy at the moment."

Lynden did not take the hint. Instead he leaned casually against the corner of the wagon. "Don't let me detain you."

Blaise pressed her lips together in annoyance. How was it that she could never manage to gain the upper hand with this infuriatingly persistent nobleman?

Not caring if she was being rude, she lowered the flap again to shut him out and proceeded to finish brushing her hair, all the while wishing there was a way to turn the tables on him. But . . . perhaps there was.

Her irritation slowly faded as the plan took shape in

her mind. A grin tugging at her lips, she changed her Gypsy clothing for the drab brown gown she'd arrived in and tied her hair back with a scarf, then donned her woolen cloak. Satisfied that she looked like any other common country girl of the servant class, Blaise hunted in the wagon for the items she would need.

When she opened the flap again and jumped down from the wagon, Lynden was waiting for her, just as she knew he would be. His eyebrow rose at the sight of her new attire.

"I don't wish to be taken for a Gypsy," she explained vaguely.

"Ah. And may I ask why?"

A gleam of mischievousness flickered in her expression. "I am going fishing . . . for chickens."

"I beg your pardon?"

"I mean to catch some chickens for supper." She held up her bounty—some long pieces of string and a small bag of corn. "There is a farm just down the road, did you notice? Well, they are sure to have a henhouse. I didn't tell you before because I didn't think you would approve."

Comprehension slowly swept across his scarred face, while his eyebrows drew together in a frown. "You cannot be thinking of stealing them?"

Blaise laughed outright. She had finally managed to disconcert the lordly Lord Lynden. "Can I not?" Her eyes were bright and amused. "You may accompany me if you wish."

"Certainly I don't wish it," he retorted dryly.

Shrugging her shoulders, she started to turn away.

"One moment, if you please." When she hesitated, Lynden shook his head. "This is absurd. I can't allow you to engage in criminal activity."

Blaise tossed her head. "I don't think you have any say in the matter, my lord."

His mouth tightened. "I'll pay for them. I can afford the cost."

So could she. And of course she would leave some coins

to compensate for whatever birds she took. She wasn't truly contemplating theft. She was merely planning a harmless prank on the persistent viscount. "But then I would miss all the sport of tricking the *gorgios*."

"*Sport?* I doubt you would find it sporting to be thrown in jail and transported for theft."

"Oh, but I don't intend to get caught. Any Gypsy worth his salt can elude detection."

His grim expression was all she could have desired. What a slowtop she had been! She'd gone about trying to dissuade him all the wrong way, allowing him to set the rules of his pursuit. But no longer. She would use his own code of honor against him, to her own advantage. No well-bred gentleman could possible condone theft. No nobleman of Lynden's obvious affluence would understand the poverty and hunger and desperation that drove people to steal. Certainly he would not excuse stealing for a lark.

And if she could manage to give him a disgust of her, perhaps then she could rid him of this determination to make her his mistress. At the very least, it would give credence to her pretense of being a Gypsy.

"You cannot have considered the consequences of your actions," Lynden said, obviously striving for patience.

"Oh, fiddle. You remind me of my—" Blaise broke off. She had been about to say stepfather. "My previous employer, the dragon lady. She was as stiff-necked as they come."

"You think me stiff-necked merely for trying to prevent you from committing a crime?"

"Exactly." In fact, she knew very few English gentlemen who were not. Laughter, bright and provocative, shone in her eyes as she turned away. "You, my lord viscount, are a stuffed shirt!" she called merrily over her shoulder.

Julian stood there for the length of several heartbeats, staring after her, torn between the desire to shake her, the urge to respond to her obvious challenge, and the need to sweep her up in his arms.

He suspected his conflicting desires had a great deal to do with those violet eyes of hers. Lively and mischievous, they were as full of life and laughter as a sunbeam dancing on an ocean wave. And trying to pin her down was just as difficult as trying to capture a sunbeam.

During the past three days, his facination with Blaise had only grown. It amazed him, the force of his attraction. She resembled none of the women he'd desired in the past. Her body was shapely and aesthetically pleasing to the discriminating male eye, but her facial features actually were quite ordinary. Certainly he'd known women far more beautiful. His own wife had been a celebrated diamond—yet Caroline had been an ice maiden compared to Blaise's fire. It was that fire, that sparkle, that gave her such an uncommon appeal. He'd moved no closer toward his goal of satisfying his carnal desires, and yet that hadn't seemed as essential as simply being near her. For the first time in years he was interested in a woman for more than the physical relief she could bring him. His elusive minx could offer him so much more. He wanted to bask in her wholeness of spirit, her natural zest for life. Simply being near her affected him like champagne bubbles in his blood. He felt *alive* again, a state he hadn't experienced during the four years since his wife's death.

Almost against his will, Julian found himself following her, while cherishing some vague notion of keeping her out of trouble . . . if he couldn't manage to shake some sense into her first.

As if she'd known what he would do, she slowed her steps and allowed him to catch up to her. Along the way, Blaise walked slowly out of consideration for his wounded leg. His leg *had* seemed much better recently. He limped less heavily now, and the lines of pain had faded from around his blue eyes. Although she doubted Lynden would have complained of the pain, in any case.

She refused, however, to listen seriously to any attempts he made at dissuading her.

By the time they reached their destination and paused

to look around the farm, he had given up trying. From a position behind a copse of willows, they reconnoitered the yard. The large main house was of timber frame, with brick and plaster overlay. Behind it stood a barn in good repair and several other outbuildings, along with what looked to be a chicken coop. Some two dozen hens were scratching in the dirt yard.

Staying well back, Blaise edged her way around the house until she came within a hundred feet of her prize. A dog began barking in the distance, yet she thought it must have been tied up, since it never attacked. There was no one in sight. She smiled when she spied a wagon full of uncured hay near the chickens, realizing it would provide cover of a sort.

When she started toward it, though, Lynden stayed her arm. "I suppose you insist on going through with this?"

"Are you turning craven, my lord?" Blaise taunted lightly. "You don't have to accompany me, you know."

"For tuppence I wouldn't."

"I don't have tuppence to give you. I told you my circumstances were sadly reduced."

Blaise ignored his annoyed snort and crept forward. Reaching the wagon, she gingerly crawled beneath it and lay flat on her stomach. The bottom of the wagon bed was nearly three feet off the ground, which allowed adequate freedom of movement.

With a resigned sigh, Julian joined her, settling on her left, carefully taking most of his weight on his sound leg, but wincing at the resulting strain on his bad thigh.

"I must be mad," he murmured wryly. "So what comes next?"

In a whisper Blaise explained the Gypsy method of stealing chickens while she worked. "First you thread the end of the string through a kernel of corn, like so . . . and secure it with a knot. Then you throw it out in the yard and wait for the chicken to swallow the bait. When it does, you reel the line in, just as you would a fish."

"I thought you said you didn't possess the usual Gypsy skills," he pointed out.

"I don't, but Miklos taught me how to do this."

"Why am I not surprised?" Julian said dryly. "But what happens if we're caught? I doubt those poor birds will come quietly."

Getting caught wasn't what worried her. She didn't fear legal redress, not with Lord Lynden as her partner in crime. She was certain he could talk his way out of any difficulty. A nobleman could get away with flagrant violations of the law, simply by virtue of his rank. But the thought of actually stealing did give her qualms.

Trying to ignore her conscience, Blaise flashed him a smile. "I'm sure you'll think of something."

"Thank you for your faith in me."

She finished tying off the string and eyed a fat hen which was clucking innocently some five feet away, ignorant of its fate. But then she hesitated, suffering an uncharacteristic attack of missishness. She, who had never stolen anything in her life, was about to commit a theft. At least the farm looked prosperous. It wasn't as if she would be taking from the really needy.

She also had an additional worry. She'd lied to Lynden about her skill in chicken stealing. She'd only watched Miklos practice, and that was years ago, when she was a child. Nor had she ever been required to kill a chicken herself. Her poultry had always shown up on the dinner table roasted or sauteed or baked in a pie. She hadn't taken that into account when designing her stratagems.

"You'll have to wring its neck," she whispered.

Beside her, Lynden turned his head to stare sardonically at her. "You *must* be jesting."

She looked down at his lean, elegantly shaped hands, at his superbly tailored coat, which was dust-stained from their long walk and from their wallowing in the dirt, and she couldn't help the choked laughter that escaped her at the image of the aristocratic Lord Lynden having to perform such a lowly chore. Even as a soldier, he would have had servants to perform such menial duties. "If you don't kill it, my lord, you'll wind up with an armful of squawking chicken, and that, I daresay, will be even less pleasant."

He closed his eyes in pained resignation. "And to think I used to have discriminating principles. Very well, my sweet Gypsy, shall we begin before the dog decides to have us for supper?"

Nodding, Blaise took aim and let the string fly. From that point on, however, her plan abruptly disintegrated.

A curious rooster came bobbing toward the corn kernel and gobbled it up before the hen could. When a startled Blaise jerked reflexively on the line, the rooster objected mightily and dug in its claws, all the while flapping its wings and trying to squawk.

Realizing she was losing the struggle, Julian grabbed the string from Blaise and pulled, but the embattled bird put up a valiant fight. When it was almost in reach, it tried unsuccessfully to rake Julian with a sharp spur, and did succeed in giving him a vicious peck on the back of his left hand.

Julian swore and let go. The rooster raced off, trailing the string from its beak and scattering the harem of hens in its wake.

Bristling with indignation himself, Julian sucked at the faint wound on his hand, while Blaise tried unsuccessfully to muffle her laughter.

"Wretch," he muttered finally with reluctant amusement. "I could be bleeding to death for all the compassion you've shown."

"I'm sorry," she said repentantly, turning brimming eyes to him. "Were you really hurt?"

"Excruciatingly."

"Let me see."

Reaching for his left hand, she peered down at the faint pink mark just above his middle knuckle. The peck hadn't even broken the skin, and was nowhere near as savage as the scar on Lynden's face.

She was debating whether to offer sympathy or a scolding when he suddenly reached up to curve the fingers of his right hand behind her neck.

Blaise froze. He hadn't attempted to kiss her in days, not since the time at the inn. Her heart began racing as those beautiful azure eyes locked with hers.

"No . . ." she breathed.

His grip tightening gently on her nape, he drew her face inexorably closer for his kiss.

Yet she knew what would happen if she allowed his lips to meet hers. She would lose control of her senses. Her limbs would turn to warm honey. Her will would vanish. She might not even be able to stop her seduction.

"No!" Blaise exclaimed in desperation, and brought her hand up to shove at Lynden's shoulder.

She used more force than she'd intended, though, and he wasn't prepared. Abruptly thrown off-balance, he lost the support of his elbow and twisted his body, taking the impact on his wounded leg.

His gasp of pain was loud and harsh as he clutched at his thigh.

No longer in danger from his advances, Blaise scrambled to her hands and knees.

Julian cursed savagely and rolled over on his back, trying to catch his breath. Blaise leaned over him with real concern. "I'm sorry . . . are you all right?"

"No," he said through gritted teeth, shutting his eyes.

"Well, it was partly your fault," she muttered in her own defense. "I don't recall giving you leave to fondle me."

He didn't reply, and a few moments went by before he opened his eyes again and looked directly at her, his gaze nearly as exasperated as it was pained. "No more trying to steal. I'm not fit for such heroics, and you haven't the skill—or the sense to know you haven't. It was an imbecilic idea, besides being *wrong*. I should never have condoned it."

"If you have such high-minded scruples, my lord," she said stiffly, "then you can always pay for the chickens."

"I intend to," he snapped.

With effort, Lynden edged out from under the wagon

and sat up. "Go and fetch the master or mistress of the house. Tell them I'll offer two guineas for the lot."

Blaise bit her tongue at his cold, authoritative tone. She had to make allowances for his pain. "Can you walk?"

"That's debatable at the moment. Now do as I tell you. Go buy the bloody chickens."

Feeling both guilty for hurting him and resentful of his high-handedness, Blaise climbed to her feet and flounced off toward the house, not giving him a backward look.

As he followed her with his gaze, Julian again experienced that conflicting desire to shake her and make love to her at the same time. After this last incident, it was even stronger. His arousal was still painful, nearly as painful as the throbbing muscles of his thigh.

His mouth tightened. He was more determined than ever to make Blaise his mistress, both to keep her from a life of poverty and crime and because he keenly wanted her in his bed.

He wanted her. It was a simple and profound truth.

And he would have her, Julian vowed. The next time he managed to get his Gypsy alone, she wouldn't get off nearly so easily.

Chapter 7

He wanted her. He couldn't remember ever wanting like this. His need was like a fever in the blood. And yet Julian knew how far he remained from achieving his desires. His lady of fire avoided him whenever possible, and when not, she appeared disappointingly immune to his advances.

Julian felt the frustration keenly—although, perversely, the delay made his sense of anticipation and excitement sweeter and added a novelty he'd never before experienced.

He'd never faced such difficulties with another woman. In the past, with his wealth and rank, his attractive features and charming address, he'd had only to express interest in a woman and she was soon his. Indeed, he usually had females fawning over him and pursuing *him*, sometimes to the point of embarrassment. He had never before faced this particular situation, having a woman avoid him and deny him his aims.

But then his fascinating Gypsy was like no other woman he'd ever known.

She seemed to be two creatures at once—a scampish minx with laughing violet eyes and a lively spirit, and a raven-haired enchantress who filled him with yearning and haunted his sleep. Not the kind of haunting he was accustomed to. He hadn't been tortured by nightmares of Caroline's death since arriving at the Gypsy camp six days ago. His dreams came quickly each night, but they were safe dreams, easy dreams.

And the pain of his wound was lessening. The liniment Panna had given him had effectively reduced the recurring spasms and aching stiffness in his leg. Some days were worse than others, but the ravaged muscles seemed truly to be healing. There were periods when he was free of pain, and hours at a time when he managed to forget he even had an infirmity. For that reason alone, he owed the Gypsies a debt of gratitude.

The chickens had gone a short way toward satisfying his debt. The farmer's son had delivered several crates of live birds that very afternoon, and Miklos had promptly declared a celebration was in order.

" 'Tis full bellies we'll 'ave tonight," the chief said delightedly, "thanks t' yer lordship's munificence."

Julian had politely demurred. It had been Blaise's idea to obtain the chickens, and although he hadn't approved of her method, she'd provided him the opportunity to purchase them.

That night the Gypies had feasted joyfully on roast fowl and fried potatoes and suet pudding, a dish for which the Rom apparently had a great fondness. They'd eaten only half of the chickens, sparing the other half to produce eggs—three of which Julian had enjoyed at breakfast that morning. They'd also found various uses for the chicken feathers and bones.

Julian was surprised to discover how frugal the Gypsies actually were. Nothing was ever wasted; everything was converted into an item of use. Indeed, during his brief time here, he'd found a good deal to admire about the Romany people. They were good-natured and open-hearted and easily excited, with a lust for life that was contagious. Loneliness, he learned, was the most terrible fate that could befall a Gypsy, a state which Julian had known quite intimately for the past four years. This tribe was hardworking and relatively clean, despite having to live out of doors with little chance to bathe.

He also discovered that the Smith's tribal surname was Petulengro in Romany. Smith was the English version, given out to keep the *gorgios* ignorant of Gypsy language and culture. Gypsies held a deep distrust of *gorgios*. Having been persecuted and vilified for centuries, they had learned to adapt to English ways when necessary, yet they held staunchly to their own heritage.

Some of the customs Julian found strange, such as having to wash utensils in a certain order, in pots reserved for certain purposes. The taboos regarding females were not unlike some that he understood were followed in India—where some scholars claimed the Rom originated. The ritual burning of a dead person's belongings resembled India's custom as well. Gypsies were incredibly superstitious, it seemed. And they believed strongly in the ability of certain persons to foretell events. Julian couldn't share those beliefs, and yet he didn't know how to explain the uncanny accuracy of Panna's vision the other day. It had shaken him when she claimed to have seen "a dark place, with stones and crumbling walls . . . death." She could have been describing the very Roman ruins where Caroline had died.

There were also, however, characteristics of the Gypsy way of life that Julian silently deplored. He had objected to Blaise's planned theft of the chickens, certainly. Yet the Gypsy philosophy seemed to be that wealth should be shared, and that poverty was only a transient state, to be shrugged off with a laugh and the hope that better days lay ahead. Theft was considered a normal way of survival, while tricking the *gorgios* was seen as entirely honorable.

Yesterday morning Julian had viewed this practice firsthand, when he'd caught Miklos in the act of doctoring a broken-winded nag to give it false vigor and make it appear years younger.

Miklos had unashamedly admitted to his tactics, his grin flashing a brilliant white against his swarthy skin. "Well, it's like this, yer lordship. You file the *grai*'s teeth and fill the holes with blacking . . . Then you feed it lard to ease its breathing . . . and apply a physic to give it spirit. And if it 'as too many gray 'airs, you paint it wi' dye."

"Amazing," Julian said, truly impressed after watching the horse transform before his eyes.

"You wouldn't peach on me, now would you, m'lord?"

"That would scarcely be the way to repay your hospitality, would it?"

"Aye, that it wouldn't. I knew we could count on you, for all that you're a *gorgio rye.*"

When later Julian mentioned the incident to Blaise, she'd tossed her head in a manner that was half laughing, half defiant, and told him it was the Gypsy way. "Miklos rarely resorts to such deceptions. He travels this route several times each year, and he wouldn't stay in business long if he couldn't be trusted. He'll find a buyer who deserves to be hoodwinked—or at least one who can afford it."

Julian had dropped the subject. There might be a good number of things about the Gypsies that he disapproved of, yet he was in no position to judge these people or their way of life. Their moral transgressions were trivial compared to his own, after all, and it smacked of hypocrisy for a man under suspicion of murder to condemn far lesser crimes.

What concerned Julian more than his discovery of the Gypsies' light fingers and shady dealings, however, was how short time was growing.

He'd been at the camp nearly a week, and he was in danger of outstaying his welcome—although no one but Blaise had seemed particularly anxious for him to leave. But Blaise was apparently in a greater danger. This afternoon it had become clear that she was being sought by someone in a position of authority. A horseman had come riding into the camp, asking discreetly probing questions about a raven-haired girl with violet eyes.

He was a tall, lean fellow dressed in casual country attire. But despite his well-fitting coat, it was doubtful he was a gentleman, since his speech was coarse and peppered with London cant. Julian suspected he might perhaps be a Bow Street Runner—those officers of the law, prime thief catchers, and purveyors of detective work. The man's sharp, assessing eyes seemed to miss little, and what he saw he appeared to disdain.

Upon the stranger's arrival, Miklos came forward to act as spokesman for the tribe, and Julian was given another demonstration of the Romany nature: Gypsies were masters in the art of dissimulation and pretending innocence, especially when it came to misleading the authorities.

No, Miklos asserted respectfully, he hadn't seen anyone fitting such a description recently. No, he would never presume to hide the truth from your honor. Would your honor wish to search the camp?

The stranger's gaze flickered over Julian and paused. "And you, sir. 'Ave you seen the lass what I described?"

Julian smiled with charming blandness. "You may address me as Lord Lynden. And no, I don't recall such a creature. If you doubt my word, and *if* you can present the proper credentials authorizing your harassment of private citizens, then I also might be persuaded to allow you to search the camp."

The fellow's mouth tightened, but he backed down rather than risk offending a peer of the realm. "That ain't necessary, yer lordship. I'll take yer word for it."

"I'm gratified," Julian responded dryly.

When the man had ridden away, Miklos flashed a cheerful grin. "I'd say 'e didn't care to challenge a fine *gorgio rye* like yourself, m'lord."

"Rank does have its advantages at times," Julian agreed pleasantly. "Why do you suppose he was searching for our Mistress Blaise?"

The Gypsy's expression went carefully blank. " 'Oo can say, m'lord?"

"I expect you could, if you wished to. And I know she could. But I won't press the issue. We should, however, do what we can to protect her, don't you think?"

"Aye, m'lord. We'll move camp tomorrow, a day sooner than planned. To pack up now would look like we'd something to 'ide."

Julian murmured a wry reply, but he couldn't dismiss the disturbing event as easily as Miklos could. He was too concerned about Blaise.

Upon close inspection she would never pass for a true Gypsy. She had pitch-black hair, true, but her long midnight tresses were much silkier and finer than theirs. Her eyes held the same luminous quality of a Gypsy woman's, yet theirs were a fierce black while hers were a soft, sensuous amethyst. Compared to their coarse, bronzed complexions, her skin was the smoothest, palest ivory. And her bone structure was much more delicate than theirs as well.

Julian only felt his frustration mount at his helplessness. He could possibly protect Blaise from whatever trouble she was in, but she would have to allow it—and she was proving maddeningly elusive.

That evening after supper, the Gypsies had gathered around the campfire as they did each night, to be serenaded by the sweet, sobbing melody of the violins. Blaise, as usual, had taken a seat as far from him as possible. And Julian, as usual, found his gaze inexorably drawn to her.

Just then, Miklos's wife, Isadore, went over to Blaise and spoke. Blaise shook her head at whatever the Gypsy woman said. Isadore then tried to draw Blaise to her feet, but she pulled back her hands and hid them behind her. A moment later Panna shuffled over.

Julian watched curiously as a conversation ensued. Because of the music, he couldn't hear what was being said, but Blaise obviously was being urged to do something she didn't wish to do.

The music stopped just then, in time for him to hear her exasperated declaration, "Oh, very well!" Rising to her feet, she took her place among the dancers around the fire.

Julian straightened on his seat. Blaise had never before joined in the dancing, and he was fascinated to see her attempt it. She wore her bright Gypsy clothing, yet she stood out from the other Rom like a polished diamond among rough-cut stones—or the beads the Gypsy women were so fond of wearing. When the first note sounded, Blaise lifted her arms high and began to sway.

The enchanted dance began with a slow sensual rhythm. Blaise avoided his gaze entirely, but Julian watched her with rapt attention. In the golden firelight, she appeared more self-conscious than the other performers, and perhaps not as incredibly fluid as the true Gypsy women, but she was every bit as graceful, and even more enticing. He couldn't look away.

The music soared, while the dancers proceeded to quick, flashing steps and flaring skirts.

Their wild beauty stirred him, but it was Blaise herself who held Julian spellbound. Life and passion seemed to sing in her body, and the exertion left her face damp and flushed. She looked like a woman who was making love and enjoying it immensely—vibrant, alive, irresistibly aroused.

He felt his own body growing hot, hard, his desire kindling to a fever pitch. His brain filled with the fire of enchantment. He wanted her with an intensity that was almost an obsession. He wanted her panting, writhing in passion beneath him. He wanted to bury himself so deeply in her sweet warmth that his past and future faded away, wanted her so badly he was unable to think of anything else.

The performance ended with the dancers whirling and leaping in joyous abandon. At the cessation of music, Blaise came to a breathless halt and suddenly became of aware of the blue eyes fixed so intently on her. Helplessly, she met Julian's gaze. She read desire there, and a yearning so strong it frightened her.

Unconsciously, she took a step back. She had obviously made a mistake. She'd only participated in the dance at Panna's urging, because she'd wanted to convince Lord Lynden she was truly a Gypsy and not just a *gorgio* guest at the camp. But her plan had somehow gone astray. He didn't look at all as if his mind was on her identity. His hot gaze caressed her, stroked her, as surely as if he had reached out his hands to touch her.

Shivering, she took another step backward, experiencing an overwhelming urge to escape. She needed to be alone, until the strange, heated, sensations racing through her body could fade.

Abruptly Blaise abandoned the campfire and disappeared into the woods.

For a moment Julian sat there, transfixed, yet he could not possibly have left circumstances as they were. The music was still strumming wildly through his blood when he went in search of her.

He found her some distance from the camp, at the edge of a meadow, illuminated by moonlight. She was humming softly to herself, now and then swaying in time to the faint strain of violins emanating from the camp.

He stood watching silently, wondering, not for the first time, if it was her purpose to drive him insane with desire. If so, she was succeeding. His fascination for her was beyond control. She was quicksilver and moonbeams, and quite the loveliest thing he could remember.

Blaise, however, would have refuted the charge had he given her the opportunity. She was not attempting to ensnare Lynden. Indeed, she had done her best to escape him. She'd fled to the meadow intending to lose herself in the shadows until she had at least gained a semblance of control over herself, over her riotous feelings. The dance she'd just performed had kindled her senses, unleashed a wildness in her that she'd never experienced before. The music was fire in her veins, sensual and pagan. She still felt feverish, restless, alive with the excitement of the night. With the promise of passion she'd seen in Lynden's eyes.

When she heard the quiet rustle of footsteps in the grass behind her, she stiffened abruptly. It could only be he. No Gypsy would willingly walk the night amid the fairies and evil spirits. A thrill of fear shivered through her.

"I grew concerned when you didn't return," he murmured from behind her.

Blaise didn't turn around. She couldn't trust herself to be near him, not when she felt this strangely, as if her whole body were alive with sensation. She was palpably aware of his presence, of the danger he presented. It would be impossible to resist him, his seduction, when she felt this vulnerable, this abandoned, when her pulse was racing so swiftly. She tried to take a step away.

"Don't go . . ."

The swift and paralyzing intimacy of his voice riveted her in place, although she managed to reply breathlessly, "I . . . I've told you before, my lord . . . there is no need for you to concern yourself with me."

"Ah, but there is. A great need." He gave a short mirthless laugh. "A need I can no longer control, it seems. I worry about you, whether I wish to or not."

"You . . . shouldn't."

"How can I not? You are obviously in trouble, hiding from someone."

"It . . . it isn't anything I cannot handle."

"What of the Runner who was searching for you today?"

"The Gypsies won't betray me."

"Not willingly. But neither can they offer you the same protection I can. I could keep you safe, sweeting."

He had moved closer, Blaise realized with dismay. His nearness alarmed her, set tension thrumming at her nerves. Yet she couldn't seem to react. She stood transfixed as he moved directly behind her. In the distance she could hear the music of the Gypsies—violins and tambourines beating a wild rhythm in time with her pounding heart.

Forcibly, she drew a shallow breath. "Did you know," she asked with feigned brightness, "that Gypsies believe fairies dance in meadows?"

"No," he replied softly, "and at the moment I don't care what Gypsies believe. Nor will I allow you to put me off and change the subject again."

She felt his warmth at her back a moment before he slipped an arm gently around her waist. Blaise inhaled a sharp breath at the primitive sensations that rippled through her. His closeness, the animal heat of his body, the soft command in his voice, all served to rob her of willpower. She knew she should step away, yet she couldn't command her limbs to move.

"I want to be the one to keep you safe," he whispered in her ear. "I want to be the man you turn to for comfort and protection. I want you in my bed, in my arms. Name your price, sweeting. I'll set you up in a house, give you your own carriage and horses . . . whatever it takes to make you mine."

A penetrating throb of pleasure raced through her at his desire. He was here to claim ownership. He wanted to possess her, to have her, to become her lover. He would make a magnificent lover, Blaise was certain. She had known it the first moment he'd kissed her in the inn.

At the memory of that potent kiss, Blaise gave a ragged shiver, fighting the sweet weakness he aroused in her, but all she could manage was a soft, breathless "No . . ."

"I want you, love. More than I've ever wanted anything, anyone."

His seductive voice flowed over her like silver moonlight, as intimate as a stolen kiss, promising exquisite passion. She believed that promise. And to her profound dismay, she couldn't resist it, any more than she could resist the treacherous, melting feeling that was stealing over her. Contrary to her will, she pressed against Lynden, savoring his warmth, his hardness at her back. She could feel his heartbeat, heavy and sensual, thrum through her body, his breath hot and caressing against her ear.

"I'm weary of war, of grief. I need peace, sweeting. I need your brightness, your laughter. I need to feel you wrapped around me. I *need* you." That bewitching voice vibrated against her skin as his lips nuzzled the sensitive area just behind her ear. "You will be my salvation . . ."

Blaise's breath locked in her throat as his mouth skimmed hot and open along her neck, and still she couldn't find the strength to move. Whatever natural instincts of self-protection she possessed seemed to have fled. Her limbs grew liquid—warm and honeyed—entirely helpless. She wanted his kisses; her body wanted the pleasure of his touch. The sensual assault of his lips was tender, carnal. It made her feel wanton, made her skin tingle with the hot flush of desire. She closed her eyes helplessly, her body trembling.

"Are you cold? Let me warm you, love . . ."

What did he mean? He *was* warming her. His feather-light kisses were flooding her veins with shuddering heat. She wanted to turn in his arms, to raise her mouth for his kiss, but even that was beyond her. She felt lost in unreality, in a thick, dreamy pleasure, while conflicting sensations rioted through her. The blood moved heavily through her veins, while her pulse raced relentlessly. She couldn't seem to think, to breathe, to do anything but feel. Dazed, Blaise swayed in his arms.

Immediately Lynden tightened his grasp and drew her closer against him. She felt the urgency of his hard male body against hers—and the resultant shock of feminine awareness that streaked through her was so powerful that it frightened her.

Of its own accord, her hand reached up behind her and curved around the back of his neck. The warm male sinew and muscle beneath her fingertips felt reassuring, and yet somehow she managed to summon a protest.

"No . . . This is madness. We are . . . too different."

"Yes . . . sweet madness." Undeterred, he raised his right arm to curve it around her shoulders, across her collarbone, while his left arm remained around her waist. "What are differences between two people destined to become lovers?" he murmured. His fingers reached up to stroke her throat. "We *will* be lovers, sweeting . . ."

His hot lips blazed a fiery trail along the taut cord of her neck. "Shall I tell you how I would go about making love to you?" He laughed softly when she shivered. "I'll teach you how to enjoy your body, how to enjoy sharing. Your body can be an instrument of pleasure for us both."

As he spoke, the hand at her waist moved slowly upward to cover her breast, tracing her shape through her clothing. Shocked, fascinated, frightened, Blaise remained frozen in immobility, even when the hand at her throat glided downward slowly to dip beneath the embroidered neckline of her blouse, beneath her linen shift. His palm nestled against her bare breast, warm and protective and incredibly exciting. She felt the nipple distend and swell abruptly, into a tight peak.

"Your beautiful body deserves to be worshipped . . . Let me worship you, sweet."

The sound of his passion-rich voice trapped her in a web of sensual anticipation; Blaise softened against him helplessly as desire unfurled all along her body. Her breasts seemed to grow heavier, fuller, lusher.

She closed her eyes as he stroked gently. It hurt where he touched—a heavy, aching pleasure that seemed to spread in hot waves throughout her entire being.

A moan hovered in her throat as his fingertips plucked at her budded nipple. She arched her back instinctively, pressing her breast wantonly against his hand, seeking release for the unnamed needs, the fierce cravings he was arousing in her. Yes . . . this was sweet madness.

"I hunger for you, love . . ."

Yes, she thought dizzily. She felt it, too. The welling hunger rising within her was as fierce as anything she'd ever known. His bold persuasions, his whispered endearments, his exquisite touch were destroying her remaining reason. The flame of desire sweeping though her set her blood on fire; her body blazed with the sweet rage of need.

So dazed was Blaise by his skillful seduction that it was some moments before she heard the distant voice calling to her.

A man's voice.

Miklos, she realized.

With a jolt of awareness and alarm, Blaise jerked herself from Lynden's embrace. A blast of chill air wafted over her overheated flesh, shattering the night magic and making her shiver, bringing with it the return of reason.

She didn't look at Lynden as she attempted self-consciously to straighten the disheveled bodice of her blouse. She didn't know how it had happened, how she could have been so blind to propriety. He had nearly made love to her. A few minutes more and she would actually have succumbed to his persuasions. And incredibly, she hadn't wanted him to stop. She felt incomplete now, somehow cheated. The abrupt cessation of his passion had left her empty and aching.

Yet she couldn't allow him to know that.

"I wish you to believe me," Blaise said unsteadily, growing minutely calmer as the sound of Miklos's voice grew closer. "I cannot accept your offer to become your mistress."

Lynden, however, seemed determined not to hear her.

Stepping closer, he took her chin between his long shapely fingers and turned Blaise to face him. The savage scar on his cheek was barely visible in the moonlight as he stood gazing intently down at her, but she could see the blatant sensuality on his features, the heated look in his eyes.

"I cannot, will not, accept your refusal." His tone was soft, confident, inflexible. "I fully expect to make love to you, sweeting. The only question is when."

She was indeed in trouble, Blaise realized as she reflected on the previous day's misadventures. First she'd been forced to hide in a cupboard in Panna's wagon to avoid detection by a stranger who was nosing around the Gypsy camp—a stranger who in all likelihood was in her Aunt Agnes's employ and had been commissioned to find an ebony-haired, violet-eyed runaway.

But more dangerous by far was last night's moonlit encounter with Lord Lynden. She had refused his proposition once again but barely escaped with her innocence intact.

Blaise shivered at the memory. She didn't know what had come over her last night, allowing him such liberties, holding her and stroking her bare breasts. Perhaps she'd been bewitched by the fairies that Gypsies believed in so devotedly. But more likely it was Lord Lynden's beguiling charm that had ensnared her. His potent combination of masculine beauty, persuasive cajolery, and sheer determination to have his way with her had nearly proved fatal.

Thankfully, she had been saved from complete seduction by Miklos's timely intervention. The Gypsy chief had not gone searching for her by accident, Blaise knew, but because he was worried about her. He had scolded her hotly the moment he had her alone.

"You must take greater care, Rauniyog," Miklos insisted. "The interest of a 'ighborn lord such as 'im can only mean one thing, and it ain't the 'onorable estate of marriage."

"Marriage!" Blaise eyed him blankly. "I should think not. Lynden considers me a Gypsy. You've told me often enough how the English feel about Gypsies."

"Aye, a nobleman of 'is rank would never stoop so low as to wed a Rom."

Blaise raised her chin. "Well, I wouldn't want *him* for a husband, either. He can be as starchy as my stepfather, undoubtedly."

"Starchy or no, 'tisn't a wife 'Is Nibs is after when he goes sniffing around yer skirts."

"I wasn't born yesterday, Miklos. I *know* what he is after. But I can take care of myself."

"Well, see that you do."

She had no need of Miklos's warning, though. She had already resolved increased vigilance in keeping up her defenses against the persistent Lord Lynden, and to remain close to either Panna or Miklos as long as he continued in camp.

Despite her resolve, however, Blaise had found herself in a state of perpetual nervousness since the previous night, quite unlike her usual high-spirited good humor. Whenever Lynden was near, she felt disconcerted and acutely self-conscious. Each time he looked at her, she remembered his brazen caresses, the warmth of his elegant hand on her breast, stroking her nipple to exquisite arousal. Each time she merely thought of him, she recalled his promise to make love to her.

With her wayward thoughts refusing to submit to discipline, Blaise could hardly keep her attention focused on what Miklos was saying now. It was late in the afternoon, a good five miles from the meadow that had nearly been the scene of her seduction. The Gypsies had pulled up camp at dawn and traveled farther west into Hertfordshire, spending the remainder of the day plying their trade in the next village. As he'd returned to camp, Miklos had spied a magnificent chestnut stallion in a neighboring pasture, and he'd come to Panna's tent before supper to discuss the situation.

Blaise was busy peeling potatoes to go in the large caldron that hung on a tripod over the cooking fire. With one ear, she listened to the Gypsy chief praising the horse's excellent qualities and lamenting the fact that he would never have the wherewithal to purchase such a fine animal. That he coveted the stallion was obvious.

"What a fine *grai* he is!" Miklos mourned as he paced the ground. "What fine colts he would sire. If I could 'ave him, I'd never wish for another thing, I vow."

Panna cackled in her raucous way as she stirred the cooking pot. "Until the morrow, when another thing struck yer fancy."

Miklos looked offended but he went on with his complaint. " 'Tis sure he was put there by the *gorgios* to torment a poor Rom."

"Aye, but 'tis the way of the world."

"If only I could 'ave 'im for a short spell."

"An' what would ye do wi' him?"

"Why, cover the red mare, o' course. 'Tis 'er time, for certain."

Panna straightened slowly, looking deep in thought. " 'Ow would ye go about it, Miklos?"

"Why, I'd take the mare to visit 'im tomorrow when they let the *grai* out to pasture for 'is run. 'Tis too late today. 'E's gone now. They took 'im back to 'is stable. I watched."

"Ye'd take the mare to 'im in broad daylight? The *gorgios* would 'ang you if you were to be caught."

"Aye." Miklos's tone was despondent.

Blaise looked up at the talk of hanging. From the conversation, she had deduced Miklos wanted the stallion to use for stud with his prize mare. As a young lady, she was not supposed to know of such things, but then she never had been as deaf and blind as young ladies were supposed to be, or as proper, either.

"I'd do better to spirit the *grai* away for a time," Miklos mused aloud.

"You want to steal the stallion?" Blaise was surprised into saying.

"It would not be stealin'," he protested. " 'Tis only borrowing I want to do. I'd give 'im back shortly."

"The *gorgios* would consider it the same thing. And if the stallion is as fine as you say, he must belong to someone of consequence. Do you really want to risk it?"

Frowning, the Gypsy stroked his chin, obviously torn. Miklos saw nothing wrong with "borrowing" another man's horse, Blaise knew. It was ingrained in the Gypsy character to take advantage of *gorgios* whenever possible, and horse stealing was an honored skill among Rom. She'd heard countless stories around the campfire about such legendary exploits. It would be a triumph for Miklos to pull it off. And a colt with such superb bloodlines would mean money for the tribe later. And it wasn't as if he didn't intend to return the horse. He wouldn't truly be stealing.

Panna interrupted her reflections. " 'Ow would ye get away wi' it, Miklos?"

"I'd make it look like the *grai* slipped away on 'is own. They'll never know 'e's gone, not if I take 'im only long enough to do 'is business."

The old woman considered for a moment. " 'Tis too dangerous."

Miklos's broad shoulders drooped, his disappointment palpable. Blaise wished there was something she could do to help.

But perhaps there was. The chicken incident had not shown her to be an accomplished thief, but if she were caught making off with the stallion, she might possibly talk her way out of trouble. Sir Edmund's highly respected position in the government would provide her a measure of protection, and her aunt's social connections wouldn't hurt, either. Of course, she would have to expose her identity then, and her good name would very likely be ruined.

And yet she owed Miklos a great deal after all he'd done for her. How could she refuse to aid him when he needed her?

"The odds will be better if I help," she said slowly. "The *gorgios* wouldn't hang me if I were caught."

Miklos suddenly brightened. "Aye, if you're caught, Rauniyog, yer stepfather's fine name would keep you safe. But no . . ." He shook his head sadly, as if he'd reconsidered. "I could never allow you to do such a thing."

No, Blaise thought, he would never ask her to help commit a crime and protect him if she were caught. Not unless she persuaded him . . .

She looked to Panna for guidance, but the old Gypsy woman was studiously avoiding her gaze.

"If the horse is what you want," Blaise said, "then of course I will do whatever I can to help."

Miklos's expression—half hopeful, half agonized—clearly evinced his dilemma. Finishing with the potatoes, Blaise set down her knife and wiped her hands on her apron, then went to him. Taking his hands in hers, she looked up at him with a persuasive smile. "You have no choice in the matter, Miklos. I won't allow you to miss this chance on my account. I intend to help."

"I dunno, Rauniyog . . ."

"Oh, come now. I never thought to see you turn down an opportunity to trick the *gorgios*. Is it possible you're becoming missish in your old age?"

Miklos gave a rumble of laughter at the absurdity of the accusation, and Blaise joined in.

That was how Julian found them a moment later—their heads close together, hands clasped, laughing like children. He couldn't believe the hot rage of jealousy that streaked through him as he watched his Gypsy minx gaze so adoringly up at the handsome chief.

"I trust I'm not interrupting anything of importance," Julian said tersely.

Both Blaise and Miklos gave a start and turned to eye him guiltily. Julian watched Blaise's smile evaporate and felt such a sharp and unexpected sense of loss, he wanted to kick himself. The wary look in her violet eyes didn't please him, either. It was clear she no longer trusted him—or perhaps she no longer trusted herself. She hadn't exactly made a determined effort to fend him off during their intimate encounter last evening, and perhaps she regretted it now.

As he glanced from Blaise to Miklos and back again, the silence was broken by Panna rapping the wooden spoon against the edge of the iron caldron. "Ye should tell 'is fine lordship what ye're planning," the old woman said. "I'll wager 'e'll help."

"Tell *him*?" Blaise exclaimed in disbelief, while Miklos scowled.

" 'Ave you gone daft, woman?"

Julian frowned. "What should you tell me?"

"There's a fine *grai* in yonder pasture what Miklos
wants to make use of. But 'e could use your help."

Miklos threw up his hands and stalked away, but after
a short distance, he stopped and returned to glare at
Panna. " 'Is lordship will never agree."

"Mayhap 'e will if you ask 'im nice."

"Agree to what?" Julian asked, more than a little curious now. When no one spoke, his mouth twisted impatiently. "I'd be obliged if you would stop being so
secretive and permit me to make my own decisions as to
what I will or won't agree to do."

Panna chuckled and shrugged, while Miklos cleared his
throat. Rather nervously then, the Gypsy chief explained
what he wanted.

"Let me see if I understand you correctly," Julian said,
his scowl deepening. "You want to steal this stallion so
it can get a colt on your mare?"

"It isn't stealing," Blaise declared defensively, ignoring the fact that Lynden was repeating her own words
of a moment ago. "We only mean to *borrow* the horse
temporarily. A few hours at most."

Grimly, Julian raised his gaze skyward, as if praying
for patience or heavenly intervention. "In the eyes of the
law it *is* stealing," he pointed out reasonably.

"Then we shall just have to make certain the law never
finds out, won't we?"

"Still, it's too risky. I cannot allow you to attempt
it."

Blaise's eyes flashed at his pronouncement. She had
originally taken up Miklos's cause because she'd wanted
to help him, but now she was determined to go through
with it, if only to defy the disapproving Lord Lynden.
He was not her stepfather. He had no authority over
her. And he had absolutely no right to forbid her to do
anything.

"You, my lord, have no say in the matter—unless
in addition to being a stuffed shirt, you mean to be
a spoilsport and peach on us to the authorities. That

would certainly show your gratitude to Miklos for his hospitality to you this past week."

"Rauniyog!" the Gypsy chief interjected, sounding horrified by her rudeness to the noble *gorgio*.

"What I had in mind," Julian replied coolly to her hot retort, "was offering to pay for the privilege of the stallion standing at stud. That is how such transactions are normally accomplished."

It was an eminently reasonable suggestion, but it came too late; Blaise had already dug in her heels. "What if the owner refuses to allow it? Then Miklos would lose the opportunity to achieve his dream *forever*."

Julian's eyes narrowed in annoyance at her exaggeration of the possible outcome. Not for the first time he found himself wanting to shake some sense into her—and her swarthy Gypsy friend. Miklos had managed to corrupt Blaise so thoroughly that her scruples were in danger of becoming tarnished beyond repair. And yet he doubted if he would be able to sway her if her dander was up—as it evidently was. It had been a mistake, Julian realized belatedly, to have used precisely that commanding tone with his Gypsy minx. But bloody hell, he hadn't been able to stop himself. Whether or not he was justified in claiming a proprietary right with Blaise, he felt keenly protective toward her. He couldn't abide the thought of her languishing in prison for stealing or, worse, being hanged. Yet that was precisely what might happen if she were caught.

"Very well," Julian said in resignation. "I shall accompany you."

"You?"

"Yes, I, sweeting. I am volunteering my services on your behalf."

"Whyever would you do that?"

"To save your pretty neck from hanging, why else? If you insist on attempting this foolish endeavor, then I shall go with you. If I am caught, I doubt I would be prosecuted for a horse thief, whereas you and Miklos would be prime suspects."

Remembering she was supposed to be a Gypsy, not a young lady of quality, Blaise couldn't immediately think of a rejoinder. Lynden's argument was the same reasoning she'd used with Miklos a moment ago—and just as valid. Indeed, given the viscount's rank, he would be more able to protect the Gypsies than she would. And she could hardly protest Lynden's offer of assistance, not after having made such a point about his evident ingratitude.

"Aye, 'tis a good plan," Panna observed. "We thank ye for yer generosity, m'lord." When Lord Lynden gave her a polite bow, she added, "You an' Rauniyog must go together."

Unable to believe what she was hearing, Blaise eyed Panna suspiciously. The old Gypsy woman seemed bent on throwing her at Lynden's head. Perhaps Panna still believed what the cards had told her—yet after that first cryptic warning, Blaise had heard no more about her fate being linked to Lynden's. Panna had kept strangely mum on the subject.

Panna still gave no explanation for her reasoning, but stood serenely stirring the stewpot.

Still, it was left to Miklos as chief to make the final decision.

" 'Tis settled then," he decreed. "Tomorrow we do the deed."

Chapter 8

The temporary purloining of the stallion, however, did not unfold as planned. The horse was never turned out to pasture the next day. Perhaps, Blaise suspected, because a tribe of Gypsies had descended on the area. With the Rom's reputation for being light-fingered, farmers and estate owners could be expected to take extra precautions to keep their livestock safe.

Miklos was heartbroken. He had set his hopes on having a colt sired by the stallion. But by midafternoon, after watching and waiting all day for an opportunity that never came, he was despondent enough to admit failure. Even Lord Lynden's suggestion that they wait until nightfall to spirit the horse away from its stable did not cheer the Gypsy chief. Leery of evil spirits and fairies, Gypsies rarely went out at night, and Miklos was no exception. It was left to Blaise to second Lynden's motion and to convince Miklos it would work.

A new strategy was agreed upon. After dark, when the grooms and stablehands on the estate could safely be assumed to be asleep, Blaise and Lord Lynden would attempt to sneak into the stables, locate the stallion, and lead it away to the pasture, where Miklos would be waiting with the mare. Still skeptical, Miklos nevertheless allowed himself to be persuaded.

Upon returning to the Gypsy camp, they discovered the viscount's traveling chaise and servants had arrived with Lynden's daily offering of some choice gift. Today it was a dozen rounds of cheese and twice that number of fresh loaves of bread. The goods were unloaded and

119

turned over to Isadore for distribution—and then, amazingly, Lynden climbed into the carriage and disappeared for several hours, leaving Blaise to wonder if he had lost his nerve and abandoned them.

He returned in time for supper, though, and Blaise cornered him as soon as he stepped from the carriage.

"Where have you been? We are supposed to leave in only a few hours."

He gave her one of those beautiful smiles that always made her think of the sun emerging from behind a cloud. "Did you miss me, my sweet?"

"Of course not! I was simply worried that you had changed your mind and didn't mean to help us after all."

"No doubt I shall regret it," Julian said dryly, "but I haven't changed my mind. In fact, I was engaged in reconnoitering. I decided some advance intelligence was in order if we are to succeed."

She searched his scarred face suspiciously but could find no sign of deception. "What do you mean?"

Julian kept his expression purposely bland. He could scarcely believe he had allowed himself to be swept up into this absurd and highly illegal venture, but he'd been unable to disappoint the large-hearted Miklos or his cohort in crime, Blaise. And yet by falling in with their scheme, he'd stumbled onto a way to further his own aims. The task now was to pull it off with his lady of fire none the wiser.

"I discovered that the stallion belongs to a Baron Kilgore," he remarked casually. "In fact, I spoke with him at length this afternoon. He's quite a pleasant fellow."

"Surely you didn't approach him about paying a stud fee?" Blaise exclaimed in dismay. "You promised you wouldn't! Now he'll only be suspicious if the stallion goes missing—"

"Calm down, minx. I said nothing to him about paying a fee. I did, however, learn everything I needed to know for tonight's adventure. I managed to lose a carriage wheel as I passed Lord Kilgore's estate, which provided the opportunity I needed to investigate the place. Kilgore was exceedingly accommodating. He invited me in for a glass of wine while his servants saw to the repair of my wheel, and afterward I toured his stables. I've seen the stallion and the stall where he's kept."

Blaise stared, uncomprehending.

"You wound me, sweeting. The least you could do is be properly impressed by the clever way I achieved it."

"I . . . Of course I am impressed, but what about our plan to borrow the stallion for Miklos?"

"Our tactics have changed slightly," Julian explained. "We aren't going to wait till tonight. You and I are leaving now, just as soon as you've changed out of your Gypsy clothes and had a bite to eat."

"Now?"

"Yes, now." His hands rose to her shoulders and turned her around, pointing her toward Panna's wagon. "Go and change your dress and put on your cloak, then return at once. In the meantime, I'll advise Miklos of the new plan." When she started to protest, Julian gave her a little push. "I'll answer your questions once we're on our way. Now go."

Blaise obeyed, even though she was still a bit bewildered and skeptical about the need for haste. She quickly changed into her brown broadcloth gown and brushed out her hair, then threw her woolen cloak over her shoulders and returned to the carriage where Lynden awaited her. Two men sat on the driver's box—both of whom Blaise recognized by now as Lynden's trusted servants—but there were no grooms hanging on behind or riding postilion. Both men were staring straight ahead, as if they'd had been instructed by their lord to ignore the unusual events that were about to take place.

Lynden himself held the carriage door open for her, and that was when she noticed his odd attire. He wore the garb of the working class—a black woolen frock coat that fit his shoulders nowhere nearly as snugly as his usual superbly tailored, form-molding coats. He was also bareheaded, and his soft curls glinted with gold and silver highlights in the late-afternoon sunshine.

It was only after Lynden had handed her inside that Blaise thought of protesting the intimacy of riding in a closed carriage with him, but by then he had spread out a supper of bread and cheese on a cloth and was offering her a drink of wine from a flask, and so she kept the comment to herself. After all, this transgression did seem rather mild following the other liberties he'd taken—his devastating kisses and shockingly bold caresses—during the past week. Besides, he *was* trying to help her.

When the carriage was moving at a steady clip, Blaise asked just what he had planned, and Lynden explained.

"You and I will be set down at the drive to the Kilgore estate, while my man Terral and my coachman Grimes continue on to the stables to deliver a cask of ale to the servants there with my compliments, in appreciation for aiding me this afternoon with repairing the damaged wheel. Terral will hint for an invitation to remain, and while they are all occupied in consuming the contents of the cask, you and I will slip into the barn and hide in the hayloft."

"What if your men are not invited to stay?"

"The cask should still provide a sufficient diversion for us to slip in unseen," Lynden said with a smile. "I've never met a groom yet who would turn down a tankard of good ale, have you?"

"Well, no, I don't suppose so."

"This plan has the added advantage of ensuring that Kilgore's servants sleep soundly tonight. With only drunken grooms to contend with, we should have no trouble leading the stallion away. I've instructed Miklos to meet us in the field at midnight, just as we planned earlier."

Blaise chewed slowly on a crust of bread and considered this new plan. The only objection she could think of was the wait she and Lynden would have until midnight. It would now be several hours before they could come down from the hayloft and attempt to take the stallion. She wondered if he had indeed planned it that way on purpose. There was no way of reading his intent in his blue eyes, however.

The sun was just beginning to sink behind the horizon when Blaise and Julian stepped down from the carriage. They watched the vehicle drive away, and then slipped behind the high yew hedge bordering the drive to make the trek to the stables.

The house came into view after a short while. It was an elegant mansion of ivy-covered gray stone, flanked by smooth lawns and towering oaks. Well in back of the manor house, in a large cobblestone yard, stood two rows of stables whose spacious box stalls appeared to be filled with blue-blooded horses. As she hid behind an oak tree, Blaise also noticed a large barn to the rear of the stables.

"Lord Kilgore must be very fond of horses to have so many," she whispered to Lynden.

"He's mad about them," Julian answered absently. "Keeps a score of hunters and owns several Thoroughbreds, which he races each season."

Blaise sent him a puzzled look. "How do you know so much about him if you only met him today?"

Julian shot her a quick glance and cursed himself silently for his slip. At this rate his careful plan for the evening would fall through before he ever had a chance to implement it. "Kilgore told me of them himself," Julian hedged. "It was all he could talk about this afternoon."

Limping slightly, he moved forward to duck behind another tree, then gestured with his head for Blaise to join him.

"Will seems to have succeeded," he murmured in her ear.

Across the yard, beyond the row of stables, a dozen men had gathered around the Lynden carriage to quaff tankards of ale. From the sounds of laughter and good-natured ribaldry, they seemed to be enjoying themselves immensely.

"The stallion is in the large barn. Let's go . . . and keep quiet, sweeting. We don't want to be overheard."

Surreptitiously, Blaise followed, her breath quickening involuntarily as they moved ever closer. Her heart had not been totally involved in this caper; she'd participated purely for Miklos's sake. And yet she was beginning to feel the same shiver of anticipation and excitement she experienced whenever she engaged in conduct that was improper or dangerous. This situation was both.

They achieved their target without a hitch, much to Blaise's surprise. They slipped inside the huge barn and found it empty of people, although the chestnut stallion whickered nervously in its stall halfway down on the right. Just inside the wide barn doors stood the ladder to the loft, and Lynden took Blaise's elbow to direct her toward it, obviously intending for her to climb up first.

"No," she whispered, shaking her head. "I'm wearing skirts."

He stared at her for an instant, and then his fingers tightened on her arm. "I promise not to look."

"That isn't the only problem. You're not supposed to walk where the hem of a Gypsy woman's skirts have been. It's considered unclean."

"I am not a Gypsy, and for that matter, neither are you. Nor do we have time to argue—"

"So don't argue. You go first."

His mouth twisted with mild impatience, but he began the climb, favoring his wounded leg and grimacing as he hauled himself up over the ledge of the loft. When Blaise followed, she found Lynden lying on his back on the wooden floor, his forearm shielding his eyes.

"Are you all right?" she whispered in alarm.

"I will be . . . in a moment. I'm not up to such exertion," he said with an attempt at lightness.

Blaise wished she could help him. Rising to her feet, she looked around her, searching for a more comfortable place for him to rest. A row of small windows under the eaves let in the last red-gold light of day, making it easy to see.

The huge loft was filled with piles of sweet-smelling hay, but there were open areas here and there that provided a walkway. Moving toward the rear, Blaise raked some of the loose hay together to form a comfortable bed, then took off her cloak and spread it out. Finally she piled more hay to form a wall to shield them from a casual observer, should someone climb the loft ladder. By the time she was satisfied, she was starting to perspire. The air was warm, although it was nearly the end of September, while dust motes danced, golden and hazy, all around her.

She turned back to Lord Lynden then, and found him watching her intently with those deep azure eyes of his. He was staring at her unbound hair, she realized, remembering that she hadn't worn a head kerchief. Blaise couldn't help but be flattered by the hot masculine admiration in his eyes, but it disconcerted her all the same, reminding her of the danger inherent in being alone with him. She forcibly had to resist the urge to tuck her raven tresses beneath the neckline of her gown, out of sight. His own curling hair, tousled by his exertions, gleamed pale gold in the muted light.

With difficulty, she managed to tear her gaze away, and without speaking, she gestured for him to join her. Lynden picked himself up and crossed the loft to her makeshift hideaway, inspecting her handiwork and noting her precautions.

"My compliments, minx. I couldn't have done better myself."

When he had settled himself on her cloak and stretched his right leg out, Blaise knelt on one corner of the cloak— as far away from Lynden as possible—and bent down, searching. Almost immediately she found what she was looking for. "There is a knothole in the floorboard," she observed, keeping her voice low as she pressed one eye to the opening. "I can see down below. We should be able to tell if anyone comes in."

"Excellent," he murmured dryly. "Tell me, sweeting, do you undertake this sort of escapade often? You seem to have a great deal of practice."

"Some," she answered truthfully, still whispering. "Not stealing—I told you I'm not a thief. But I have frequently been in situations where I didn't wish to attract notice."

"I don't doubt it. Have you ever been apprehended?"

"No. It was a near thing a few times, but I've always managed to come out unscathed."

At least until the last time, Blaise amended to herself. She hadn't been caught sneaking out of the house even then, but when Sir Edmund learned of it, he had read her a lecture in that chill, impersonal tone he reserved strictly for her, and banished her to England, into her aunt's custody. Which might not have been so bad, if not for Aunt Agnes's deplorable choice of suitors. As much as Blaise disliked her Aunt Agnes's harping, she found it preferable to her stepfather's critical disapproval. At least Aunt Agnes acted as if she truly cared. Yet she no doubt would have an apoplectic fit if she could see her errant niece now.

Thinking of her aunt's probable reaction, Blaise found herself swallowing a smile. Really, it was too bad Aunt Agnes was so far away. The uproar the outraged lady would cause would likely make Lord Lynden wish he were back in the Peninsular Campaign in the thick of battle.

He did not seem to be relishing the current situation much now, Blaise realized when she heard him mutter, "How did I ever allow you to talk me into this?"

She glanced over her shoulder at Lynden. He was massaging his lame leg gingerly, as if it was causing him pain—in which case she had to forgive him his sour mood. She was even willing to try and distract him from it, if she could. "But this was *your* plan, if you recall."

His dark golden brows rose. "You can't possibly mean to place the responsibility for this scheme on my head."

"Well, no, but I credit you with superior tactics."

"Pray don't remind me."

Blaise bit back a laugh. "Come now, my lord, where is your spirit of adventure?"

"It vanished with the threat of prison."

"Faintheart."

She said it softly, teasingly, with more than a hint of mischievous laughter in her eyes—and Julian found himself captivated all over again. Desire stung with fresh insistence. He wanted this hoydenish, glorious, violet-eyed witch with a fierceness he could scarcely believe. Those beautiful eyes were sparkling with intrepid amusement, and it was all he could do to refrain from pulling her down beside him in the hay and giving his passion free rein.

Knowing the moment was not yet ripe for seduction, though, he summoned a frown instead. "You, wench, are enjoying yourself far too much for my peace of mind."

"Am I, my lord?"

It was said with an arch smile and a coy toss of her head, before she turned back to peer through the knothole. Julian took a steadying breath and disciplined himself to be patient. There would be time enough to implement his plan. They had the entire evening ahead of them. "There is no need to watch. We'll hear anyone who comes in."

She didn't respond.

"You'd best make yourself comfortable," he said after another moment. "We have a long evening ahead of us."

Realizing the wisdom of his suggestion, Blaise abandoned her post and settled with her back against the hay to wait.

A few moments later, Lynden casually shifted his position and leaned back beside her. Blaise tensed at his nearness, but he merely closed his eyes, as if prepared to catch a nap before the evening's business of horse stealing began.

A peaceful silence ensued, broken occasionally by the soft thud of hooves as the stallion moved restlessly in its stall below. Evening eventually stole over the loft, leaving them in darkness. Blaise could hear Lynden's quiet breathing, yet she didn't think he was asleep. The relaxed, steady rhythm somehow comforted her. She had

feared being alone with him, worried that he might take
advantage of their enforced intimacy. But his stillness
set her mind at ease. At the moment he didn't seem the
dangerous, predatory nobleman who had nearly seduced
her.

At length, the moon rose outside and sent faint beams
of silver light through the small loft windows overhead,
permitting her to make out her surroundings. Against her
will, Blaise found herself watching Lynden in fascination, studying the sensual features etched by moonlight.
He was a beautiful man but for the scar. That slashing
disfigurement made a woman yearn to offer him comfort,
to run her fingertips tenderly over his ravaged cheek. It
was all Blaise could do to remind herself how dangerous
such a caress might prove.

It was perhaps an hour later when she heard someone
enter the barn and caught the faint glow of a lantern.
Lynden's eyes opened at once, confirming her belief that
he hadn't been sleeping.

Cautiously, Blaise bent to put her eye to the knothole.
Apparently one of the grooms had returned to check on
the stallion and to secure the barn for the night. Blaise
held her breath until the servant retreated with the lantern
and she heard the large double doors swinging closed on
their hinges. Even then she couldn't quite relax. This was
almost too easy.

Lynden didn't seem to share her concern. His eyes
had closed again and the soft rhythm of his breathing
resumed, reassuring her. Blaise sank back against the
hay, prepared to wait.

She couldn't have pinpointed the exact moment that
she sensed a change, but she became aware that Lynden's
eyes were open and he was watching her. The atmosphere seemed suddenly charged with a subtle tension.

"I'm pleased you took off the scarf. Your hair is too
lovely to be confined."

His murmur was a husky half whisper, as seductive
as it was dangerous. Every nerve Blaise owned became
suddenly taut with alarm, yet she couldn't seem to move.

Just as two nights ago in the moonlit meadow, she felt herself being drawn into the same hypnotic spell that had trapped her then.

He seemed to understand the extent of his masculine power over her, for he showed no hesitation as he reached up possessively to twine his fingers in her hair. For a moment that was all he did, rubbing it, savoring the texture, letting it glide sensually through his fingers. Then he turned his attention to Blaise herself, lifting his gaze to her face, and his hand, too, running the backs of his knuckles lightly, lightly along the delicate curve of her jaw, down the line of her throat.

Blaise couldn't draw back. The intimacy that radiated from the shadows wrapped around them, holding her immobile. She knew what was coming next, yet she was powerless to stop it.

With unhurried grace, Lynden bent toward her. A shaft of moonlight momentarily illuminated his face, defining the savage scar that branded his cheekbone, yet Blaise's gaze was drawn not to that, but to his mouth. The temptation of his beautiful mouth made her breathing go shallow.

She felt his hands, warm on her shoulders, and made an attempt at sanity. "My lord . . ."

"Call me Julian, love."

"I couldn't. The stallion . . . We have to—"

"The stallion isn't going anywhere. We have time . . . all the time we need."

"But . . . someone might come . . ."

"No. We're entirely alone." He wasn't concerned that they might be interrupted. He'd gone to great lengths that afternoon to stage this seduction, and he was determined to use his time alone with Blaise to complete advantage. Before the night was through, his Gypsy would be totally his. "Now, hush. I'm going to kiss you."

He drew her to him slowly, bringing her face close to his. Yet he didn't kiss her at once. He drew out the moment, tantalizingly. His mouth hovered just above hers, heating her lips, caressing them with his breath.

Involuntarily, quite against her will, a small frustrated sound issued from Blaise's throat. Julian smiled, satisfied, and complied with her unspoken need, finally covering her lips with his. Blaise was barely aware that the faint sigh she heard came from her.

The coaxing pressure on her mouth deepened as he delicately teased her into parting her lips. When she did, he softly thrust his tongue within her welcoming warmth. He stroked her mouth gently with his tongue, learning the shape, the unique contours, the flow of her breath. His hands came up to cradle her head as he took his time, varying the kiss in texture and pressure.

A delicious languor overwhelmed her, and Blaise lost all awareness of time. Her world narrowed to the scent of him, the taste, the wet warmth of his mouth, the exploring movements of his tongue. When finally he lifted his head, his breathing sounded soft and even to her, while she could barely pull the air in and out of her lungs. And still she remained powerless to resist what she knew would follow.

She heard the soft rustle of hay as he shifted his weight to make the surface of the cloak available to her.

"Your pallet, my sweet."

It required only a gentle tug of her hand to draw her down to lie beside him. Helplessly she watched him through half-closed eyes. His gaze swept over her slowly, with lingering thoroughness. Then, with languid sensuality, he reached up and spread her dark hair in silky disarray.

"It seems I've waited forever to do this," he whispered.

"You can't have," she answered him thickly, her head swimming. "You've known me for only a week."

"Eight days and . . . some seven-odd hours. I've counted every moment. And strained every ounce of ingenuity I possessed to arrange this meeting."

"You planned this—"

His shadowed smile was sweet and lazy as he stretched out beside her, his weight supported by his elbow. "Let's just say I hoped I might have the opportunity to have you to myself. You belong in my bed, sweeting," he said with conviction. His right hand drifted over the vulnerable column of her throat. "I merely need to convince you."

"You . . . won't be able to. It is useless to try."

His laughter was quiet, enticing. "Shall we see?"

He lay on his left side, mostly in shadow, yet she could see the glint of moonlight on his hair, and the curling lock that tumbled over his forehead as he bent to her.

Blaise's body tensed as he began his assault, tracing the shell curves of her ear with his hot open mouth, following the inward swirl with his tongue, nibbling away her resistance, her doubts, with his gentle lips. His tender, erotic caresses sent shuddering thrills through her pleasure-flushed veins. Her eyes closed in surrender. Heat spread within her, throughout her body, while her breath came in shallow pants.

Hearing the soft sound, Julian knew he was succeeding in his desires. Boldly he carried his seduction to the next level, his fingers working gently at the buttons of her gown's bodice.

Moments later, Blaise felt an abrupt coolness as he gently tugged her chemise down and bared her breasts. Her gasp was loud in the darkness, and yet her thoughts were a restless blur. She knew she should make him stop, knew she should fight the insistent throb swelling inside her, but instead she softened against him helplessly, even as she murmured an inarticulate protest.

"Hush, sweet." He filled his palm with her lush breast, slowly kneading, feeling the soft, graceful swell.

"No," she managed to breathe as her head moved restlessly from side to side.

"You don't enjoy this, minx?"

"No . . . I can't . . ." Her nipple was hard and aching under his curving fingers. "It hurts . . ."

"A pleasurable hurt?"

She didn't reply, and yet he knew the answer already. He knew because his mouth had found her throat and he felt the wild cadence of her pulse as he pressed his lips into her silken flesh. "For days now you've tormented me," he whispered. "It seems only fair that I should do the same to you now. Is it torment, my fiery Gypsy?"

"Yes . . . yes," she panted, arching her back as she responded to his touch.

"Good."

His clever, eloquent fingers began a brazen exploration of her unrestrained breasts. He seduced her with light sidelong touches, with slow erotic strokes, lightly contouring the taut flesh, embracing the frantic, tumbling thunder of her heart, moving upward over her collarbone and along the line of her throat, finding and lightly massaging her pulse points with his fingers, exhibiting the sureness of a man who knew how a woman's body would respond to his caresses.

Dazed, Blaise found herself straining weakly toward him. A moan hovered in her throat when he bent his head to her breasts, a moan that became a reedy gasp as he gently kissed the erect nipples. And when he filled his mouth with the tip of her breast, she gave a genuine cry at the arrow of pleasure that shot through her.

She knew what desire was then. Her body felt heavy and tense with wanting, with craving. His mouth was tender and urgent on her skin, his tongue a lash of fire.

It was an act of instinct that made her raise her arms and twine her fingers through his golden hair, holding his mouth to her breast. She no longer wanted to resist him. She knew what it was to feel *desired*. His passionate attentions made her feel wanted, needed, valued—a heady experience after so many years of feeling unwanted, unloved.

Blaise was only marginally aware when he slowly raised the hem of her gown. The cool air on her bare thighs made her go rigid, but his whispered words of encouragement overshadowed her alarm.

"My lady of fire . . . Don't fight me, sweeting . . . I only want to pleasure you . . . Let me love you . . ."

His searching hand grew bolder, making slow kneading circles along the silky length of her bare legs, stroking her flushed skin.

His breath was hot against her ear as he issued a soft command: "Open your legs for me, sweeting."

When hesitantly she obeyed, he moved upward purposefully, gliding his fingers through the dark triangle of downy hair between her thighs to cup her femininity.

Her gasp was smothered by his mouth as it took hers again. His lips and tongue working in concert with his hand, he gentled her. Her body went soft and wet and languid under his caressing, probing fingers. Those warm fingers were bolder now, stroking her, exploring her, parting the quivering folds of flesh and sliding inside her, lingering, only to withdraw and stroke her slick flesh again.

Moaning whimpers of pleasure, Blaise arched against him, her head thrashing feverishly. She couldn't comprehend what he was doing to her. He seemed to know her body better than she did herself . . . just where to touch and caress, to tease and torment, to make her quiver and throb, to make her go wild.

Incredibly aroused by the frenzied, restless woman beneath him, Julian drew a steadying breath of air into his tight, aching chest and forced himself to go slowly. He wanted desperately to cover her and bury himself so deeply in her lush heat that he lost any sense of self, yet he wanted more for her to glory in this moment. He wanted to show her every pleasure that had ever been between a man and a woman.

Her head falling back, Blaise allowed him his way. There was no thought of resistance or surrender; there was no thought at all. Only a keen awareness of his scent, his taste, the vibrant rhythm of his heartbeat, the urgent, erotic movement of his stroking fingers. She couldn't seem to remain still. She was panting, quaking against him. And then suddenly her body went rigid. Deep muscles clutched inside her as she shuddered violently in his arms, as he brought her to a climax so shattering she thought she was dying.

He captured her cries with his mouth, muted her sobs of ecstasy with his kiss. His hand stilled on her love-slick flesh. And when her racking shudders had subsided, he gathered her trembling body tenderly in his arms. His loins were full and aching for her, his own breathing heavy, his wounded thigh throbbing from the exertion and the need to stretch, yet he simply held her, allowing her time to recover.

After a few moments, Julian lifted his head to watch her, his gaze caressing. Her face was pale and delicate, framed by the night shadows of her hair.

When finally her eyelids lifted, his breath caught in his throat. She was looking at him, her eyes wide with shaky-hot uncertainty and wonder.

"You've never felt that kind of passion before," he said huskily, a statement rather than a question.

"N-no."

"Your previous protectors could not have been very proficient lovers if they neglected to see to your pleasure."

A deep blush flooding her cheeks, Blaise shut her eyes in dismay. Lynden thought she had done this before, had taken lovers before him. But she hadn't. Until meeting him, she'd been the recipient of nothing more than a few chaste kisses. She might be prone to scandal, but she wasn't abandoned. At least not until now, until *him*.

Dear heaven, how could she have tumbled in the hay with a near stranger in this wanton fashion, allowing him such intimacies it made her squirm with shame to recall? Her supreme self-confidence was to blame. She'd thought she could handle Lord Lynden—this *situation*— yet it had gotten totally out of hand. By *design*, if she understood him correctly. He had planned her seduction tonight, had somehow managed it so that he would have her alone. As adept as she was at scheming, he was evidently even more so. And she had fallen in with his plans like a witless sheep to slaughter.

Quivering, Blaise shut her eyes tightly and buried her face against his shoulder, wishing she had never heard of Lord Lynden.

Julian felt her tremble and mistook it for delayed reaction to the explosive passion she had just experienced. Tenderly, he lifted the disheveled sweep of raven hair that had fallen across her breast, letting the ebony skeins of silk pour over and through his fingers. The thought of having that silken mass wrapped around him made him shudder with need and arousal. His body was hardened in tense, coiled readiness to take her, yet he was willing to let her grow accustomed to the newness of her own passion. He needed a few moments himself to become accustomed to his own strange feelings.

Awakening her sexually had affected him in an entirely unanticipated way. Holding her, making love to her, he had felt more alive than at any time in the past four years. He felt *alive*—with eagerness, with anticipation, with want. Ever since meeting her, he'd felt a new awareness of his surroundings, a fine-tuning of nerve endings he had lost four years ago, a honing of faculties. His senses seemed somehow fresher, more acute, almost as if he had finally emerged from a deep sleep—which perhaps he had. His lady of fire had awakened him to life, just as he had awakened her to ecstasy—

This last thought was interrupted by a commotion that sounded from somewhere outside the barn: muffled shouts, followed by grunts and the sound of scuffling.

"Dear heaven!" In alarm, Blaise pulled out of his embrace and sat up abruptly, looking around her frantically.

Julian pushed himself up more slowly, his healing thigh muscles fiercely protesting the movement. He placed a cautionary hand on her arm while he tried to listen. At first he couldn't make out the words, but one shouted accusation was clearly legible.

"She's in there, I tell you! I saw 'er go in myself with that gentry cove. I waited an' waited—"

Blaise was trying unsuccessfully to fasten her bodice. Julian gently pushed her hands away and undertook the task himself. He wondered what had gone wrong. He'd gone to great lengths to see they wouldn't be disturbed, and yet it seemed that something had interfered with his plans.

"Perhaps it has nothing to do with us," he murmured reassuringly in Blaise's ear, although he couldn't quite believe it. She didn't seem to believe it either, for her body was rigid with tension, and she wouldn't meet his gaze. When he was done fastening her buttons, she hastened to move away from him, as far as the confined hideaway of hay would allow.

Julian's mouth tightened. It would no doubt be awkward to be discovered in such a compromising position, making love in a barn. It was quite obvious they had been tumbling in the hay. Even in the dim light he could see his Gypsy's lips were swollen and passion-bruised from his kisses, her hair wild and tangled with wisps of hay.

They waited in the darkness for quite some time, occasionally catching the sound of voices, but more often there was nothing but silence. Finally they heard the heavy barn door creak open.

Putting his eye to the knothole in the floorboard, Julian saw someone enter. He was carrying a lantern and he moved straight to the loft ladder. To Julian's surprise and chagrin, the intruder was Lord Kilgore himself.

"Julian?" he called up quietly. "Julian, old fellow, are you there?"

He had no choice but to reply. "Yes, Richard. What is it?"

"I regret to interrupt your revelry, but I think you'd best come down. It seems you have a problem you never anticipated."

"What problem?"

"There's a chap here who claims to be a Bow Street Runner. Apparently he followed you here. My people caught him lurking outside the barn, attempting to enter, so they came to fetch me. He claims your . . . er . . .

companion is the missing young lady he's been searching for."

"What if she is? I'm not inclined simply to turn her over to him on a whim."

"It might be more complicated than that. You see . . . it seems the missing girl is a *lady*, Julian."

Chapter 9

There was a profound silence while Julian stared at Blaise in the moonlit darkness.

"You had best explain," he said finally, his tone tightly controlled.

He had addressed her, but his friend apparently heard and took the command to be meant for him.

"The missing young lady is a Miss St. James, of Stevenage. Evidently the Bow Street Runners have been combing the countryside for her, commissioned by her aunt, Lady Agnes Waite. The minion of the law who was found lurking outside my barn suspects your friend of being the girl he is searching for."

Julian rose slowly and moved to stand before Blaise. His silence seemed ominous as he searched her face; even in the dimness she could see the dawning fury on his features. When he grasped her hand to draw her to her feet, she came reluctantly.

"Is it true?"

"Is what true?"

She winced as he seized her shoulders. "Don't play games with me!" he demanded, his voice deadly quiet. "I want to know your real identity."

"I don't live at Stevenage, if that is what you're asking."

His hands moved convulsively upon her shoulders, making Blaise stifle a gasp at the pressure of his grip. She thought about trying to make an escape, but she didn't think he would give her the chance. "All right! My aunt and cousins live there."

"Your aunt is Lady Waite?"

"Yes."

"And the dragon lady you were running from the day I met you at the inn? She is your aunt?"

"Yes."

His grip loosened carefully, as if he didn't trust himself to touch her without resorting to violence. He took a step back.

Blaise rubbed her bruised arms and watched Lynden warily, wondering why he was so angry. She'd done nothing more than keep her name from him, and perhaps shade the truth a bit. But her reasons for not divulging her identity had been entirely justified.

"Perhaps," Richard called up quietly, "you should come down here to discuss this. You will naturally wish to handle this discreetly. You wouldn't want the lady's name bruited about."

"No, we wouldn't want that," Julian replied brittlely. He bent to scoop up Blaise's cloak, but rather than give it to her, he draped the garment over his arm. "Shall we go?" he asked her mockingly, with a sweeping gesture indicating the direction of the loft ladder.

She thought better of refusing. The look in his wintry eyes made her shiver.

When they had both descended the ladder, they were met by a dark-haired, ruddy-cheeked gentleman of approximately the same age as the viscount.

"This," Julian said to Blaise, "is the stallion's owner, Lord Richard Kilgore. We attended Eton together." His mouth twisted as he turned to his friend. "Forgive me, Richard, if I cannot complete the introduction. I don't know the lady's name."

"Miss St. James, I presume?" Baron Kilgore said uncertainly.

"Yes, my lord, that is correct," she admitted with a stiff bow.

Julian swore savagely under his breath. She had *lied* to him. She was in fact a lady of quality—by birth if not deportment—rather than the adopted Gypsy she had pretended to be. And he'd fallen for her deception like the veriest simpleton, a callow youth gulled by an experienced doxy.

The sense of betrayal he felt was as powerful as anything he'd ever experienced with his late wife. Worse, for he'd known what to expect from Caroline. He hadn't counted on such dishonesty from his Gypsy. He'd believed Blaise was different. He'd thought her lively and vital and pure of heart, full of laughter and brightness. Those qualities, even more than her sexual appeal, had attracted him to her from the first.

Discovering that his lovely minx was not so pure, that she'd played him for a fool, was like being kicked in the chest by that bloody stallion they'd planned to pilfer. He had been so wrapped up in the wonder of her, so smitten by her freshness and high spirits that he'd been blind to her real nature.

Yet it was the possible *consequences* of her deception, even more than the deception itself, that turned his blood cold.

All the warmth he'd felt in her presence, all the light and happiness, left him abruptly. All that remained was a cold, sick rage.

Blaise, meanwhile, was beginning to feel her own form of rage as she comprehended how completely she had been manipulated. Bristling with resentment at Lynden's high-handedness, she turned on him before he could speak. "Eton? You were in this together, weren't you?"

His eyes could have been chips of ice. "In what together?"

She waved her arm. "This! This scheme to borrow Lord Kilgore's stallion. He knew about it, didn't he? Because you told him."

"Yes, I told him," Lynden replied tersely. "It was his horse. I thought he deserved to know."

"You betrayed us!"

"If I had, you and your Gypsy friends would now be languishing in jail. When I discovered the stallion belonged to Richard, I decided upon a plan to protect his interests and yours."

"*My* interests? You weren't protecting my interests!"

"I was, you little fool. I didn't want you to be hanged for a thief."

"I would *not* have been hanged."

"You planned to steal from this estate."

"It wasn't stealing!"

"It was close enough to put you in real danger. When I couldn't persuade you to abandon your idiotic scheme, I called on Richard and asked his permission to borrow the stallion."

"That wasn't the only plan you concocted, was it?" Her face was flushed with anger and embarrassment. "You arranged it so that you and I would be alone together in that loft, didn't you? We never were in any danger of being apprehended. Oh, to think how I allowed you to dupe me!"

"*I* duped *you*?" For a moment Julian's famous address deserted him entirely.

"Yes! You tricked me into coming here with you."

He gritted his teeth in fury. His sense of outrage at her deception was only compounded by her accusation—and further aggravated by his aching thigh and the discomfort of being left sexually frustrated by a scheming hussy. "That is hardly the issue," he said icily. "What matters is that you deceived me about your identity."

"Perhaps I wasn't as forthcoming about my circumstances as you think I should have been, but my name really was none of your concern!"

"It became my concern," he snapped, "the moment you allowed me to compromise your reputation."

Blaise's chin rose. Her reputation might be in tatters now, but that was *her* problem. It was certainly not his place to lecture her. "That, my lord, is hardly your affair."

Lord Richard interrupted their impasse. "Perhaps we should adjourn to my study and sort out the truth there.

There is no need to turn this into a spectacle for the servants."

"Yes, by all means, let us avoid a spectacle," Julian observed caustically.

Rather roughly, he draped Blaise's cloak over her shoulders and pulled up the hood to shield her face. It would offer her little protection from recognition, however, since his own servants knew her by sight. And after tonight's farce, there was little chance of keeping her identity quiet. The thought made Julian clench his teeth.

Blaise had to repress a gasp as he escorted her outside; his grip on her arm was tight enough to be painful.

A burly groom armed with a sporting gun stood guard outside the barn door, while some ten yards away, another towered menacingly over the Bow Street Runner who, bound and gagged, lay struggling on the ground.

"What do you wish me to do with the fellow, Julian?" Richard asked uncertainly.

"You'd best set him free and give him a place to sleep for the night. I'll speak to him in the morning, after I decide what is to be done."

A muffled growl met this pronouncement, but Julian ignored it as he marched Blaise across the stableyard and through the rear door of the manor house.

The interior of the manor was as elegant as the exterior, she noted as they moved along a corridor and passed several stylishly furnished rooms. Lynden seemed to know exactly where he was going—and his familiarity only reminded her of his perfidy. To think that she had allowed herself to be gulled by this . . . this profligate! And then he had the audacity to be miffed at her, simply because she hadn't advertised her name and circumstances for all and sundry to gawk at. Really, it was enough to make her gnash her teeth!

Moments later Lynden paused before an open door and glanced over his shoulder at his friend, who had followed. "You will allow us the use of your study, Richard? I'm sure you will understand why I wish to keep our discussion private."

Lord Kilgore looked a bit disappointed, but he agreed politely. "I shall be in the drawing room upstairs if you need me. Just ring for a servant if you require anything else."

Forcibly Julian ushered Blaise into a large study. A fire burned merrily in the grate and several lamps had been lit. Still gripping her arm, he led her to a wing chair and pushed her down. "Don't move," he commanded.

Striding with an obvious limp to a side table, he poured himself a snifter of what looked to be brandy, but offered nothing to her. He stood staring down at the dark golden liquid for a moment before turning to impale her with a level gaze. "Now, I want a full explanation. Who are you and what the devil were you doing with a traveling band of Gypsies?"

Blaise kept her lips tightly closed, a mulish expression on her face.

"You *will* tell me, Miss St. James. I intend to learn the truth if it takes all night. You won't leave this room until you answer my questions to my satisfaction. Who are your people?"

She decided from his harsh tone that he meant what he said. For a full minute the quiet crackle of the fire in the hearth was the only sound in the room. But then Blaise shifted uncomfortably in her seat. Perhaps it was best to get this unpleasantness over as swiftly as possible.

"My father was American," she finally murmured.

Julian nodded. "That explains the odd accent. You say he *was* American?"

"He died when I was ten."

"And your mother?"

"She was English. She passed away five years ago."

"And this aunt of yours, Lady Waite?"

"Aunt Agnes is my mother's sister. She lives in Stevenage."

"Which is an hour or so north of here, if I'm not mistaken. I suppose that was where you were headed when I discovered you at the posting house in Ware?"

"Yes."

"Is Lady Waite your legal guardian?"

"No . . . not precisely."

His mouth thinned. "Then what, *precisely*?"

"My mother remarried shortly after my father died," Blaise said with a bitterness she couldn't hide. "My stepfather is my guardian. He is a career diplomat, currently attached to the consulate in Vienna. Sir Edmund St. James . . . perhaps you've heard of him? He was instrumental in persuading Count Metternich and the Austrians to join the Allied coalition against Napoleon this past summer. With his busy schedule, though, Sir Edmund had little time for me, so he turned me over to Aunt Agnes."

Which was perfectly true, Blaise thought with silent defiance. She didn't add that she had driven her stepfather to the end of his patience by causing one near scandal too many, or that she had been banished to England in disgrace.

"The name isn't familiar to me," Lynden replied. "What is your connection with Miklos?"

"My father was from Philadelphia, in Pennsylvania. He was fascinated by the Gypsies there, so when he came to England on tour, he decided to study the Gypsies here, to investigate their differences. He spent the summer traveling with Miklos's tribe. When they wintered near Stevenage, he met my mother at an assembly. They were married six months later and returned to Philadelphia."

"And your claim that you were adopted by Miklos's tribe? What of that?"

Blaise had the grace to blush. "That . . . wasn't quite true. My father was very close to Miklos, and they always treated me like a daughter, but I was never officially adopted."

"You lied to me," Julian stated flatly.

Refusing to be intimidated, Blaise returned his hard gaze. "I was afraid you would turn me over to my aunt if you knew who I really was."

"I don't enjoy being played for a fool," he said very, very softly.

Blaise shivered. The brandy seemed to have done little to improve his mood. Lord Lynden was as angry as her stepfather had ever been over one of her escapades, but somehow his careful control seemed far more ominous.

"Why the Gypsy disguise?" he asked finally. "Was it merely for a lark?"

"No. I didn't want my aunt to find me. You see, she wished me to marry a certain country squire, and I disagreed with her choice. So I took refuge with Miklos, just until Aunt Agnes could be brought to see reason."

"You should have known better. No lady behaves the way you have."

"Perhaps I don't really wish to be a lady. All right," she said defensively when he shot her a sharp glance. "I'm sorry I deceived you, but there really was no harm done."

"No harm—!" He broke off, his jaw tightening till the muscles stood out in rigid relief. "You allowed me to fondle you, to bare your body—I nearly seduced you tonight! You call that *no harm*?"

Her cheeks flooded with crimson at the reminder of what had happened between them barely a half hour ago. She had absolutely no excuse for the brazen way she had behaved. "I did try to warn you away," she said lamely, "but you wouldn't listen."

"I accept some measure of the blame. If I had known who you were, though, I certainly would never have pursued you as if you were a—" He caught himself in time. He had started to say "a field whore in Spain," but such language was hardly appropriate for the ears of a young lady—which, he was beginning to believe, was what Miss St. James was. Bloody damnation, but he should have known it from the first. What a fool he had been to be taken in by her deception! Obviously he had been thinking with his groin rather than his head.

Julian ran a hand raggedly through his bright hair as the enormity of the situation began to sink in. He had compromised a gentlewoman. And he would have to pay the price.

He couldn't afford to have another scandal attached to his name. Not when he had his own scandal to live down. He was living under the black cloud of Caroline's death, and he had yet to figure out how to resolve it. His chief purpose in returning home was to face the past—to end, if possible, the hell of the past four years. How could he possibly put his life in order, how could he manage to restore his reputation, if he had to defend the added charge of ruining a young gentlewoman's virtue?

"How many people know of your disappearance?" he asked suddenly.

She shook her head warily. "I don't know. My aunt, certainly. My abigail. Perhaps others."

Julian shut his eyes as he fought the suffocating feeling of being entrapped. Servants couldn't be trusted to remain quiet. And there were others involved—the Bow Street Runner, for instance.

Devil take it, but he didn't want to marry again! Particularly not *her*.

He shook his head as he thought of being tied for life to a guileful wench who had deceived him from the first. Even if he could manage to stomach it, even if he could have overlooked Blaise's artful conniving, even if he weren't vehemently opposed to marrying again, his Gypsy minx would be a particularly poor choice of a bride. She offered beauty, spirit, excitement—everything a man could want in a mistress—but if her recent scandalous behavior was anything to judge by, she would make him an abominable wife. Under even normal circumstances, taking her home to Lynden Park would be a disaster—and these were not normal circumstances. His jaw clenched as he considered the bitter irony. If he married a willful hoyden like Blaise St. James, his family name would doubtless only be tarnished further.

Julian ran a hand raggedly down his face, his spinning thoughts chasing themselves in circles as he searched for a way out. But it always came back to one crucial point. He was trapped. He was truly trapped. Her deception had forced his hand.

He had no other option. He had compromised the reputation of a young lady. Ergo, he was honor-bound to marry her. Even if the last thing he wanted was another wife. Even if the thought of wedding a deceiving schemer made his blood boil.

He had no choice in the matter. He would have to wed her, to protect not only *her* name, but his own.

In bitter resignation, Julian swallowed a fiery mouthful of brandy. "Do you realize what this will do to your reputation when it becomes common knowledge that you spent a week in my company, under the dubious chaperonage of a tribe of Gypsies?"

"I don't see why it can't be kept quite."

"Servants talk. The Runner who was paid to search for you may not be willing to keep silent, especially after the way he was treated tonight. And in any case, rumors can be just as devastating as the truth."

"I will think of something," Blaise said stiffly. "I usually do."

He studied her grimly over the rim of his brandy glass. "Are you a virgin?"

Her gasp made it clear how shocking she considered the abrupt question. "Yes, of course I am!"

"How was I to know? Your behavior during the past week was not exactly what one would call circumspect. In fact, I'd say you deliberately led me to believe you were other than a gentlewoman."

She maintained a guilty silence.

"Well . . ." He forced himself to take a deep breath. "It seems I have no course but to offer you marriage in reparation."

"Marriage!" Blaise stared at him. "You must be mad!"

His mouth twisted bitterly. "I imagine you could find several others who would venture to agree with you, but I assure you I am quite sane. And despite current popular opinion, I *am* a gentleman. My sense of honor obliges me to offer for you, and propriety demands it."

"Propriety be dammed."

Julian would have liked to entertain the same sentiment, but he couldn't afford to. "I assure you, I like being forced to wed even less than you do. But it will be a marriage of convenience, nothing more."

"Whose convenience, my lord?" Blaise asked, a hint of bitterness edging her tone.

Julian's eyes narrowed, but otherwise he ignored her comment. "I won't countenance any dalliance, but otherwise I don't care if you seek your own amusements. I never intended to marry again, but I—"

"Again?" She drew an audible breath. "You are married?"

"Was. I am a widower."

His tone was dark, while something hard and bleak in his eyes tugged at her heart, despite his current animosity toward her. Blaise steeled herself, though, against the sympathetic urges she felt. She didn't want to feel sympathy for Lynden. She needed to preserve all her resources for herself if she expected him to see reason. She wouldn't accept his offer. The last thing she wanted was a marriage of convenience. Indeed, that was what had led to this predicament in the first place.

Taking a deep breath, she forced herself to remain calm. "Thank you, my lord, for your kind offer," she recited, "but I must respectfully refuse."

His lips twisted in a mirthless smile. "Clearly you misunderstand me. I am not making you an offer in form. I am simply stating a fact. We shall be married in order to contain the damage done to your reputation."

"But I don't *want* to marry you!"

"You should have thought of that before you allowed yourself to be compromised."

"I never expected you to marry me!" Blaise said with growing frustration. "I never once considered it."

"I realize that. If I thought you had purposely lured me into proposing to you, I would leave you to society's vultures. This way you will at least have the protection of my name."

"I don't need your protection!"

"Nevertheless you shall have it. I won't accept your refusal, Miss St. James. We shall be married tomorrow— or the day after. It will take me a day or so to procure a special license."

"You can't make me!" She had risen to her feet and was glaring at him, her fists clenched in fury. Julian's own fury, however, had reached explosive proportions. It was bad enough that he'd been forced into this untenable situation, but now she had the temerity to spurn his noble gesture.

"I think I can," he said softly, forcibly controlling his temper.

"Indeed? How?"

"Quite simply. I shall merely use my influence to have your Gypsy friends transported . . . unless you agree to an immediate marriage."

"You wouldn't!"

"Would you care to put it to the test?"

"But . . . that is blackmail!"

"Call it what you will, but those are your options."

He never raised his voice, yet his pronouncement seemed more unequivocal than if he had shouted at her. Blaise stared at him in dismay.

"After the wedding, if you behave discreetly, we can go our separate ways, but you *will* become my wife."

The coldness, the flatness of his tone stopped her protests. She knew she wouldn't succeed in persuading him to change his mind, at least not tonight. She might do better to wait until morning to attempt it. "What about Miklos?" she asked lamely.

"What about him?"

"We . . . you were supposed to bring the stallion to him at midnight. He had his heart set on it."

"I don't see why that cannot go forward as planned— *after* we are wed. I will, of course, send someone to inform him of the change of plan."

She would have to be satisfied with that, Blaise reflected, gritting her teeth in frustration.

"Now," Lynden said as if the subject were closed,

"you are no doubt weary." He walked over to the bellpull and gave a tug. "I shall summon a maid who will escort you to bed. In the morning I shall send for your aunt and we can discuss plans for the ceremony." He drained his glass, then turned away to refill it.

He had dismissed her like a troublesome child, Blaise realized. It was that ignominy, as much as the coldness in his eyes, that cut her to the quick. Yet she blinked back the sudden tears that blurred her vision, and lifted her chin, vowing that tomorrow she would take up the battle again.

An august butler appeared almost at once, in answer to Lord Lynden's summons. On his lordship's orders, Blaise was turned over to the housekeeper, who showed her to an elegant guest bedchamber and remained to assist her. Her every comfort was provided for—a generous fire in the hearth, hot water to wash with, a nightdress obtained from who knew where, a cup of mulled wine.

Blaise suffered the attention in silence, weariness and tension draining her of the will to fight. Yet the moment she snuffed the candle and her head touched the pillow, her eyes refused to close.

She lay in the strange bed, staring at the ceiling, pondering Lynden's absurd determination. He was being overfastidious about observing the proprieties, of course. He couldn't possibly *wish* to marry her. Half American by birth, she possessed a bloodline that was questionable at best. She was certainly no proper candidate for a viscountess, not with her propensity for scandal and her disdain for the cold formality of the English upper crust. He would do infinitely better to look elsewhere for a bride.

But he didn't intend to look elsewhere. He meant to have her.

A feeling of cold dread knotted Blaise's stomach. Usually she managed to find a way out of the scrapes she fell into, but she wasn't at all certain she could manage her way out of this one.

Chapter 10

Panna did not view the turn of events as a catastrophe, Blaise learned to her dismay the following morning. Rather, the old Gypsy woman considered the hand of fate to be at work.

Arriving directly after Blaise's breakfast tray had been removed, Panna was shown up to her bedchamber (much to Blaise's surprise) on Lord Lynden's orders (much to her disgust). A sleepless night had left her in a foul humor, unable to summon any of her usual optimism. To further exacerbate her raw mood, the gown and half boots she had been wearing the previous night had disappeared, reducing her only attire to a high-necked flannel nightdress. No doubt Lord Lynden was worried that she might try to escape.

Relieved to see a friendly face, she flung herself into Panna's bony arms and blurted out the story, omitting only the most intimate details about what had happened up in the hayloft.

"It was meant to be," Panna stated cheerfully at the conclusion.

Blaise drew back abruptly and stared. "You cannot be serious."

"Aye, child. Did I not tell you that the *rye*'s future was entwined wi' yer own? You should never scoff at the cards, Rauniyog."

Her look of amazement turned to suspicion. "Did Lord Lynden send you up here to try and persuade me?"

"No, there was no need o' that. I'd already made up me mind."

"Panna, how *could* you?" Blaise exclaimed, feeling abandoned. "Don't you see what a villain he is? I told you, he threatened to have all of you transported if I didn't agree to marry him."

"Well, then, it seems you must agree."

Blaise threw up her hands and turned away. Without waiting for an invitation, Panna lowered herself into a chair and watched the girl restlessly pace the bed-chamber.

"What objections do you 'ave to weddin' the fine *gorgio rye*?"

"He only wants a marriage of convenience, for one thing."

"And that is not what you want?"

"Certainly not. When I marry—*if* I marry, I want my husband to love me. And I want to love him. I want the kind of love Mama and Papa had." Perhaps she had idealized her parents' relationship, but she didn't want to settle for less.

"And you may find it still, with the *rye*."

Blaise's scoffing expression clearly described how unlikely she considered that possibility. "And he's . . . he's an *Englishman*."

And if there was one thing she believed wholeheartedly, it was that Englishmen were cold fish. She had only to look at her stepfather and her English cousins to be convinced of that. And she'd seen too many other examples to be entirely mistaken. Perhaps her feelings were irrational. Certainly it would be difficult to explain her prejudice to Panna when she herself had never put it into words. But her disparagement of an entire class of males, she knew, was based in fear. She dreaded being tied for life to a man she couldn't love, who didn't love her, imprisoned in a marriage that resembled the cold relationship she had with her stepfather. Sir Edmund barely tolerated her, while she had developed a reckless, devil-may-care attitude in sheer defiance of his stiff formality, as well as to better endure her lonely

existence. She couldn't bear to think of having a husband
who was anything like her stepfather.

And while Lord Lynden might not possess the usual
passionless, phlegmatic temperament of the British aristocrat, when he'd learned of her deception last night, he'd
responded just like her stepfather. Indeed, he'd been even
worse than Sir Edmund at his coldest—dictatorial and
heartless. The charming, sensual man she'd known at
the Gypsy camp had vanished, leaving behind an icy
stranger.

Panna, however, reminded her that under the present
circumstances, her alternatives were few.

"What choice d'you 'ave if you don't wed 'im? Do
you want to live under yer aunt's thumb forever? After
this, 'tisn't likely yer aunt will be too fond of you."

Blaise shuddered at the mention of her shrewish relative. Aunt Agnes would never forgive her this time. She
had disgraced herself beyond redemption. And with her
reputation ruined, she would be unable to make any kind
of suitable match at all, which meant she would have
to live with Aunt Agnes for the foreseeable future. Her
aunt would no doubt be happy to lock her in the wine
cellar and throw away the key—with daily visitations to
the prisoner to shriek invectives at her.

"Her scolding will be unbearable," Blaise muttered.
"I'm sure that's the reason Mama married so soon after
Papa's death—so she could escape Aunt Agnes's con-
stant harping."

"Mayhap your mama wanted to be wed because she
wanted to be wed."

"No, she loved Papa too much."

"Mayhap she also loved Sir Edmund."

Blaise shook her head stubbornly. She had viewed her
mother's remarriage barely a year later as a betrayal,
and she would never admit that Frances had borne any
real affection for her second husband. Sir Edmund could
never take the place of her adored papa.

" 'Tain't fittin' for a woman to be alone," Panna
observed, trying another tack. "A woman needs a man,

and children, too. You may not see the *gorgio rye* as the 'usband of your dreams, but you'll come to rue refusing 'is offer to wed, mark me words."

Blaise ceased pacing and sank down on the edge of the feather mattress, staring at her hands dejectedly while she considered Panna's advice. What a mess she had made of it! She had achieved her purpose in running away; she would be able to avoid her London season and marriage now. But she would also be a pariah in society. She wouldn't weep over missing the festivities—the countless balls, soirees, Venetian breakfasts, and musicales; she could live without those and the fashionable company that London offered. But she would definitely regret losing the freedom to mingle in society. She was a gregarious creature by nature, and to be cut off from any companionship but that of her aunt and her aunt's three stiff-necked sons ... Well, she would sooner run away with the Gypsies for good.

Which was probably not even a valid option now. If she tried to run, Lord Lynden would very likely pursue her. And the consequences would doubtless be unpleasant. He had threatened to have her Gypsy friends transported, on some trumped-up charge, no doubt, unless she agreed to the marriage. She wasn't certain he would really do so terrible a thing, but neither was she sure she wanted to chance it.

"Life does not end at wedlock, Rauniyog."

"I know that. It's just that ..."

"Just what?"

"Lynden doesn't really want to marry me. He only offered because he felt guilty about compromising me."

"There's many a good marriage that've begun with less. And for sure there's one thing you 'aven't considered. You might be good for 'im."

Blaise looked up at that. "I?"

" 'E's a troubled man, don't ye know it. There's a darkness in 'is soul that needs the light o' love."

Coming from anyone else, such a pronouncement would have sounded melodramatic and perhaps foolish, but Panna's declaration only sounded matter-of-fact. And Blaise had known the old Gypsy far too long to doubt there was at least a grain of truth in her predictions.

Then Blaise suddenly recalled a certain conversation two days before and her eyes narrowed. "You wanted this to happen, didn't you, Panna? You told Lynden about our plan to borrow the stallion . . . and it was at your suggestion that he accompanied me. You *wanted* him to compromise me."

The old woman cackled softly. "I only gave fate a nudge."

Blaise didn't know whether to be outraged or merely indignant at being betrayed. Yet Panna had always had her best interests at heart. She couldn't believe this time was any different. Nor did she believe it would do much good to resist any longer, not if Panna and Lord Lynden had joined forces.

"I suppose," Blaise said slowly, "that I have no choice but to agree to marry him."

"Aye, but 'twill be for the best, you'll see."

She glanced away wistfully, wondering if Panna could be right. Lynden might be different from the other Englishmen she knew. It was just possible that he wasn't a cold fish like her stepfather. Even if last night his reaction to discovering her identity had been icy fury, she couldn't help remembering the warmth and passion he had shown her with his kisses, or the devastating effect they'd had on her. Their attraction was purely physical, of course, but that might be enough to base a marriage on.

Thinking about it, Blaise felt the first stirrings of hope. Just possibly they might somehow make a good marriage. It was even possible, she realized with tentative optimism, that eventually they might, just might, even come to love each other.

The shrill voice echoing throughout the house late that afternoon alerted Blaise that her outraged aunt had arrived. Steeling herself for the dreaded interview, she waited in her bedchamber until a footman knocked on the door with the message that Lady Agnes Waite requested the presence of Miss St. James in the Blue Parlor.

Resignedly, Blaise tucked back into place a loose tendril of ebony hair that had escaped its moorings and smoothed the skirts of her drab brown gown. Her clothing had been returned to her, cleaned and pressed, but the two sturdy footmen stationed outside her door made it clear that she had not been trusted with the freedom of the house—a worthless precaution, Blaise thought indignantly. If she had wanted to elude them and escape, she would have found a way, but she had decided not to attempt it.

The footman escorted her downstairs to an elegant room that was apparently the Blue Parlor, as evidenced by the blue flocked wallpaper, damask draperies, and brocade furnishings. Aunt Agnes, still dressed in bonnet and traveling pelisse, stood waiting impatiently by the fireplace, obviously quivering with rage. She was a tall, handsome woman with lustrous dark hair lightly sprinkled with gray—or at least she would have been handsome had not her fierce scowl pinched her features into a sour mask resembling a prune.

For the sake of appearances, she greeted her niece through stiff lips and held her tongue until the footman withdrew. The moment the door closed, however, she delivered a blistering tirade, denouncing Blaise's disgraceful behavior and berating her for her ingratitude, calling her, among other things, an outrageous, discreditable girl and a wicked, headstrong, scandalous wretch. White-faced, Blaise endured the denunciation without uttering a word in her defense, knowing that to do so would only incite her aunt to further rage.

Ten minutes later, Lady Agnes collapsed on the settee, fanning herself with her hand. "To think all this time I have cherished a serpent in my bosom. You cannot *know* what you have done to my poor nerves!"

"I am sorry," Blaise muttered, only marginally repentant, "for any inconvenience I might have caused you, Aunt."

"Sorry! *Sorry!* Is that all you have to say for yourself? You worry me nearly to death, making me think I had lost the daughter of my dearly departed only sister, you cost me a *fortune* in fees to hire those worthless Bow Street Runners, you spoil the house party I spent *weeks* arranging on your behalf, you put me in an insupportable position with your stepfather, you force me to lie to Squire Featherstonehaugh so he won't develop a disgust for you—"

"I never asked you to go to such trouble for me," Blaise interrupted stiffly. "Nor did I ever wish for the squire as a suitor."

Lady Agnes suddenly pressed her lips together, as if forcing herself to bite her tongue. "Well, I must say you've done better for yourself than I could have done for you, nabbing a rich viscount. From what I understand, Lynden could buy Digby twenty times over and never miss the cost. And the title is vastly superior and centuries older. Seeing how it turned out so well, I am willing to overlook your disgraceful behavior."

It was all Blaise could do to keep control of her temper. "I did not *nab* Lynden," she retorted. "I certainly never targeted him for a husband—"

"Oh, pooh, you are mincing words. Now tell me the particulars. Lynden's letter said the marriage ceremony is to be held tomorrow. I cannot approve of such haste, but I suppose there is little hope for it. We must be thankful he is willing to take responsibility for dishonoring you."

"He did not dishonor me!"

"Why would he offer for you otherwise? His letter said he felt he had compromised your honor beyond what was proper and he felt obliged to rectify matters."

"He may feel that way, but I disagree about how serious the damage was."

"You spent the entire week in the company of those nasty, heathen Gypsies—I call that highly improper."

"Lord Lynden wasn't to blame for that. And," Blaise added with a measure of truth, "he behaved toward me as any gentleman would have." She didn't know why she was defending Lynden except that Aunt Agnes was attacking his integrity.

"A gentleman would have restored you to your family."

"He didn't know who I was. I never told him. He only discovered it last night."

Lady Agnes sniffed. "I should have known it was your fault, you disgraceful girl, but that is neither here nor there. We must discuss the wedding preparations. I've brought your gowns with me and your abigail. There will be no time to hire a dressmaker to outfit you in the latest fashion, so you will have to make do with a ballgown as a wedding dress."

Blaise shook her head. Garvey would be genuinely welcome, not merely for the services she performed as maid, hairdresser, and companion, but because Blaise truly liked the quiet older woman. But it was too soon to be discussing wedding attire. She wasn't totally certain she would marry Lord Lynden. And she refused to be browbeaten by her aunt into making what was likely to be the most important decision of her life.

"You presume too much, Aunt. There may not even be a wedding."

"Whatever do you mean?"

"I mean that nothing is settled. I was told that Lynden went to London to obtain a special license, but I have not agreed to accept his proposal."

Lady Agnes's blue eyes grew round. "You *refused* him? Are you mad?"

"I don't consider it mad to be certain of my feelings before taking a husband for life."

Her aunt's expression went from thunderstruck to thunderous. "Your *feelings*? What have your feelings to say to the matter? You have disgraced us all! You *will* marry Lynden, and that is that." She must have recognized the stubborn set of her niece's jaw, for she exclaimed, "Listen to me, you wicked child! I shan't face Sir Edmund with the knowledge that I failed in my duty to you. If you think you can pretend this never happened, you can just think again!

You've gone too far this time. Your reputation is in ruins. If you think I will take you in after this, you are entirely mistaken. I won't tolerate a disgraceful baggage in my home!"

"I will thank you, madam, to keep your voice down."

Both Blaise and Lady Agnes turned at the interruption to find Lord Lynden himself standing in the doorway. Blaise was dismayed at the sudden leap of her pulse that just seeing him brought about. He wore his overcoat and his boots were dull with road dust.

He stepped into the room and shut the door pointedly behind him. "I don't care to have my affairs broadcast to the entire household, particularly when neither the staff nor the house is my own."

"You must be Lord Lynden," Lady Agnes said with an ingratiating sweetness that contrasted remarkably with the shrill tone she had used just moments before with her niece.

Lynden made the semblance of a polite bow, but his features were drawn into a cold mask. Blaise noted the lines of pain about his blue eyes, though, and when he moved farther into the room, he couldn't disguise his halting gait. The grueling journey he'd undertaken today must have aggravated his wounded leg, she realized.

Lady Agnes appeared not to notice his limp, or the scar that marred his noble features. "I was merely impressing upon my niece her duty in wedding you, my lord, and taking her to task for putting us all to so much trouble."

"As my betrothed, Miss St. James is no longer your concern."

"But . . . she is—"

"I will discipline her myself, if it is warranted. And I don't care to have my future wife termed a 'disgraceful baggage.' "

Blaise had started to bristle at the notion that he was now her disciplinarian, yet she was mollified somewhat to see Lynden come to her defense and stand up to her shrewish aunt.

Aunt Agnes looked unusually flustered. "Of course I

didn't mean to call her a 'baggage,' my lord. I sometimes lose control of my temper and say things that I don't mean. My niece can be a bit willful at times—which is often tiresome. And sometimes she acts the hoyden. But she isn't truly wicked. She was outrageously spoiled by her father, you see."

Blaise was amazed to see her aunt showing such deference to Lord Lynden, yet he met her overtures with cool disdain.

"Indeed." It was a curt reply, no doubt intended to depress pretensions.

"Yes, it hasn't been easy to manage her all these years—"

"I can very well understand why Miss St. James was eager to escape your control, madam. Indeed I can only applaud her restraint. If I had had to deal with you, I would no doubt have been driven to commit mayhem."

Lady Agnes's complexion turned red, but she was not easily intimidated. "From what I understand, sir, you already have!" She turned to Blaise with a haughty look. "You were concerned about the sort of husband he would make. Well, let me tell you, miss. Lord Lynden is not the paragon he appears. Not only are his affairs with the demimondaine legendary, but I understand there is strong evidence he murdered his wife!"

Blaise drew a sharp breath and sent a shocked look at Lynden. She expected him to refute the wild accusation, but he didn't say a word. He stood like a statue, his jaw clenched so tightly the corded muscles stood out.

"I trust you are happy, niece," Lady Agnes said with obvious relish. "I have warned you for years about your disgraceful behavior, and now you must pay the piper. You will just have to lie in the bed you've made. Literally."

She stalked to the door then and threw it open. Her gaze alighting on a footman, she pointed. "You there, you will show me to my rooms at once. I don't intend to put up with such rudeness for a single moment longer than it takes me to do my duty."

When she had swept from the room, Blaise turned questioning eyes to Lynden. "What did she mean, you murdered your wife?"

His haunted gaze met hers, but it was a moment before he answered. "I don't intend to discuss it."

"Not discuss it!"

"My late wife," he replied grimly, "is none of your concern, and neither are the circumstances of her death. At the moment there are more important matters that should interest you. I have the special license, and I've arranged for the ceremony to begin at eight o'clock this evening."

She stared at him blankly, trying to shift her thoughts from murder to marriage—a marriage she had yet to agree to. "This evening! But that is only"—she glanced at the ormolu clock on the mantle—"three hours away!"

"Yes, it is, but I see no reason for delay. I trust you will be ready."

With the briefest of bows, he turned and quit the room, limping discernibly, leaving Blaise to stare after him in bewilderment and dismay.

Chapter 11

❧⌇❧

In the end, she capitulated.

The wedding took place precisely at eight o'clock that evening in Lord Kilgore's drawing room, with the local vicar presiding and a very few oddly assorted guests in attendance. The special license Julian had obtained eliminated the necessity of reading the banns and permitted the marriage to occur at any convenient time or place. In this case, a time and place that was primarily convenient for Lord Lynden, Blaise thought with vexation at his high-handedness.

The ceremony was a solemn, swift affair, certainly not the cherished ideal of a young woman's dreams. The entire event seemed unreal to Blaise—almost as if she were merely an observer rather than a prime participant. She felt as if she were standing outside herself looking on.

Item: The bride wore a high-waisted wedding gown of ivory satin with a tulle overskirt shot with silver threads. Her raven hair was artfully arranged high upon her head, and threaded with a satin ribbon.

Item: The groom wore a superbly tailored blue coat that accentuated his lean elegance and enhanced the intense color of his eyes.

Item: Neither of them appeared overjoyed.

Certainly she didn't *feel* joyous on this, the most significant day of her adult life. She could scarcely believe this was happening. After exerting such effort to avoid an arranged marriage to a suitor of her aunt's choosing, here she was, repeating vows to honor and obey a man

162

who was nearly a stranger, and one who was rumored to have murdered his wife, at that.

Blaise glanced covertly up at Lord Lynden standing beside her, appraising his hard, unsmiling features. That he did not wish to marry her, she was humiliatingly aware. She had spent the past three hours wrestling with the decision whether *she* wished to marry *him*. Despite the pressure of his threat against her friends, her certain ruination if she spurned his offer, and Panna's obvious support for the marriage, Blaise refused to go meekly to her fate without careful consideration.

It was certainly a point in Lynden's favor that Aunt Agnes didn't appear to like him. Her aunt had visited her room barely an hour ago to finish the tirade she'd started, first scolding Blaise again for causing such a scandal, then proceeding to enumerate Lynden's faults and express her shock at his limp, saying that cripples gave her palpitations. Blaise had been incensed for Lynden's sake and overly defensive, considering the current state of her own conflicted feelings toward him. Yet she thought the condemnation highly unjust.

It was not as if he were exactly repulsive, either. Aside from his war wounds and the scar that marred his cheek, Lord Lynden was physically everything a young bride could wish for. His lameness, in her opinion, while limiting his natural grace, did not detract from his appeal. If anything, his suffering only made him a more sympathetic figure. Indeed, most young ladies would have been delighted to become the wife of a wealthy, exceedingly handsome viscount. Even one with such a dark cloud hanging over his head.

Shifting her gaze, Blaise studied the long-fingered, lean hand that was presently clasping her own. Had those tapered, well-manicured fingers committed murder?

She wanted to doubt it. She didn't want to believe he had done something so terrible as kill his wife. That afternoon, Lynden had refused to answer her questions about the accusation against him, or even to defend himself. Yet, oddly, his reaction reassured her more than protestations might have done. And nothing in his behavior during the past week had led her to believe him capable of such violence. Even at the height of his anger after discovering her duplicity, he had exhibited nothing but the most careful control. The previous consideration he had shown her, his concern over her welfare, the tenderness in his kisses, all supported her instinctive belief in his innocence.

Besides, she had satisfied her doubts to a small degree by the simple process of interviewing his manservant. A personal servant would likely know better than anyone if there was any credibility to the hideous rumors.

Before going upstairs to dress for the ceremony, Blaise had asked a footman to summon Lord Lynden's servant to the Blue Parlor. Her position in the house was questionable, but she evidently held enough authority to have her simple request obeyed. Or perhaps it was just that while Lynden had ordered her not to leave the house, he apparently had not forbidden her freedom of speech.

The burly Will Terral arrived shortly, and at her request, closed the door behind him. He doffed his hat respectfully, but watched her somewhat warily.

Taking a step forward, Blaise gave him what she hoped was a reassuring smile. She had no reason to expect him to tell her the truth. A loyal servant would never betray his master or reveal dark secrets. But she hoped to watch his expression closely, to see if he gave anything away, to gauge his reaction for any hint of dissimulation.

"You may find it odd that I asked to speak to you, but I . . . have a question which I must put to you. Mine is not idle curiosity, either, for your answer affects my future directly. You have heard, no doubt, that I am to marry Viscount Lynden?"

"Aye, miss. May I wish you every happiness, miss?"

She hesitated, surprised at the sincerity in his tone. She hadn't thought Terral would want her to marry his master. She'd had the impression that he didn't approve of her, although he'd never done anything overtly disrespectful during the past week to warrant reprimand. And his expression was nothing but deferential now, if a bit guarded.

"Well, my question . . . I wouldn't ask you to betray your master's confidence, but . . . I don't know how to put this delicately, so perhaps I should simply say it. The rumors about Lord Lynden . . . are they true? Did he . . . murder his wife?"

"That he did *not,* miss."

"No?" She was surprised by the adamance of Terral's tone, by the fierceness of his sudden frown.

"No. 'Twas a riding accident that killed her ladyship."

Blaise searched his scowling face. "Do you have any proof of his innocence?"

"I don't need proof, miss! I've known his lordship all my life and he's not one to do murder. No matter that there's some who've spread rumors otherwise."

"If it isn't true, then why would anyone say it was?"

"He and her ladyship wasn't on the best of terms. They fought sometimes—just before the tragedy happened, too. But he didn't solve his problems by doing for her. She rode out with a storm brewing, and he went after her. By the time he found her, she was already dead."

Terral's reply might be the blind loyalty of a faithful servant, Blaise realized, or one who had been well-paid to conceal the truth, but she didn't think he was lying to her. His defense was too *intense.*

He hadn't finished championing Lord Lynden, either, it seemed.

"He took her death hard, miss. Wasn't the same man afterward. For sure he blames himself for what happened. Why else would he go off to war and try to get himself killed, not caring whether he lived or died?"

Startled, Blaise didn't reply at first. Had Lynden been so devastated by his wife's death that he hadn't wanted to live without her? Had he loved her so very much that he couldn't bear the grief of her loss? Or was it guilt that had driven him away? Had he killed her and then regretted it?

Blaise desperately wanted to know the answers to those questions, but she didn't think Terral could supply them, not on so deeply personal a subject. Yet she sensed that some reaction was expected of her. "Thank you, Mr. Terral," she said finally, quietly. "I appreciate your candor. I will think carefully about what you've said."

Terral nodded brusquely, but rather than accepting his dismissal, he stood there for another moment, twisting his hat in his hands, looking uncomfortable. "By your leave, miss . . . as long as you're inclined to speak plainly . . . I own I thought his lordship was making a mistake, staying with the Gypsies and you . . . ah . . . He had meant to go home, see? I could tell he was putting it off. And his leg and all—I didn't think it could help for him to go tearing off here and yon. But I warrant I was wrong. That Gypsy cure worked far better than anything I knew to try. And you . . . Begging your pardon, miss, but this past week . . . he's changed. I've not seen him so carefree since it happened. I don't know what it is you've done to him, but for sure it's a good thing. He needs you, miss."

Again, Terral left her speechless, but this time her muteness was accompanied by a strange, tight feeling in her throat as Blaise suddenly, unaccountably felt as if she wanted to cry. "I . . ." She swallowed hard and turned away to hide her discomposure. "If I do become Lord Lynden's wife, I hope I may count on your support, Terral."

"Aye, miss, that you may."

He left her alone then, shutting the door softly behind him. Blaise stood there for a long moment, the burly servant's words echoing in her ears. *He needs you, miss.*

Panna had said much the same thing.

It was an unsubstantiated yet compelling notion, one that struck a responsive chord deep within Blaise's heart. No one had ever *needed* her. She'd been a burden to her stepfather and her aunt, and even her mother at times. The thought that she might actually help Lord

Lynden by marrying him seemed incredible—and incredibly appealing. She found herself, for the first time, entertaining the idea with a strange sense of excitement.

Lynden couldn't be guilty of murder. She wouldn't allow herself to believe it. She had no factual confirmation of his innocence, nothing but the assurance of a personal servant and her own instincts to guide her, but she was almost certain the accusations were false. Terral had insisted as much—implying that Lynden was the victim of rumor and vile gossip, that he'd been greatly wronged.

But whether or not Lynden was to blame for his wife's death, he had been deeply affected by it.

That, in fact, must be the reason for his "troubled soul." Blaise had thought "the great sorrow" Panna alluded to might be the result of Lynden's experiences in war and the pain he'd suffered from his wounding, but now she knew his scars went even deeper than his war wounds.

And her feelings for him went deeper than compassion. She had always been physically attracted to him. From the first, she'd been in danger of losing any semblance of willpower whenever he merely looked at her. But now, knowing about his past tragedy, she was in danger of losing her heart to him. She understood now the quiet anguish she had sensed in him at times. His suffering aroused her most protective instincts. A *woman's* protective instincts. She wanted to help him if she could, to soothe his grief and comfort him. She wanted to love him. She wanted him to love her. She wanted him to need her. She simply *wanted* him.

It had always been there, the attraction, the indefinable bond between them. It pulled at her now, with a strength that amazed her. And she believed it was reciprocated. Judging from his ardent pursuit of her this past week, Lynden seemed to desire her. And she hoped that eventually, someday, desire could lead to love.

That was why, in the end, she had agreed to the marriage. Why she had allowed Garvey to bathe and dress her and arrange her hair. Why she was standing here now beside Lord Lynden, repeating the solemn, binding vow, "I will."

She hoped to find love.

It surprised her, therefore, to feel herself trembling now. She was frightened, not of Lynden himself, but of the unknown. Would it be possible to achieve what she most wanted? Would it be possible to make him fall in love with her?

He had said theirs would be a marriage of convenience, nothing more. Blaise shuddered at the thought. She had always despised the notion of such unions. But for noblemen like Lynden, it was a common occurrence. Had his first marriage been like that, one of convenience, as marriages of the upper class so often were? If so, had he ever come to love his wife? Or had it been a love match? More crucially, Blaise wondered, could he ever grow to love *her*?

As the vicar intoned the final words that would join them in holy matrimony, Blaise stole another glance at Lynden and shivered. He looked so forbidding, this man who was nearly her wedded husband.

"You may kiss the bride."

She barely heard the final pronouncement. It was only when Lynden turned to her that Blaise realized he intended to kiss her to seal the vows. His eyes were a chill, glittering blue as she raised her face to his, and when he bent briefly, his lips were cool and impersonal. Blaise felt her heart sinking.

The celebration afterward was awkward and uncomfortable for everyone present. Blaise's closest Gypsy friends, Panna and Miklos, had been allowed to attend the wedding ceremony, but they stood tense and wary, unaccustomed to being in such a fine house. Lady Agnes bristled, incensed at being contaminated by such riffraff and still in a dudgeon because of Lynden's earlier rudeness. The vicar looked bewildered by the hostile atmosphere. Both the abigail Garvey and the manservant Terral seemed anxious. The bridal couple barely exchanged a word. And Lord Kilgore appeared eager for the unusual event to end so his home could return to normal.

The guests partook of refreshments—champagne and delicate cakes served by footmen. Julian wished for something stronger to drink, but repressed the urge, just as he forced himself to stand there and receive the polite good wishes of the guests.

After the proper toasts were offered, the conversation dwindled.

As if recalling her duty as the eldest lady present, Lady Agnes bestirred herself to address Lord Lynden stiffly. "May I inquire as to your travel plans, my lord?"

"We shall spend the night here, and tomorrow leave for my home."

"Your family seat is near Huntingdon, is it not?"

"Just south of there."

"An excellent estate it is, too," Lord Kilgore offered. "Lynden Park puts my place to shame."

Blaise, who had barely heard anything after "We shall spend the night here," tensed with a sudden feeling of nervous excitement. This was her wedding night. Tonight she would become fully a woman in the arms of her husband. She would learn the secrets of which genteel females were kept in abysmal ignorance. She would discover the passionate conclusion to the mysterious proceedings Lynden had begun the previous evening in the hayloft. Her pulse quickened as her gaze sought him out.

Wrapped up in watching him, Blaise barely caught Lynden's cool reply to some question. "I wouldn't know. It has been four years since I've been home."

The admission of such a long absence surprised Blaise until she remembered what Terral had told her. Lord Lynden had gone off to war and tried to get himself killed. Had that been four years ago? she wondered. Had that been when he'd lost his wife and stopped caring whether he lived or died?

The torturous celebration dragged out for an obligatory half hour before the guests began to disperse. Blaise accompanied Panna and Miklos downstairs to the front door and hugged them both.

" 'Tis a good day, Rauniyog," Panna declared. "Ye'll thank me for this one day, mark me words."

"Perhaps so," Blaise replied with less confidence.

Miklos, who had ventured barely a word since arriving at the lordly manor house, promised to bring the tribe to visit Blaise at her new home in a month or so. It cheered her only marginally when Miklos expressed his gratitude for helping him achieve his heart's desire. He was to breed his prize mare, after all; Lord Kilgore had offered to make the stallion available on the morrow.

At least her sacrifice hadn't been all for naught, Blaise thought glumly—even if it didn't escape her notice that she had been bartered for the price of a future colt.

There were tears in her eyes as she watched her dear friends leave, but she had brought herself under control by the time she mounted the stairs to return to the drawing room. To her surprise, Aunt Agnes was waiting for her at the upper landing, looking oddly subdued.

"I know there have been times when you have resented me," the older woman said tentatively, "but I only want what is best for you, child."

"I know, Aunt. And I am sorry for all the trouble I've caused you."

"Well . . . I don't suppose you could help it. You always were too high-spirited for your own good. Do you . . . need me to instruct you? For tonight, I mean?"

Blaise was spared a reply, however, by her new husband, who had stepped out into the corridor. "That will be unnecessary. I will instruct my wife on whatever she needs to know."

A blush staining her cheeks, Blaise avoided looking at Lynden as she thanked her aunt.

Lady Agnes had sniffed at Lynden's pronouncement. "I shall wish you good night, then."

Watching her aunt move down the hall, Blaise wondered if her racing pulse would ever come under control again. Lynden's declaration that he would teach her about lovemaking had sent heat streaking through her entire body. She *knew* he would make an excellent instructor. Memories of what he had done to her in the hayloft crowded into her mind, making it difficult for her to think of anything else.

She was aware that he awaited her attention, though. Uncertain whether to join him in the drawing room again, Blaise glanced up at him and received the answer to her unspoken question.

"It is time you retired. I shall come to your bed-chamber in half an hour. I presume that will allow you adequate time to prepare?"

The shock of meeting his narrowed azure eyes nearly took her breath away. There was anger there, and impatience. None of the anticipation or tenderness expected of a man bedding his wife for the first time.

"Yes . . ." she murmured meekly, unsure what she had done wrong, not knowing what else to say.

He left her then to return to the drawing room, his gait stiff and halting. Before the door shut behind him, though, she heard Lord Kilgore's relieved sigh, accompanied by what sounded like a friendly slap on the back. "Thank God that's over," Kilgore said. "You look in need of a spot of brandy, old man."

"More than a spot," her husband replied grimly. "I need an entire cask."

His answer did not, Blaise thought despondently, bode well for their future marriage.

Garvey was waiting for her when she reached her bedchamber.

"May I wish you well on your marriage, my lady?" the abigail said in her quiet voice.

Blaise gave a start at the elite form of address, having forgotten that she was now a viscountess. "Thank you, Garvey."

"Shall I help you undress?"

She glanced involuntarily at the canopy bed. The velvet curtains had been drawn back, and the covers turned down invitingly. Absently, Blaise nodded. "Yes. My husband . . ." She hesitated over the word, thinking how strange it still sounded. "Lynden will be here shortly."

She allowed herself to be undressed and garbed in a high-necked, virginal nightdress. Then she sat at the dressing table while her long hair was taken down and brushed till it gleamed. Blaise was grateful for Garvey's steadying presence and the familiar tasks of preparing for bed, for it kept her mind off what was to come.

Finally, however, there was nothing more the abigail could do for her mistress. Garvey fed a shovelful of coal into the fire, then turned out all the oil lamps but one, leaving it burning low on the small bedside table.

"I'll leave you now, my lady, if there is nothing else you require."

"Yes, thank you, Garvey."

When she was alone, Blaise continued to sit there at her dressing table, wishing she had thought to bring a glass of wine with her to bed. She was so nervous she was trembling. Her deflowering was only moments away, and she—

Do get hold of yourself. There was no reason to be so apprehensive. Lynden's lovemaking in the hayloft had proved him to be an incredibly skilled, considerate lover, and there was no reason to believe he would be different tonight . . . except for the cold anger she had seen in his eyes. Forcing herself to rise, Blaise climbed into bed and pulled the covers up to her chin.

It was perhaps ten minutes later when she heard the door to her bedchamber swing open without so much as a knock. Blaise tensed, wishing she had never agreed to this hasty, unwanted marriage. Yet it was too late now for second thoughts. The grim, beautiful, scarred man watching her from the doorway was her husband.

He had changed his attire and now wore a floor-length dressing gown of burgundy brocade. A half-filled snifter dangled from his fingertips.

Shutting the door behind him, he leaned against the wooden panel and raised his glass to his lips. He drank

a large swallow, then held the crystal glass up to the light
to inspect its contents.

"I usually refuse to drink brandy," he observed with
careful emphasis. "It's certain to have been smuggled from
France, and I didn't spend four years fighting Boney's
armies only to line his pockets."

Forgetting about her own apprehension, Blaise gazed
at him with sudden suspicion. "Are you foxed?"

"Not nearly enough."

Which was entirely true, Julian reflected. He had
imbibed more than was wise, but he'd needed the potent
liquor, not only to dull the ache in his thigh—aggravated
by countless hours of riding in a swaying coach—but to
help him face this damnable situation with a measure of
control.

His fury hadn't abated during the past twenty-four
hours. If anything, it had only increased. He'd been forced
into this marriage, tied for life to a wench who at best was
a scandalous romp, at worst a heartless schemer. Blaise
had trapped him, lied to him, given him no choice but to
offer her the protection of his name. He'd never intended
to marry again, not after his first marriage had ended in
tragedy, but Blaise had left him no alternative.

He'd come here tonight with some dim idea of punishing her for it.

Swallowing another mouthful, Julian regarded her with
hooded eyes. He felt far differently toward Blaise than he
had toward his first wife. He still wanted her, more than
he'd ever wanted any woman. But never as his wife.

That was the hell of it. She was his now. He had the
legal right to take her, to touch her, to make love to her
any time he chose. Except for the understood rules of his
class. A gentleman was expected to control his lustful
urges toward his wife. A gentleman never allowed his
base instincts free rein with a lady.

And Blaise claimed to be a lady. Young, innocent,
sweetly virginal.

Julian clenched his teeth at the sight of her lying
there. There she was, his *wife*, hiding behind the covers,

cowering in her bed as if he might ravish her or, indeed, murder her.

Murder. It outraged him that she could believe him capable of such a crime. But her bitch of an aunt had wasted no time ensuring that Blaise learned of his unsavory past and the allegations against him.

His impotence only heightened his rage.

"Not too foxed," he added finally with an edge of mockery, "to perform my husbandly duties."

"I . . . If you wish to . . . put off your duties," Blaise said in a small voice, "I wouldn't object."

"Oh, no. I intend to consummate our marriage tonight, dear *wife*, so there will be no possible grounds for an annulment. I won't have you trying to get out of it. You've put me to enough trouble as it is."

"*I* put *you* to trouble?" Incensed by the injustice of the accusation, Blaise abruptly sat up in bed, clutching the covers. "I didn't ask you to marry me!"

"No, you only made it impossible for me to do otherwise."

"You couldn't regret our marriage any more than I."

A muscle twitched warningly in his jaw. Draining the rest of his brandy in a single fiery gulp, he pushed himself away from the door and strode awkwardly toward her, but as he passed the wing chairs in front of the fireplace, he somehow stumbled on the carpet and wrenched his leg before he caught the chair back and righted himself. Cursing violently, Julian clenched his teeth in pain.

Blaise immediately felt contrite, seeing him suffer so. She wished there was something she could say to make amends for losing her temper and exacerbating an already flammable situation.

"I know you didn't murder your wife," she began tentatively. "I'm sure—"

"You know nothing of the kind."

She was startled as much by his contradiction as by the savagery in his tone, but she had obviously touched a raw nerve. Trying to vindicate him had only angered him further.

"Terral said she was killed in a riding—"

"Shut up." His blue eyes were as cold and glittery as glaciers. "I told you, I won't discuss my wife."

Her chin rose stubbornly. "I am your wife now, and I think I have a right to—"

He set the empty snifter down on the reading table with enough force to shatter the crystal. In three strides he had closed the distance between them and reached for her.

His dark, angry face loomed over her as he grasped her shoulders. "For all anyone knows, I throttled my first wife in her bed—just as I might do to you if you don't keep your tongue between your teeth!"

Blaise could feel the threatening grip of his fingers as he moved one hand to her throat, but she glared back at him militantly. "If you're trying to frighten me, it won't work! I don't frighten."

His narrowed eyes dropped suddenly to her breasts, which were hidden by the covers she was clutching to her chest. "Good," he said tersely. "Then we can get this over quickly."

His hand slid forcefully behind her nape then, and he yanked her toward him.

He kissed her roughly, the gentleness she'd known in him entirely gone. He raped her mouth, his tongue surging and stabbing, assaulting her senses with the taste of brandy. It was a seizure that punished, that dominated her mouth with almost reflexive expertise, that ravished without ardor. The fierce power of it left Blaise quivering with fright and a nameless longing.

She was panting for breath when he abruptly drew away. His fingers hooked over the edge of the covers, and in a single swift motion, he dragged them down, exposing her flannel-clad body to his gaze. Blaise instinctively covered her breasts with her crossed arms.

"Take off your nightdress."

She hesitated, instinctively rebelling against his icy tone. And yet only a short while ago, she had promised to honor and obey him.

"Take it off or I'll rip it off."

She thought he might just be angry enough to do it. With trembling fingers Blaise reached for the hem of her nightdress. Shifting her hips, she tugged the garment over her head.

She would have used it to cover herself, but her husband yanked it from her and tossed it on the floor. Naked and vulnerable, her cheeks flaming, she remained silent, enduring his cool scrutiny of her body. His gaze surveyed her everywhere, his eyes touching her boldly, intimately, his expression mortifyingly impassive.

"Lie down."

Blaise stared at him warily, but she didn't resist when, with one hand on her shoulder, he pushed her back till she lay full-length on the bed. She tensed when he abruptly sat down beside her, his hip crowding her threateningly, then sucked in her breath when his hand moved down her chest and cupped her right breast.

He lingered there, his thumb and forefinger arousing the nipple, making it contract in shocks of pleasure, making Blaise shiver uncontrollably. Then he shifted his hand and began a slow, insolent exploration of her body. His palm was warm and slightly rough with calluses, and it was all she could do to keep from squirming under his skillful touch.

He knew exactly what effect he was having on her, too, Blaise was certain. Beneath partly closed lids his brilliant eyes watched her coolly, while his hand moved down her tense abdomen to the silkiness of her womanhood.

"Spread your legs."

Her face flushed hotly at his crude command, but Blaise closed her eyes and obeyed, unwillingly accepting the pleasure he was giving her.

Her sharp intake of breath was loud and rasping when his finger finally slid inside her. He held it there a moment, making her want to writhe with frustration at his inaction——before finally he began stroking again, gliding through the hot, slick wetness seeping from between her thighs. With a strangled gasp that was almost a sob, Blaise let her hips arch wildly against his probing fingers.

It was not his intent to give her pleasure, though, but merely to ready her for his invasion. When he withdrew and stood up, her eyes flew open.

His hard, tense face seemed to loom over her as he shed his dressing gown and bared his lean, graceful body. In the dim lamplight she saw his scarred thigh but caught only a glimpse of the thick manhood jutting out from a nest of dark golden hair, yet she was startled by the size and power of it.

He gave her no time to contemplate what was to come. Wordlessly, he positioned her legs apart and mounted her, settling himself between her thighs, covering her chest to thigh. Rather than experiencing fear, though, Blaise felt a tremulous wave of longing rack her body at the unfamiliar weight pressing her down. She was acutely aware of his overpowering maleness, of the keen sensations he aroused within her: the fierce blue gaze that bored into hers, the sensitive ache where her breasts touched his hard body, the warm skin of his chest, the hard pressure of his belly, the rasping friction of the gauze bandage against the skin of her inner thigh, the thrusting shaft probing for entrance.

"Open your legs to me," he ordered harshly.

Dazed, she obeyed, and then gasped at the shock of him. The sudden assault of his bigness, his maleness took her breath away. The hard, stretching pressure that parted her flesh and invaded her made her whimper. A flash of pure panic opened her eyes wide. His teeth were clenched, making the scar on his cheek stand out vividly. Then one powerful thrust and he was inside her.

Blaise's cry mingled with his low curse.

He held himself still while she grew accustomed to the stabbing pressure. When her hot flesh swelled tightly around his shaft, he began to move. He thrust with quick, urgent strokes, his possession swift and dispassionate as he finalized the consummation. Her fingers clung to him, clutching the bunched muscles of his shoulders while she gritted her teeth and endured.

A dozen pounding heartbeats later, she heard his groan as he drove into her, felt the lean body go rigid against her. His muscles clenched for an eternity, before he finally collapsed upon her with a rasping breath. Blaise bit back a sob and buried her face in the sweat-dampened skin of his shoulder, grateful that it was over.

Another long moment passed before he shifted his weight to his elbows and raised his head, the taut skin of his cheekbones flushed with spent passion and pain.

Averting her face, Blaise lay still and limp beneath him, feeling the hurtful ache between her thighs, her body throbbing with unfulfilled desire.

Julian drew back, surveying her dark tousled hair, her trembling mouth. Her face was very white, her eyes shimmering with unshed tears. He rolled off her, trying not to hurt her or his damaged thigh further. His gaze ran down her slender body, past the firm, high, rose-tipped breasts and narrow waist, along the flat belly, and lower, to the gleaming wetness at the junction of her thighs. Her pale skin was smeared with the milky fluid of his seed and the darker tinge of virgin blood.

He muttered a violent oath. He was not proud of himself. He'd taken his innocent young wife swiftly and coldly, with no tenderness and very little consideration for her virginity.

Raking a hand through his hair, Julian climbed wearily to his feet, ignoring the fierce ache of his wounded thigh and the stronger ache of his conscience. Self-recrimination was a familiar companion. He'd lived with guilt eating away at him for four years. One more black mark to his credit would hardly make a dent.

He fetched a dampened cloth from the washstand and, much to his new wife's apparent dismay, proceeded to wash away the telltale stains from her thighs, brushing aside her hands when she attempted to shield herself. Then he pulled the covers up over her naked body and drew on his dressing gown.

She watched him in wide-eyed silence.

"Go to sleep," he said brusquely as he turned away.

He had made it nearly to the door, carefully favoring his cramping right leg, before she spoke in a hoarse whisper.

"Where are you going?"

"To my own rooms," Julian threw over his shoulder. "I intend to explore at great lengths the salubrious effects of brandy, Boney's pockets be damned!" He let himself out of the bedchamber, barely controlling the urge to slam the door behind him.

Alone, Blaise stared after him with shocked incomprehension. Realizing that Lynden had actually left her, she turned on her side and drew her legs up to her chest, curling into a ball, a chill, sick feeling in her stomach.

For a long moment she lay there quivering with mortification and anguish. Her husband had left her bed on their wedding night. He had used her body roughly and then abandoned her.

Remembering, Blaise moaned into her pillow. She had made a *terrible* mistake. Lynden's coldness had been worse than anything her stepfather had ever shown her. How wrong she had been to hope that he might be different. He was just like every other cold Englishman of her acquaintance. No, he was worse. He was hardhearted and *cruel*. She must have been temporarily insane to have agreed to wed him. She had wanted his love, had yearned for it, but it was apparent now that Lynden would never open his heart to her in return. What a fool she had been!

Fiercely Blaise brushed away the tears welling in her eyes. She had to pull her battered emotions together. She had to quit pitying herself and do something.

Abruptly she threw back the covers. She winced at the ache between her thighs as she stood up, but she determinedly found her clothing and began to dress in the brown broadcloth gown she'd arrived in. She wouldn't stay in this absurd marriage. She wouldn't stay tied to a man who didn't want her, who saw her only as a burden to shoulder.

Her gaze found the curtained bedchamber window. It would be relatively easy to escape that way. The oak tree just outside had thick sturdy limbs that would support her weight till she could drop to the ground. She would seek refuge with her Gypsy friends for the night, and tomorrow she would—

She didn't know what she would do tomorrow, but whatever she chose would be better than staying here to face the cold, heartless stranger who was her husband.

Chapter 12

"You cannot mean it!" Blaise stared at the Gypsy chief in disbelief. It had never occurred to her that Miklos would refuse her shelter. She had arrived at the Gypsy camp a short while ago, interrupting the wild revelry celebrating her nuptials.

Both Miklos and Panna had been disturbed to see her, but they took her aside, away from the music and dancing, and heard her out in silence as she confided her woes, leaving out only the intimate details of her marriage's rough consummation.

When Miklos learned she had run away, he eyed her with severe disapproval. "The Rom gave you refuge before, Rauniyog, in memory of your sacred father, my *pal*, to save you from your aunt. This time, 'owever, I cannot aid you. You are wed to a fine lord now. You must obey yer 'usband."

Blaise turned pleadingly to Panna, but the old woman merely shook her head. "You may stay the night, child, but in the morning, ye'll return to your 'usband— if 'e doesn't come to fetch you first. 'E won't be 'appy that ye've bolted. Now, come sit by the fire and warm yourself."

Stunned by their refusal to help her, Blaise followed blindly as Panna led her to a log and gently pushed her down. She felt betrayed by her friends. They had taken Lynden's side without question, abandoned her to his authority, evincing not even the least regard for her plight or her feelings.

Now she was truly desperate. She could try to run

away, but the dangers inherent in such a foolhardy action would be monumental. A young woman alone, with very little money, with no means of survival, would be prey to every vagrant and vandal on the roads. And she had no one else to turn to. She had little choice but to return to her cold-hearted husband, a man who didn't want her.

Shivering, Blaise stared morosely into the leaping flames, the plaintive sob of a violin mirroring her misery and despair.

Attempting to drown his own feelings of anger and despair, her husband sat drinking alone in the darkened drawing room. But not even Kilgore's finest brandy could dull Julian's senses enough to prevent guilt from flaying his conscience. He'd never been so cruel to a woman, so purposely savage, as when he'd taken his young wife in their bridal bed.

He'd been angry—indeed furious at being trapped into a marriage he'd never wanted, but with his emotions in such a state, he should never have visited her bed. It had been necessary to consummate the marriage so it couldn't be anulled, yet that was no justification for taking her so coldly. Blaise was his wife now, and as such, deserved the respect due her station.

Knowing he would somehow have to make amends, Julian finally set down his glass and forced himself to his feet. Reluctantly, and rather unsteadily, he groped his way down the dimly lit hall to Blaise's bedchamber and let himself in. The silence that met him struck him as ominous, as did the chill draft wafting in the open window.

Limping across the room, Julian stared down at the empty bed, at the pale crimson streaks that stained the tousled sheet. She was gone.

A terrible feeling of déjà vu assaulted him, flashes of long-held nightmares dancing before his mind's eye. *Caroline had fled from him like this. And Caroline had died.*

Instantly sober, with a familiar feeling of dread knot-

ting his stomach, Julian returned to his own bedchamber
and threw on breeches and boots and redingote. Logically
he knew he was overreacting. Blaise was no doubt with
her Gypsy friends. She'd gone to ground like a wounded
vixen, almost certainly. But he wouldn't rest easy until
he'd found her.

He made his way rapidly to the stables and saddled
a horse himself, so as not to broadcast the news of her
flight. His secrecy was not merely to spare his pride. Her
disappearance on their wedding night would doubtless
make him look like a fool, but he could bear being
branded the rejected bridegroom. He hoped to avert further scandal, though. He had wed Blaise to save both
their names from savage gossip, but the rumormongers
would have a field day if it became known that his new
young wife had fled from him, that he had driven her
away with his cruelty. The comparisons to his previous
marriage would be inevitable. Blaise's flight could only
give credence to the belief that he had murdered his first
wife. Yet it was to lay those ghosts to rest that he had
ended his self-exile and returned to England.

A half hour later when Julian rode into the Gypsy
camp, he spied Blaise sitting before the campfire looking
strangely forlorn, despite the throng of dancing, drinking
Gypsies that surrounded her. His jaw hardened, while
a turmoil of emotions flooded through him. Relief at
finding her safe. Fury at her defiance. Remorse for the
unnecessarily harsh way he'd treated her.

He dismounted slowly, awkwardly, cursing the stiffness in his right leg. In the past day and a half, the savaged muscles had been subjected to more exertion than
was wise, and the strain was beginning to take a toll.

Just then the Gypsies became aware of his presence.
The exuberant celebration suddenly ceased, the violins
and tambourines quieted. Julian saw his wife's back stiff-
en. Still seated, she glanced over her shoulder at him. Her
face was pale, her expression stony.

Tommy, the chief's son, came running up then to hold
his horse. "Shall I take the *grai,* m'lord?"

"Yes, if you please. I shall be staying awhile—if I have your permission, Mr. Smith?"

Miklos, who had followed, bowed low. "Aye, m'lord. You are always welcome in my 'umble camp."

"I wish to speak to my wife."

"O' course."

Blaise jumped up from her log then, and after a betrayed glance at the Gypsy chief, whirled and stalked away from the campfire, toward the wagons.

Julian followed, although with his leg troubling him, he couldn't move as quickly over the rough ground.

"Blaise!" The sharp command in his tone was unmistakable.

She came to a reluctant halt, some ten yards from Panna's wagon, but she didn't turn around. Hearing his uneven gait as he came up behind her, Blaise pulled her cloak more tightly about her in a self-protective gesture. Away from the firelight, the darkness seemed more intense. She had made a tactical mistake, leaving her place by the campfire. There was safety in numbers, but she was here, alone with a vengeful husband. She felt his presence behind her. In the distance she could hear the Gypsy revelry begin again, but she had never felt less like celebrating.

"Have you come to drag me away by my hair, my lord?" she asked, her voice unsteady.

There was a taut silence. "Is that really necessary?"

To her shock, she felt his fingers reach out to stroke her unbound tresses. Blaise flinched. "Don't touch me!"

"You are my wife now." She could almost feel his effort at patience. "I have the right to touch you whenever and wherever I wish."

She remained bitterly silent, knowing it was true. English law made her little more than chattel, for her husband to treat as he would.

"Did I hurt you earlier?"

She could have sworn there was an edge of tenderness in his tone. "Yes." She stiffened when his hand came to rest lightly on her shoulder, but she didn't pull away.

"The pain will go away. For a woman it is always difficult the first time."

The pain was not only physical! Blaise wanted to shout, but she refused to let him know how deeply he had hurt her. "Are you such an expert on deflowering virgins then, my lord?"

"You are the first." His reply was curt, and the chill was back in his voice.

"Indeed? My aunt gave me to believe that your conquests are legion."

"Bloody hell . . ." The muttered oath was savage and low. His grip tightening on her shoulder, he turned her to face him.

Her eyes had adjusted by now to the moonlight, and she could see his shadowed features. His expression was hard and sensual and more than a little fierce. "I regret that I used you so roughly, but that cannot be undone now. Nor can our marriage. That will not change, no matter how you dislike it. You are my wedded wife now, and as such your behavior is my responsibility. And I warn you now, I won't tolerate your usual misconduct. You will cease these childish antics of yours immediately, do I make myself clear?"

Hurting, miserable, Blaise only wanted to strike out at him. She would never forgive Lynden for their horrible wedding night, or for coercing her into this loveless union. He would rue the day, she vowed silently, that he had insisted on this marriage.

"Or what, my lord? Will you murder me like you did your first wife?"

He dropped his hands abruptly, as if she had struck him. The sudden shuttered look on his face hid his thoughts, but Blaise was certain she had hurt him as deeply as he had hurt her. Her small victory, however, didn't satisfy her as much as she would have expected, perhaps because she knew how underhanded her tactics had been, attacking his vulnerability. Yet she was too upset to care.

"Are you ordering me to your bed, my lord?" she

asked with forced sweetness. "If not, I should like to return to the dance."

His fists clenched, but he replied with only a terse word. "Go."

Blaise turned and walked away, conscious of his eyes watching her all the while.

Julian stood there in the darkness, seething at her defiance, still reeling from her accusation. Did she truly believe him capable of murder?

Moments later his reflections were rudely interrupted by a soft clumping sound. Spinning around, he realized he was not alone. Panna emerged from the back of her wagon, shaking her gray head and causing her long gold earrings to swing.

"You'll not win her obedience wi' commands, me fine lord."

His mouth tightened at the old Gypsy's confirmation that she'd been eavesdropping. "Indeed? I don't recall asking you to advise me on how to deal with my wife, Mistress Smith."

His quelling tone had no apparent affect on Panna. " 'Tis obvious somebody must. You're goin' about it all wrong. You must first earn her loyalty and love. Rauniyog will do anything for you then, take any risk, bear any burden. But if you act the ogre, you'll only drive 'er away."

"I am not an ogre."

Panna cackled, her black eyes gleaming. "Nay, that you're not, m'lord. Ye're a 'andsome gent 'oo 'as a way wi' the ladies. You can do far better, I'll warrant."

She shuffled off in the direction of the campfire, while Julian cursed under his breath. How had he managed to find himself in such an impotent position? He was the one who had been wronged, forced into this damnable marriage for honor's sake.

And yet he *had* wronged his young wife, as well. She might be a maddening chit, but he had indeed treated Blaise with more cruelty than she deserved.

Julian dragged a hand through his hair. So how did he

proceed from here? He was saddled with her now. Unless he banished Blaise to one of his lesser estates—a certain mistake if he wished to exercise any control over her and prevent her from getting into untold mischief—he would have to keep her by his side.

And if he wanted their relationship to be at all bearable, he would have to make peace with her. For her to accept their marriage, he would at least have to show her more warmth than he had in the past two days . . . so that she would remain with him willingly . . . so that he wouldn't fail her the way he had Caroline.

Caroline. His face contorted momentarily at the agony of her memory, but he forced the haunting image from his mind. He had a new wife to concern himself with now.

Panna was indeed right. He could do far better when dealing with Blaise. He had made serious mistakes with her. Even so, the damage was not irreparable.

His lips compressing in a thin line, Julian gazed determinedly toward the campfire where the Gypsies were celebrating his nuptials.

No, not irreparable. He hadn't begun to employ his powers of persuasion.

Blaise heard the excited whispers, even over the sound of the music and revelry, but it was several moments before she understood the cause: the *gorgio rye*, her husband, had joined in the dancing around the campfire.

She sat fully upright on her log, her eyes widening in astonishment. Lynden had been a guest in the Gypsy camp for over a week, but he had never before attempted to dance.

His limp scarcely noticeable, he stepped lightly, snapping fingers to the music, his arms raised above his head. He wore no coat, so the fine cambric of his shirt strained visibly across his lean-muscled chest and shoulders.

He was watching her intently, his eyes a brazen cerulean-blue as his feet skimmed over the packed earth, to the beat of a shaking tambourine.

Blaise watched him in return, transfixed by the wild beauty of his dance. It was pure sensuality—blatant, raw, graceful. A true Rom might be more athletic, more powerful, but this was magic. His curling hair glimmered molten gold in the firelight, a Gypsy prince surrounded by his tribe. The masculine allure of his movements called to everything in her that was feminine, that yearned for passion.

Her blood ran hot with the quickening tempo. She was aware of her surroundings—the other dancers, the clapping hands, the wild soaring music of the violins—but she and Lynden might have been alone. She watched his gyrating hips, his flexing thighs, and remembered vividly what had happened only a few short hours ago between her and this beautiful man. The feel of him moving between her legs. The fiery sensation of being deeply penetrated. The hard, thrusting rhythm. Her body started to throb, while a hot, insistent ache flared between her thighs.

The cheers and the applause grew louder as the exotic music built to a frenzy. Lynden began to whirl, his head and shoulders thrown back, his arms outstretched. Then suddenly his right leg buckled. He fell hard, landing on his left side, his performance not part of the dance. The music came to a crashing halt.

Blaise stared in horror to see Julian collapsed on the ground, so very near the fire. With a cry, she leaped to her feet and ran to him.

He was doubled over, clutching his thigh, his teeth clenched in agony while the muscles of his leg knotted in pain. Her hands fluttered helplessly as she knelt beside him.

When she tried to touch him, to urge him away from the fire, he groaned hoarsely, so she drew her hands back. He lay there panting, his eyes shut, the white tautness of his face frightening her.

Panna spoke from behind her. "Take 'im to 'is tent, while I fetch the liniment. You'll tend to your 'usband, Rauniyog."

Blaise nodded, temporarily forgetting her vengeful intentions and her vow to make Lynden sorry for wedding her. She couldn't bear to see him suffering so. No matter how despicably he had treated her the past two days, she had to help him now.

Two strong Gypsies assisted him to his feet, but his face twisted in pain and he gasped, "Wait!" He stood there rigidly, his head bowed as he waited for a spasm to pass. She could see sweat molding the thin cambric shirt to his back.

Finally, though, he nodded.

They helped him to a tent on the outskirts of the camp, the same tent he had used during his previous stay. The moment he was inside, Julian collapsed on the pallet and lay there on his back, trying to catch his breath.

Blaise entered after him and sat beside him on his right. Unable to bear seeing him in such pain, she sought his hand, trying silently to offer him comfort. When his fingers clutched hers spasmodically, though, she couldn't bite back a sharp remark. "Whatever were you thinking of, dancing like that with your wounded leg?"

His mouth twisted in the semblance of a mocking smile. "I was attempting . . . to be like the Gypsies . . . you so admire."

His reply took her completely by surprise. He had staged that riveting performance in order to impress her? It had worked, certainly, but he should have known better. She shook her head, wondering what it was that made him want to hurt himself.

"I never . . . should have tried such a foolish stunt . . . not after all the leg's been through today."

Blaise agreed entirely, and yet she held some of the blame. If he hadn't had to travel to London, if he hadn't had to stand during the ceremony and the formal celebration afterward, if he hadn't had to consummate their marriage . . . Her mind shied away from that memory.

"Where did you learn to dance like that?" she asked to distract herself as much as him.

"In Spain. In winter quarters . . . we had too much time

on our hands. We often hired dancers to entertain the
regimental officers. I learned the flamenco from them."

"That was a Spanish dance? It looked so similar to
our Gypsy dances."

"I imagine it has similar origins. The flamenco dancers . . . in Spain are mostly Gypsies."

Blaise averted her gaze, wishing she had contained her
curiosity. She had no trouble picturing her golden-haired
husband surrounded by a dozen dark Spanish beauties . . .
women who would no doubt fall all over themselves in an
effort to see to his every need.

Panna came a moment later, bringing with her the
special liniment, several lengths of muslin, and a small
lamp which she hung from a hook just inside the tent.

Her black eyes looking from Blaise to Julian, she
chuckled and pronounced, "You'll not be needing me."
Then, backing out, she let the tent flap fall.

Alone with her husband, Blaise felt herself flushing.
The rest of the world had been shut out, enveloping them
in a quiet intimacy. He was watching her intently.

"Do you . . . require assistance, my lord?"

"Don't you think it's time you called me by my given
name? It's Julian."

"Julian," she repeated, her breath a thin whisper.

"I would be grateful for your help."

As she reached for him, Blaise tried to quell her embarrassment, telling herself this man was her husband.

With difficulty she drew off his boots, and then his
stockings. Much to her relief, he unfastened the buttons
of his breeches himself, and raised his hips so she could
tug them down. She had averted her gaze, but his grunt
of pain brought her eyes back up.

His cambric shirt covered the most intimate parts of
him, fortunately. Yet she didn't need to remove all his
clothing to know what lay beneath. She had only glimpsed
him before, but the image of that hard-muscled, beautifully
formed male body was seared into her memory. Against
her will, she found herself staring at his bare legs, at the
powerful horseman's thighs that were dusted with golden

hair . . . at the right one that was horribly scarred.

She hurt when she saw those scars. The flesh was scored with deep indentations and thick, savage puckers. Trying not to think of the pain he must have suffered, she uncorked the bottle of liniment and poured a small amount of the thick liquid into her cupped palm. Then she hesitated. The fresh scent of mint filled the interior of the small tent while she debated with herself and gathered her courage. There was no hope for it. She was going to have to touch him. She lowered her hand to his thigh, palm down.

When he flinched, she froze.

"Did I hurt you?"

"No, it's just cold."

Relieved, she began slowly massaging his wounded thigh, tracing the unsightly scar tissue, lightly stroking her slick fingers over the damaged flesh, pressing gently.

He let his head fall back. "God . . . that feels good."

Unaccountably, it felt good to her, too. Touching Julian's warm skin filled her with a hot, physical yearning, a need to know more of him. She lowered her other hand to his leg. She could feel his vitality coursing beneath her fingers, the power of firm, vibrant musculature.

She pressed harder.

She could feel him begin to relax under her ministrations. Slowly, thoroughly, she kneaded the tight, knotted muscles, trying to relieve, to soothe, working the pain from him with the heels of her hands, her palms, her fingers, her thumbs, in slow rotating strokes.

When once he emitted a low grown, she hesitated.

"No . . . please don't stop."

Her fingers began moving intimately again.

"Where . . . did you learn to do this so well?" His voice was husky.

"In the Turkish bathhouses. My stepfather was posted to the East for a short time."

"And you accompanied him?"

"I had to. It was that or live with my Aunt Agnes."

She thought Julian might not have heard her. His eyes were closed and he lay completely pliant beneath her caresses, as if he'd fallen asleep. And yet the strange movement beneath his shirt, at the junction of his thighs, declared quite openly that his body at least was awake.

Blaise watched with shocked fascination as his erection slowly grew to jutting proportions, pushing aside the thin cambric to expose his entire groin to her view. The protruding shaft was long and thick, rising straight up from a swirling nest of dark golden hair, the swollen sacs beneath flushed as if from heat. She felt her heart begin to beat in slow, thudding strokes. The sight of his huge masculine sex was alien but not frightening. Indeed, just the opposite. The memory of having that stiff length of flesh moving inside her aroused a throbbing ache in her that she couldn't deny.

Suddenly realizing her brazen fascination was being observed, Blaise felt hot color flare in her cheeks. His eyes were open now, his gaze riveted on her face.

"You'll have to fashion a bandage," he said huskily.

"Yes." Her own voice was just as husky.

Unsteadily she wiped her hands on a muslin cloth and bent over him, carefully wrapping a clean length around his thigh. When she finished, he was still watching her.

"Touch me," he whispered.

Her breathing ceased. Her lips parted, but no sound came out.

"I'm your husband now, Blaise."

When still she hesitated, his fingers curled purposefully around her hand and moved it up his thigh to his burgeoning rod. The intimate connection with that hard arousal shocked and thrilled her at the same time. The satin skin was fiery hot, sheathing flesh as rigid as steel.

He grimaced at her light touch, but when she tried to pull away, his fingers clamped around her hand, pressing her harder against him.

"I didn't mean to hurt you earlier, Blaise."

She had difficulty focusing on what he was saying. "Didn't . . . you? I thought you meant to punish me because you had to wed me."

He smiled a slow, sad smile that made her hurt inside. "Perhaps so." He gave a weary sigh. "But it's done now. Ours . . . may not have been the most ideal circumstances for a marriage, but it can't be changed. We can only try to accept it. And perhaps make a new beginning."

She searched Julian's face, wondering if he truly meant it. "I would like that."

His fingers tightened over hers, reminding her that she still held the most intimate part of him. She drew in a sharp breath, while his eyes grew shuttered. The charged tension within the small tent was suddenly almost tangible.

Drawn to him, almost against her will, she leaned forward. She had meant only to give him a brief kiss, but his lips were warm and tasted of desire. She found herself straining toward him, trying to press her suddenly heavy breasts against his chest.

Julian stopped her by gripping her arms, holding her lightly in his hands. "No. It's too soon. I'll only hurt you again."

"How do you know?"

"I just know. You're not ready for me."

"Then," she whispered, her black hair tumbling over her shoulders as she bent to him again, "make me ready."

For a long moment he didn't respond. For a long moment he merely lay there rigidly, as if fighting conflicting urges within him.

Shocking even herself with her boldness, Blaise settled the conflict: she gently squeezed her fingers around his swollen shaft.

His hoarse intake of breath was audible.

Relying on purely feminine instinct, she hesitantly resumed her massage, stroking along the full, hard length of his manhood . . . caressing . . . exploring his body the way he had done hers in the hayloft. She thought her brazen action must have been at least partially successful,

for after a moment he groaned softly, while his hips came
up off the pallet, thrusting himself into her hand.

"God . . . enough!" Julian rasped suddenly as he pulled
from her grasp.

Startled by his abrupt withdrawal, Blaise blinked in
bewilderment. But he didn't offer any explanations.
Instead, he reached up and caught her nape in a taut
grip. Drawing her face down to his, he captured her
mouth in a fierce, sensual kiss.

Blaise gave a small whimper and melted against him.
She could feel his hands tangling in her hair with a
hurting pressure, but she didn't care. His hot, thrusting
tongue was mimicking the most intimate act of passion.

Then one hand left her hair and she felt it groping for
the hem of her gown. She sighed and raised herself up
to make his task easier. At once, his searing fingertips
glided up her leg, along her inner thigh, to where she
was already hot, damp, throbbing.

His burning lips freeing her, he drew back to stare at
her. "I can't believe how wet you are."

"I'm s-sorry," she stammered in embarrassment. "I
didn't . . . but you made me that way."

"No, sweeting. There's nothing to regret. I'm pleased
you're so easily aroused. Now take off your dress."

She stiffened at the command. It was too much like
the cold order he'd given her earlier that evening, when
he'd made her strip off her nightdress. But unlike earlier,
the harsh tone he'd used just now held no coldness,
no detachment. Instead, there was an urgency to it that
matched the hungry heat in his eyes.

"I . . ." She glanced helplessly at the hanging lamp. "I
should put out the light."

"No, I want to see you."

She wanted to see him, too, Blaise realized with an
honesty that should have shocked her but didn't.

She watched in fascination while he unbuttoned the
front opening of his shirt and drew the garment over his
head tossing it aside. Then he lay back, sprawling on
the pallet, his graceful, smooth-muscled body completely

naked, his skin glowing golden in the pale light. Blaise couldn't tear her eyes away.

It was with great difficulty that she removed her gown and her underclothes—her garters and stockings and shift. She was shaking so badly that her fingers kept missing the buttons and catching clumsily in the fabric. And all the while her husband was watching her, waiting.

His azure eyes flamed with raw desire when she finally tugged off the shift and bared her body to his gaze.

"I want you," he said softly. "Come here."

Keeping her eyes closed, she lay down shyly beside him, not quite touching his naked skin. But that wasn't what he had planned.

"No, climb on top of me, sweeting."

Startled, Blaise lifted her eyelids and turned her head to stare at him quizzically.

"I want you to straddle me with your legs. It will cause less strain on my thigh that way."

"Can you . . . can it be done that way?"

His smile was patently amused. "I'd forgotten such innocence as yours existed." Her brow furrowed in indignation, but before she could defend herself, he added, soothingly, "That was not a criticism, minx. A man wants his wife to be virginal." The sudden grim look that shadowed his expression confused her, but it was gone in a moment. "Don't argue, sweeting," he said, losing patience. "Mount me the way you would a horse."

Her chin lifted. "I don't think you really mean that. A lady rides sidesaddle."

That gave Julian pause, but he smiled again. "Are you being deliberately obtuse? Use your obvious talents for improvisation to accommodate me."

Her shyness faded in her determination to meet his challenge. Sitting up, she turned to face him, and then hesitantly moved her right leg over him.

"Carefully," he murmured. He aided her . . . cupping her soft, rounded bottom with his hands . . . drawing her knees up on each side of his narrow hips.

It was shocking, to be sitting on him this way, naked flesh against naked flesh, his thighs hard and hair-roughened between her trembling legs. And his manhood . . . She didn't even need to lean forward to have that rigid throbbing length press against her belly.

"Am I . . . hurting your leg?" she managed to ask.

"No . . . not at all."

He was staring at her bosom, she realized. At her bare breasts jutting between her tumbling black tresses. But it was the heated look of a man anticipating gratification. In response, she could feel her breasts swell painfully, the nipples tauten with desire.

He seemed to sense her need, though, for he cupped the aching globes in his hands, making her draw a sharp breath. "It was all wrong the last time," he said softly. "I promise you it will be different. I won't seek my release without ensuring your pleasure first."

She believed him as slowly he drew her down till he could capture a distended nipple with his lips. The wet heat of his mouth sent a shock of pleasure streaking through her that made every nerve in her body tingle, every muscle tense. Blaise braced her hands against his shoulders and clung to him while he feasted.

He tugged the crest, lashed it with the rough, wet surface of his tongue, kneaded it with his lips, nipped softly with his teeth till her body throbbed. Then he proceeded to give the same exquisite attentions to her other breast. The soft sound of his sucking was somehow powerfully erotic, as was the feel of the long, thick shaft rubbing between her thighs, against her woman's mound.

All too soon, though, he drew away, his voice low and husky when he spoke. "Lift your hips, sweeting, and take me inside you."

She obeyed eagerly, her desire so intense she was willing to do anything he commanded. With trembling need, she raised herself up, and with his hands guiding her hips, slowly impaled herself on his male hardness.

"Carefully . . . that's it . . . all the way . . . Ah, love."

She panted softly, her eyes closed, and sat very still, afraid to move with that enormous arousal deep inside her.

"Look at me." When she complied, he smoothed back her raven hair from her face. "Does it hurt?"

"No," she murmured breathlessly. "Not much."

"What does it feel like?"

She hesitated, trying to find the words to describe the sensations she was feeling. "Full . . . hot . . . as if I might burst if I move the wrong way."

His smile was pure sensuality. "No, love, you'll burst if you move the *right* way."

He began to thrust then, slowly, showing her precisely what he meant by *right*. Blaise whimpered at the incredible sensation. He was so hard inside her, so fiery hot, an exquisite shaft of fire spearing through her. She writhed, but his grip on her hips tightened and he drove upward into her abruptly, mercilessly.

Suddenly she couldn't seem to hold still. Need took control of her quivering body and she rocked her hips against him mindlessly, trying to get closer, clutching at his shoulders with feverish strength that turned to frenzied abandon. A sob tore from her throat at the building pressure.

"Let it come, sweeting."

Her body ignited at his soft command. She quaked and shuddered with the pulsating, wrenching release, while he held her shaking form. Finally she went limp and collapsed on his chest, gasping for breath.

It was several moments before she regained her awareness to find her face pressed in the warm curve of Julian's shoulder. Except for his hand slowly stroking her naked back, he hadn't seemed to move. But he was still enormous inside her, his arousal hard and throbbing.

It confused her for a moment, until she remembered his promise and comprehended that he hadn't shared the exquisite pleasure he had given her. A flaring sense of excitement kindled anew within her, reigniting the fevered ache. He wasn't finished making love to her.

"Did I hurt you?" he murmured.

"No." Her voice was a hoarse rasp. She felt his lips brush her temple and knew he still wanted her.

"Do you think you can bear to let me come inside you?"

She turned her face up to his. "Yes . . . please . . . please."

He smiled at her eagerness and kissed her briefly. Then he raised her up slightly, letting his lips trail down her throat to her breast.

In only moments, his slow movements and erotic mouth brought her back to a fever pitch of passion. His hungry suckling forced a shuddering moan from her, a moan that turned into a sob as he thrust himself deeper, deeper into her. Then her passion exploded, her body racked by a climax so shattering she could do nothing but cling to him.

Julian felt her joy and responded with one final fierce thrust, and then his body clenched in savage contractions as he poured himself inside her. She fell limply against him before he had finished. His arms came around, holding her still as his seed continued to pump into her.

When it was over, they both lay there breathing harshly, drained of all energy, their sweat-dampened skin sticking together.

Too exhausted to move, Blaise gave a weary, replete sigh and closed her eyes. There had been tenderness this time. They had made love, not merely coupled. And the experience had been more incredible, more shattering than she'd ever dreamed possible. The sensuality Julian had shown her, the fervent passion, had proved he was nothing like the cold-fish Englishman she had dreaded marrying. No, he wasn't at all cold. Perhaps she hadn't made such a terrible mistake after all.

That was her last conscious thought before she drifted off to sleep.

Julian lay there in tranquil sensuality, ignoring the pain in his aching thigh and savoring the feel of her warm naked body curled against him. His thoughts drifted.

He hadn't wanted to wed this scandalous, free-spirited hoyden, but possessing her had more than satisfied his intense physical desire. It had been a stunning experience, this second mating between them. Better even than he had dreamed. Her body had come alive in his arms, but his soul had come alive in hers. The soul that had been dead since Caroline's demise . . .

But he wouldn't allow himself to think of the past—or even of the future. Tomorrow would be soon enough to face his ghosts. Tomorrow, when he returned to Lynden Park with his new, unwelcome young wife.

Easing Blaise gently onto her side, he sat up and snuffed the lamp, then resumed his place on the pallet. After covering them both with a blanket, he gathered his sweet Gypsy in his arms and buried his scarred face in her hair. Slowly breathing in the fragrant scent, Julian allowed himself to slip into slumber.

Chapter 13

⌒◯◯⌒

A blustery rain slashed his face as he rode through the
deepening gloom. His mind still reeled at Caroline's
taunts, at her defiant admission of adultery, at her betrayal
with his dearest friend. But once his fury had ebbed enough
for rational thought, he'd realized he had to pursue his
reckless wife. Caroline was far from being an accomplished horsewoman, yet she had galloped blindly away
from the house, with no thought for the brewing storm
or the waning afternoon light.

The gray outline of the Roman ruins crouched in
the distance. The pile of crumbling stone walls was
her favorite retreat on the estate. She would have
come here, he was certain. Yet with the gusting
rain, he could see no sign of either Caroline or her
mount.

Then he spied the dark, crumpled shape at the base
of the wall. Fear speared through him at the sight of her
slender form lying so still and silent.

His heartbeat pounding in his ears, he forced himself
to dismount, to kneel beside her. With trembling fingers, he touched her rain-wet face, her pale lips, the
base of her fragile throat, feeling for a pulse, any sign
of life.

Please, God . . .

His wordless prayer remained unanswered. Beneath
her fair hair he could see the jagged indentation in
her skull, could see the dark blood mingling with the
chill rain.

Dear God, she was dead . . .

The vivid nightmare jolted Julian awake with heart-pounding panic. Lunging upright, he hauled in a jagged breath.

When he realized where he was, though, the shudders that racked his naked body began to dissipate. In the darkness of the Gypsy tent he could just make out the slender form of a woman in his bed. His wife, he remembered. His *new* wife. Blaise, not Caroline. Her hair was ebony, not blond.

She hadn't awakened at his thrashing, apparently. Just to make certain who she was, though, he reached out to feel the base of her throat. Her pulse was warm and steady and reassuring.

He lay down again, staring into the darkness, forcing the vivid images from his mind.

He was gone from the tent by the time Blaise stirred awake early the next morning. The process was slow, for she was reluctant to relinquish the pleasurable dreams she'd been having, or to acknowledge the unfamiliar aches and twinges in various parts of her body. Yet perhaps this was the way a new bride was supposed to feel.

Wonderingly, Blaise raised her fingers to her kiss-swollen mouth. A bride. Viscount Lynden. *Julian.* Her husband.

Her face nuzzled the blanket that still bore his scent as she lay there remembering the incredible events of last night—her passionate lover and the brazen things he'd done to her. A warm glow suffused her entire body. If this was marriage, then she was willing to give it a fair chance. She was about to begin a new life with a man who was virtually a stranger, yet not even the daunting thought of leaving her Gypsy friends and traveling to her husband's ancestral estate could subdue her spirits.

Eagerly, Blaise threw off the blanket and sat up. She could smell the woodsmoke of the cooking fires and knew the Gypsy camp had begun the day. She washed quickly, using tepid water from the basin that had been left just inside the tent, and after dressing, made a trip to the woods to take care of necessities.

She was returning to the tent to search for Julian when she spied him moving slowly across the camp toward her with the aid of his cane. Wishing to spare him further effort, Blaise hurried toward him. Her pulse rate quickened the closer she came. He had changed his clothing of last night for more formal attire, and he looked every inch the nobleman in a pristine white cravat and high shirt points, dark blue frock coat over gray pantaloons and matching waistcoat, gleaming black boots, and high-crowned beaver. His sheer beauty took her breath away. Morning sunlight speared his hair, turning it a pale burnished gold, while his eyes appeared a deep, rich sapphire against the blue of his coat.

"Good, you're awake," Julian observed tersely. "I've just returned from Kilgore's, where I ordered the carriage and our luggage. Be prepared to leave directly after breakfast."

Disconcerted, Blaise gazed blankly up at him. Perhaps it was too much to expect him to shower her with words of tenderness, but a greeting of "good morning" would not have been unreasonable.

His grim, shuttered expression, however, gave no hint of tenderness. A scowl drew his brows together as he surveyed her briefly, taking in the ill-tailored brown broadcloth. "And get rid of that disreputable gown before we leave."

Blaise's chin rose instinctively at his command. "This gown was perfectly acceptable when you thought I was a Gypsy."

"I beg to differ. It was never acceptable—and you were never a Gypsy. Once we arrive at Lynden Park, I will expect you to find a modiste to outfit you properly. As my viscountess, you have a certain position to uphold."

He turned abruptly on his heel then, and walked stiffly away, leaving Blaise to stare after him in hurt and bewilderment, wondering what she had done to earn Julian's wrath. This ill-tempered man was certainly not the same tender lover who had shown her such concern and passion last night. This was the same cold stranger who had wed and bedded her so perfunctorily yesterday evening. The abrupt reversion dismayed her more than she would have thought possible. Not even Sir Edmund at his most chilling could have been more cutting.

But, Blaise thought, taking a steadying breath, she was married to Julian now and she would have to learn how to deal with his violent swings of mood. With growing disquietude, she went in search of Panna and breakfast.

Shortly, the Lynden traveling chaise drew up, followed by another coach bearing Blaise's abigail, Garvey, and Julian's manservant, Terral. Garvey did not appear surprised or disapproving to find her mistress at the Gypsy camp. Indeed, just the opposite.

"His lordship said you had decided to spend the wedding night here with your friends," Garvey said serenely. "I thought it kind of him to allow it, and rather romantic."

"I suppose it was," Blaise prevaricated, torn between indignation that Julian had manipulated the truth so easily and relief that he'd managed to keep the news of her flight from becoming common gossip.

After claiming the portmanteau Garvey had brought, Blaise returned to her tent to change her drab brown broadcloth gown for the clothes folded inside: a traveling suit of forest-green corded muslin, with a cream-colored shawl of worsted cashmere and soft kid gloves. To complete the outfit, she settled a low-crowned bonnet of cream gros de Naples over her smooth chignon and tied the green ribbons under the chin.

Her new husband apparently approved, for when he next laid eyes on her, he nodded briefly. "Are you ready?"

"Yes . . . if I might say goodbye to my friends first?"

He didn't interfere with her farewells to the Gypsies, but stood looking on impatiently. He did manage, however, to unbend enough to thank Miklos for his hospitality. "I should like to repay you for your kindness. Be assured that you and your tribe are welcome to camp on my estate if you ever find yourself in the vicinity of Lynden Park. It's just south of the town of Huntingdon."

"Aye, m'lord, I ken the area," Miklos replied. "And we'll be mighty pleased to accept—in a few weeks, though, when we make our way north. We 'ave a 'orse fair to attend first."

Blaise felt lonely already, knowing it would be weeks before she saw them again. She entreated Miklos as she gave his hand a final squeeze. "You'll come north as soon as you can?"

"Aye, m'lady, that we will. But you need time to learn the ways of your new life. And 'aving the Rom on your doorstep would not be to your advantage with the *gorgios*."

"You know I don't care about that."

"Aye, but you're a fine lady and you've a fine name to live up to now."

Panna's final farewell was briefer: "May the fates bless you, Rauniyog."

"You, too, Mother." Her eyes blurred with tears, Blaise gave the old woman one last hug and turned away blindly.

Julian handed her into the carriage and climbed in after her. Their servants would follow behind in a coach borrowed from Baron Kilgore.

Almost immediately the traveling chaise began to move. Blaise clung to the strap and watched the Gypsy camp fade from sight. It was several moments before she regained enough composure to glance at her husband beside her. He had settled into his corner and stretched his right leg out carefully, bracing himself against the rock and sway of the coach.

Swallowing the ache in her throat, she roused herself to make polite conversation. "It was kind of you to invite Miklos to camp on your estate."

Julian shrugged. "After accepting their hospitality all this time, it was the least I could do . . . even if they are likely to poach me blind. I shall have to alert the game-keepers to look the other way once your friends arrive."

"Is your leg paining you?" Blaise asked, seeing him grimace.

"No. It's merely stiff."

She didn't quite believe him. She could see the lines of strain around his eyes, and suspected he was suffering the ill-effects of his exertions last night, even if he wouldn't admit it.

"Would you like me to . . . rub it for you?"

"Thank you, no. It will do well enough if I'm not required to chase after my errant wife."

Blaise flinched as if struck. He could have refused her offer without reminding her that she was partly to blame for his pain. Looking away, she pressed her lips together. Because of his wound, she was prepared to make allowances for his foul temper, but she hoped it wouldn't last.

His grim humor, however, did not abate as the day wore on. If anything Julian only became more uncommunicative. The journey was as comfortable as a well-sprung, richly appointed traveling coach drawn by excellent horses could make it, but if Blaise had wished for a considerate, loving husband to entertain her and fawn over her, she was destined for disappointment. Julian virtually ignored her. And yet she didn't think it was due to deliberate rudeness. His mind was obviously occupied, his thoughts far away. Willing to allow him that measure of privacy, Blaise settled back on the luxurious squabs and watched the autumn countryside fly past.

A few hours later they stopped for luncheon at a posting house, but Julian was no more forthcoming then than he had been all morning. Blaise had felt his tension rising, the closer they came to Lynden Park. He drank more wine than usual, and returned to the coach in brooding silence for the final leg of their journey.

When Blaise did at last press him, she soon wished she hadn't spoken.

"Will I get to meet any of your family when we reach your home?" she asked.

"I have no family."

"None? No relatives at all?"

"Some distant cousins who aren't on speaking terms at the moment. Except for my heir, of course. He considers my fortune worth overlooking any scruples."

Blaise could tell she had chosen a poor subject, so she tried another. "Don't you think you should tell me something of Lynden Park if I am to live there?"

"You'll see it soon it enough. We should arrive within the half hour."

She wanted to bristle at his surly reply, but she quelled the urge. "You aren't eager to return home, are you?"

"No."

"Why not?"

The hard glance he gave her was hardly inviting. "It would be an understatement if I said it holds . . . unpleasant memories for me."

"Memories of your late wife?"

He didn't answer, merely looked away, focusing his gaze on the passing scenery.

"Perhaps it would be better for you to talk about it. As your wife, I should know what happened in any case."

"I told you, the subject is not open for discussion."

"You couldn't have done what they accused you of doing. Terral said—"

His oath was harsh and low. "I won't have you gossiping with the servants, do you understand me?"

"I was not gossiping. I was merely expressing a natural trepidation. If you *had* killed your first wife, I think I deserved to know it before I became your second."

"I did kill her."

Blaise stared, shocked by his bald statement. "I don't believe you," she returned flatly.

"You know nothing about it."

"Well, I'm trying to learn!"

When Julian glowered at her with fierce blue eyes, Blaise took a steadying breath. "If you did do such a preposterous thing—and I don't believe it for one minute—it had to be an accident. There had to be extenuating circumstances."

Julian gritted his teeth to hear her loyally defending him. He *was* to blame. And he resented Blaise for trying to absolve him of his guilt.

He sat there in smoldering silence, remembering in vivid detail that terrible day, hearing the echo of Vincent's anguished accusation. *You killed her, you bloody bastard! You* killed *her!* Vincent Foster. His friend and neighbor. His wife's lover.

Julian had wanted to deny the accusation even then, yet he couldn't defend himself against the truth. He might not have struck the deathblow, yet he was to blame. Caroline's death never would have occurred except for his violent fury. He had driven her out into the storm . . .

Blaise left him to his tormented thoughts; masking her hurt, she retreated to her own corner. She regretted that she had forced the issue, regretted that she had ever married him. He had obviously shuttered his heart against her. She was an unwanted intrusion in his life.

A short while later, however, Blaise was prodded out of her bitter reverie when the traveling chaise slowed and turned off the road. They had been driving through sloping uplands flanked by grassy meadows and dotted with wooded copses. Now they passed through an ivy-covered lodge gate and traversed a long gravel drive, through a beautiful landscaped park. As they rounded a bend, the manor house came into view.

Magnificent was her immediate thought. The tall rectangular mansion consisted of a long main wing and two shorter side wings surrounding a paved court, all built of golden stone that exuded a mellow warmth. Serene, regal, it stood basking in the haze of autumn sunshine, the numerous windowpanes gleaming with quiet brilliance.

Blaise found herself drawing a deep breath. She had expected the house to be shuttered and closed, like its master, but the overall effect was a stately grace that was welcoming rather than imposing. Behind the main house, there appeared to be a vast number of outbuildings, and across a green sward where cattle grazed peacefully, she could glimpse gardens and orchards. It was quite obviously the ancestral seat of some great lord.

"It's beautiful," she murmured. She sat forward on the edge of her seat, peering eagerly out the coach window. She had forgotten her husband's noble rank and apparent wealth, and could scarcely believe she was to be mistress of this magnificent estate.

She had also forgotten Julian's reluctance to return to his ancestral home. His tension was palpable as the carriage drew to a halt before the front entrance.

She looked at him expectantly, but he was staring at the mansion and made no move to descend, even when a footman opened the carriage door wide and stood at rigid attention.

"My lord?" Blaise said tentatively. "Julian?"

He seemed to shake himself mentally, before fixing her with a brooding gaze.

"Are you quite all right?"

"Yes."

"Then shall we go in?"

At his nod, she accepted the footman's assistance and stepped down onto the pavement. Slowing her pace to match Julian's uneven gait, she crossed the court and mounted the flight of gracefully curving stairs.

Before they reached the top landing, however, he stayed her with a hand on her arm. "Before we proceed any further," he said in a low voice, "I feel I must remind you of the responsibility you incurred upon our marriage. You are the Viscountess Lynden now, and as such you will behave with circumspection and propriety, as befits your exalted station."

Blaise blinked up at him. She could hear her step-father's chill tones in his warning, but she thought Julian's assumption that she would forget what was due his rank entirely unjust. And yet he wasn't finished, it seemed.

"I've done enough to drag my family name through the muck. I don't want it tarnished beyond repair by another scandal. I won't be made a laughingstock by any of your ill-conceived escapades. Are we understood?"

"Yes, my lord, of course," Blaise muttered, even as she stiffened in outrage. He hoped to avoid scandal, did he? He wanted a proper viscountess? Well, she might be unable to escape being tied to him, but she could certainly make him regret coercing her into becoming his wife. And if she wished to, she would cause any number of scandals.

Head held high, Blaise marched up the final steps and gave a start when the door was thrown wide by a stolid-faced butler.

Ushering her inside, Julian introduced the man as Hedges. "This is my wife, Lady Lynden. I'm sure you will do your utmost to make her welcome."

Hedges bowed formally. "Naturally. Welcome, my lady. May I be permitted to offer best wishes on the occasion of your nuptials? And may I say, my lord, how pleased we are to have you home?"

"Thank you, Hedges."

The upper servant's manner with her, Blaise observed, was polite and formal, but there was genuine affection for her husband in his tone. She also noted that while Julian had responded easily to the butler's welcome, he had not expressed any gladness to be home. Indeed, his expression was wary, his attention fixed on his immediate surroundings, as if he thought a ghost might leap out at him any minute.

The surroundings *were* something to gape at, Blaise admitted, impressed. The interior of the house appeared just as magnificent as the exterior. The large central foyer boasted two sweeping staircases with gleaming mahogany banisters and a huge crystal chandelier that reflected light in an array of glittering rainbow-hued prisms. Everywhere Blaise looked, she glimpsed furnishings proclaiming wealth and exquisite good taste.

The butler's formality apparently extended to the other Lynden retainers, she deduced, for a short line of liveried servants stood at rigid attention to one side of the entrance, headed by a thin, metal-haired older woman whom Julian introduced as the housekeeper, Mrs. Hedges.

Mrs. Hedges curtsied and welcomed the lord and lady home with the same stiff deference the butler had exhibited, before allowing Hedges to present the rest of the servants.

"The staff is quite small at the moment, my lady," Mrs. Hedges commented at the conclusion, "as you can see, but the house has been closed. With his lordship away for so many years, there was no need for more servants. Now that he has returned to take up residence, however, perhaps you will wish to engage others?"

Wondering if the comment was a veiled criticism of Julian's long absence, Blaise looked to him for guidance, but his attention had strayed back to the entrance hall. Curious as to what held such fascination for him, she murmured a noncommittal reply to the housekeeper, saying that she would discuss such arrangements with his lordship and let her know.

The woman gave a cool nod. Mrs. Hedges evidently was prepared to reserve judgment on the new mistress, but Blaise was not inclined to reciprocate. She longed for something to relieve the starched atmosphere.

Julian turned back to her just then with a glance as cool as those of his servants. "I'm sure you will wish to rest and refresh yourself. Mrs. Hedges, will you show her ladyship to her rooms?"

Blaise felt her face flame at his obvious dismissal. What better proof could she have of his indifference toward her? She was a stranger here, unwanted, unwelcome. A new bride without a husband to champion or support her.

She held her head high, though, as she addressed the butler. "Hedges, please send my abigail up to me when she arrives."

"Certainly, my lady. As you wish."

She heard Julian dispersing the staff as she followed the housekeeper up one of the curving staircases, but didn't catch the murmured conversation that followed between him and the butler.

When she was out of sight, though, Julian turned and strode directly into the nearest room, the library. The sideboard held several decanters of liquor. Choosing the first one with indifference, he poured a full measure into a glass and drank swiftly, grimacing as the potent sherry burned a path to his stomach. The ghosts he had wanted to face were very much alive and dwelling in his house. The ghosts of his past. Caroline's spirit. The entrance hall where he had last seen his wife alive had been filled with her haunting image.

Every detail of that hideous day was etched forever on his mind. He'd arrived home from London unexpectedly one afternoon, just as Caroline was preparing to meet Vincent. He could still picture her standing on the lower steps of the west staircase, attired in a crimson riding habit, brandishing a riding crop. He could still hear her anguished voice making that last irrefutable charge.

You don't love me, you never have! You care only for your London lightskirts!

No, he couldn't say he loved her. He felt a mild fondness for Caroline, but merely that. He'd left her alone too frequently, intent on pursuing his own pleasures.

They had married for convenience, as people of their station often did. In the beginning their expectations were clear. He would provide wealth and an exalted title; she would give him an heir in exchange. The fact that children were not forthcoming at once hadn't troubled him greatly. There was still time. He was satisfied with their relationship. Caroline was as well, or so he'd believed. Not until the final year of their three-year marriage had she even intimated that she wanted more from him. He'd thought he was doing her a kindness, sparing her his amorous attentions. She had always received him coolly during his infrequent visits to her bed, so he'd sought passion from his mistress with a clear conscience.

They might have continued that way into old age, except that Caroline's expectations changed. She'd wanted him to play the devoted lover, the attentive husband. She'd resented his London friends, his pursuits, his liaisons—which had provided fodder for many a bitter argument. He'd given up his London mistress, but that hadn't satisfied her. She'd demanded his heart, his obeisance. Which had only driven him farther away.

And a lonely, resentful wife was a prescription for disaster.

"Well, *I've* taken a lover!" she'd screeched at him that final afternoon.

The shock of her defiant taunt momentarily robbed him of breath, before fury streaked through him. He grasped her by the shoulders and shook her violently, his rage ungovernable as he shouted at her, demanding to know what she meant.

Weeping, she broke away. *"Vincent adores me! He would never treat me so abominably!"*

The name was like a fist in his stomach. His boyhood friend and neighbor, his wife's lover? Vincent's betrayal struck him more forcefully than even the knowledge of Caroline's adultery. When she rushed sobbing from the house, he simply stood there, too stunned to follow. All he could do was picture his wife and his friend together . . .

After abruptly sloshing more wine in the glass, Julian carried it across the room to the cold fireplace and threw himself into a chair. Bowing his head, he buried his face in one hand, the self-reproach and recriminations swamping him with familiar ease.

He hadn't loved her enough. He'd allowed her too much freedom. He'd ignored her far too often. By the time he had understood the depth of her bitterness, it was too late.

If he had been a better husband to her, Caroline would still be alive, and he wouldn't be hounded by this savage guilt. Vincent would have made her a better husband. Vincent had loved his wife more than he himself had.

He didn't think Caroline had loved the man in return. Self-centered, pampered from birth, his beautiful wife was accustomed to getting whatever she desired, and her husband's indifference was more than she could stand. By taking a lover, she had been trying to arouse his jealousy, Julian had finally realized. Or perhaps she saw it as revenge, turning him into a cuckold and Vincent into a fool. She'd used Vincent as cat's-paw—and yet his love for her had been genuine. Vincent was the one most devastated by her death, and bitter enough to fabricate those wild accusations of murder.

Julian, mired in a turmoil of regret and self-blame, had made little effort to refute the charges. So the rumors, fanned by Vincent's grief, persisted.

And there was cause for suspicion, after all. The vast servant staff at Lynden Park had heard that last violent argument, had witnessed Lord Lynden's furious pursuit of his fleeing wife. Nor did he help his case afterward by shutting himself away from his friends and neighbors. His own servants had rallied around him, but he'd found their pity and concern almost as unbearable as the un-spoken accusations by less familiar acquaintances, or the bewildered grief of Caroline's family. They hadn't known whom to blame, but he had. It was guilt, eating at him like acid, that had made him leave his ancestral home and ride off to war—to make himself pay for being alive when Caroline was dead. He had never forgiven himself.

And now? He had returned home in order to deal with the past, to end his long exile, to try and restore his family name, his savaged reputation. Yet at the present moment, his earlier optimism seemed laughable. His guilt was as sharp-edged, as taunting, as ever. His ghosts were just as real. And he had a new wife to contend with as well.

It was perhaps half an hour later that Julian roused himself from his grim reflections to remember Blaise, and another twinge of guilt prodded at his conscience. He owed his new bride at least the courtesy of his attention on her first day in his home. The least he could do was ensure that Blaise was settling in. He hadn't wanted to enter Caroline's rooms, but his reluctance now seemed both craven and rude. His preoccupation with the past was no excuse to forsake common civility. Nor was it wise to treat his second wife with the same casual indifference he'd shown his first. By now he should have learned his lesson.

Julian rubbed his forehead wearily as he recalled how inconsiderate and ill-tempered he'd been all day. With his own personal devils driving him, he'd totally forgotten the resolve he'd made the previous night to handle Blaise with more care.

With a heavy sigh, Julian set down his empty glass and struggled to his feet. He had just reached the west stairway in the entrance hall when he heard an odd swishing sound and a soft cry, *"Watch out!"*

Startled, he looked up to see a flying projectile come rushing down the stairs at him.

Barely having time to register that it was not a cannonball but a young woman—*his* young woman—streaking toward him along the banister, Julian desperately sidestepped, at the same time reaching out to try and catch her. He stumbled and muttered an oath as he nearly fell, but he did manage to check Blaise's speed, and miraculously she landed on her feet. Gripping her arms, he stood staring down at her a full five seconds before he realized what had happened; the incorrigible girl had actually slid down the banister, nearly bowling him over in the process.

It was all Julian could do to hold his temper in check. His grasp on her arms tightened as he hissed, "What the devil were you doing?"

Blaise glared up at him defiantly, her violet eyes flashing. "What does it look like I was doing?"

"I suppose," he ground out, "you have a good reason for disobeying my express wishes and acting the hoyden not an hour after you arrive?"

"Your commands, you mean!"

"Very well, my commands!"

Blaise wrenched out of his grasp and took a step back. She would have departed entirely, except that it savored of retreat. "I am not your servant to be ordered about, my lord."

"No, you are Viscountess Lynden, and I'll thank you to remember it."

"How can I possibly forget with you reminding me every two minutes?"

At precisely the same moment, they both became aware they weren't alone. Hedges had entered the hall, evidently intent on investigating the shouting match. Standing at attention, he had assumed the carefully blank expression of a superbly trained servant.

At the awkward silence, he cleared his throat. "Is there something you require, my lord?"

"Thank you, no, Hedges. I'll ring if I need you."

The butler bowed and made a dignified retreat.

Taking a deep breath, Julian made an effort at control and returned his attention to his wife. "It isn't only your lack of propriety that concerns me. You might have hurt yourself—or me."

"You weren't there when I started down," Blaise said defensively. "And I wasn't in any danger. I've ridden the banister hundreds of times in other houses."

"Other—you make a practice of this?"

"Well . . . no. I haven't since I was a child."

"Which was such a long time ago," Julian muttered sardonically. "Would you mind telling me why, then, you found it necessary to do it in my house?"

"Because it was fun! And because a joyless house needs *some* kind of relief occasionally. Your home is magnificent, Julian, but the atmosphere here is as stuffy and staid as anything my stepfather could have dreamed up."

The blistering rebuke he'd meant to give her died on his tongue. A joyless house was what she'd termed his home. And the hell of it was, she was right.

Julian glanced up at the grand staircase with its gleaming mahogany banister. It would be an alluring sight to an undisciplined, capricious girl with spirits as lively as Blaise's. And if he were truly honest, he couldn't help but find her daring misbehavior a bit humorous. As a boy he had yearned to slide down that same banister. Unfortunately, the one time he'd tried it, his illustrious father had given him a stout whipping with a birch rod.

He certainly couldn't discipline his young, ungovernable wife that way. Even if he were so uncivilized a brute as to beat his wife, he doubted it would be effective. Blaise needed a lighter hand on the bridle. A fact he kept forgetting. He'd snapped at her just now, not to mention that he'd forced her to put up with his grim temper all day. Obviously he hadn't yet learned how to manage her.

His tone moderated to a mild warning. "I would be gratified, minx, if you would refrain from such dangerous starts. I don't relish seeing you break your neck."

And losing another wife to tragedy. The unspoken thought seemed to hover between them. Julian found himself looking up at the stairway again. It was with a sense of amazement that he realized Caroline's haunting image had vanished. Blaise's childish escapade had somehow relieved the terrible tension he'd felt upon entering the house.

Blaise, however, didn't care at the moment what tensions Julian was or wasn't feeling. "Do I need to gain your permission for my every action?" she demanded.

"No, of course not."

"Good. Then I should like to walk in the gardens."

He suddenly realized she had changed her gown to a walking dress of jonquil sarcenet with a short-waisted spencer of blue velvet. "Now?"

"Do you have some objection?"

"I suppose not. But I would expect you to be weary after the long journey."

"After being confined in a carriage all day, I think a brisk walk would be refreshing."

."I'm afraid it will be difficult for me to accompany you. My leg——"

"I shan't need your escort. In fact, I would prefer *not* to have it."

A semblance of the charming smile she remembered wreathed Julian's mouth. "I haven't been the best company, have I?"

"You've been perfectly *miserable* company."

"I beg your pardon."

Rather than being mollified by his apology, however, Blaise was nettled by his swiftly changing moods. Just because he suddenly chose to be pleasant to her now did not mean he deserved to be forgiven for his earlier odious treatment of her. "And tomorrow I should like to go riding, if you have a suitable mount in your stables. I don't intend to run away, if that is what concerns you," she added when he didn't reply.

His mouth twisted. "I should hope I don't have need to be concerned about that. How well do you ride?"

"I'm credited with having an excellent seat, and I'm experienced enough to handle most horses without difficulty."

"Very well, then, I don't have any objection. My horses were sent ahead, so Grimes should be able to provide you with a suitable mount. And it should be safe enough, as long as you take a groom with you and remain within the boundaries of the park. I don't wish you to ride out alone."

Blaise pressed her lips together. "Thank you, my lord. You needn't trouble yourself about me further. I'm sure I can find the gardens. I saw them from my rooms, and Mrs. Hedges gave me a general idea of the layout of the house."

Turning, she marched from the entrance hall, leaving Julian to stare after her.

Blaise made her way without difficulty through the main wing of the house, bypassing rooms that boasted lofty ceilings and long windows, inlaid floors and handsome tiled fireplaces, Axminster carpets and damask draperies. She paid scant attention. The Holland covers had been removed from the furniture in preparation for their arrival, she'd been told, but at the moment she didn't give a fig about the grand manor house where she was now to live. Her seething thoughts were focused solely on her dictatorial husband.

Shortly she found a footman who was eager to aid the new mistress. Following him to a rear door, she soon found herself outside on a polished flagstone terrace, overlooking a magnificent garden laid out in formal geometric designs and splashed with the colors of autumn flowers—asters, dahlias, hollyhocks, and late-blooming roses.

Still simmering, Blaise descended the steps, swept past a fountain flanked by marble benches and topiary yews, and started blindly down a smooth gravel path. Julian said she had to have the supervision of a groom, did he? *Well, we shall just see about that, my lord husband.*

Not only did she resent his high-handed, autocratic commands, but she was still smarting over his cold treatment of her, still hurt that he wouldn't allow her into his confidence in the matter of his late wife, and still incensed that he would scold her in front of the servants.

Well, she wouldn't put up with it! In the future, Blaise vowed, whatever he ordered her to do, she would do the exact opposite. She had to make a stand now, at once, before Julian got the notion that he could run roughshod over her. If she allowed him to begin their marriage by commanding her every movement, she would be miserable.

Blaise glanced over her shoulder at the splendid house. Legally, Julian might be her lord and master, but he would soon discover he hadn't married a meek-mannered child or an obedient hound who would roll over at his every command.

Chapter 14

"But, m'lady, I don't know if I should," the groom objected the following afternoon. "I was told to attend you."

"Which you have done masterfully," Blaise replied. "But I would prefer to be alone, truly."

"I don't know . . ." They were well out of sight of the stables, and the servant was obviously reluctant to accept his dismissal.

"I shall take full responsibility." Blaise gave him a cajoling smile, making the young man blush. "Really, it isn't necessary for you to shadow my footsteps. I have a keen sense of direction, and you have given me an excellent description of the area, so I won't become lost. And if it should happen, I can stop at a cottage and ask the way. I shall be perfectly safe."

Her manner was firm but kind, but if that didn't succeed, she was prepared to resort to drastic measures. She had every intention of escaping the groom's escort and galloping over the countryside alone—if only to prove a point. Not that she didn't require the accompaniment of a groom, but that she refused to submit to her lordly husband's dictatorial commands.

The groom, however, proved no match for her determination. After a few more moments of silent debate, he gave in and turned his horse around, heading back to the stables.

Elated by her success and the prospect of an afternoon's freedom, Blaise nudged her mount forward. When after luncheon she had asked that a horse be brought around, she could not have been more delighted with the choice. The sweetly spirited bay mare matched her mood exactly—eager for the challenge of exploring the countryside.

Blaise breathed deeply as she took in the splendid view. The sunshine of yesterday was gone, leaving the overcast skies dreary and chill, yet even so, Julian's estate still looked magnificent. The rolling pastoral landscape was interspersed with newly harvested fields and well-tended orchards and, occasionally, clumps of farm buildings and tenant cottages.

Blaise greatly admired his land, his home, and couldn't understand how Julian could have stayed away so long. How could he have given up all this? He'd been born and bred to this land, but evidently he didn't appreciate his good fortune. Having been rootless herself for so many years, she had yearned for a place to call her own. She wanted roots, a settled home life, love . . .

Her mind shied away from the thought. It wouldn't do to raise her hopes, or she would be devastated when she had to accept reality. This was her home now, and the idea was incredibly appealing, but she might never be able to win Julian's love, or build with him the kind of future she had dreamed of having. Not with such a terrible beginning to their marriage. Not with the mysterious tragedy of his past.

She had been given his late wife's rooms, Blaise knew. Mrs. Hedges had made it a point to inform her that the first Lady Lynden had designed the suite herself—a bedchamber, a dressing room, and a sitting room that connected with the master's rooms. It was all quite elegant and expensive, done in brocades and velvets of ruby-red and rich gold. But the heavy materials and dark colors were not to her taste, and the thick draperies kept out the light. Blaise had found herself wanting to escape the oppressive atmosphere.

Her walk in the gardens the day before had raised her spirits, but they had fallen again when evening came.

Supper with her noble husband had been a quiet, sober affair. They had dined alone in the large formal dining room, separated by the tremendous length of the polished dining table. There was little chance for meaningful conversation, even if Julian had been so inclined—which, by all appearances, he was not. And neither was she. She was still too vexed at his high-handed treatment of her. The food had been superb—clear turtle soup, fillets de Turbot, braised neck of veal, pigeon pie, as ell as broiled mushrooms, buttered salsify, spears of asparagus from the Lynden forcing houses, and several other removes, with a sponge cake and stewed pears in cream as the sweet—but Blaise had been in no mood to do justice to the meal.

They had retired directly afterward, to their individual suites, and Blaise had not seen Julian since. He had not visited her rooms last night, and she didn't know what to make of it. Either he was being considerate and concerned with overtiring her, or he was wary of intruding on her after their contretemps that afternoon, or perhaps he simply didn't wish to make love to her again—a possibility that greatly depressed Blaise, despite all her intended defiance.

He had already breakfasted by the time she had come down that morning, she learned, and was closeted with the estate steward. Blaise ate in solitude and spent the next several hours interviewing the housekeeper, Mrs. Hedges, and becoming familiar with the house.

Her new home.

The thought was rather daunting. To think that *she* was responsible for the supervision of what would soon be a vast household, once a complete staff was hired. Blaise had never applied herself to any task of such magnitude, although her mother and her aunt—and her abigail, Garvey, too, for that matter—had attempted to train her in the duties expected of a highborn lady.

"But you never paid them the least mind," Blaise scolded herself aloud, making the mare flick back her dainty ears. "You were too busy playing childish pranks and plotting how best to annoy Sir Edmund to gain his attention."

Remembering, she felt a bit ashamed of herself. But she was grown up now, and beyond such immaturity. She hoped.

Then again, Julian might not wish for her to take responsibility for his home. He had married her merely to prevent a scandal, not because he wished for a manager to oversee his household, or a gracious hostess for his guests. He hadn't wanted a helpmate, or someone to provide him with children, either. As for a companion in his bed . . . She doubted he had married her for *that*. Her ignorance and inexperience in matters carnal would not hold much allure for a worldly, sophisticated man like Julian. He had even remarked on her naiveté on their wedding night. Besides, noblemen did not look for pleasure in their wives' beds, but sought it in the arms of lightskirts or actresses or mistresses—or Gypsies. It had been the Gypsies' undeserved reputation for promiscuity—and perhaps the challenge of her refusing his initial advances—that had caused Julian to pursue her so single-mindedly during the first week of their acquaintance. He had been laboring under the misapprehension that she was no lady.

But he had no reason to pursue her now that she was his wife. Blaise knew that he could, and possibly would, seek his pleasure elsewhere. And with his combined advantages of masculine beauty, noble title, and excessive fortune, Julian, she was certain, would not have to look far in order to find willing female companionship. Indeed, he might have a mistress in keeping even now.

At that realization, Blaise felt a sudden sharp pang of what she recognized as jealousy. She did not want her husband conferring on other women the shattering physical intimacies he'd shared with her. She wanted his kisses, his caresses, to be hers and hers alone. Such proprietary sentiment might be considered provincial and ill-bred in fashionable circles, but if so, then she didn't want a modern marriage. Or a marriage of convenience, either, where they each went their separate ways. She wanted her husband to be lover, friend, confidant. She wanted the kind of joyous marriage her mother had known with her father.

What kind of marriage had Julian enjoyed with his late wife? Blaise abruptly wondered. She had to admit to a rabid curiosity. Julian had refused to speak of Caroline, which could mean absolutely anything. He could have loved her to distraction, or hated her with equal passion.

"And it makes not the least bit of difference," Blaise muttered defiantly, remembering her current grievance with her overbearing husband.

With a shake of her head, she spurred the mare into an easy gallop.

She stayed primarily to the lanes, once crossing a gaily tumbling brook to investigate a lovely glade. Occasionally she passed groups of men in farm laborers' attire who eyed her surreptitiously. Blaise suspected they were Julian's tenants. She was certain he must have an excellent steward. The estate looked too prosperous to have been abandoned by an absentee landlord.

She calculated she was perhaps five miles from the manor house when she came across a wide, grassy field half hidden by a copse of elms. The place was rather eerie for all its charm. Thick walls of crumbling gray stone gave it an abandoned look. It was apparently some kind of ruins—perhaps an ancient monastery or a fortress fallen into decay.

Blaise was halfway across the field when she realized she was not alone. A man lay on his back in the grass, near one of the ruined walls, one arm shielding his eyes, a book by his side. He was dressed as a country gentleman—which must have been his status if he had the leisure to spend in this manner.

He must have heard the muffled hoofbeats, for he gave a start and sat up, running an elegant hand briefly through his dark hair.

Blaise drew the mare to a halt several yards away. It was perhaps unwise to stop and speak to a strange man, especially when she hadn't even the protection of a groom. Indeed, she should have ridden on. But she was mounted on a swift horse, after all, and she was curious why he would be lying there when it threatened to rain.

"Forgive me, I didn't mean to disturb you," she apologized. "I thought this was my husband's property."

"Your husband?"

"Lord Lynden."

"Ah." His expression immediately became shuttered. "I heard he had brought home a wife from his wanderings. News," he explained at her surprised look, "travels rapidly in this small neighborhood." As he spoke, he climbed gracefully to his feet and tendered her a polite bow. "You aren't mistaken, my lady. This is Lynden land. I fear I am guilty of trespass."

He was an astonishingly handsome man, Blaise realized. He was approximately the same age as Julian, she guessed, but there the similarity ended. This man was much more slender, with a brooding air and a disheveled lock of mahogany hair that fell over a pale forehead, half covering his heavy eyebrows. She couldn't tell the precise color of his eyes, but they were dark also, brown or almost black.

Gathering her wits, Blaise started to make a noncommittal reply. But he spoke again. "Allow me to introduce myself. Vincent Foster, at your service, my lady."

Blaise had the odd impression he was watching her closely to determine her reaction.

"Your husband has not told you about me?"

"No, but then I don't know many of his acquaintances. We have only been married a short while."

Mr. Foster seemed to relax. "I am your nearest neighbor. We grew up together, your husband and I. I live not far from here with my sister, Rachel." Mr. Foster gestured in the distance. "Our estates join at your western border."

"In that case," Blaise said with a smile, "I doubt that

my husband would object to your making use of his field."

He hesitated. "I wouldn't be so certain of that. Julian and I are not exactly on the best of terms." At her curious look, he added, "Perhaps I *should* leave. Julian would not approve of your stooping to acknowledge me."

Nothing he might have said could have made Blaise more determined to pursue the acquaintance. She was just irked enough with her noble husband to defy common sense and propriety by remaining here alone to converse with a perfect stranger.

"I do hope you mean to explain such a cryptic statement, Mr. Foster. Why would Julian disapprove? I confess you have me greatly intrigued."

"Perhaps you should ask him."

"I shall, when next I see him. But in the meantime you have me on tenterhooks."

"On second thought, perhaps it would be better if you said nothing to him of our meeting"

"Are you suggesting I *deceive* him?"

"No. I merely wish to keep from causing trouble for you. Julian would not be pleased to know you had spoken to me, or met me here, even if it was a chance encounter. Especially here."

He seemed determined to give her vague answers, but despite his frustratingly enigmatic allusions and brooding disposition, Blaise felt attracted to the gentleman. She would like to strike up a friendship, if possible, and to learn more about his sister. "Did you say you have a sister named Rachel?" she asked politely, taking a different tack.

"Yes. My only sister, who is a few years younger than I. I'm certain she would be pleased to meet you, but . . . it might be rather awkward. As I said, we are not exactly on speaking terms with your husband. Nor is the rest of the neighborhood, for that matter. I regret to say you are not likely to have many callers at Lynden Park. You may find yourself frequently shunned."

She wondered if the first Lady Lynden's death might

have something to do with his warning. "Because of what happened four years ago?"

Mr. Foster gave her a sad smile. "Yes. It is unfortunate that you should be made to suffer for it. If you find yourself lonely, you may ride here, to these ruins. They say this was once a Roman garrison fort."

"Why do I feel that you are attempting to change the subject, Mr. Foster?"

His smile turned bitter. "Perhaps because I am. It is painful for me to reflect on the past."

"Well it is totally *confusing* to me. And I would be grateful if you could enlighten me."

"I am not the one to tell you."

"How am I to learn what happened if no one ever speaks of it?"

He didn't reply.

"Did you know the late Lady Lynden well?"

"Yes. Quite well."

"Then perhaps you will at least tell me what she was like."

"In appearance you are very different from Caroline. The exact opposite, in fact."

"Indeed?"

"Caroline was extremely beautiful."

"And I am not? How unflattering, sir," Blaise said with a smile. She was not flirting with him, merely attempting to lighten the mood. But Mr. Foster did not seem even to hear her, his thoughts were so far away.

"Her hair was a golden color, like sunlight. She had such grace . . . like a swan. And her sweetness . . . She was much too good for Julian."

Mr. Foster sounded as if he had been highly enamored of the late Lady Lynden, and as if he held strong feelings against Julian, as well. Blaise could not help asking, "And you blame my husband for her tragic accident?"

He gave a sad smile. "Caroline's death was not an accident. It was murder."

Blaise gave a start at the bald statement.

"This was where it took place. Her body was lying

there . . ." He pointed to the main bulk of the ruins. "I came upon them shortly after it happened. There was a storm that afternoon. It was raining torrents; the wind was gusting hard."

"What were you doing out in a storm?" Blaise demanded skeptically, even though she knew she should not have encouraged him. This conversation was highly improper, and faintly disloyal, besides. Julian was her husband now. She owed him the benefit of the doubt.

"The rain came up suddenly. But I often take long walks, even in inclement weather. I frequently happened upon Lady Lynden here. This was one of her favorite places. That afternoon she had asked me to meet her here. And when Julian learned of it, he followed her here and killed her."

"I don't believe it," Blaise retorted automatically. "And I don't appreciate your making unfounded allegations."

"They are not unfounded."

"I understand there was never any proof of foul play."

"No bill of murder was brought against him, but he killed her, all the same. She had become an inconvenience. That afternoon he was in a rage because Caroline dared defy his orders."

Blaise could believe Julian had lost his temper if his wife defied his orders—she had been in the same position herself. But losing one's temper was not the same thing as murder. She came hotly to his defense. "He is not a murderer!"

"You defend him with passion."

"He is my husband, sir."

"He was Caroline's husband as well."

"If you are trying to turn me against him, I assure you it won't succeed."

"Your loyalty is commendable, my lady, but sadly misplaced." Foster stepped closer to her horse, looking up at her intently. "I truly hope you don't regret your decision to marry him."

It had not really been her decision, Blaise thought irrelevantly. "You are presumptuous, sir."

"Perhaps, but if my warning you now can save you, it will be justified. I beg you to take care, Lady Lynden. I should hate to see you come to harm at his hands. If ever you have need of a friend, if you are in need of refuge, you may count on me."

She couldn't doubt his obvious sincerity. He seemed truly concerned for her. But he believed those absurd tales about Julian killing his wife. "If I have need of a *friend,* sir, I will choose someone I trust to impart the truth, not scurrilous accusations. Perhaps it would be best if you stayed off Lynden land after all. Good day to you."

With that Blaise wheeled the mare around and rode away, but she could feel his dark eyes following her until she was out of sight.

The pleasure had gone out of her day. And for that she blamed Vincent Foster. She didn't believe his accusations in the least. Indeed, she was more intrigued than intimidated by Julian's haunted past. But it disturbed her to realize Mr. Foster believed them. Was this what Julian had been up against when he'd left here four years ago to fight a war?

Her thoughts were so occupied with such sobering questions that Blaise at first didn't see the tall, golden-haired man standing in the stableyard. When she finally noticed him, it was too late to turn around and ride away again. Julian was obviously waiting for her, and one look at his hard expression warned her of her mistake.

With trepidation, Blaise drew her mare to a halt barely a yard from him. She had expected Julian to be angry when he discovered she'd flouted his authority by riding through the countryside without a groom, but she had never seen him so coldly furious.

He didn't ask her if she required assistance dismounting, but reached up and plucked her from the sidesaddle, setting her jarringly on her feet. He kept a tight grip on her waist as he glared down at her.

"Where have you been, madam?" he demanded, his voice fierce and low.

"I should think that would be evident. I've been riding, of course."

"I expressly ordered you never to go out without the accompaniment of a groom."

Blaise swallowed hard, remembering her resolve to stand up to Julian's dictatorial commands. "So you did," she replied with forced sweetness. "But I decided I preferred solitude this afternoon."

She saw him grit his teeth and take a deep breath, as if struggling for control. "I was not acting out of idle whim. I am concerned for your safety. If you were hurt, I would blame only myself."

Blaise felt her own hot anger at being scolded cool dramatically. But it flared up again immediately at Julian's next comment.

"But that will be the last time you ride without a groom, I assure you. I will refuse you the use of my stables entirely if I must."

Her eyes sparking militantly, Blaise glared up at him. "Why don't you simply lock me in my room and keep me on a diet of bread and water? Then you wouldn't have to worry about me!"

"If that is the only way to ensure your obedience, then I shall."

"How barbaric! And to think I was just defending you to your neighbor only a short while ago. I told Mr. Foster you didn't murder your wife in a fit of rage, but now I'm not so certain!"

She didn't imagine the way the blood suddenly drained from Julian's face; his complexion turned pale, making his facial scar stand out vividly across his cheekbone.

"You spoke to Vincent?" His voice was oddly hoarse.

"At length. I came across him on my ride this afternoon. He showed me the Roman ruins, in fact."

Julian's face turned even whiter, if that were possible. "You met Vincent Foster at the ruins?"

Blaise felt a sudden twinge of alarm at his look of sheer horror. "I didn't *meet* him exactly. I mean I did . . . he introduced himself . . . but it wasn't a planned meeting. He said you wouldn't approve."

"What . . . was he doing there?"

"Reading a book of poetry, I believe. He looked quite harmless."

Julian turned away abruptly and stood with his back to her. His head was bowed, his hands clenched into fists. When he next spoke, his voice was so low Blaise could barely make out his words, although she could tell he was deadly serious.

"You are not to see or speak to him again, do you understand me? I forbid it. You are to stay away from him entirely. I refuse to allow Vincent Foster to step one foot on Lynden property. If I have to set patrols to guard the ruins, I will."

"Don't you think those measures might be rather drastic?" Blaise asked, bewildered and frightened by Julian's barely contained fury.

"Perhaps not drastic enough, given your propensity for scandal. If you think I mean to allow you free rein to cause another, you much mistake the matter. I won't tolerate such disgraceful behavior in my wife."

"You are mistaken, my lord," she retorted, her anger swelling again, blotting out her fear. "I haven't *begun* to misbehave. If I truly wanted to disgrace you, I would become an actress and take to the stage. That would show you what *real* scandal is!"

He walked away from her. Simply walked away without replying or looking back over his shoulder. Or rather, he limped.

Blaise bit her lip as she stared after Julian. She felt somehow as if she had taken unfair advantage of him, like kicking a wounded animal when it was most vulnerable.

The remainder of the day she spent in a similar turmoil of conflicting emotions—guilt, anger, uncertainty, resentment, depression, unhappiness. She didn't understand Julian and his terrible hostility toward her, and didn't know if she wanted to.

She had a supper tray brought to her room that evening. She didn't know where her husband was, and was convinced she didn't much care. All she knew was that she felt very much like crying, that she was miserable. But then, misery had become a commonplace state of mind for her since her marriage.

That evening Blaise went to bed alone and feeling wretched. She missed Julian—the *real* Julian. The charming, seductive, persuasive, golden nobleman who had pursued her with such intent purpose at the Gypsy encampment. She was lonely in this great house, at the prospect of living with the cold stranger he had become. So lonely she might even be glad to see Sir Edmund just now. Her stepfather's aloofness, his cool disdain, was not as bad as the sheer enmity her new husband had shown her. She didn't think she could bear to maintain such a soul-chilling relationship for even another week, let alone for the rest of her life.

Yet it didn't look as if her circumstances would improve greatly in the near future. If Julian were like other landed noblemen of means, he could absent himself for months, to partake of the social season in London, or the endless rounds of house parties in the country, or the various sporting seasons, or simply to get away from her. He could leave her all alone here, with nothing but her thoughts for company, unless she was fortunate enough someday to have children to comfort her—

At that startling reflection, Blaise turned over in bed, staring up at the darkened canopy overhead. By marrying Julian so hastily, she hadn't had time to consider what the future might hold. The notion of bearing him a child was strangely thrilling and sobering at the same time. Did he want children?

Did he even want *her*?

Did he ever again intend to visit her bed? She would regret it profoundly if she never again experienced his sensual kisses, his caresses. He had given her a tantalizing taste of ecstasy that had only left her craving more. For a few brief, blissful moments he had made her feel desired and wanted and loved. Even if his wanting her had been an illusion, it was an illusion she wanted to hold on to.

Yet it would be at least partly her own fault if their estrangement deprived her of the physical side of marriage. By challenging his authority, by flouting his commands, she might very well have forfeited any right to his respect, destroyed any desire he had once felt for her.

Perhaps, Blaise began to think, she would be smarter to change her tactics. If she hoped to derive any happiness from her marriage at all, she would have to take responsibility for trying to make it work. It was clear Julian would not. No doubt he thought of her as a burdensome nuisance, as a scandal waiting to happen.

Restlessly, she punched her pillow, trying to reach a comfortable position for her head. The root of her troubles, it seemed, was the past—the terrible demise of the first Lady Lynden. Accident or not, Julian clearly blamed himself for Caroline's death. Responsible or not, he had allowed the tragedy to nearly destroy him.

What she didn't know was *why*?

Had he loved the beautiful Caroline? Had he grieved for her so much that he had wanted to die? Or had his burden of guilt simply been too heavy to bear?

Why had he returned home after all these years? To clear his name? To find forgiveness? To answer the charges of murder? Would he ever come to terms with the past? Would he ever be free, Blaise wondered, to love *her*?

Until she had the answers to those disturbing questions, she doubted her marriage to Julian would ever have a chance to succeed. Deceased or not, Caroline was her rival.

Blaise winced at a painful thought. She was jealous of a ghost.

Yet she couldn't fight a ghost, Blaise realized. She

would have to find out precisely what had happened to the first Lady Lynden, what events had led up to her death. And then she would have to make Julian see that he had suffered long enough.

She didn't know if it could be done. Four years was a long time for a man to build unbreachable walls of guilt and self-condemnation around himself.

But she had to try. And no one had ever accused her of lacking determination or mettle.

Consoling herself with that thought, Blaise began to develop a plan.

Chapter 15

Blaise implemented her campaign as she did everything else in life, with determination and vigor and
the careful strategy of a seasoned military veteran. Julian,
as a former field commander, might even have been
impressed by her skillful planning, had he known what
she was up to. Fortunately he did not, or his already
strained patience would have exploded.

She began by questioning the servants—subtly, of
course—about the late Lady Lynden and about Julian
himself. Under the pretext of examining the state of
the household stores—linens, silver, china—and learning
the management of a new household, she interviewed the
housekeeper at great length about the previous mistress's
way of doing things. Even so, Mrs. Hedges remained
frustratingly closemouthed. At least, that is, until Blaise
challenged her directly.

"You don't approve of me, do you, Mrs. Hedges?" she
asked baldly one afternoon while they were discussing
which staff positions needed to be filled now that the
viscount had taken up residence.

For the first time since Blaise's arrival at Lynden Park,
the woman actually looked taken aback. "It is not my
place to approve or disapprove of you, my lady."

"Stuff and nonsense. You know as well as I that my
acceptance here will depend in large measure on your
opinion of me."

Her smile took the sting from her words, but Mrs.
Hedges stiffened visibly. "If you are not satisfied with

my service, my lady, you may, of course, dismiss me."

"Whyever should I wish to dismiss you? From what I can tell, your service has been excellent. It would be foolish of me to turn you away simply out of pique. Especially since I need you. I've never managed a household anywhere near this size, and I haven't the least idea how to go on. I *need* you, Mrs. Hedges, probably much more than you need this post. But I would be gratified by at least a pretense of support from you."

The housekeeper blinked at such plain speaking.

"I can understand your loyalty to the first Lady Lynden," Blaise went on, "and I'm terribly sorry about what happened to her, truly, but what concerns me now is the future. I don't mean to pry, or ask you to betray any confidences, but I should like to know what I am up against. Rumor has it that my husband murdered his first wife, and I mean to—"

"Malicious lies!" the housekeeper exclaimed with the first show of passion she'd exhibited in Blaise's presence. "His lordship never would have raised a hand to harm the mistress."

"*I* believe he is innocent, but there are clearly others who do not. And Lynden won't speak a word in his own defense. It seems unfair that he should have to suffer so unjustly, especially after he was so terribly wounded during the war."

"Indeed, he's been hurt enough."

"Exactly. But I'm a stranger here and can do little alone. Yet I should think that working together we can manage at least to foil the gossips and perhaps even prove his innocence. It would help to discover how those rumors began."

Mrs. Hedges looked at her new mistress with a dawning respect, and became a reluctant confidante.

It was then that Blaise learned about the violent argument that had driven Lady Lynden to ride out in a storm. It had occurred directly in the main entrance hall late one afternoon in June, after his lordship had arrived home unexpectedly. Most of the staff at that time had heard the voices raised in anger, but not the content of the speech. The next thing anyone knew, Lady Lynden was galloping away from the house on the horse she used for her daily ride. His lordship had to go all the way to the stables to saddle a mount before he could follow her. He'd found her body near the Roman ruins. Apparently Lady Lynden had fallen from her horse, her skull crushed by a rock.

"It could have been an accident then?" Blaise asked Mrs. Hedges.

"It *was* an accident, my lady."

"So how did the rumors of her murder get started?"

"I'm not certain, except . . . Mr. Foster had some harsh words with his lordship before the funeral, and afterward they never spoke again, to my knowledge. Which is odd, considering how close they once were. Like brothers, they were."

Mrs. Hedges then told Blaise more about their neighbor, Mr. Vincent Foster, and his sister, Rachel. They were landed gentry and had run tame at Lynden Park while they were growing up, almost as if they were Julian's siblings.

"Did Mr. Foster have reason to wish Lord Lynden ill?"

"Not that I know, my lady. It was his sister, Miss Foster, who was the spiteful one. It's not my place to judge my betters, but it seems that she once fancied becoming Lady Lynden."

"She wanted to become Julian's wife?"

"Yes. Before his lordship married—the first time, I mean—Miss Foster used to lord it over all the servants here. More than once she gave me orders that she had no right to be giving."

Mrs. Hedges's husband, the butler, had little more to add to Blaise's increasing store of knowledge, except to confirm that Lord Lynden and Mr. Vincent Foster had indeed had a falling out, and to express his willingness to help prove Lord Lynden's innocence.

"His lordship is a good man, my lady," Hedges pronounced solemnly.

"Then you don't believe he killed Lady Lynden, either?"

"Would I stay to serve him all these years if I thought such a heinous crime had been committed?"

Blaise had to admit she couldn't see the possibility of the stately Hedges condoning anything so improper as murder.

Mr. Marsh, the elderly steward who had managed the Lynden estates single-handedly during the past four years and had served Julian's father for twenty years before that, had absolutely nothing to say on the subject of the tragedy, however. His loyalty was entirely to his current employer. Blaise tried to question Marsh one morning as he reviewed the household accounts with her, but he seemed immune to praise, prodding, or persuasion, much to her frustration.

There were limits, Blaise began to realize, to what she could achieve on her own, no matter how intrepid or resourceful or determined she might be.

Her lack of information sources was a major obstacle to her plan to uncover the truth and prove Julian's innocence. His servants could provide her with only so much enlightenment. She was cut off from her peers, and therefore privy to none of their insights or gossip or collective reasoning. In the six days she'd been at Lynden Park, no one except the kindly vicar and his wife had come to call—and then only, Blaise suspected, because the vicar was not about to risk offending the wealthy patron who provided his excellent living. None of the neighbors had welcomed Lord Lynden home, or accepted his new bride into the parish community, or congratulated them on their marriage, or simply inquired as to their health. The lack of hospitality—indeed, the pointed neglect—was more than rudeness, Blaise was beginning to apprehend. She and Julian were being deliberately shunned.

Another obstacle was the subject of her intense investigations himself: her husband. She had seen very little of Julian during this first week as his wife. All his time he spent in the company of his steward, Mr. Marsh. She applauded Julian's industry, to a point. He had thrown himself into the work of the estate, driving himself relentlessly to refamiliarize himself with his responsibilities and perhaps make up for his long absence. Yet he seemed to be purposely avoiding her. And his huge house was large enough that a determined man could lose himself for quite some time.

When Blaise did manage to meet him, it was usually at mealtimes. The atmosphere between them was strained, his conversation curt, cool, and distant. It was as if he no longer cared what disasters she created or scandals she involved herself in. As if he were intent on ignoring the fact that he now had a wife.

Will Terral, fortunately, was much more helpful. Terral had assumed the position as his lordship's valet, and while not exactly loquacious, was more forthcoming than any of the others about Julian himself, perhaps because he knew his master best. Blaise, surprised to learn she had not been forbidden the use of the stables as long as she was accompanied by a groom, secured Terral's escort one afternoon and used the opportunity to learn about the man to whom she was married.

Before the tragedy of his wife's death, according to Terral, Julian had been a renowned sportsman, a leader of the Corinthian set, as the premier sporting gentlemen of the day were known. He'd been a member of the Four-in-Hand Club, the famous coaching club where horse-mad young bucks held frequent races along the London roads. He had also been known to spar with Gentleman Jackson himself, the celebrated pugilist who now instructed wealthy men in the science of fisticuffs.

The "golden Lord Lynden," as Terral had heard him called, had been a favorite with the ladies, a revelation which Blaise, with a stab of jealousy, could well believe. But according to Terral, Julian was well-liked by men and the lower classes as well. To a one, his servants had thought him noble and kind and good, and believed that he could never have killed a woman, much less his beautiful wife.

Until the tragedy, Julian had seemed to lead a charmed life. Even on the battlefield, despite his heroic and often foolhardy acts of daring, he had kept off the casualty lists—until several months ago during the battle for Vitoria, when the French forces in Spain had finally suffered a defeat so overwhelming they might never recover.

" 'Twas a close one for sure," Terral reminisced. "The sawbones were going to take his leg, but I stopped 'em."

"He must be profoundly grateful to you," Blaise suggested.

Terral forgot himself so much as to grunt. "Aye, he's grateful, for all the good it does. He shouldn't be in the saddle at all right now. His leg's in no condition to bear such punishment. But will he listen to me? *No*. He says he has to ride over his land to inspect the farms and fields. Maybe you can get him to cease, m'lady?"

She knew what Terral was referring to. Just that morning, she had spied Julian from her bedchamber window, leaving the house with Mr. Marsh, dressed in beautifully cut riding clothes. Despite his need to inspect the estate, though, his wound hadn't healed enough to withstand such strain.

"I don't know that he will listen to me, either."

"Well, somebody has to make him see sense. And I daren't mention it again. Just this morning, he threatened to cashier me and send me back to Spain if I didn't cease mollycoddling him. But you've seen his limp. It's worse now than it was a month ago."

It was true that his limp had grown more pronounced in the past few days. And she harbored the strong suspicion that his rash behavior was intentional, that it was merely a way to make himself suffer more.

"I'll try to see what I can do," Blaise promised without much conviction.

"It's all because of what happened to her ladyship that he won't see reason. It's like there's a powerful devil driving him."

Blaise was acquainted with her husband well enough

now to agree. There *was* a devil driving Julian. His past. And she wished she could somehow help him conquer it.

Julian gritted his teeth against the pain and poured a third brandy for himself. The Spanish vintage was much inferior to the French wines he refused to buy from England's enemy, but at the moment he wanted the most potent liquor he could find. Swallowing a fiery mouthful of the stuff, he sank wearily into a leather armchair before the cold hearth and carefully eased his right leg onto a brocade footstool.

He had been unable to sleep with the fierce ache in his thigh, and so had closeted himself away in his study, intending to drink himself senseless. The hour was late, and he was as dispirited as he was physically drained and battered. He'd spent the countless hours since morning visiting his tenants, and then his damnable horse had shied and rammed his wounded leg into a fence post— the perfect culmination of a hellish day.

His tenants' reactions to him had been more painful than his riding accident, though. Where once they had shown him intense loyalty, now they treated him with sullen wariness. He couldn't blame them, considering how he'd neglected them during his four-year absence. And he doubted his reputation as an alleged murderer had helped matters much.

Julian flexed his fist in simmering fury at his impotence. Damn and blast it, what a bloody coil! Perhaps, he reflected savagely, it was a mistake to have returned home. Perhaps he should have remained in London and opened his town house. At least then he wouldn't have to endure the resentful and suspicious looks of his people, or the defiant challenges of his wife. His wife. Blaise, the beautiful Gypsy witch who seemed determined to cut up his peace. If he had stayed in London, he would never have met Blaise. Did he want that? Would he rather have never met her?

He'd done his utmost to avoid her this past week.

He didn't trust himself to be near her and not act in a manner he would regret. His rage when Blaise had defiantly announced that she'd met Vincent Foster at the ruins had been nearly as great as his instinctive horror. His reaction was even more violent than it had been four years ago with Caroline, when she'd taunted him about her adulterous affair.

Julian ran a hand roughly through his disheveled curls. Whatever had happened to his claim to good breeding and refined manners? He was a gentleman, for God's sake. Or he'd once been. Four years ago he would never have allowed his temper to override his good judgment. He'd never felt an ungovernable need to commit an act of violence—not until his final altercation with Caroline. He'd lived his life on an even keel, the typical, indulged life of a wealthy nobleman, taking pleasure where it was offered and rarely concerning himself with the future. He'd never imagined the possibility that his comfortable existence could be shattered.

And yet it had been. And now it was being threatened again. By his disobedient, willful, unmanageable new wife. Blaise managed to arouse his fury in a way Caroline never had, just as she aroused his body. Ever since the disastrous beginning to their marriage, he'd been torn between wanting to throttle her and the savage desire to tumble her in the nearest bed or haystack and thrust into her so deeply that he forgot who and where he was.

It was on that thought that Julian heard the slight sound of a door opening.

He turned his head to find Blaise standing in the doorway, holding a branched candlestick aloft. Her virginal nightdress was covered almost entirely by a wrapper of amethyst velvet, nearly the same shade as her beautiful eyes, while her unbound raven hair spilled in lovely disarray over her shoulders. The reaction of his body was instantaneous; his lions felt suddenly heavy and tight as he remembered the last time he had removed that nightdress and bared that exquisite body.

Julian closed his eyes against the vision, wishing she would go away. He couldn't deal with the alluring contradiction Blaise represented just now. His physical resources were at a dangerously low level, and just now he didn't want to deal with the turmoil their confrontations caused.

She didn't take the hint. Instead, she moved a step farther into the room. "I missed you at dinner."

He didn't reply.

"Do you mean to drink yourself into oblivion?"

In answer, he took a long swallow of brandy. His uncontrollable young bride was enough to drive any man to drink, he thought. "If I can, yes. And I would prefer that you leave me to it in peace."

Blaise stared at Julian uncertainly. An oil lamp burned low on the mantel, wrapping the room in a soft glow and illuminating the beautiful man sitting alone before the empty hearth. He wore a dressing gown of sapphire-blue brocade, the same shade as his eyes. The lamplight shone on his gilded head, muted the scarred face, but it couldn't mask the dark aura of disillusionment that surrounded him. A golden archangel imprisoned in his own private hell, she thought with anguish.

"What are you doing here?" he demanded in a chilling tone.

Blaise bit her lip. She had sought him out, hoping to effect a reconciliation, but it was clear she had chosen a bad time. The look of desolation that was often present in his eyes was even more pronounced now, and she sensed a terrible weariness in him that wrung her heart. Then again, there might never be a good time to say what she needed to say.

She shut the door softly behind her and set her candlestick down on the nearest table. "Your leg must be paining you."

"I'm not ready for a bloody Bath chair yet."

She winced at his savage tone, but she refused to retreat. He was her husband. She didn't want him to shut her out of his life or keep her at arm's length.

Moving the short distance across the room, she knelt at Julian's feet, beside the footstool that supported his right leg. He might not want her to tend his wound, but she was determined to ease his suffering if she could.

She reached for his outstretched leg, which was covered completely by the long blue dressing gown. He didn't pull away, to her surprise, but sat there tense and wary, as if he didn't want her touch but couldn't bring himself to refuse it.

Her fingers discovered warm bare skin. The shocked realization that Julian was naked beneath his dressing robe made her hesitate an instant. Then she slid her hand over his bare knee and up the muscled leg, to the tight, puckered flesh of his ravaged thigh.

"Go away, damn you. I don't need you."

His entire body was clenched, his voice rough, impatient. But Blaise wouldn't allow herself to be intimidated. He did need her. He needed someone to forgive him, to relieve him of the burden he carried. He needed someone to drum some sense into his head. Her fingers began to move gently over his wounded thigh, pressing deep into the hard muscle.

"Are you sitting here feeling sorry for yourself?" she asked, not looking at him.

"Perhaps." He laughed softly, a harsh whisper of sound edged with self-mockery. "Why not?" He waved a hand expansively. "I think I have the right to feel anything I bloody well please. I can afford to wallow in maudlin sentiment if I choose."

Blaise took a deep breath. "I think you're acting like a spoiled little boy."

His blue eyes suddenly focused and narrowed on her.

"My father—my real father—used to say a man's character is tested by adversity. Well, yours was tested when your wife died, Julian, and it was found wanting. I doubt you ever faced true adversity until then."

There was an ominous silence.

"You're trying to destroy yourself," Blaise forced herself to continue, "as penance for whatever crime you feel you've committed. But you didn't kill your wife. Her death was an accident. You have to stop blaming yourself for it."

He had grown quite still. When Blaise looked up, it was to meet the glittering blue anger in his eyes.

"What is this, my little Gypsy?" Julian asked with slicing sarcasm. "Have you suddenly turned philosopher?"

"I'm only expressing what is common knowledge."

"You've been gossiping with the servants again, I take it." He brought his glass to his lips and drank deeply. "So," he said almost conversationally, "what did you learn, sweeting? I'll wager nothing of real note. I imagine my servants are too discreet to tell you all the sordid details."

"What do you mean?"

"You haven't heard the whole tale, have you? You don't know about Caroline and Vincent. My wife and my friend. They were lovers."

Blaise's sharp inhalation was audible. He had meant to shock her, she was certain, but she wasn't really shocked. After hearing Vincent Foster speak so reverently of Caroline that day at the ruins, she'd known there was more to the tale than had been publicly acknowledged. And it made sense now, knowing the two of them were lovers. What didn't make sense was why Julian was so willing to shoulder all the blame for her death.

"You didn't kill her," Blaise repeated with conviction. "You aren't a murderer."

"I was angry enough that day to commit murder. Don't you think I had a right to be angry, sweeting? To be cuckolded by my closest friend?" The bitterness in his tone was edged with self-derision, but Blaise couldn't accept it.

"Yes, you had a right to be angry. At Caroline. At Mr. Foster. But not at yourself. You have no right to bludgeon yourself for what wasn't your fault."

"Caroline died because of me. If I'm not to blame, who is?"

"Fate . . . God . . . who knows?"

"Vincent blames me."

"Vincent is *wrong*."

Julian leaned his head back wearily. Her hands were lulling him with their unremitting, gentle caresses. "You thought I was being arbitrarily dictatorial by telling you to keep away from Vincent. I wasn't. I know him. He'll do his damnedest to turn you against me."

Blaise kept up her determined stroking while she considered her reply. She understood now why Julian felt such bitterness toward Vincent, but he didn't know her at all if he thought she would cease believing in him simply because someone else tried to poison her feelings for him.

"He couldn't turn me against you. I won't see him again. Or visit the ruins. I won't go there again, I promise."

"Those damnable ruins." Julian closed his eyes. "Do you want to know why I hate that place?"

"Because . . . Caroline died there?"

"In part. I see them in my nightmares. But that was also where she and Vincent carried on their affair."

"How do you know?"

"He told me. In vivid detail. He described to me how they used to meet every afternoon and shed their clothes and couple in the grass like animals. So I would realize how passionate Caroline could be in the arms of a man she loved. So I would know how much of herself she had given him."

Dismayed, Blaise stared at Julian.

Abruptly, he opened his eyes. "And now you feel pity for me, don't you, sweeting?"

Blaise shook her head at his savage mockery. "I could never feel pity for a man with your advantages and talents. What I feel is anger—anger to see you wasting your life this way. You have so much . . . you have so much to give. And you won't even try!"

"Devil take it—you know nothing about it!"

Blaise rose suddenly to her feet, her fists clenched as she stood over him.

Julian's forbearance fractured. Kicking the footstool out of the way, he reached up and wrapped a hand in her long black hair, twisting so that she was imprisoned in his grasp. He hated her for making him remember, for making him feel, when all he wanted was oblivion from his haunted dreams, from the devils driving him.

She looked startled by his hold, but she didn't try to free herself. Her hair felt as cool and soft as watered silk against his skin.

"Is that the reason you pursued me here, sweeting, to upbraid me for the lamentable flaws in my character?"

His savage tone was intimidating, his expression threatening. But he wasn't going to drive her away, Blaise thought defiantly. She refused to be driven away. "I came here to comfort you."

He stared at her a long moment. "Then comfort me."

He tugged her hair, pulling her off-balance, between his spread thighs. Instinctively, with a startled exclamation, Blaise clutched at Julian's shoulders for support. To her shock, she found her breasts pressed directly against his face. Her nipples tightened at the sudden contact before she managed to right herself. She drew back as far as his grip on her hair would allow, for the first time feeling an edge of fright.

His expression was hard and sensual, a promise of impending danger, as he stared up at her. "Take off your robe."

"Why?" Blaise eyed him warily. "What do you intend to do?"

"You wanted to comfort me. I'll make it easy for you. Now do as I say."

With trembling fingers, she complied, unfastening the buttons along the front of her wrapper, letting it slide over her shoulders and fall to the carpet.

"Raise the skirt of your nightdress."

"Wh-what?"

"You heard me, sweeting."

Yes, she had heard him, but she couldn't believe he wanted her to do anything so brazen; beneath her nightdress she wore nothing.

When she remained rigidly uncooperative, he took over, drawing up the soft flannel, bunching it at her waist. She was standing directly in front of him, and his action left her completely bare, open to him, entirely too vulnerable. Every nerve in her body tensed.

"Hold up your nightdress."

Hardly knowing what she was doing, Blaise obeyed, clutching at the fabric of her nightdress as if it might give her strength.

Still holding her gaze, Julian slipped his hand between her thighs and spread her legs slightly. Then, with a single finger, he touched her sex.

Her gasp was loud in the quiet room. He watched with slitted eyes as he stroked her, drawing the entire length of his finger slowly along the yielding warm folds of her flesh, fondling the aching bud of her femininity. Blaise felt as if she had been touched by a flame. The muscles of her belly and thighs clenched involuntarily in response, even as her hips strained uncontrollably toward him, seeking the pleasure he had taught her was possible. He stroked her again, this time probing deep inside her. In only a moment her hot flesh grew slick with heated nectar.

There was a dark light in his eyes that acknowledged her body's instinctive response. Releasing her hair so that both hands were free to hold her hips, he leaned forward to press his lips against her quivering belly. Blaise made a soft murmur of protest. "Julian . . ." She shook her head, her heart pounding so hard that she thought she might faint.

He ignored her plea. Cupping the back of her knee, he drew her right leg up to rest her slippered foot on his left thigh, exposing her totally to his heated, glittering gaze. Unbalanced, Blaise had to clutch his shoulder to keep from falling.

"What are you—" Her voice faltered as he trailed his wet tongue softly, intimately, along the shivering surface of her inner thigh.

"Oh!" The choked whisper was all she could manage as he kissed the dewy, throbbing center of her. Then she felt the soft slither of his tongue and her legs nearly buckled.

"No . . . no . . ." She gasped weakly. "You . . . shouldn't . . ."

"Yes, I should. I shall." The words were almost a growl. His hands slid around the soft curves of her bottom to hold her to him, gripping her while his probing kiss invaded her. The damp heat of his mouth was a scalding brand.

Blaise shuddered, throbbed. She had never imagined a man doing anything like this to her, had never imagined feeling anything like this. Her hand came up to clutch the gilded curls of his hair but otherwise she couldn't move. His tongue assaulted her with savage, sensual determination, licking, lapping, intent on driving her into a frenzy of arousal. When she whimpered, he only pulled her closer, burying his face in the vee between her legs, his hands gripping the roundness of her bottom, lifting her hard against his mouth. All she could do was endure his caresses of fire.

Her breathing grew ragged and fast. Her hips writhed, straining under the lash of his tongue, the expert attentions of his experienced mouth. A sob built inside her, catching in her throat.

Her muscles locked against the unendurable sensation, the savage heat, the explosive pressure mounting inside her. She clung to him as he pleasured her, knowing a desperate, burning craving for release . . .

A release he wouldn't let her have.

He drew back suddenly. If not for his hands at her hips she would have fallen.

Eyes blind with passion, she stared down at him, at his lips that were wet with her dew. He was freeing himself, she realized. Pushing the folds of his dressing gown aside to bare his groin. His engorged manhood stood bold and blatant, an erotic invitation.

He took her hand and placed it on his throbbing erection. "Do I need to tell you what to do?"

"No." Her reply was a rasping whisper.

With a heart-pounding rush of need, she mounted him. A sigh of painful pleasure shuddered through Blaise as she impaled herself on his rigid shaft. This was what she wanted from him, this ecstasy of being joined to him, in the flesh if not the heart.

Her head fell back; her eyes closed. Whimpering, she rotated her hips, grinding against him, using him brutally against the swollen seat of her need.

Feeling her frantic gyrations, Julian forgot his own anger, forgot everything but the feverishly aroused woman in his arms, his need to have her. He thrust upward, deeply, driving into her, filling her again and again.

He felt her shuddering climax and groaned aloud, and then went violently out of control himself, arching his back against the fiery explosion in his body, pouring into her hot, moist interior, drenching her with the hot flood of his release, his anger and guilt flowing from him like a burst dam.

The silence afterward was punctuated only by their gasping breaths.

Blaise regained awareness first, to find herself collapsed limply on Julian's chest. His hair was damp at his temple and neck where her face was pressed.

It was a long, long moment, though, before either of them moved.

She felt his jaw brush across her hair, and then his lips, as if in apology for the savagery of their lovemaking. Blaise murmured a contented sigh.

She was satisfied. The comfort she had given her husband had been more than just physical release, she was certain of it. His passion had held a hint of desperation, she had felt it. She had made Julian lose his careful control, had driven him beyond the realm of discipline and restraint and sanity, beyond remorse and guilt and self-blame, to a world where only sensation and desire reigned.

That was enough for now. She couldn't expect to achieve victory overnight, after all. Julian had worn his guilt for so long, it had become a part of him. It would take time before he became whole again, before his heart healed enough to allow anyone else to share it.

But she meant to be there when it finally happened. He needed her, whether he realized it or not. And with that she would have to be content.

For now.

Chapter 16

S he spent the remainder of the night in his bed, in his arms. Not because Julian wished her to, but because Blaise refused to be dismissed. After expending the last of his energy on explosive passion, he had been too drained to fight her. With quiet obstinacy and a minimum of fuss, she'd helped him from the study to his bedchamber, and then tucked him into bed with all the tenderness of a mother caring for her child.

Now Blaise knelt on the thick feather mattress beside him, watching Julian sleep. The day was well-advanced—after noon, she suspected—but the room was still dim with the heavy velvet window draperies drawn against the sunlight. The fire in the grate had died down to a smoldering glow after chasing away the October chill.

She had drawn back the bed curtains, and occasionally Blaise lifted her gaze from her sleeping husband to let her attention wander around the master bedchamber. It was a handsome room, boasting a masculine elegance that only great wealth could attain. Decorated in shades of ivory and gold and deep sapphire-blue, the chamber was tastefully filled with exquisite Sheraton furnishings of mahogany and satinwood, and dominated by a huge canopy bed. Velvet and chintz fabrics, expensive flocked wallpaper, and gilt-framed oil paintings completed the effect of richness and grace. In the week since her arrival, she had never been invited to her husband's apartments. The connecting door between their suites had remained locked.

251

It didn't bode well for their relationship, Blaise thought, that she'd had to scheme her way in. But now that she was here, she was determined to stay. She wasn't about to waste the small measure of progress she'd achieved last night. She had chiseled through the walls Julian erected around himself, and wouldn't allow him to rebuild them.

When she'd awakened that morning, she'd washed quickly and then donned the blue brocade dressing gown he'd worn last night, since her own wrapper was undoubtedly still on the study floor where she'd dropped it. She brushed her hair and left it to fall loose and free down her back because Julian seemed to like it that way. Afterward, she rang for a breakfast tray and ate buttered scones and drank hot chocolate by the fire. Then she made certain Julian would not be leaving his bed anytime soon, and settled down beside him to wait. She meant to be there when he awoke. And she meant for him to listen to her.

He had to have been exhausted to have slept so deeply and so long, Blaise thought with a fresh surge of compassion. His cheeks and jaw were roughened with a dark golden stubble; his curling hair was wildly disheveled, while shadows of weariness lay beneath his eyes.

Seeing those faint shadows hurt her. She would have felt the same for any suffering creature, but this man was her husband. The man she was coming to love.

She loved him.

Frowning, Blaise hugged the folds of his dressing gown closer to her body. Her growing feelings for Julian disturbed and worried her. She hadn't meant to fall in love at all. Especially not with a man who kept his heart so closely guarded.

"An Englishman, of all people," she murmured in disbelief. She buried her nose in the soft brocaded silk of his robe, breathing in the subtle masculine scent that was distinctly Julian's. What she felt for him was love, she was afraid. She had suspected it last night when she'd found him sitting so alone and vulnerable in his study, and known it for certain when he'd accused her of pitying him. It wasn't pity she felt, but love. A fragile, fledgling love that Julian seemed determined to crush before it had a chance to bloom.

Because he considered himself unworthy.

Despite his despicable behavior toward her during the past week, she was willing to forgive him. She was willing to prove to him that he deserved to be loved. She was willing to fight for his soul, even if he was not.

It might be a difficult task. Not only had he forgotten how to enjoy life, he believed he didn't deserve happiness. But it was time he got on with the business of living.

It was nearly a half hour later before Julian at last stirred awake. He was lying on his side, facing her, so that Blaise, kneeling on the bed, was in his line of vision when his eyelids fluttered open. It took a moment for his blue eyes to focus on her.

"I didn't dream you last night," he murmured, his voice scratchy with sleep.

He didn't seem disappointed to find her here, Blaise decided. Wary, perhaps, but not as if he might abruptly order her to leave.

"What . . . are you doing here?" he asked.

She smiled. "Watching you. I've never watched a naked man sleeping before."

Julian blinked, as if not comprehending.

"Do you always sleep that way, without a nightshirt?"

His brow furrowed. "Sometimes. Except in winter." Then his eyes narrowed, squinting. "Is that my dressing gown you're wearing?"

"Yes. I appropriated yours because you made me take mine off last night. You do remember last night, don't you, Julian?"

"Yes." Averting his gaze, he turned his head on the pillow, groggily surveying the room over his shoulder.

"Terral isn't here," Blaise informed him. "I took the liberty of sending him away. And I told him you would not be joining Mr. Marsh today."

"Did you? I trust you mean to tell me why you would issue orders to my servants without consulting me."

"Because you need to rest."

Julian started to raise himself up on one elbow and discovered that the braided cord tied around his wrists did not allow him enough mobility. "Good God." The silken gold cord, the kind used to secure draperies, ran from his bound wrists to the upper right bedpost. "What the devil have you done?"

"I should think it obvious," Blaise replied sweetly. "I'm ensuring that you remain in bed. It wasn't difficult to do. You were sleeping so soundly that I had to check your heart to see that it was still beating."

"Untie me, Blaise. *At once.*"

"Not until you promise to stay here and rest today, Julian. If you won't take care of yourself, I shall have to see to it myself."

He gave a vicious tug on the cord, but only succeeded in drawing the knots tighter. "Damnation, do as I say."

"Or what?" Still kneeling, she edged back on the bed a bit, keeping well out of range. "Will you ravish me as you did last night?" She regarded him with wide-eyed innocence. "As a threat, it lacks substance—I think I rather like being ravished by you. But if you intend to do it every time I anger you, then it will likely occur with great frequency. And it still won't settle anything."

"What," he said through clenched teeth, "do you want?"

"I want you to promise that you'll remain in bed today and give yourself a chance to rest. It won't be unpleasant, I promise you. I have a pot of coffee waiting for you, although it's likely cold by now. But I can ring for more, and some breakfast, as well. Or perhaps you would prefer luncheon? I can order a bath for you, too, if you like. It might do your leg a deal of good to have a long hot soak. And afterward I'll massage your wound. I found the bottle of liniment Panna gave you. Terral will doubtless be jealous that I've usurped his duties, but I think I might make better progress than he has of late."

Julian stared at her as if she had lost her wits. "And if I don't agree?"

"Well . . ." Blaise smiled apologetically. "You could always shout for help, but I imagine you would find it rather ignominious if your servants had to rescue you, a war hero, from your own wife. It won't be easy, in any case. I locked both doors, so they will have to break them down."

"Mrs. Hedges has a key."

"I propped a chair beneath each handle."

Julian let his head fall back on the pillow in an apparent gesture of capitulation. "Very well. Since you leave me no other choice, I'll remain here to rest. Now untie me."

"Not yet, if you please, my lord husband. I have other conditions. We need to come to an understanding, and I'd like to be certain you will listen. The issue, you see, is fairness."

"No, blast it, I don't see!"

His bound hands curled into fists, and Blaise suspected that if Julian were loose, he might very well have tried to throttle her. She hastened to present her case.

"My concern is our respective responsibilities in our roles as lord and lady of the manor. It seems highly unfair that you have two very different standards of behavior, one for you and one for me. I am expected to conduct myself with 'circumspection and propriety, as befits my exalted station'—those were your exact words, I believe. But you are free to behave any way you please, no matter how detrimental it might be to *your* exalted station."

Julian closed his eyes as if struggling for patience. "My wits have obviously gone begging. What the devil are you talking about?"

"If I'm required to comport myself as befits Viscountess Lynden, then I think it only fair you should be required to behave with similar regard for your position as Lord Lynden."

"Blaise, I won't tell you again . . . Untie my hands."

"Certainly, when I have your assurance that you will give me a fair hearing."

His smoldering silence lasted longer than Blaise considered comfortable. Finally, though, he heaved a sigh and held up his bound hands. "All right."

"You'll listen to what I have to say and not get angry?"

"I'll listen."

She suspected she would have to be content with that. Bending over him, Blaise deftly unknotted the cord and freed his hands. For a moment afterward, she wasn't certain if Julian would keep his word. But when he had finished rubbing his wrists, he sat up in bed and propped the pillows behind his back, regarding her grimly.

"Now, what is this all about?"

The covers had slid down his bare chest almost to his waist, and Blaise found the fascinating sight rather distracting. "Well . . . the fact is . . . I am your wife."

"I won't argue that point."

"But you certainly seem determined to forget it. You've turned me over to your staff as if I were a servant who needed training."

His silence suggested no disagreement with that argument, either.

"And I think it's time I stand up for myself," Blaise observed. "I've been meek and yielding long enough."

One golden eyebrow shot up. "You call your behavior this past week *meek and yielding*?"

"Yes. And I've been remarkably patient, considering how you've neglected your duties toward me."

"Indeed. What duties might those be?"

"Well, shopping for one."

"Shopping?"

"Yes. I want to visit the shops in town."

"You don't need my permission to do so."

"I don't really need new clothing, either. Despite your scorn for the gown I wore when I first met you, my wardrobe is quite adequate. Sir Edmund is no skinflint, and he required me to dress in a manner befitting his station, too. But it would be politic to patronize the local modistes and milliners."

"Do you need more funds, is that it?"

"No. The clothing allowance you authorized Marsh to give me is more than generous. What I need—what I want—is your escort."

"Mine? Why? Can't your abigail accompany you to the shops?"

"Yes, but that is precisely my point. Your habit of leaving me to the servants. I am a stranger here, Julian, and I need the support of my husband."

Julian's eyes shuttered with sudden understanding. "My support will likely be a disadvantage to you, sweeting. The shopkeepers will take flight when they see me coming."

"Not if they know you intend to spend a great deal of money on behalf of your new bride."

"Are you suggesting I *bribe* them to accept me?"

Blaise smiled at him bewitchingly. "No, merely persuade them to consider your point of view. I expect money will open blind eyes far more readily than protestations of innocence."

"Blaise . . ." He hesitated, trying to control his annoyance, his exasperation, his sense of helplessness. "I appreciate your concern for my welfare, but I doubt spending a fortune will make anyone believe in my innocence."

"That is only because you don't have the soul of a merchant, Julian. Trust me, it will work. You can have the shopkeepers eating out of your hand within the month."

"I'm not certain I even care to try."

"*I* care. And combating those awful rumors about you is better than sitting here doing nothing. I'm not ready to give up without a fight. I don't want to spend the rest of my life here at Lynden Park shut off from the rest of the world."

Even before she saw the anguish leap into his eyes, Blaise knew her tactics were underhanded, but she believed playing on Julian's guilt was her best chance to prod him to action.

"It would be simpler," he said finally, "to have the merchants attend you here at home."

"But then we wouldn't be seen together."

"And I suppose that is your point? For us to appear together as a loving couple?"

"Exactly. We have nothing to be ashamed of or forgiven for, and we should behave accordingly. If we act as if we're guilty, then people will assume we're guilty. But we're not, so we shouldn't."

He smiled faintly. "*We?* You are assuming a liability that has nothing to do with you."

"It has everything to do with me now. I'm your wife, Julian. I belong at your side."

He reached up to caress her cheek gently. "I had no right to involve you in this devilish mess."

"If I recall, it was precisely in order to get me *out* of a devilish mess that you married me. So I consider us even. Will you come shopping with me?"

"Yes, minx, if it will make you happy."

"It will." Blaise smiled brightly. "And I want to begin attending church on Sundays, also. You have a family pew, don't you? The vicar looked highly disapproving during his visit when I had to beg off, so I'm sure he'll welcome us."

"I suppose attending church would not be out of the question."

"And I want to start visiting your tenants with you. It is time someone took up the reins as mistress, in any case. I can do it, I think. My mother taught me some things, and I've watched Aunt Agnes often enough to know what is expected of a lady of rank. Dispensing calf's-foot jelly for the ill and christening gifts for new babies shouldn't be too difficult."

"I doubt if your playing Lady Bountiful will have much effect on my tenants. The disposition of the English yeoman is celebrated for its stubbornness."

"Americans can be just as stubborn."

"We'll see," Julian equivocated. "Those are your conditions?"

"Actually, there is one more." The blush that stained her cheeks suggested embarrassment. "I would like to have a normal marriage."

"Normal?"

Blaise had difficulty meeting his gaze. "You promised to cherish me when you wed me—how did the ceremony go? 'With my body I thee worship'? I confess I was not paying close attention just then, but I'm certain that worshipping me has been the farthest thing from your mind this past week."

For the first time in a week, the graveness left Julian's eyes, to be replaced by a hint of amusement. "You want us to establish full conjugal relations, sweeting, is that it?"

Her blush deepened. "Well, yes."

"You believed you had to tie me up in order to persuade me to make love to you?"

"Well, I did have reason to doubt you would listen to me otherwise. You've hardly spoken to me lately."

"I concede your point. Still, if a *normal* marriage is what you want, you shouldn't be here. It isn't normal for you to be in my bed in the middle of the day, minx. The proper course is for the gentleman to visit his lady's rooms."

"I didn't say it had to be *proper*. Aunt Agnes is always accusing me of being highly improper, in any case. Besides, I had to come here. If I had waited for you to come to me, I might have grown old and gray."

His thumb softly stroked her cheek. "I'm afraid you may not be getting such a bargain. I'm not quite the dashing lover I was before the war. I'm far less mobile, and I wasn't scarred then."

She raised her hand to caress his ravaged cheek. "I think your scar lends your features character."

His smile was gentle, rueful, poignant; it made her ache inside with the need to touch him. "I recall you

saying just last night that my character had been tested
and found wanting."

"Don't . . . I was angry when I said that. But I'm not
going to allow you to fall prey to self-pity again."

"No?"

"No, not even if I have to resort to more drastic measures than tying you up."

"Good God. Please, that won't be necessary. I surrender."

"Then you mean to rest today?"

"I mean to stay in bed at least."

Blaise looked at Julian questioningly. "I don't wish to
become a scolding fishwife, Julian, but—"

"How fortunate. I don't wish you to become one,
either."

"—but I will if that's what it takes to make you see
reason."

"I told you, I surrender. I agree to your demands."

"Would you like me to ring for your breakfast then?"

"No."

"Do you need me to massage your wound?"

"No."

Her expression turned to disappointment. "Would you
prefer that I call Terral to do it?"

"No, sweeting."

"Then what would you like?"

His hand moved down her bare throat, stroking softly. "I would prefer to begin work on your last condition."

"Oh." Her violet eyes widened innocently as she realized his meaning. "Can one do that in the daytime?"

"Yes, sweeting. One can, most assuredly."

"Isn't it a bit scandalous?"

His laughter, rusty from disuse, rang out for the first
time in a long while. "Since when have you ever been
concerned about causing a scandal?"

"*I* wasn't, but I thought *you* might be. You've been so
stuffy and disapproving lately, my lord, that I feared you
might object merely on principle."

Julian smiled, his slow, sensual, golden smile. "I think we can make an exception in this case. Shall I show you how it's done in the daytime?"

"Yes . . . please."

Not waiting for him to act, though, she trailed her hand down his chest, touching him, feeling the intoxicating warmth radiating from his bare flesh, the erotic tension in the muscles of his breast. Without conscious thought, she moved closer, stroking the sleek warm skin beneath her palms.

When she felt his masculine nipples tighten, her eyes widened in real surprise. "Yours do that, too? I didn't know."

"I hope there is still a great deal you don't know about lovemaking," Julian murmured dryly.

"Will you teach me?"

"It would be my pleasure, sweeting." He pushed aside the folds of the dressing gown she wore to bare her naked breasts, and his eyes darkened. "You aren't wearing your nightdress."

"I didn't want you to go to the trouble of having to remove it."

"Very considerate."

With both hands he slowly began to caress her, his thumbs stroking the aching tips of her breasts, his long fingers gently kneading and arousing. When he began to tease her taut nipples with plucking motions, Blaise sucked in a sharp breath at the feel of those clever, elegant hands, unprepared for the answering flood of warmth between her thighs. "Julian . . ."

Hearing the plea in her husky voice, he drew her unresisting against him. "With my body, I thee worship," he whispered against her lips.

Suddenly feverish, she sought his mouth, whimpering as she pressed hard against him. It was an act of instinct, of aching hunger, that brought his hands up to anchor her head as he drank from her mouth.

It was like drinking a life-sustaining elixir, a rejuvenating, invigorating balm for the spirit.

Julian drove his fingers deeper into her tresses, trying to understand the powerful force that his sweet Gypsy wielded over him. He had returned home to reclaim his soul, and Blaise was giving it back to him.

Julian groaned. He wanted her. He wanted desperately to lose himself in her passion, to let her warm the cold places inside his heart, to fill the aching hollow.

"Comfort me, Blaise . . . heal me . . ."

His voice was raw, rasping, and Blaise responded with all the passion of which she was capable. She wrapped herself around him, shutting out the cold, pouring her own warmth into him, driving away ghosts and demons and tormenting memories.

Chapter 17

Their relationship changed significantly that day, much to Blaise's profound relief and pleasure. Except for a brooding melancholy she sometimes glimpsed in Julian, he seemed to have mastered his anger and despair at the past, in favor of rebuilding his future. He made a concerted effort to carry out his duties, not only as lord of the manor, but as lover and husband as well.

She slept in his bed each night. She was there to chase away his haunted nightmares when he awoke gasping, to cradle and comfort him when he cried out another woman's name. She was there to massage his thigh, to ease the taut muscles and smooth away the throbbing ache. But although he turned to her for comfort, the physical pleasure he gave her in return surpassed her wildest imaginings. Propriety and reservation played no part in their lovemaking; sensuality and uninhibited joy reigned supreme in their marriage bed. Julian taught her about her body, and about his, and how to transform feverish desire into explosive ecstasy.

Despite her sheltered upbringing, Blaise knew the intensity and frequency of their lovemaking was unusual for married couples of their class. She confessed her surprise one night when she lay curled in her husband's arms, replete and drowsy with spent passion.

"No one ever told me . . ." she said with a languorous yawn, "how nice this part of marriage could be."

"I should hope not," replied Julian with amusement, slowly stroking her bare arm. "Young ladies aren't supposed to know about carnal matters."

"It doesn't seem fair," she murmured, and then forgot about fairness and anything else as Julian bent to nuzzle her breast again.

It was a fresh beginning, Blaise realized with gratitude. Julian seemed to have decided to make the best of a marriage that he had never wanted. She could have been content if not for the specter of the past hanging like a black cloud over her husband's head.

The difficulty of his situation was forcibly brought home to her the first afternoon that Julian escorted her shopping. Sitting beside him as he tooled his gleaming yellow curricle along the country road, Blaise spied a horse and rider approaching at a sedate pace. Even from a distance she could tell the rider was dressed as a gentleman—high shirt collar and white cravat, well-cut bottle-green coat, gleaming top boots over buckskin breeches. But only after she felt Julian stiffen beside her did she recognize Vincent Foster.

Vincent halted his horse at the same moment Julian pulled up his team. For the space of several heartbeats, the two men stared at each other, the only sound the jingle of harness. Blaise could feel the animosity radiating between them. This was, she suspected, their first meeting in four years.

Vincent's handsome mouth curled in an expression much like a sneer. "So you've returned."

"As you see," Julian said quietly. "Hello, Vincent."

"I wonder that you dare show your face. You must truly have no conscience."

Julian seemed willing to ignore the pointed insult. "I've been away too long. I decided it was time to get on with my life."

"A pity Caroline was not afforded the same opportunity. Have you warned your new bride that she has taken a murderer to her bed?"

Blaise could see Julian's gloved hands tighten into fists as he gripped the reins. She laid a gentle restraining arm on his sleeve, but repressed the urge to leap to his defense. This was one battle she didn't dare interfere with.

"You've succeeded well enough," Julian replied tightly, "in filling her ears with your version of the story. I saw no need to expound on it."

"I doubt you told her the truth."

"Vincent . . ." Julian's voice held the edge of strained patience. "No one blames me more than I blame myself, but it is long over."

"On the contrary. *I* blame you entirely. You should never have been allowed to get away with it. And if I have any say in the matter, you won't."

Julian's gaze narrowed to shards of blue ice. "It matters not to me if you poison the good opinion of every person in the country, but I give you fair warning: in future, keep away from my wife."

He snapped the reins then, giving the horses the office to start, and drove away rapidly, leaving a cloud of dust behind. Out of loyalty to Julian, Blaise refused to look back to confirm that Vincent Foster was watching, but she fancied she could feel his dark brooding eyes boring holes in her back.

Immediately she launched into a bright but meaningless discussion detailing the purchases she intended to make, but her chatter did little to divert Julian's attention. He remained preoccupied and uncommunicative for the rest of the day. It was all she could do that evening to coax him into receiving her in his bed. Yet the incident with Vincent only made her more determined to champion Julian's cause.

At least her strategy for conquering the prejudices of the neighboring community proceeded apace. Julian escorted her shopping several times during the following week.

A pleasant country market town, Huntingdon was situated on the banks of the River Great Ouse. Surrounded by leisurely lanes, it was filled with brick-and-timber houses and handsome Tudor buildings rich in history. According to Julian, the coffin bearing Mary, Queen of

Scots, had rested in St. George's Church on its journey to Westminster Abbey. Huntingdon was also the birthplace and childhood home of one of the most powerful men in British history, Oliver Cromwell, while the neighboring village of Godmanchester had begun its days as a major Roman crossroads.

They entered nearly every shop in Huntingdon, spending lavishly and making their presence felt. No establishment was too small or too unimportant for Lady Lynden's patronage. Besides mercers and modistes and milliners, they visited the market square to inspect the vegetable and flower stalls, as well as the bakeries and butcher shops to discuss possible deliveries to Lynden Park. And despite the initial shocked stares and worried glances Julian received, Blaise could see her plan beginning to bear fruit.

She began each assault by requesting a personal introduction to the proprietor, then lavishing praise on the wares offered, while at the same time giving the impression of being highly selective. And then she would hesitate, pretending indecision. After soliciting the shopkeeper's opinion, Blaise would smooth Julian's sleeve and gaze up at him adoringly and say something like, "Which should I choose, my darling? The powder-blue, or the rose?"

With a gleam of repressed amusement in his eyes, Julian obediently returned the reply she had instructed him to give. "Why, both, my love. You must certainly have both."

"Oh, darling you are so very good to me. I don't deserve so kind and generous a husband."

Thus she added extensively to her wardrobe—gloves and slippers, fans and reticules, embroidered silk stockings and knots of ribbon, fringed shawls and gauze scarves and countless bonnets—and laid in stores at Lynden Park that would take six months to deplete. With very few exceptions, her warmth and liveliness and genuine interest won over the proprietors, while her husband received the credit for being lavish with his purse. His tragic history, at least for the moment, was forgotten.

Julian, after watching his young wife in action several times, quit shaking his head at her shameless tactics and merely laughed at himself for doubting her abilities. "Perhaps you should take to the London stage after all, minx," he said one afternoon. "Your talents are obviously wasted here in the country."

Blaise smiled archly. "I told you it would work. Although I do hope you weren't planning to take your seat in the House of Lords anytime soon. I imagine your peers wouldn't be impressed to see the golden Lord Lynden in a butcher shop, surrounded by sausages and legs of mutton."

She took the battle to his tenants later that same week. On Thursday morning when Julian's attention was occupied with London business, she coerced his estate steward to escort her around the tenant farms—which was a violation of Julian's wishes, if not his direct orders. He had refused to take her himself, saying that he didn't wish her to be exposed to further hostility.

By now, however, he should have known better than to trust Blaise to conform to his notions of compliance or obedience, or to expect her to retreat when confronted with adversity. Yet this time she wasn't flouting his authority merely to be contrary or to gain his attention or even to prove a point. This time she was doing it for his own good. She wasn't about to surrender yet. And after all, she rationalized, Julian hadn't *forbidden* her to call on his tenants.

With Mr. Marsh driving her in the gig, Blaise visited the cluster of charming red-brick and yellow-stone cottages some half mile from the manor house where the majority of his tenants lived, calling at each dwelling to meet the occupants.

Even with the respected and much-liked Mr. Marsh to make the introductions, though, Blaise received the same cold treatment to which her husband had been subjected—wary and sullen silence. She inquired after families, remembering names exactly, down to the most recent great-grandchild, but her most charming manner had little effect. Nor did the little gifts of foodstuffs from the kitchens at Lynden Park which Mrs. Hedges had helped her pack, or any of the countless geegaws she'd purchased in the shops of Huntingdon. She'd brought wooden soldiers and rag dolls for the children, hair ribbons and handkerchiefs and kitchen utensils for their mothers, and for the men, pipes or penknives. But while received politely, her bribes didn't induce these sturdy English farm people to become any more talkative or accepting. Disheartened, Blaise had to admit Julian might have been right: this was a battle she might not win.

She had taken her leave from the last cottage and was about to accept Marsh's assistance into the gig when she overheard a muttered remark from behind her. She couldn't make it out clearly, but it sounded something like " 'ide behind 'is lady's skirts."

Turning abruptly on her heel, Blaise found herself facing a man with only one leg, supported by a crutch. He was youngish, perhaps a half-dozen years older than she, and wore what looked like a permanent scowl on his ruddy face. She hadn't met him during her calls, although she had been told of him.

She pinned him with a flashing violet gaze. "I should like an explanation of your comment, if you please."

The young man lowered his eyes, but refused to answer directly. " 'Twas nothing, m'lady."

"Lord Lynden is *not* hiding behind my skirts," Blaise declared. "In fact, he didn't want me to come here today, precisely because he wished to shield me from the kind of hostile reception he knew I would receive."

His expression remained one of belligerence and anger.

"Your name is John Weeks, is it not?" When he regarded her warily, she added, "I met your wife and son a moment ago. Why do you think his lordship is hiding behind my skirts?" When still he didn't reply, her mouth tightened. "Perhaps it is time for a bit of plain speaking. Lynden warned me not to expect a warm welcome—he said it has nothing to do with me, but with what happened four years ago. You blame my husband for the first Lady Lynden's death, is that it?"

Suddenly looking uncomfortable, Weeks lowered his eyes. "They say 'e killed 'er."

"*Who* says?"

"Why, everybody."

"And you believe everything you hear?" Blaise placed her hands on her hips. "I don't deal in scurrilous rumors and innuendo. And I don't believe for one moment that he killed her."

The silence was damning.

"Come now, do I look like a fool? Do you really believe I would be idiotic enough to marry a murderer?"

By this time a small crowd had gathered near—a woman holding a baby, another clutching the hand of a toddler, several more who were simply listening intently, a youth carrying a pitchfork, an elderly man who was bent and wizened.

"Lynden did *not* kill his wife," Blaise repeated emphatically. "Those rumors of her murder are totally unfounded. Lady Lynden's death was a tragic accident."

"Begging pardon, m'lady," Weeks muttered, "but you wasn't 'ere."

"And I suppose you were? You saw with your own eyes what happened to her?"

Weeks lowered his gaze again.

"They had an argument," Blaise went on. "A violent one, to be sure—but I defy you to find a single person who has never lost his temper with his spouse." She glanced at the crowd, aware that she had their rapt attention. "And anyone could fall off a horse in the middle of a storm. I've done it myself a few times, in fact."

Someone nodded. Sensing her argument was beginning to have an effect, she glanced over her shoulder at Julian's steward, who was standing frozen by the gig, looking both bewildered and aghast. "Mr.

Marsh, has anyone ever produced a shred of evidence to indicate that Lord Lynden killed his wife?"

"N-no, my lady."

"Have you ever known his lordship to behave in any manner that would suggest a propensity for violence?"

"No, my lady, I have not."

She turned back to John Weeks. "Do you consider Mr. Marsh a poor judge of character?"

"No, but 'e's beholden to 'is lordship for 'is livelihood."

"So he is, but I doubt he would have remained here all these years if he believed Lord Lynden guilty of murder."

"Then why did 'is lordship leave so sudden-like? And stay away for so long if 'e 'ad nothing to 'ide?"

"I expect because he was devastated by her ladyship's death. He holds himself to blame—not because he caused the tragedy directly, but because he felt he should somehow have prevented it."

" 'E was gone for a long time," Weeks observed, still scowling.

"It's true Lord Lynden has neglected you far too long, but he regrets it and means to make it up to you, if he can. And it's not as if he's been engaged in frivolous pursuits. For the past four years he has been off fighting a war, risking his life for his country."

The expression on Weeks's face suddenly turned bitter. "I risked my life in the war, too," he muttered. "I fought for King and country as a soldier, and look where it got me. I'm a cripple."

Blaise glanced down at his leg that had been cut off above the knee, and her expression softened a degree. "Lynden was luckier than you. He nearly lost his leg in the battle of Vitoria, but he managed to keep it. He still suffers pain and walks with a limp, but at least he can walk."

"I can't do even that. I got no livelihood any longer. I'm not fit for work. I can't get behind a plow or chase after a sow."

"Perhaps you should speak to his lordship about it. I'm sure he would be sympathetic. He understands better than anyone the plight of injured soldiers."

"I ain't asking for charity. It's honest work I want."

"Well, I didn't think you meant *dishonest*," Blaise replied with a smile so sudden and disarming that it made Weeks blink. "What kind of work were you engaged in before?"

"Farming is what I know."

"Can you wield a hammer?"

"Aye, m'lady."

"Can you operate a bellows?"

"Mayhap I could."

"Then instead of guiding a plow, you could learn to build one. Or if smithing isn't to your fancy, I'm certain Lynden can find you gainful employment in a field that will suit your limitations. If, that is, you aren't too proud to learn a new trade?"

His shoulders came back stiffly. "I ain't too proud, m'lady. I'd be right grateful."

"Well then, I suggest you present yourself to my husband tomorrow morning so you may discuss what is to be done."

For the first time since the conversation had begun, the scowl left John Weeks's face. His expression was still wary, but he tugged his forelock respectfully. "Thank you, your ladyship."

"You may save your thanks for his lordship." Blaise glanced at his leg. "Has your amputation healed fully?"

"No, m'lady. It still pains me something fierce."

"Lord Lynden has an excellent liniment that heals wounds and softens taut muscles. I expect he would be happy to share it with you to help ease your suffering."

"That would be kind of 'im, m'lady."

"I would only ask the same of you, that you show him the least measure of kindness in return. He's suffered enough during the past four years. And then to come home to this kind of reception—well, I would be ashamed to treat anyone so shabbily."

She could see by Weeks's disconcerted expression that her point had been taken.

"I'm right sorry, m'lady," he mumbled.

"I don't care about myself," Blaise said truthfully. "I'm half American, so I don't expect you to accept me easily, especially since our countries are at war. Indeed, your opinion of Americans is probably no better than mine of the English—you think we're all unmannered savages, and I think you're all cold and stuffy. But I've always believed the English were fair-minded. It doesn't seem at all fair-minded, though, to condemn Lynden without giving him the least chance to defend himself or to tell his side of the story."

"Mayhap we've been too quick to judge," John Weeks said grudgingly.

"Perhaps you have. But I will forgive you if you will try to make it up to him."

"Aye, m'lady, that we will."

Julian heard from Marsh later that same afternoon about how his wife had charmed, bullied, and shamed his tenants into accepting her. He shook his head in admiration then, and again when John Weeks offered what seemed to be a sincere apology to him and to her ladyship. And yet again when he rode out the next morning over his farms. He could scarcely believe the drastic change in his reception. Rather than eye him with sullen wariness, his tenants greeted him with sympathetic nods and bashful smiles.

It was when they attended church on Sunday, however, that the battle was truly joined. The small victories Blaise had achieved to date had not totally satisfied her. Their neighbors had continued to shun them; not a single member of the gentry had paid a call at Lynden Park. Their pointed snubs didn't particularly distress Blaise since she was accustomed to being scorned for her outrageous conduct, but she was incensed for Julian's sake.

Her ire only increased on Sunday. The small stone church was nearly full when she and Julian entered, but the silence seemed deafening. As they walked up the narrow aisle to take their place in the Lynden family pew, Blaise could feel every eye on them.

The vicar gave a sermon about forgiveness and brotherly love, but after the service, no one except he and his wife made the least effort to approach them or speak to them. Blaise recognized Vincent Foster, who fixed Julian with a dark, brooding stare. The cool, elegant, chestnut-haired lady on his arm was possibly his sister, Rachel, Blaise guessed, a fact that was confirmed by Julian. Unlike her brother, though, Rachel Foster looked straight through them, as if their presence were beneath her notice.

Blaise's response to the woman was immediate and unusual: intense dislike, laced with jealousy and relief. If, as Mrs. Hedges suspected, Miss Rachel Foster had once wished to marry Julian, then Blaise decided he'd had a fortunate escape.

Julian, however, did not seem as concerned about himself as for her.

"I regret that you are being made to suffer for my reputation," he murmured soberly as he handed her into the carriage.

Blaise's chin came up in defiance. "You have nothing to apologize for, Julian, least of all the deplorable manners of those rude people. They have no right to treat you that way. But they won't continue in that vein, not if I have anything to say about it!"

Faintly amused to hear his madcap of a wife complaining about someone else's deplorable behavior, Julian settled back among the cushions and regarded her quizzically. He'd frequently underestimated Blaise's talent for getting her own way before this, and he didn't mean to be caught flat-footed again. "And just how will you contrive to change them, minx?"

"I don't know yet, but I'll think of something." Her slender jaw hardened with a determination Julian was beginning to recognize. "This means war!"

Chapter 18

D espite her declaration of war and her determination, Blaise did not decide on a specific plan of
action until two mornings later as she lay in Julian's
bed, thinking. She sat up abruptly, clutching the sheet
to her naked breasts. "A ball! We can hold a ball at
Lynden Park."

Julian, replete after an hour of passion with his ener-
getic and eager young wife, stretched lazily and reached
out to run a languid finger down her spine. "A ball?"

Thinking furiously, Blaise wrapped her arms around
her drawn-up knees. "This situation calls for bold measures, Julian. We shall send out invitations for a ball and
see who dares refuse."

He frowned as he tried to switch his focus from lovemaking to war tactics. "Have you considered the possibility that no one will attend a ball held here?"

"They'll attend."

"And just how do you propose to accomplish that,
sweeting? Tie our guests hand and foot and drag them
here bodily?"

"Nothing so drastic . . . not yet, at any rate. But if I'm
right, we won't have to. People admire anyone audacious
enough to thumb his nose at society. And that's precisely
what we would be doing by holding a ball and inviting
the entire neighborhood. Besides, the old cats will come,
if only because they are curious to find out what kind of
woman would dare marry an alleged murderer."

Feeling his fingers stiffen against her back, Blaise
glanced over her shoulder to see the bitter smile that

twisted his lips. She sent him a bright smile in return. "Don't you see, Julian? Our neighbors have snubbed us because we've allowed it. What we must do is make it impossible for them to ignore us. If they just could see you, speak to you, they would see you are exactly who you've always been and have not turned into some terrible villain."

What he could see was the flush of excitement on Blaise's face, an excitement he couldn't bring himself to quash, even if he thought her idea deplorable and destined to fail. "I think you will need a more compelling reason than mere audacity or my vindication if you hope to lure anyone here," Julian said finally.

"Very well, then . . . What if we held a *charity* ball? What could be more compelling than charity? We can create a fund to benefit soldiers wounded in the war— to help them learn new skills so they may earn an honest living, or if they're severely incapacitated, to provide support for their families. Just like you did for John Weeks. You made it possible for him to use his talent for woodcarving by apprenticing him to a cabinetmaker. If you did it for Weeks, you could do it for others. There must be scores of other wounded men who are just as deserving, who have suffered just as dreadfully. Their sacrifice has gone ignored by the very class of people whose way of life they were protecting—*your* sacrifice has gone ignored, as well. But it's time the English nobility faced up to their selfishness."

Julian remained silently thoughtful.

Taking heart when he didn't refuse her outright, Blaise rested her chin on her knees and worried her lower lip. "I think I could bring it off. I do have *some* experience as a hostess. I've presided at balls occasionally for my stepfather. It's one of the few things Sir Edmund allowed me to do, one of my few talents he appreciated. And after years of watching him, I've learned a thing or two about diplomacy. But it might also be wise to hedge our bets and make certain we have at least a few guests. Perhaps we should invite some of your London friends to stay

with us beforehand. We could arrange a house party. And
ask your military friends—you do have some cavalry
friends, don't you?"

"One or two," Julian murmured dryly.

"Well ask then, that will be just the thing. It will give me a
chance to meet your friends, and you will have someone
to commiserate with if my plan doesn't work as well as I
hope. And the shopkeepers will be pleased. We can order
all our foodstuffs from them, and I can commission a
new ball dress—" She broke off as she recognized the
hesitation on his face. "Please, darling Julian . . . don't
be a faintheart."

She had half turned to face him, letting the sheet
droop slightly—whether by accident or by design, he
couldn't tell. He wouldn't put it past his scheming minx
to use her physical charms to get her way, but he wasn't
sure he cared just now that she might be manipulating
him shamelessly. He only knew that the sight of her
bare swelling breasts, so pale and enticing, stirred his
loins.

He smiled then, a rueful admission of surrender as he
stroked her naked back. "I think you could manage to
persuade me."

At the sensual touch of his fingers on her skin, Blaise
momentarily forgot what point she had been trying to
win. Her gaze was arrested by the sight of Julian reclin-
ing there against the pillows . . . the gilded, softly curling
hair; the aristocratic, fine-boned features of his face;
the graceful, lean-muscled body. He was so virile, so
beautiful, so blatantly male. His blue eyes had darkened
slumbrously in a way she was beginning to recognize. He
wanted her, and the knowledge turned her pulse wild and
erratic.

Then he reached up to caress her bare breast, slowly
rolling the rigid nipple between his long fingers. With
a sighing murmur, Blaise arched against his hand, an
instinctive movement that was half feminine, half feline.
She made not the slightest protest when Julian drew her
down to him.

He pulled her close, until her naked breasts teased his naked chest, until her pliant lips molded to his. At the same time, his hand slipped beneath the sheet, gliding between her thighs. His intimate, dexterous fingers began moving against the slick threshold of her femininity . . . just as a quiet knock sounded on the door.

The interruption shattered the heated mood. Blaise stiffened, while Julian muttered a low oath of annoyance.

Ceasing his caresses, he raised his head and sent a dark look at the bedchamber door. "Yes, what is it?"

"Forgive me, my lord," his butler's voice solemnly intoned from without, "but there is a *person* who insists upon seeing her ladyship. He says you gave him permission to camp in your fields. I believe, my lord, that he is a . . . *Gypsy*."

Hedges pronounced the word as if it were contaminated, while Blaise scrambled to her knees with an exclamation of delight. "Miklos! They've arrived!"

Julian groaned silently. He had hoped for a few more weeks of calm before having to deal with the corrupting influence his bride's Gypsy friends had over her. But it was too late now to change matters; Blaise had already called out to Hedges, telling him to inform Miklos she would be down in an instant. Then she turned to him, her face bright, her amethyst eyes shining like jewels.

"Oh, famous! Julian, this is the very answer. Miklos's tribe can provide the entertainment for the ball. We'll have a Gypsy theme, with dancing and music and even fortune-telling—oh, it will be splendid! If our neighbors wish to be treated to a spectacle, we will give them one!"

She jumped up from the bed and scooped up her wrapper from the tangle of clothing on the floor, yet didn't take the time to don it. "I have to dress at once and persuade Miklos to let me hire his tribe."

She bent down to plant an excited kiss on her husband's temple, but when she started to turn, Julian caught her wrist to forestall her. "Shouldn't you give a bit more thought to this enterprise, minx, before you go rushing ahead?"

"What is there to think about? It won't deplete your purse, if that's what worries you. The Rom work cheaply—"

"I rather had in mind the impact on our neighbors."

"Oh, pooh, don't be a stuffed shirt. It will work, Julian, trust me. All *gorgios* are curious about Gypsies, and they are fascinated by fortune-tellers. I have to ask Panna if she will do it . . ." Blaise was still talking to herself as she hurried across the room and disappeared behind the door to her suite.

Feeling as if he had just been swept aside by a whirlwind, Julian lay back with his hands clasped behind his head. His exasperating, bewitching young wife had left him aroused and aching . . . and yet the pleasure he'd received watching her excitement had almost made up for it. Her eyes shining, her expression alive with hope and vibrancy, her lovely body naked to his gaze, Blaise had looked utterly enchanting. He'd wanted nothing more than to haul her down into his arms and bury himself deep inside her—a desire which was overtaking him more and more frequently of late. His need for her had become a physical craving, almost an addiction.

Julian stared up at the canopy overhead, wondering how Blaise had managed so quickly to gain such a powerful hold on him. Weeks. Had it been only a matter of weeks since he'd been compelled to wed her? It seemed too short a period for anyone to have affected his life so profoundly.

The carnal pleasure she gave him did not fully explain the strength of his attraction, either—although that did indeed provide a measure of her appeal. Blaise might have come to his bed innocent and untutored, but she was as passionate and hot-blooded as any man could wish, and more satisfying than any lover he'd ever known. Her hungry, uninhibited response to his lovemaking, so surprising in a wife, was all that he could have wished.

Yet it was her unfettered zest for living that drew him so inexorably to her. Her warmth, her spirit, her fire. He felt as if he were slowly coming back to life in her presence. As if the frozen numbness that had debilitated his senses and left him dead inside after Caroline's passing was slowly thawing. He couldn't bring himself to regret wedding Blaise, despite having to endure her outrageous, unconventional, unpredictable, and occasionally infuriating conduct.

Remembering her latest scheme, Julian squeezed his eyes shut. The thought of holding a ball at Lynden Park, complete with heathen entertainment and fortune-telling for his neighbors to gawk at, filled him with acute dismay. Nor did he at all like the idea of his viscountess consorting with Gypsies.

But it didn't appear as if he had much choice. His past attempts at controlling Blaise's behavior had usually misfired. And he was coming to realize that to forbid her anything would only ensure that she flouted his authority and did precisely the opposite of what he wished.

Perhaps he would be wise, Julian decided, to refrain from voicing his objections about a ball. And at least undertaking such a vast project would give Blaise something upon which to focus her tremendous energies. And—he hoped—something to keep her out of mischief.

Blaise's reunion with her friend Miklos was a joyful occasion. Hedges, who had hovered protectively within view of the entrance hall to ensure the caller didn't make off with the Lynden silver or anything else of value, looked appropriately shocked and disapproving to see her ladyship race down the stairs directly into the embrace of the swarthy Gypsy. But Blaise remained oblivious to the butler's disapprobation. Laughing in delight, she hugged Miklos and asked a dozen questions at once as she pulled him into the nearest parlor.

Miklos answered as best he could while gaping at the exquisite furnishings. "Ye've done well for yourself, Rauniyog. I kenned the *gorgio rye* was plump in the pocket, but not *this* plump."

Blaise dimpled. "I could have done worse. Lynden is quite generous with his purse. You should see all the purchases he's made for me during the past weeks."

After discovering that her Gypsy friends were well, Blaise rang for refreshments. While they ate buttered scones and drank tea, Miklos told her of his tribe's travels during the past weeks, and the fair where he'd made several profitable deals horse trading. He also said he thought his prize mare might be breeding a colt by Baron Kilgore's stallion, but it was still too soon to tell.

When they had finished eating, Blaise ordered her horse saddled so that she could visit the Gypsy camp. Just then her husband, resplendent in dove-gray pantaloons and claret frock coat, put in a brief appearance to greet Miklos. Julian declined to accompany them, however, pleading another engagement. As he bent and fondly kissed the top of Blaise's head, he admonished her to take a groom.

"Is that really necessary—to waste a servant's time?" she objected. "Miklos can see me home."

"Aye, that I will, m'lord," the Gypsy agreed.

Julian smiled briefly. "I am obliged for your kindness, Mr. Smith, but I must consider appearances. It won't benefit Lady Lynden's reputation to be seen alone with a Romany gentleman, no matter how close the friendship."

"Aye, that's the way of the world," Miklos replied without rancor.

"Well then, I shall leave you to your own amusements. Be home in time for supper, sweeting. Afterward we can resume the exercise that was interrupted a short while ago," he added with a wicked gleam in his eye, before taking his leave.

Blaise couldn't repress a blush at his veiled reference to their lovemaking. "Julian is very protective of me," she explained to Miklos when her husband was gone.

Miklos nodded sagely. "As well 'e should be. And you should learn to obey 'im now that you're a married lady, Rauniyog."

Although wrinkling her nose at that advice, Blaise did take a groom as instructed. Miklos's tribe had set up camp only a short ride from the manor house, in a choice bit of pasture, beside a sweetly flowing brook. Blaise counted some two dozen more wagons than she remembered.

"We 'ooked up with another tribe," Miklos explained. "It seemed right selfish to accept 'is lordship's generous 'ospitality without sharing our good fortune with other Rom."

Inviting another tribe to camp on Lynden property was an abuse of Julian's kindness, but Blaise didn't protest Miklos's shameless exploitation, knowing it was an ingrained habit of Gypsies to take full advantage of *gorgios*.

Panna greeted Blaise like a long-lost daughter, embracing her and then drawing back to search her face. "Are ye 'appy in yer marriage, Rauniyog?"

Blaise smiled, as if hugging a secret to herself. "It isn't as terrible as I thought it might be."

Panna merely cackled and looked smug.

An hour later, after Blaise had greeted all the members of Miklos's band and met the leaders of the other visiting tribe, she was able to speak to Panna and Miklos alone and enlist their help with her ball.

She didn't mention her reason for holding it, or that Julian was suspected by some of murdering his first wife. Panna already knew of the shadows surrounding his past, in any case, and Blaise wasn't certain how Miklos would take the news. Gypsy men were extremely protective of their women, and he might not care for the notion that she had wed an alleged murderer, no matter how false the charges.

Knowing the Gypsies' love of bargaining, Blaise began the discussion by explaining her need and making an outrageously low first offer. After some arguing, she managed to negotiate a reasonable price, hiring Miklos's tribe to entertain her guests with music and dancing and fortune-telling at a ball to be held week after next. Even though it would mean rushing, Blaise had taken Panna's advice and settled on the Saturday before All

Hallow's Eve, so as not to compete with any Halloween festivities.

They had just concluded the spirited deal when she spied a small brown animal scampering at the side of a Romany gentleman two wagons away.

"A monkey!" Blaise exclaimed in delight. "I haven't seen one of those since Philadelphia."

" 'E dances and does tricks," Miklos informed her.

A thoughtful gleam entered Blaise's eyes. "Please, Miklos, will you introduce me to his owner? I think having a performing monkey at my ball would be just the thing."

She told Julian about her success that afternoon, only mentioning hiring the monkey as an afterthought. Julian bit his tongue and refrained from comment. When Blaise deliberated about whom to invite to the ball, he even went so far as to help compile the guest list, although he did manage to convince her not to write his friends in London requesting them to attend a house party. If her plan turned out to be disaster, he preferred to have as few witnesses as possible.

Only when she proposed inviting Vincent Foster and his sister, Rachel, did Julian put his foot down. "No, absolutely not, minx! I won't have him in my house."

Blaise argued that it was only wise to extend the olive branch. The Fosters had a good deal of influence in the neighborhood, and if it could be seen Julian had patched up their differences, his acceptance would be assured. Blaise eventually won the argument, simply by wearing down her husband's resistance with reasoned, unrelenting persuasion.

Yet during the fortnight that followed, Julian watched her progress with growing trepidation. Blaise threw herself heart and soul into the elaborate preparations, and he worried that she was destined for disappointment. At least, though, between planning for the upcoming ball and her daily visits to the Gypsy camp, she remained too busy to undertake any new schemes.

At the end of the week, Julian received a letter from Blaise's stepfather in Vienna. Sir Edmund extended congratulations on their marriage that were couched in terms of condolence for having been saddled with his stepdaughter, and offered advice on managing her. The tone of the letter annoyed Julian. Blaise wasn't *quite* as bad as Sir Edmund claimed. And the gentleman's recommendation for keeping her on a tight rein, Julian considered nonsense. He had come to know his unconventional wife and her stubborn determination well enough during the past month to realize such tactics would only encourage Blaise to rebel. The only way she would curb her excesses and obey him, Julian suspected, was if she did so willingly.

Her abigail, Sarah Garvey, confirmed as much. Julian had requested an interview with Miss Garvey shortly after Miklos's arrival in the neighborhood.

Miss Garvey defended her charge with affection and calm good sense. "You see, my lord, Blaise had a delightful childhood growing up in Philadelphia. She was spoiled by an adoring father, and his death when she was ten devastated her. Then her mother remarried and Blaise spent her formative years living in countless foreign countries. Because of Sir Edmund's career, they moved frequently and she had little opportunity to make friends her own age. And then her dear mother departed, too. Not only was Blaise motherless, but she had no real home, and she was left with only Sir Edmund and me to guide her. With her American upbringing and her rootless existence, it is scarcely a wonder she turned out a bit wild."

"I'm certain you did your best," Julian murmured sympathetically.

"I did indeed. But she has been in my charge for only three years, and I have no formal control over her, merely the power of influence."

"I do not hold you to blame for my wife's conduct, Miss Garvey."

"No, I did not think you did. But I wished you to understand why Blaise sometimes acts a veritable hoyden. It is due both to her nature and to her rearing."

"I understand."

"She has very little regard for propriety, I fear."

Julian smiled wryly. "An understatement, surely. It would surprise me to learn that Blaise has ever willingly conformed to a rule of propriety in her life."

"She possesses irrepressibly high spirits, true, and at times she is a bit headstrong and willful. But there is not an ounce of real wickedness in her. I implore you not to be too severe with her."

"I think I've shown remarkable restraint," he replied in a wry undervoice. "Even so, it would behoove me to learn how best to deal with her, unless I wish to spend the rest of my life being driven to distraction. Perhaps you could advise me?"

"Yes, indeed. If I might be candid, my lord?"

"I wish you would."

"Sir Edmund did not deal at all well with her. I believe Blaise undertook many of her escapades merely to gain his attention, but he responded by ignoring her and keeping her at arm's length. What she needs, more than discipline or chastisement, is affection and understanding."

Julian steepled his fingers as he reflected on the abigail's advice. In the past he had thought of Blaise only in terms of *his* needs. Not once since compelling her to wed him had he considered what she might need from him. He would have to think on it.

"I promise you," he told Miss Garvey, "I will endeavor not to make the same mistakes with Blaise that Sir Edmund did. Although I cannot guarantee any more success than he had."

"That you will try is all anyone can ask, my lord. Blaise is young still, and she has had no one to cherish, or to cherish her."

Her choice of words left Julian strangely disturbed. When the abigail had gone, he remained in his chair, pondering her advice.

Panna had said much the same thing on his wedding night, after Blaise had fled from him: to win her obedience he must first earn her loyalty and love.

Love. It was true, Julian realized. Blaise would be far more malleable if she were in love with him. And very likely he could manage it. He could make his young wife lose her heart to him if he applied himself. Most females found him hard to resist when he bothered to exercise his famous charm.

But the starker truth was, he didn't *want* Blaise to love him. Indeed, love had been the primary source of dissension in his first marriage. Caroline had fancied herself in love with him—and demanded what he couldn't give in return. His heart. He hadn't returned her love, and she'd bitterly resented him for it, enough to turn to another man. He wouldn't go through that horror again.

Julian shook his head. He didn't want Blaise's love. He wanted her respect and obedience, merely that. And he had no intention of loving her in return. Theirs was a marriage of convenience, nothing more. The best he could give her was understanding, and perhaps the attention she craved.

Absently he stroked his facial scar with his fingertips as he decided on the course he should take. He would steer a middle ground, allowing Blaise enough free rein to give her high spirits latitude for expression, but not so free that she caused a scandal. He would not neglect her, though. He wouldn't leave her alone and lonely the way he had Caroline.

He would give Blaise attention and understanding, but he wouldn't allow her to love him.

Chapter 19

Blaise received very few replies to her invitations, despite the ball's billing as a charity function to benefit wounded war veterans. She knew the community was discussing the event, for the vicar told her so, but being the heated topic of discussion on everyone's lips did not guarantee endorsement, nor did even a noble purpose ensure participation.

As the day loomed closer, Blaise began to worry that perhaps she had miscalculated. Even Baron Kilgore, who had been instrumental in bringing about her marriage to Julian, sent his regrets, explaining that he was promised to friends in London. She had counted greatly on Lord Kilgore's support, knowing her husband needed every possible ally.

Julian faced the upcoming event with stoicism, prepared for the worst. While his young wife might possess the determination and tactical brilliance of a female Napoleon Bonaparte, not even she could work miracles. Only the vicar had faith in such things. Reverend Nethersby predicted the community would relent and attend en masse.

The day of the ball dawned cold and clear. Blaise woke with nervous dread curling in the pit of her stomach and spent the remainder of the day seeing to last-minute details. By five o'clock there was nothing more for her to do. She went upstairs to bathe and dress for the evening, hoping she wasn't headed for disaster. She wanted Julian to be proud of her organizational abilities, but she wanted more desperately for him to be accepted once more by his peers.

Her abigail arranged her hair in an elaborate coiffure and helped her don her ballgown. When Garvey had gone, though, Blaise sat frozen at her dressing table. What would happen if she failed? Would Julian come to hate her? Would he abandon any effort to bury the past and build on the future, a future with her?

She gave a start at the knock that sounded at her dressing room door. Bidding entrance, she turned slightly in her seat to see her husband enter, using his cane with one hand and carrying a long slim box in the other.

Julian took two steps into the room and came to a halt, letting out a breath of relief and appreciation. He had been half afraid Blaise might attend her ball dressed as a Gypsy, merely out of defiance. But as she rose and turned to face him, he could see that her high-waisted gown was exquisite, entirely appropriate for a lady of fortune and rank. The ivory lace tunic fastened at the bodice and fell gracefully over a lilac satin slip, the delicate hues pro- viding a superb contrast to her raven hair and violet eyes. The gown boasted short full sleeves and a rounded neckline cut low to emphasize her breasts and show off her milk-white skin to advantage. Julian's eyes darkened at the sight.

"Will I do?" Blaise asked worriedly.

His smile, slow and sensuous and blatantly admiring, gave her all the answer she needed. "You are devastating."

His murmured reply added the extra measure of praise she desperately needed to bolster her confidence.

He held out the slim velvet-covered box. "The Lynden jewels. They are yours now. Your abigail suggested these might go well with your gown, but there are others in the safe, if you don't care for them."

Blaise accepted the box and opened it eagerly. "Oh!" The soft exclamation of reverence escaped her lips at the sight of the stunning necklace of glowing amethysts and the pair of matching earrings resting on a bed of velvet. "They're *beautiful*."

"Allow me, sweeting."

Leaning his cane against the dressing table, he lifted the necklace from its case, and when Blaise gave him her back, fastened it around her bare throat. His fingers lingered caressingly on her naked shoulders as he bent and kissed the sensitive skin at her nape.

Trembling at his touch, Blaise attached the earrings to her ears and stared at herself in the cheval glass. The effect was regal, enchanting, but it was Julian's gesture that gratified her more deeply. By giving her the Lynden jewels, he had publicly claimed her as his viscountess. She was truly his wife. She belonged to him.

"You will be the envy of every woman there," Julian said softly.

She met his gaze in the mirror. She might be envied tonight, but it wouldn't be due to her appearance. Rather, it would be because she could claim this beautiful man for her husband. His softly curling hair gleamed like burnished gold in the lamplight, while his eyes shone like sapphires. He was dressed in shades of gray and silver. In his form-fitting, charcoal-gray coat, pale gray satin waistcoat embroidered with silver thread, matching light gray satin knee breeches, white silk stockings, and black patent pumps with silver buckles, he presented an extraordinary figure of masculine virility and grace— elegant and overwhelmingly male.

"You will be the one to set feminine hearts aflutter," Blaise replied.

His mouth twisted wryly. "I'm more likely to give them heart shock when they view my face for the first time."

Sensing his vulnerability, she turned and reached up to touch the scar on his cheek, gently tracing the savaged flesh. "I've grown quite attached to it. It gives you an element of fascination. It's true," Blaise said when his eyebrow rose skeptically. "Trust me, Julian, not a woman who sees your scar will be able to resist the urge to comfort you."

"Well, I suppose we will soon find out." Retrieving

his cane, he offered her his arm. "Shall we go down, my lady?"

Blaise took a deep breath and accepted his escort, her heart suddenly in her throat now that the moment was at hand.

The cacophony of the orchestra tuning up met their ears as they descended the stairs.

"I thought you intended to have your Gypsy friends play their violins tonight," Julian observed.

"Yes, and dance as well, but not at first. I don't want to cause too great a shock at once and frighten away our guests. We'll begin with the traditional ball dances."

"I trust you don't intend for me to dance any reels, minx. Such feats might prove a strain on my leg, despite the remarkable progress your massages have achieved."

She smiled up at him bewitchingly. "No. In fact, you are forbidden to dance at all, Julian. It will disappoint the ladies, of course, but it will also remind them of your wound and that you're a war hero, and render you a figure of sympathy."

He grimaced. "Do you mean I'm to provide entertainment for those who've come to gawk?"

Blaise laughed. "In a manner of speaking. But you won't be alone. Miklos's tribe will be here. And so will John Weeks. I intend to have him tell his story about the horrors of war and the suffering he and other soldiers endured. I hope to make our guests feel guilty enough to contribute generously to our fund. Still, you no doubt will be the prime attraction. Everyone will be curious to know where you have been the last four years."

"With such delights in store," Julian murmured dryly, "it will be a wonder if anyone comes at all."

Blaise didn't mention that she, too, had begun to harbor severe doubts that anyone would attend. Instead, she drew Julian into the ballroom to show him the result of her efforts.

The light of hundreds of candles reflected brilliantly off crystal chandeliers and the gleaming wood floor, while the unusual trappings gave the huge room an exotic atmosphere. At the far end, a great marquee of blue and red striped silk had been erected, complete with small booths in front to emulate a fair of sorts.

"Well?" Blaise demanded anxiously.

"I confess my admiration, minx," Julian said with dry amusement. "I would never have thought to turn my home into such a spectacle."

Relieved that he wasn't angry, Blaise wrinkled her nose at him. "Only because you are a stuffed shirt, your lordship."

She led him across the floor to the tent, to where Miklos waited, resplendent in bright red coat, full blue trousers, and shiny black boots. A golden earring dangled from one ear.

The Gypsy swept them both an elaborate bow. " 'Ow fine you look, Rauniyog . . . er . . . m'lady. M'lord, I'm honored to 'ave the opportunity to serve you. The Rom welcome you. If you will follow me, please . . ."

The tent had been partitioned into small rooms by long curtains. Within the rooms, Panna and several other brightly garbed Gypsy women sat upon silken cushions before low tables, prepared to read palms and tell fortunes from the tarot cards.

Panna, decked out in vivid shawls and a huge green turban, gestured invitingly to Julian, her golden bangles jingling. " 'Ow do you do, me fine lord? Care to 'ave yer fortune told? I'll even waive 'alf the fee in yer case. The rest goes to the Wounded Veterans Fund."

Julian declined with a smile. "Thank you, Mother, but one such experience is more than enough for me."

Panna cackled. "No matter, I'll tell you anyway. You'll be pleased to learn ye're about to have a change of fortune. Luck will be with you tonight!"

"I advise you to tell that to all your customers. You're bound to have a successful evening if you do."

The old woman wagged a finger at him. "You don't believe in the Sight, but you'll see I speak only the truth."

This time Julian had to force his smile. Wishing the

old Gypsy well, he continued Blaise's tour. John Weeks had been given the largest partitioned area within the tent, all to himself, with chairs set up in a semicircle. Blaise explained that the gentlemen guests would be escorted here, to be told about the Fund, while their ladies had their fortunes told.

When they entered the room, Weeks reached for his crutches and struggled to his feet. "Oh, m'lord," he said in a tone bordering on awe. " 'Tis a wondrous thing you're doing, helping out the poor devils like me who suffered in the war. I'm right grateful, and so will all the others be."

"Don't thank me, thank my wife. She deserves all the credit."

The praise in Julian's tone warmed Blaise, but she hastened to disavow any responsibility. "Oh, no, it was Lord Lynden's idea entirely." She let the two men talk for a moment before she drew her husband away.

In the adjacent supper room, tables lined the wall, groaning with aspics and lobster patties, hot-house strawberries and marzipan confections, as well as countless other delicacies and delights.

"I hope our guests do come," Julian remarked. "We shall have a great deal to eat, otherwise."

The vicar and his wife arrived a few moments later, just as Blaise had arranged.

"How very clever, Lady Lynden," Mrs. Nethersby remarked hesitantly upon seeing the decorations. "I daresay no one has ever thought of using *Gypsies* in quite this way before."

Knowing *gorgio* prejudices, Blaise forced a smile and refrained from defending her friends.

With the orchestra playing to an empty ballroom, they formed a reception line just inside the entrance doors and spent a tense half hour engaged in desultory conversation, waiting to see if any guests would arrive. Normally possessing nerves of steel, Blaise felt perspiration dampen her palms.

Her confidence slipped with every tick of the clock,

until finally Hedges stepped into the room and intoned in his most formal voice, "Lord and Lady Ackerton."

With a brief glance at her husband, Blaise summoned a bright smile and turned to greet her first guests, a large portly gentleman and his silver-haired wife.

They were followed by several announcements in quick succession.

"The Misses Denby and Mr. Charles Denby."

"Sir James and Lady Waters."

"Mr. Reginald Bascomb."

"Mr. and Mrs. Carstairs."

A steady flow of elegant people streamed into the room after that, to Blaise's vast relief. Most were long-time acquaintances of Julian's, although a few were new to the neighborhood since his departure. They exhibited a wide range of expressions as they greeted her husband for the first time in four years: skepticism, curiosity, trepidation, disdain, and occasionally pleasure to see him after so long an absence. Their mere presence, however, Blaise considered a triumph; now at least Julian had the opportunity to win them over.

It soon grew apparent that he was succeeding. His charm and wit, as well as his casual unconcern about the savage rumors concerning his past, went a long way toward persuading many of the guests of his innocence. When the reception line eventually disbanded, more than a few ladies and gentlemen circled eagerly around Lord Lynden to listen to him relate tales of the Peninsular Campaign and to learn how he had come to be wounded.

Blaise smiled to hear the exclamations of sympathy and dismay over his suffering from the ladies. She had been right; no female under the age of eighty could resist wanting to hold this beautiful, tormented man to her breast and offer him comfort.

He made no effort to disguise his halting gait in front of the guests, nor, when the dancing began, did he join in. Yet he expressed his apologies in so chivalrous and charming a manner that a half-dozen young ladies declared on the spot that they would also abstain from dancing in order to keep him company.

Blaise commanded her own coterie of admirers, as well—so many that Julian hardly had an opportunity to speak to her. With regret he relinquished his wife to the gallants forming around her, and for the next several hours, he watched with mingled jealousy and pleasure as partner after partner claimed the vivacious Lady Lynden's hand for a dance. She moved from cotillion to contra dance, from boulanger to waltz—still considered risqué since being introduced from the Continent the previous year—with hardly a pause.

Yet she didn't neglect her other guests, either. Obviously on her best behavior, Blaise exhibited the diplomatic skills she claimed to have learned from her stepfather, and managed to charm even the haughtiest of the dowagers present.

One such elderly noblewoman rapped Julian on the arm with her fan to demand his attention. "Wherever did you find that outrageous minx, Lynden?"

"I suppose you are referring to my wife, Lady Fitzsimmons?" Julian replied warily.

"Indeed, I am. How splendidly refreshing to find a young miss who can say two words for herself! When she told that tale of her father and the porcupine, I thought I would split a seam. I haven't laughed so much in years. I daresay my heart will suffer for it tomorrow. I shall send you the doctor's bill, unless you have her visit me and entertain me with more of her delightful stories."

"I shall endeavor to oblige you, my lady," he said with a bow.

He shouldn't have been so surprised at Blaise's success, Julian knew. He'd had firsthand experience of her unrelenting pursuit of her aims and her determination in championing his cause.

Her victory gratified him, for Blaise's sake, even more than his own. She didn't deserve to be shunned and made to suffer because of him. It was clear, though, that he no longer needed to be concerned for her. After this evening she would have acquaintances and callers aplenty.

Even the presence of the Gypsies was well-received. Although there had been a few raised eyebrows at first, most of the guests seemed to be enjoying the entertainment, especially Panna's fortune-telling. More than one young lady could be heard effusing about the mysterious fate in store for her.

The skilled musicians and whirling dancers with their flashing movements and dark enticing eyes were much admired. The monkey, too, seemed to be a big hit. Wearing a red jacket and hat, the animal solicited donations in a tin cup while blinking its large, soulful eyes, and was pronounced to be "adorable" and "a cheeky little devil."

With few exceptions, Blaise could claim the entire evening a triumph. Those few exceptions, however, threatened to spoil the ball for her. They all involved Vincent Foster's sister, Rachel.

Mr. Foster had not shown up for the ball, but Miss Foster had deigned to attend without him. Blaise had met the elegant chestnut-haired beauty in the reception line, and then spoken to her briefly on the sidelines after the Gypsies' first scheduled performance. Neither occasion gave Blaise any pleasure.

"How very . . . original," Miss Foster remarked of the wild entertainment. "But I confess surprise that Julian would allow *Gypsies* into his home. Caroline would never have tolerated such riffraff."

Blaise bit her tongue and responded with a forced smile. "Then it is fortunate Caroline is no longer here to see it."

Miss Foster's eyes narrowed. "I trust your wedded bliss lasts longer than poor Caroline's, Lady Lynden."

"I beg your pardon?"

"It devastated her to learn her husband was unfaithful to her."

Blaise felt herself stiffen and her facial muscles grow rigid. "Indeed?"

"Oh, yes. It was common knowledge that Julian kept

a mistress in London, but poor Caroline never did come to accept it. They fought about it constantly, even on the day she died."

Blaise tried to take a steadying breath. She could hardly believe how much the bald intelligence about Julian's mistress wounded her. She hadn't imagined that he had led a chaste life; any man as sensual and physical as he would no doubt enjoy the pleasures available to a nobleman of his class and wealth. But to be told outright that he had betrayed his wife . . . Blaise felt as if a knife had been thrust into her stomach, as if she couldn't get enough air.

Yet she would swallow live coals before letting this . . . this harridan know of her pain.

"That is the one thing so distasteful about common knowledge, Miss Foster. It is so *common*."

Rachel Foster smiled archly. "No doubt you are made of stronger stuff than Caroline was."

"Perhaps. I never had the pleasure of meeting her, so I couldn't say."

"At least I trust you are more open-minded than she. Caroline's possessiveness destroyed her marriage. You would do well to allow Julian to pursue his . . . *other* interests without interference. He isn't the type of man to brook being kept on a tight leash."

Blaise clenched her teeth. She had to remember that this woman had once wanted to marry her husband, that jealousy was no doubt the motivation for her viciousness.

She summoned a false smile. "How kind of you to advise me on managing my husband, Miss Foster. But I truly doubt Julian would wish to sport a mistress now. I can't count the times he has told me how . . . satisfying he finds our marriage bed." Blaise had the gratification of seeing Miss Foster's pink mouth curl in a sneer. "Oh, but do forgive me. I should not be speaking of such things to an unmarried lady . . . even one of your age. If you will excuse me now? I must see to my other guests."

Feeling that at least she had held her own in their verbal encounter, she left Miss Foster standing there fuming. But the evening had been virtually spoiled for her; all Blaise's insecurities came rushing back with disturbing force. Julian had never wished to marry her; certainly he didn't love her. At the moment he needed her help in overcoming his past, but once he had conquered his demons, what then? He would be free to pursue his "other interests," as that insufferable Miss Foster had suggested.

How could she hope to hold the attention, the affection, of a man who no doubt could have the most beautiful, most fascinating women in the country?

Just then Blaise spied Julian moving across the crowded ballroom floor toward her to escort her in to supper. She gave him a brilliant smile that hid her uncertainties and took his arm, determined not to dwell on her disturbing thoughts.

It was after the supper break that Blaise had occasion to speak to Miss Foster again. The music had ceased temporarily, so that the muffled shriek from within the Gypsy tent was heard by much of the assembled company.

The next instant, Miss Foster came rushing out, white-faced. "That . . . that witch in there . . . She should be horsewhipped!"

Reacting as dutiful hosts, Blaise and Julian reached her side at nearly the same moment, but he provided more help by supporting the lady's arm. "What is it Rachel? What is the trouble?"

Visibly shaken, Miss Foster glanced over her shoulder, as if she feared pursuit. "That horrid Gypsy—she shouldn't be allowed to tell such lies."

"Perhaps you misunderstood," Blaise said soothingly. "Fortune-telling is not an exact science."

"I did *not* misunderstand!" Her tone reverberated with an edge of hysteria. "She—"

Panna came out of the tent just then, a grave intensity drawn on her lined face.

Rachel Foster's slender hand went to her throat, as if in fear, and she backed up a step. "I won't stay here to be insulted a moment longer!"

She whirled toward the door and promptly stumbled over an object in her path, falling to her hands and knees. The frightened monkey beneath her spilled its coin cup and set up a raucous screeching as it flailed its gangly arms.

With a muttered oath, Julian waded into the tangle and tried to separate the two of them, but the monkey was still screeching as it made an escape. Racing away, it scrambled up the leg of the swarthy Gypsy who owned it, hiding its face in the man's shoulder.

With a wild sob, Miss Foster struggled to her feet and shook off Julian's assistance. "He attacked me! That beast *attacked* me!"

"Miss Foster, please," Blaise murmured, "I'm certain he didn't mean you any harm. If you will only calm down—"

"I don't want to calm down! Oh, look at my gown!"

Blaise glanced down at Miss Foster's elegant ballgown of gold tissue over white crepe, which had been ripped at the high waistline. "I'm terribly sorry. Of course we will make reparations—"

"Oh, shut up, you abominable little snip! Vincent warned me I was mistaken to come here tonight—"

"That is quite enough, Rachel," Julian interjected, his tone suddenly hard.

She broke off, gazing up at him wildly through her tears. "How *could* you? How could you marry that heathen Yankee?" Abruptly, she turned and flounced away, pushing through the shocked company and out the wide doors.

The silence in the crowded ballroom fairly shouted uneasiness.

Blaise felt scarlet color flood her face. She'd never been one to embarrass easily, but just now she wanted to sink through the floor. She had longed so fervently for this evening to be a success, but now she had created a scene that was disgraceful even by her usual scale.

Dimly she heard her husband direct a nearby footman to follow Miss Foster and see her safely to her carriage. When she felt Julian's scrutiny, Blaise kept her face averted, reluctant to meet his eyes. He foiled her intent, however, by placing a finger under her chin and forcing her to look at him.

He smiled grimly. "Don't let it concern you, minx. You accomplished just what you set out to—giving the gossips something else to worry over besides my tarnished past."

Before she could decide if his anger was directed at her, or even think of a reply, the aging dowager Lady Fitzsimmons came rustling up to them, muttering. "Such shameful behavior! I never would have expected it of that Foster chit. Always holds herself so high in the instep."

Startled that she wasn't being held to blame for the contretemps, Blaise sent the elderly lady a grateful smile. She was more grateful still when the orchestra struck the opening chords of the next dance number, which turned out to be a waltz.

To her further surprise, Julian handed his cane to another footman and then took Blaise in his arms.

"Julian, you shouldn't!" she exclaimed as he swept her onto the ballroom floor. "Your leg . . ."

"Hush, sweeting, my leg will survive. I wish to dance with my lovely wife . . . heathen Yankee or not." He smiled, this time with pure sensuality. "Of course, such exertion will require you to massage my thigh later."

The suggestiveness in his husky tone made Blaise's heartbeat quicken. Julian couldn't be too furious with her if he was already thinking about what would happen later in their bed.

The commotion stirred by Miss Foster's abrupt departure eventually died down; the laughter and music and gay conversation resumed. Yet it was more than an hour later before Blaise at last found the opportunity to ask Panna what had occurred to make Miss Foster react so violently.

"Whatever did you say to her, Panna?"

"I only told 'er what I saw in the cards," the old Gypsy replied grimly. "That one day her evil deeds would become known."

"What evil deeds?"

Panna shook her head, making her gold earrings jangle. "Time will tell," she said cryptically.

It was nearly three in the morning before the ball ended and the last carriage drove away. Before retiring for the night, Blaise spoke to the butler and housekeeper to commend them for their hard work—praise that Julian seconded.

"My compliments, Hedges, Mrs. Hedges, on an excellent job," Julian remarked.

The housekeeper beamed with satisfaction, while Hedges went so far as to shed his imperious expression and allow his stiff lips to curve in a smile. "Thank you, my lord. And may I be so bold as to offer our congratulations on the success of the evening?"

"Thank you, but all the credit must go to Lady Lynden."

Blaise protested modestly, but she couldn't repress a smug smile.

Exhausted, yet too stimulated to sleep, she ascended the stairs on Julian's arm. "It *was* a success, don't you think?"

"A complete rout, my love. Wellington would have been proud of you."

A warm glow filled her at his praise. "You don't think Miss Foster ruined it?"

"Not at all. Rachel Foster only made a spectacle of herself, no one else."

A muffled spurt of laughter escaped Blaise as she recalled the scene. "I shouldn't laugh. It seemed so serious at the time, her falling. She could have hurt herself. And she nearly crushed that poor monkey."

Julian chuckled with her. "But it was amusing. Particularly since Rachel has always suffered from an excess of pride."

And an excess of jealousy, Blaise remembered with distaste. Just then she also remembered the rest of her disturbing conversation tonight with Miss Foster, about Julian having a mistress in London. Blaise paused before the door to her bedchamber, debating whether to voice the question that burned on her tongue.

And yet all her thoughts suddenly fled as Julian carried her hand to his lips and kissed her fingertips lingeringly, one by one. She knew what those slow caresses meant. And she understood the sudden heated look of desire in his azure eyes. He wanted her. And he would have her. Soon.

Suddenly breathless, Blaise preceded him into her room.

Garvey had waited up for her, but Julian dismissed the abigail, saying he would attend to her ladyship himself. When they were alone, he closed the door firmly, shutting out the world. Then he turned to face her.

Blaise reached up to unfasten the magnificent necklace he had given her, but Julian shook his head. "Leave it on." His voice was low and husky.

Her eyes widened. "My gown, too?"

"No, the gown isn't necessary. I want to see you wearing nothing but amethysts."

Her heart began beating in slow hammering strokes at the burning look in his eyes. Obediently she abandoned the necklace and started to remove her gown, but Julian shook his head again as he closed the distance between them. "Allow me the pleasure."

He began to undress her slowly, attentively, occasionally bending to kiss an exposed inch of pale skin. Whenever she tried to help, his hands came up to stay her. He removed the lace tunic of her gown first, then the satin slip. Leaving Blaise standing in only her sheer lawn chemise, he focused his attention on her numerous hairpins.

"What is this I hear about your father and a porcupine?" Julian asked casually.

Blaise had difficulty comprehending the question. She

could see the blatant bulge in his satin breeches, and it was all she could do to refrain from reaching out to stroke him. "It was in America. A porcupine is a prickly creature similar to a hedgehog, only much larger, and with much longer spines. Papa tried to catch one once and got into difficulties."

"Why would he wish to catch a porcupine?"

"Gypsies consider roast hedgehog a delicacy, and he wanted to see if they tasted alike. He had learned to hunt hedgehogs when he was here in England—Miklos taught him how—but he discovered to his sorrow how dangerous porcupines can be."

"Ah." He dispensed with the last of the hairpins and arranged her gleaming mane of raven hair to fall freely down her back. Then he eased her chemise over her head, leaving her naked except for her slippers and stockings and amethyst jewelry.

Blaise shivered, despite the generous fire crackling in the grate, because of the heat in her husband's eyes.

His gaze moved over her with raking leisure, assessing her intimately, before returning to lock with hers. "The jewels don't do you justice." He ran his hands lightly over her naked skin, stroking her bare swelling breasts, her flat belly, her silken thighs above her stockings. "Have you tasted this Gypsy delicacy—roast hedgehog?"

"What? Oh, yes. Several times." She couldn't think when he was touching her like this, his hands a murmur against her body, arousing, tantalizing.

He didn't undress her further, but instead took her hand. Anticipation made her quiver as he led her to the bed. The covers had been turned down invitingly, yet rather than tucking her in, Julian merely pressed Blaise down to sit on the edge of the bed. Then he moved around the room, snuffing out the lamps, leaving the bedchamber lit by only the warm glow of the fire. Finally he returned to her side and unhurriedly began to disrobe.

Impatient, eager, Blaise watched as Julian shed his

formal garments one by one, fascinated by the elegant play of firelight over his lean-muscled body. He moved with a grace that was spellbinding. At last, though, he stood before her magnificently naked, his erection huge and swollen. Blaise caught her breath at the thought of that hard hot length thrusting deep inside her.

She held out her hand in invitation. "Julian, *please* . . ."

He merely smiled, unwilling to rush. He felt strangely proud of his unconventional wife, and profoundly grateful—for her triumph this evening, for her success in persuading his neighbors to accept him again. His heart lighter than it had been in years, he wanted to repay her for standing his defender and friend.

With care for his wounded leg, he knelt before her, and slowly drew off her slippers, one by one. Then her garters, taking his time. Next he rolled down each silk stocking, intent on drawing out the pleasure, pressing his mouth lightly against the satin flesh of her inner thighs.

Then, holding her gaze, he spread her legs wide. Blaise sucked in her breath as he began caressing her, her entire body clenched. He noted her reaction with satisfaction. She was all wet and warm, the slick, hot flesh responding erotically, eagerly, to his stroking fingers.

"Julian . . . ?" The word was a breathless gasp.

"Hush, sweet. I want you to lie back and enjoy this." Gently he pushed her down till she was lying supine on the mattress, her legs dangling over the edge of the high bed.

Trembling, heady with need, Blaise closed her eyes. She could feel his breath on her, could feel him inhale the scent of her, then his feather-light touch . . . just his tongue flicking out to tease her feminine cleft. She thrashed under the delicate lash.

"Easy, love." His voice soothed as his hands gentled her, but she wouldn't be still. When his tongue stroked her again, her hips came up off the mattress in a wild lunge.

Determinedly he draped her legs over his shoulders to allow him better access and slid his hands under her buttocks to hold her immobile. Then he pressed his warm lips against her, sucking softly in a kiss.

Blaise nearly sobbed. The moist warmth of his gentle mouth was driving her mad. His mouth was magic, tender and demanding, and his tongue . . . His tongue was a fiery spear as he slowly thrust into her.

She writhed, trying to have that hot, probing tongue touch different sides of her, straining to escape the sweet torment. There was no escape, though. He kept his face buried between her parted thighs, loving her with endless caresses of fire.

Panting, her head thrown back, she raked the sheet with her nails, clenched the delicate linen in her fingers, not caring if she shredded it to ribbons. Her body aflame, she whimpered mindlessly, begging him to end it.

Finally he did. A scream of pleasure tore from her throat as wave after wave of raw, shuddering passion washed over her. Even before her savage climax ended, though, he stood abruptly and thrust into her with restrained force, filling her deeply with his thick shaft, his own body clenched with need. Pumping, he drove into her, clutching her hips and grinding himself against her until a rich, wrenching release shuddered out of him.

"My lady of fire . . ." Julian rasped hoarsely as he followed her down, collapsing beside Blaise on the mattress, drained and limp.

Some time later he became aware of the chill assaulting his damp body. Slowly rousing himself, Julian repositioned them both under the covers.

Blaise seemed half asleep. "I should take off this beautiful necklace," she mumbled. "I don't want to damage it."

"Um-hm." Considerately, he reached up and unfastened first the earrings and then the necklace. The slow, somnolent smile she gave him in appreciation was as lovely and glowing as the string of amethysts that had adorned her throat, Julian reflected.

He set the jewels on the bedside table and gathered Blaise in his arms, pillowing her head on his shoulder. Satiated, drowsy, he started to fall asleep.

Blaise couldn't sleep, though. Now that she had recovered from the shattering passion, her restlessness returned and her eyes opened. She lay awake, her mind returning to the disturbing revelation about her husband, like a dog worrying a bone.

"Julian?"

"Yes?" His voice was slow, sleep-laden.

"Would you be angry if I asked you something?"

"Don't suppose so."

"I want to know . . . about something Miss Foster told me. She said . . . Well, she said it was common knowledge that you kept a mistress in London. Is it true?"

Julian's peaceful, relaxed state quietly vanished. He squeezed his eyes shut. Only Blaise would bring up such a subject at such a time. Didn't she know that gentlemen never discussed their mistresses with their wives? Especially not directly after making love. But then, she'd never been one to follow established rules of propriety and convention.

"I did, at one time, a long time ago," he said finally.

"While you were married to Caroline?"

"Yes."

Suddenly feeling vulnerable, Blaise buried her nose in his chest. "I wouldn't like it if you had a mistress." She hesitated. "I couldn't stop you, I wouldn't even try. But I wouldn't like it. I just want you to know."

His hand came up to stroke her hair, but he remained conspicuously silent.

When he didn't give her the reassurances she yearned to hear, Blaise's heart sank. She had no desire to share her husband with a gaggle of opera dancers, and yet she had no power to prevent it if Julian wished to pursue a gentleman's pleasures. She couldn't force him to be faithful, or even to make her such a promise.

Yet it wasn't the threat from opera dancers or actresses or Cyprians that worried her most. It was the hold his late wife had on him. Even dead, Caroline held sway over Julian's dreams and his past—and therefore his future. Sometimes she felt as if she were battling Caroline for his soul.

"Would you be angry," she asked in a small voice, "if I asked you a question about Caroline?"

He gave a heavy sigh. "No."

"Did you love her?"

Wide awake now, Julian extricated himself from their tangled embrace and rolled over on his side, giving Blaise his back. Staring morosely into the fire, he considered her question. "I was . . . fond of Caroline . . . but love? No. She wasn't the kind of woman a man could easily love."

Blaise was conscious of a sweeping feeling of relief. "Then why did you marry her?"

"For the usual reasons . . . To provide heirs to the title. Because she was beautiful and young and had the breeding necessary to become my viscountess. It was a marriage of convenience, nothing more. We both understood that. Yet after a year or so, her . . . affections changed. She began to demand more of me than I would give. And I made mistakes with her. I left her alone too often." There was a moment's pause. "She turned to Vincent Foster for comfort."

His voice held a raw edge of pain that Blaise could feel, and yet she had to press. "Your pride was hurt by Caroline's betrayal."

"Yes, that," Julian acknowledged quietly. "I was outraged that my pure, virtuous wife had taken a lover. Especially my closest friend." His lips twisted. "And I preferred that my heir be my child, not some other man's. I could have borne it better, perhaps, if I'd thought her heart was engaged. But she chose Vincent merely to repay me for my negligence—and to try and arouse my jealousy."

"But . . . you never murdered her." Blaise bit her lip, wondering how he would respond.

There was a long silence. "No."

She let out her breath slowly. It was a measure of how far Julian had come that he could admit he wasn't guilty of murder. He had tempered his self-reproach enough to relinquish some measure of responsibility for the tragedy. That was small progress at least. She reached out to stroke his naked back, offering him silent comfort.

He seemed lost in his thoughts. "Vincent blamed me for her death. He truly loved Caroline. His grief was real . . . greater than mine."

"And you feel guilt for that, too. Because you didn't love her enough."

There was a long pause. "Yes."

"So when Vincent accused you of murder, you didn't refute him."

Her perceptiveness surprised him. Slowly he turned over to face her. "My clever minx. Do you claim to have the Sight like your Gypsy friends?"

"No." She didn't need the Sight to understand what drove him. She loved Julian enough to know what was in his heart.

The bleak sadness in his eyes made her ache. When he reached up to stroke her cheek, Blaise turned her face to press her lips into his palm.

She was going to erase those shadows from his eyes, she vowed silently. She would help Julian to break free of the past, to claim a future without guilt or grief gnawing at the edges of his happiness.

If it took the rest of her life, she would convince him he had a right to be loved. And somehow, some way, she was going to make him love her in return.

Chapter 20

"What is it that has you in the mopes, Rauniyog?" Panna asked a sennight later.

Shaking her head, Blaise stared broodingly at the cooking fire before Panna's tent, unable to explain why she was so dissatisfied with her wonderful life.

She hadn't lacked companionship during the past week. On the contrary, she'd received dozens of calls, as well as invitations to various functions. And she'd achieved her most urgent goal: Julian had been welcomed again into even the best homes—the black sheep accepted back into the fold. His social calender had filled completely, despite his having to decline numerous offers of shooting and hunting because of his healing leg. His leg was improving steadily—she had to watch him closely even to tell when he was suffering—yet she knew he still felt pain from time to time.

Blaise could also feel proud of their philanthropic endeavors. Their neighbors had made generous contributions to the Wounded Veterans Fund, and plans were well under way. Under the direction of Reverend Nethersby and Lord Lynden, the largess was being used to alleviate the suffering of numerous needy families and to establish an apprenticeship program to train disabled soldiers for new work.

Blaise's Gypsy friends had prospered, as well. It seemed her ball had started a fad in the district for the Romany arts. Fortune-telling, palm reading, and dancing to wild Gypsy music had suddenly become the craze. Several ladies had ordered costumes made up in the Gypsy fashion for a future masquerade. There was even talk of holding a village fair.

The great demand benefited Miklos's tribe financially. His horse trade business was booming. Indeed, the Gypsies commanded such excitement and attention that when Blaise visited the camp, she seldom could find anyone home. That afternoon she'd waited two hours for Panna to return, with only Bruno the dog for company. Bruno's soulful black eyes, however, offered undemanding, silent sympathy, for which Blaise was grateful. She much preferred it to the prodding she was undergoing from Panna now.

" 'Tis not like you to mope," Panna observed, attempting to rouse her from her depression.

"I suppose so."

"I ken what your trouble is. You're in love wi' the *gorgio rye*, your 'usband."

Blaise nodded morosely. That was precisely the trouble. She was in love with Julian. Helplessly, hopelessly smitten.

She hadn't wanted to fall in love with him. She'd known how unwise it was to give her heart to a dispassionate, proper Englishman, especially one so preoccupied by a tragic past. And yet she hadn't been able to prevent her downfall.

The state of her own heart didn't worry her as much, though, as the state of Julian's. He didn't seem at all eager to acknowledge her love. Rather, he treated her with fond tolerance.

Oh, he was always polite and charming and exceedingly amiable. He was perceptive to her moods and generous to a fault. In their marriage bed, he was as ardent a lover as any woman could wish. But she wanted more than just a civil, perfect gentleman for her husband. She wanted Julian's love. She wanted him to need her. She wanted his body filling all the aching places inside her.

In the past weeks, he'd shown no signs of succumbing to overwhelming passion. He didn't hang on her every word or ply her with sweet nothings, the way an amorous suitor might. He didn't act as if he couldn't live without her. Her absence wouldn't devastate him.

Instead, he kept her at arm's length, giving her just enough of his attention to frustrate her.

Ever since the second week of their marriage, she'd acted a model of propriety, virtue, and decorum, yet her most excellent behavior hadn't worked in winning Julian's affection. In the past, she might have embarked on some outrageous act to gain a reaction from him. Julian, however, was too considerate of her wishes for her to revert to such childish tactics. He never ignored her the way Sir Edmund had, nor did he try to dictate her actions. He allowed her nearly complete freedom to do whatever she wished.

And yet his very amiableness disgruntled and worried her, for she was very much afraid his tolerance was merely indifference. Indeed, she wouldn't even be upset if he lost his temper with her occasionally, if only to show that his affections were engaged more deeply than he acknowledged.

"Here," Panna said, holding out a small red satin bag. " 'Tis just what you need."

Blaise gave a start, only just now realizing that Panna had gone to her tent and returned. Accepting the bag, she opened it and found a wood knot inside. "What is this?"

"A love charm, o' course. Willow knots are twined by the fairies, and whoever undoes them undoes the luck of the person 'e thinks of and opens 'is 'eart to love. When you cut this knot, think of your 'usband. Then secretly 'ide this in 'is bed, and you'll soon win 'is love."

Blaise clutched the charm to her breast possessively. She didn't have a Gypsy's faith in love charms and potions, but she was desperate enough to try nearly anything.

The love charm failed to work.

Blaise dutifully untwined the willow knot and hid it beneath Julian's mattress, but she detected no significant

change in his behavior toward her, or in his regard.
During the next week, the closest thing to jealousy or
possessiveness he exhibited was his response to a heedless remark made one evening by the hostess of a formal
dinner they attended at a neighboring estate.

When the ladies had left the gentlemen to their port
and removed to the drawing room, the conversation centered on the ways of modern marriages, about how it
was acceptable, even fashionable, for a wife to take a
lover. Blaise listened uncomfortably and hid her distaste
of such a subject. She had no experience with adultery—
nor did she wish to. Her own parents had been so much in
love, they would never have contemplated dalliance with
another partner, no matter how fashionable. Blaise was
grateful when the gentlemen entered the drawing room
and Julian joined her.

Their hostess, however, evidently was not yet willing
to drop the subject. Lady Abercrombie gazed up at Julian
teasingly, while sending Blaise a sly glance. "Of course,
I can't imagine that *you* would wish to take a lover,
Lady Lynden, not with such a handsome husband at
your command."

Blaise, feeling Julian stiffen abruptly beside her, caught
her breath at the insensitivity of the remark. Perhaps the
woman had meant to deliver a compliment, but with
Julian's past, it could only be taken as cruelty.

With an admirable semblance of urbanity, though,
Julian bowed, while Blaise forced a polite smile. Yet
when Lady Abercrombie had turned away to speak
to her other guests, Julian focused his attention on
Blaise.

His blue eyes narrowing at her in warning, he bent to
murmur in her ear with a savagery that left her gasping,
"Perhaps you find it amusing to contemplate taking a
lover, madam, but I assure you, I won't tolerate the
merest hint of impropriety from you on that score."

Then he turned on his heel and stalked away, leaving
Blaise to stare after him in wounded bewilderment.

His jealousy was not for *her*, Blaise was certain. Obviously he was thinking of Caroline. But his implied accusation stung. The idea that he had so little faith in her constancy hurt and infuriated her. Julian didn't know her at all well if he thought she could betray her marriage vows, or her love. She *loved* him. She would never give herself to any man but him. Certainly she would never behave as foolishly as Caroline had, taking a lover for revenge or in an attempt to arouse her husband's jealousy.

What worried Blaise even more, however, was that Julian still hadn't conquered his obsession with the past. He still couldn't forgive himself for his role, however unwitting, in Caroline's death. His guilt still haunted him, and until he conquered it, Blaise doubted he would ever be free to return her love. And he needed to be free. Whether he knew it or not, he needed her love as desperately as she needed his.

If only it were possible to prove Julian's innocence, he might come to believe in it himself. Yet she didn't know how to begin such a daunting task. The tragedy had occurred over four years ago, and according to rumor, there had been no actual witnesses. Even Vincent Foster, who claimed to have come upon Julian holding Caroline's lifeless body, had admitted he'd arrived too late to see exactly what happened.

Blaise discussed her dilemma with Panna and Miklos one afternoon at the Gypsy camp. She first had to tell Miklos about the suspicions against Julian, though, and he didn't take kindly to the revelation.

"They say the *rye* killed 'is wife?" Miklos demanded ominously.

"He didn't!" Blaise replied hotly. "He isn't a murderer. Lady Lynden fell from her horse, that was all."

Miklos glanced over his shoulder warily, as if he feared a ghost might suddenly appear—which indeed he did. Gypsies never spoke of the dead if they could possibly avoid it, for the soul of the deceased might return to haunt the living.

She'd been right, though, to worry about Miklos's protective instincts. If he believed Julian might harm her, he would feel obliged to take vengeance first.

"Then why would the *gorgios* say such a *joobly* thing about 'is lordship?"

"Because Vincent Foster started the lies, that's why. Mr. Foster was in love with Lady Lynden and grieved over her death. But I wouldn't be surprised if that haughty sister of his helped fan the rumors. Rachel Foster had every reason to be jealous of Lady Lynden—and naturally she would support her brother. I know Julian is entirely innocent, though. I just wish I could prove it."

"So why do you not ask the Foster *rye* to tell the truth?" Panna interjected.

"I would like to, but Julian has forbidden me to speak to him. Still . . . perhaps you're right. I should discuss it with Vincent Foster. I know he could shed more light on the tragedy. He was there at the ruins that day. I must give it some thought . . . He may very well refuse to speak to me, though. His sister will doubtless have her back up over that disastrous incident at the ball—"

Blaise stopped suddenly, remembering that particular disturbance. Panna never had adequately explained what she'd meant by Rachel Foster's "evil deeds." "You know more than you're letting on, don't you, Panna?"

The Gypsy woman's black eyes suddenly became veiled, but she shook her kerchiefed head. "Only time will tell. You'll 'ave to learn patience, child."

But Blaise found it harder and harder to be patient when her very future was at stake.

If Blaise had difficulty containing her impatience, Julian did also. He was far less sanguine than he appeared about the havoc the Gypsies were wreaking on the district. Complaints about their "tinkering" and "thieving" poured in. The impromptu fair held in Huntingdon at the end of the week only made matters worse, for it attracted Romanchicals from all over the countryside. Scores of chickens disappeared from his tenants' yards each night, and Julian found himself in the awkward position of having to defend the Gypsies' light fingers as well as pay for their transgressions, since he was responsible for inviting them there, and since he wished to keep the peace.

When he questioned Blaise about the thefts, though, she disavowed any knowledge.

"Why is everyone so quick to blame Gypsies for a missing chicken?" she asked with a wide-eyed look of innocence which he didn't quite believe.

"Don't try to cozen me, minx. I have firsthand experience that your friends' reputation for lifting poultry is well-deserved. You didn't participate in any of the raids, by any chance, did you?"

She laughed. "Of course not. I would never steal from you. And neither would Miklos. He wouldn't violate your hospitality. It would be against Gypsy law. It must be some other band."

Julian took Blaise at her word, yet he doubted he could count on her continued good behavior. For someone with her lively spirits, she had been quiet far too long. And as long as her Gypsy friends were near, the temptation to revert back to her scandalous habits remained strong.

He would have liked to send the Gypsies packing, and yet Blaise took such pleasure in their company that he hesitated. He didn't want to deprive her of her only friends, at least not until she made new ones from among her peers. He deplored the influence the Gypsies had over her—and yet he had to admit to a certain fascination for the woman she became whenever she was with them. Blaise was never so animated as when she was in their company.

But then his young wife fascinated him under any circumstances. Her behavior was a study in contradictions. At times she seemed wise beyond her years, at others a mere child. Julian caught himself smiling at the memory of Blaise delightedly munching on hot roasted chestnuts and buttered taffy at the fair.

He'd found it much more difficult than he'd expected to pretend indifference to her during the past weeks. He'd tried to chart a middle course, wanting to win merely her respect and obedience, not her love. He didn't want her becoming overly dependent on him for her happiness. Nor did he wish to be dependent on her.

Yet the tremendous force of joy Blaise exhibited, the sheer exuberance in living, the teasing and tenderness, were impossible to ignore. She was as vivid and alluring as a sunset to a man who had been blind all his life—or a man whose soul had been dead for the past four years. She was slowly bringing him back to life, Julian knew. Healing him with her laughter, her enchanting liveliness, whether he wished her to or not.

He found it difficult to refuse her anything, as well. Especially since she asked for so little for herself. Her primary concern usually was for others, and most often *him*. He couldn't help comparing her to his first wife. Caroline had always demanded the best in life—the most beautiful gowns, the most luxurious carriages, the most expensive jewelry. Blaise, on the other hand, was perfectly content tramping through the woods with the Gypsy children, searching for nuts and late bramble berries, dressed in rags and beads—as long as they were Gypsy rags and Gypsy beads, and she could tramp with her friends. Noble titles never impressed her, nor did the English in general.

When one morning toward the middle of November, Blaise tried to persuade him to go hunting for hedgehogs with Miklos's tribe the next day, Julian didn't immediately refuse.

Seeing his hesitation, Blaise pouted attractively and wrapped her arms about his neck, even though they were engaged in serving their plates from the sideboard in the breakfast room, with the stately Hedges and two footmen hovering nearby.

"Please, Julian, you have to come."

"And why is that, minx?"

"Because you're always too serious. You need to learn how to enjoy life more. You don't always want to be a stuffed shirt."

"I haven't the slightest idea how to hunt a hedge-hog—"

"We'll teach you."

"—nor am I at all certain I wish to learn."

"Oh, Julian, *please*?"

"And I have an interview with Marsh tomorrow."

"Surely you can put it off for one day."

"I doubt my leg is up to it."

"I promise we'll go slowly. Besides, your leg is much better. You hardly limp at all anymore. And if it starts to ache, I'll give you a massage. You know how much you like my massages."

The bright eagerness in her violet eyes was his undoing. Julian gave in gracefully and prepared to endure an ordeal he had no expectation of enjoying.

The following day dawned brisk but remarkably clear. Blaise awoke excited, and stayed that way all through breakfast and during the short drive to the Gypsy camp. To his surprise, she had arranged for the gig to be harnessed, and for blankets and a picnic lunch to be packed. "For later," she informed him with the secretive laugh of a child anticipating a great treat.

When they reached the camp, they found the entire tribe assembled to greet them. When the Gypsies spread out over the countryside, Miklos himself took the lord and lady under his wing. Carrying a burlap sack and a stout stick, he led them over several fields to an area he'd previously scouted out, while Bruno the dog bounded beside him.

Exhibiting a childish excitement, Miklos explained that the catching of the *hotchi* was an important event, and the hedgehog feast was one of the high points of a Gypsy's life. The prickly creatures lived under the hedgerows, but only in autumn were they fat enough to eat. The meat, a delicacy coveted by the Rom, tasted even better than chicken, Miklos swore.

Bruno the dog proved invaluable in sniffing them out, so Miklos could kill them with a smart blow to the snout with the stick.

Blaise winced when the first little creature met its fate, but Miklos expressed satisfaction, saying with firm conviction as he gingerly stuffed the animal into his sack, "A hedgehog would rather be eaten by a Gypsy than scorned by a *gorgio*."

By the time two hours had passed and they had bagged several hedgehogs, Julian's leg ached with the cold and he was grateful to return to the camp.

Blaise, claiming wifely privilege, teased him about his infirmity and offered her shoulder for support. Julian accepted, not because he needed help in walking, but simply because he wanted an excuse to hold her. He thought she had rarely looked lovelier, her cheeks flushed by the wind, her eyes sparkling with high spirits. Her effervescence left him feeling young and exhilarated, as if this were the beginning of spring, rather than the middle of fall. He found himself regretting the lack of privacy and the necessity of spending the entire day in the company of the Gypsies. At the moment he wanted nothing more than to find a secluded meadow and show his young wife the pleasures of making love in the open air.

The Gypsy camp was bustling with activity, with the women taking charge. The hedgehogs would be prepared for cooking, Miklos explained, their spines singed in the fire and removed with a sharp knife, the meat skinned and cleaned, then spitted on a stick and roasted over a glowing wood fire.

Blaise, with that secretive sparkle dancing in her eyes, tendered their excuses for the remainder of the afternoon, saying she was taking her husband on a picnic but they would return in time for the feast. Miklos, rather than looking disappointed, actually beamed with approval.

When she and Julian were settled in the gig, Blaise commandeered the reins and drove away from the camp, but just before reaching the lane, she brought the horse to a halt. Searching in the picnic basket, she unearthed a kerchief and turned to Julian with an apologetic look.

"I'm sorry, Julian, but you will have to wear a blindfold. I don't want to spoil the surprise."

His eyebrow rose warily. "What the devil are you up to, wench?"

Blaise laughed, an infectious sound that made him ache with the need to hold her. "Trust me, this won't hurt."

Giving in to the fierce desire that had been swelling in him all morning, Julian drew her, unresisting, into his arms and proceeded to kiss her breathless. Only then did he pull away and allow her to blindfold him.

As she drove away, Blaise launched into the story about her father's first disastrous experience of hunting porcupines in America, which soon had Julian chuckling. She kept up her gay chatter, but as time went on, Julian had the distinct impression her tone had taken on an edge of nervousness.

He could tell when they left the lane some ten minutes later, for the gig began to sway as it rolled over uneven ground. It was several more minutes, though, before she drew the vehicle to a halt again.

Blaise looped the reins around the dash rail to secure the horse, but then simply sat there a moment, gathering courage. Finally, taking a deep breath, she removed Julian's blindfold.

He looked around at the secluded meadow containing the ancient ruins of a Roman wall, and froze. The terrible memories assaulted him, crowding into his mind: *The slashing rain. The crumpled form of his wife lying so still on the ground. Her blood on his hands.*

For a moment he said nothing at all.

Blaise watched him nervously. His entire body had gone rigid, while his face had set like flint, making his scar stand out vividly. Yet his thunderous expression couldn't obscure the bleak look in his eyes that she had come to dread. Perhaps bringing him here hadn't been such a wise idea after all.

She had known she needed to do something more drastic than simply rely on a willow-knot love charm.

She'd hoped that by forcing Julian to confront his past, she would help banish his haunted memories. This was where Caroline had died. Yet the tragic past was nowhere in evidence. The Roman ruins didn't look so sinister in the bright autumn sunshine. Rather, they appeared picturesque and somewhat charming.

Julian didn't seem to notice. He was staring blindly at the scene, as if reliving one of his nightmares.

The taut muscles in his jaw flexed like steel ropes as he turned to her. "I suggest," he said tightly, with an obvious effort at control, "that you tell me the meaning of this."

"I . . . I only wanted to prove to you there are no ghosts here."

His blue eyes pierced her like daggers. "I suppose you think you are being helpful."

"I'm trying, truly. The past is over, Julian. You have to forget about it—and Caroline. She has haunted you for too long."

He curled his hands into fists, as if he wanted to strike out at something; at his memories, at her. But he didn't touch her. He merely said harshly, "Let's go."

When he reached for the reins, though, her gentle hand on his arm forestalled him. "*Please*, Julian, please . . . Don't make us leave just yet. Five minutes, that's all. I promise, I won't ever ask anything else of you. Not ever again."

His curse was low and fluent. But when Blaise repeated her fervent plea, Julian gave up his attempt at escape and dropped the reins. "Five minutes." Sitting back in his seat, he leaned his head back and squeezed his eyes shut.

"You won't exorcise Caroline's spirit if you don't look."

He swore again. "I don't want to exorcise her spirit, blast it!"

"I know. That has always been the trouble. You want to punish yourself for her death. But you've suffered enough, Julian."

The silence resonated between them.

"It's a pretty meadow."

He shook his head, not agreeing. He couldn't contemplate the pastoral beauty. All he could see was the driving rain, Caroline's lifeless body, the blood in her pale hair. He smiled bitterly. "Lovely."

"You're angry with me."

His snort of laughter was harsh, cynical. Yes, he was angry with her. For forcing him to relive the past. His horror, his hatred of this damnable place, was as strong now as it had been four years ago. Stronger, perhaps, for having been bolstered by four years of nightmares.

He ran a hand raggedly down his face. Feeling the scar tissue on his cheek reminded him of how he'd earned his wounds—on a bloody battlefield in Spain. He *had* suffered for his sins. Physically, and with his soul. His body was healing, at least, but his soul? He had returned home to face his ghosts, and yet he hadn't followed through with his plan. Instead, like a bloody coward, he'd avoided this meadow. He'd avoided anything to do with the past. If not for the prodding of his stubborn, exasperating chit of a wife, he would never have come this far.

He forced himself to open his eyes, to look at the ruined wall.

"It isn't so horrid now, is it?" Blaise said quietly.

Julian slowly let out his breath. Surprisingly, the horror had diminished. He still felt chill tremors crawling up his spine at the sight of that ancient stone wall, yet the image of Caroline lying there no longer seemed so stark, so vivid.

Dragging his gaze away, he looked at Blaise. "Very well. Five minutes is up. Now may we go?"

"I thought we might have our picnic here."

"*No.* Not here." His tone was adamant but not as harsh as it might have been.

"Really, Julian, it would be better if we stayed. The idea is to replace your nightmares with pleasant memories—"

"Don't press me, Blaise. I've done as much as I can today. Perhaps some other time I'll be able to return and face Caroline's spirit, but I'd prefer to take it slowly."

Acquiescing with a sympathetic smile, Blaise put her arms around him and raised her lips to his. "Are you terribly angry with me?"

"Furious."

"Do you mean to beat me?"

"Unmercifully."

"Will you at least wait till *after* you make love to me?"

She had planned this, Julian realized. His seduction was to be his reward for braving the meadow. His mouth curved in unwilling amusement. "Just moments ago, you vowed you would never ask anything of me again, sweeting. Now you want me to make love to you?"

"I don't always mean *exactly* what I say, Julian. You should know that by now. Sometimes I shade the truth in order to get my way. It's a dreadful failing of mine, I admit."

"You infuriating, outrageous brat . . ."

"You don't want to make love to me?"

Her look of abject disappointment made him smile, yet this time the smile was genuine. "Of course I do, devil take you. But not here." When he made love to Blaise, it would be in a place that held none of the terrible associations this meadow had. Not only was this where Caroline had met her end, but where she and Vincent Foster had betrayed him, carrying on their adulterous liaison. He didn't want those memories tarnishing his passion for Blaise.

He took up the reins and turned the gig around. As they left the dreaded ruins behind, he could feel the tension draining from his body with each passing yard. He drove to a remote area several miles away, a private grassy glen surrounded by a copse of leafless willows and alders and bordered by a rushing stream.

"How lovely," Blaise exclaimed. "You were right, Julian. This is much nicer."

Julian unloaded the gig and arranged the blankets and picnic basket while Blaise took off her bonnet and struggled to remove her half boots and stockings.

"You won't get cold?" he asked when he saw what she was doing.

She flung him an arch, purely feminine smile. "I had hoped you would keep me warm."

He returned the sensual smile. "I trust I can manage."

He settled on the blanket, anticipating her joining him, but to his surprise, Blaise lifted her skirts and waded into the stream, gasping at the freezing temperature.

"Look, Julian, a trout! We should have brought a line and some bait. My papa taught me to fish—only I never did like tying on the worms."

"You've doubtless scared all the fish away, minx."

He uncorked the flask of wine and drank as he watched her play. The taste was sweet and pungent on his tongue, and somehow new, as if his senses had suddenly awakened after a deep sleep. He was suddenly conscious of small things: the sweet smell of crushed grass, the throaty coo of a wood pigeon, the gurgle of the stream, Blaise's laughter, gay and uninhibited. The air held a chill, but the sun beat down, warming him, while the clear golden rays brought out the shining blue highlights of Blaise's midnight hair.

He was so aware of everything, as if he were seeing the earth and sky newly defined. The day was clean and crisp, untarnished, free of the horrors of the past. For the first time in four years he felt unfettered.

And he had his Gypsy minx to thank for his freedom. Tomorrow, perhaps, his guilt would return, but for this rare magical moment, he could enjoy the simple pleasures of being alive on a glorious autumn afternoon.

He lay back on the blanket, waiting for her to join him, desire thrumming through his body like wild Gypsy music.

Blaise didn't stay long in the water, but ran out laughing. When she reached the blankets, she sank to her knees beside him.

A fierce longing kindling inside him, Julian reached up and caught her nape, drawing her lips down for a kiss. His tongue plunged deep into her mouth, sharing the warm taste of wine, making clear his intent, his need for her.

"Are you hungry?" she whispered, suddenly breathless.

"Famished . . . but not for food."

The enchanting color that tinged her cheeks told him she felt the same anticipation of their lovemaking.

He gave her the flask, allowing her to drink only so he could lick the wine off her lips. A husky rasp of laughter escaped her, but then she pulled back. "There's no need to rush."

"Yes, there is, sweeting." Deliberately he took her hand and placed it on his groin, letting her feel the rigid length of his arousal. "I want you."

She smiled that enchanting feline smile. "You'll have me . . . eventually."

Holding his gaze, she went to work on the buttons of his coat and waistcoat, pushing aside the lapels. Then she slowly drew up his shirt.

She had planned this, he remembered as he felt her cool fingers stroke his bare chest. His seduction. He didn't want to spoil her pleasure, or his. He only wanted to savor the incredible feeling. He shut his eyes.

Her slender hands explored his body, as curious and uninhibited as a kitten. She relearned his skin, the supple firmness underlaid with steel, the silky expanse of his chest, the pebble hardness of his masculine nipples, the lean strength of his rib cage, the taut musculature of his flat abdomen.

Her fingers shook slightly as she reached for the buttons of his trousers, belying her appearance of calm. His underdrawers she opened next, revealing the dark golden hair at his groin and his thick, burgeoning erection. Her breath caught at the sight of his aroused, beautiful masculinity.

Boldly, Blaise pushed the fabric down over his lean hips, exposing the scarred flesh of his thigh, but no farther. With a soft murmur of sympathy, she bent and pressed her lips there, against the puckered, ravaged flesh, as if by doing so she might heal his wounds. Julian made a hoarse sound deep in his throat, a sound that broke off in a choked moan as she closed her fingers around his throbbing shaft.

Without hesitation, she fondled him, intimately caressing as he had taught her to do, teasing and arousing, yet with her own enchanting brand of torment, stroking his long rigid length, squeezing the stiff sacs beneath, until his aching manhood swelled to the point of bursting.

"Blaise . . ." His fingers closed around hers impatiently, trying to discourage her from setting off the imminent explosion.

She gently disentangled her hand and brushed his away. "No," she murmured defiantly. "You do this to me all the time. I want to do it to you."

She shifted slightly and bent to kiss him again, this time pressing her lips tenderly, adoringly along the rigid column of his erection. Julian went totally still, all the muscles in his body tightening.

Emboldened, Blaise let her tongue flick out to caress him. She had kissed him there before, but never had she gone so far in an attempt to give him pleasure. When he harshly sucked in his breath, she ventured further into the realm of forbidden passion, exploring, instinctively experimenting with her unskilled caresses, driven by desire and love.

Julian remained rigid while she tongued him, as if afraid to move, yet his hand involuntarily came up to cradle the back of her head, offering guidance. Blaise lavished him with hot little kisses and long strokes of her tongue, defining his hot satin skin inch by inch with her mouth, delighting in his response, relishing her momentary domination, the control she held over him. It was a heady experience, having her sensual, sexually sophisticated husband at her mercy.

And then she took him in her mouth.

She heard his hoarse gasp and wanted to shout in triumph. She felt so powerful, so feminine, so deliciously wanton. She sucked at him gently at first, then with more confidence, drawing her lips slowly, tantalizingly over the huge swollen tip of his erection, deliberately, consciously trying to drive him mad with desire the way he had done to her so many times in the recent past.

Julian squeezed his eyes shut tighter and groaned. When a moment later she drew back slightly and glanced up, she could see the dark flush of passion on his face.

"Are you falling asleep?" she whispered huskily, yet with an edge of laughter in her voice, knowing full well he was as far from sleep, as completely, passionately aroused, as a man could get.

"No, you little wretch." The words were a hoarse rasp. He was only feeling, glorying in the sensual splendor of her adoration, the exquisite, tormenting fire of her touch. His body was a mass of sensation, his senses honed to razor sharpness, every nerve and fiber and muscle focused on what she was doing to him, what she made him feel.

Yet it went far, far beyond mere carnal pleasure. He felt as if he had never been alive before this day, before Blaise. He felt so *alive*. He could feel again . . . The air swelling in his lungs. The blood coursing through his heart. The need pumping through his loins. The chill breeze where her warm lips and hot wet tongue had been. The aching yearning in his soul where the bleak emptiness had been. He felt full and complete. He felt whole.

His face contorted with pleasure and pain as she bent to him again. His hips strained involuntarily toward her, while slow tremors racked his body.

It was not long, though, before Blaise became caught up in her own game. Her playing took on an element of urgency; her breathing quickened, her own skin grew hot and flushed. Soon her fevered trembling matched Julian's shudders.

Even so she was startled when he suddenly grasped her shoulders and repositioned her to lie beneath him.

Urgently fumbling, he dragged up the skirts of her gown, heedless of the expensive merino fabric, yet her impatience seemed as fierce as his. She was hot and ready for him. His blue eyes darkened to hot cobalt as his fingers found and stroked the slick cleft between her legs.

"Julian . . . please . . . take me . . ." she implored on a sob.

With a low groan, his body shaking, he fitted his mouth over hers while he spread her knees wide with his thighs. He entered her abruptly, sinking into her in a long continuing thrust that filled her to the hilt. God, but he needed her. She was like air to him.

He heard her whimper, but her body surrendered at once, enveloping him, swelling tightly around his large possession. Ignoring the ache of his healing muscles, he clutched her buttocks, trying to pull her closer, tighter.

Sweet Gypsy, how deep can I get inside you? he wondered.

Oblivious of anything but their joining, Blaise wrapped her long legs around his hips and bucked against him. Her soft panting told him how dangerously close she was to the edge.

He rocked hard against her sensitive flesh, ramming himself into her. His next powerful thrust ignited her body into flames. She convulsed around him, catching him in the shattering climax. His own body clenched fiercely, contracting in ragged jolts, and he gave a rasping cry of release as he flooded her with the liquid warmth of his lovemaking.

Dazed, gasping, Blaise felt his crushing weight collapse heavily upon her. Yet she didn't mind. She held him in her arms, in the clasp of her thighs, cherishing the intimacy of their joining.

I love you, she murmured, but silently. *I love you.* He wasn't ready to hear her confession yet. But soon.

She sighed in contentment, burying her face in the curve of his shoulder to hide her sated woman's smile. His passion had been different this time, she had felt it. Julian had given her part of himself. A small part, perhaps, but it gave her reason to hope that someday, somehow, some way, he might give her more.

Chapter 21

❝The Gypsies must go, my lord," the vicar insisted two days later. "They have caused untold havoc, and now this outrage . . ." He gestured wildly at the bay mare that stood in the stableyard of Lynden Park. The black stockings on the horse's lower legs had faded to a dirty shade of gray, while the black mane had turned to dark chestnut.

"Indeed," Squire Ratcliff added indignantly. "It is bad enough that my horse was *stolen* from my pasture, but to cheat a man of the cloth—it is beyond insufferable!"

Julian repressed a sigh. The two irate gentlemen had arrived on his doorstep a half hour ago, complaining bitterly about the Gypsies' theft of the horse and the fraudulent scheme they had played on the Reverend Nethersby. The vicar had bought the bay mare at the fair last week from a Gypsy horse trader for twenty guineas, but Squire Ratcliff claimed the horse belonged to him. There was no question the animal's stockings and mane had been dyed black to disguise its distinguishing white markings, turning it from chestnut to bay.

"Who precisely sold you the mare?" Julian asked the vicar. "Did you learn his name?"

"One of those swarthy Gypsy fellows, I don't know which one. I thought you might know, my lord, since you are on such good terms with them."

"I'm not familiar with them all," he murmured. "But you were right to apply to me. I regret that you were inconvenienced so, Reverend. I hope you will allow me

326

to repay you the purchase price. And to recompense you, Squire, for your trouble. Now that your horse has been safely returned, though, there should be no need for prosecution."

"It is much more than a question of twenty guineas," the squire declared. "They should not be allowed to get away with such skulduggery!"

"Indeed," Julian said soothingly. "You have my word, I shall certainly investigate and try to get to the bottom of this."

The vicar shook his head. "It is one thing to be charitable, my lord, and to extend forgiveness to the repentant, but I fear these vagrants will never repent. There is only one satisfactory solution," he repeated. "The Gypsies must go."

"I promise I shall give careful consideration to your suggestion."

It took some doing, but Julian managed to slightly mollify their outraged sensibilities. When the two gentlemen had taken the bay/chestnut mare away, Julian glanced at his estate steward.

"It would indeed be best, my lord, if the Gypsies moved on," Marsh suggested with his usual calm good sense.

Julian nodded reluctantly. He wanted peace with his neighbors, if possible after his turbulent past, but as long as the Gypsies were fleecing the district, peace would be impossible. Besides, he owed Nethersby a debt of gratitude. Except for Blaise, the vicar had been his staunchest supporter during the past month. He couldn't idly stand by while the poor gentleman was hoodwinked.

And for that matter, he also had Marsh's sensibilities to consider. Marsh had patiently borne the brunt of the complaints about the thieving Gypsies without a word of reproach, but his long years of faithful service didn't deserve to be rewarded by having his recommendations dismissed out of hand.

Julian sighed. He would have liked to think Blaise could exercise greater control over her Romany friends, but he suspected it wasn't possible. The habit of tricking *gorgios* was ingrained in the Gypsy soul.

The vicar no doubt was right. The Gypsies would have to go.

Julian rode over to the Gypsy camp that morning. The children set up a mad dance when they saw him, begging for pennies and sweetmeats. A beaming Miklos shooed them away and welcomed the *gorgio rye* to his humble camp.

Julian forced a pleasant smile in return. "I'm afraid I am here on a matter of business, not pleasure."

"Well, then, you must take a glass of ale with this poor Rom."

Dismounting, Julian joined Miklos at the campfire, while Miklos's wife, Isadore, went to fetch the refreshment.

When they were both settled with a glass, Julian began. "It seems that the vicar purchased a bay mare at the fair last week, only to discover its coat had been disguised. In fact, the bay was a chestnut with three white stockings, which was spirited away from Squire Ratcliff's pasture two weeks ago. I promised to investigate the matter. Do you perhaps have any knowledge of how this came about?"

Miklos looked more dismayed than wary. " 'Tis sure I know of such tricks, m'lord—painting a *grai*'s coat to 'ide its identity. But 'twas not one of us, I swear."

"I did not think it was. Blaise assures me I can count on your goodwill. But perhaps one of your colleagues might have been involved."

Miklos shook his head sadly. " 'Tis the *gorgio* way to blame all misfortune on the poor Gypsies."

"An unfortunate truth, I agree. But the fact remains that the horse was stolen and then fraudulently sold to a man of the church. I have reimbursed the vicar for the theft, but I would be more pleased to offer him reassurances it will not happen again."

"There are many more Rom 'ere than my tribe. I've little power over the others. I cannot speak for them all."

"I feared as much. But something must be done, Mr. Smith. This is no longer a matter of a few chickens. I needn't remind you of the punishment for such a crime. And while I perhaps can manage to dissuade the vicar and the squire from taking legal recourse, they will only be satisfied by the removal of the Rom from this neighborhood."

The Gypsy's face fell, but then he gave a pragmatic shrug that managed to dismiss his disappointment. "Ah, well, I fear we've outstayed our welcome, anyway. We should be movin' on. A Traveler never stays in one place for so long as we've done 'ere."

Julian eyed him gravely. "I regret the necessity, but I believe it is for the best." He hesitated, choosing his words so as not to offend Miklos's pride. "You are a shrewd businessman, Mr. Smith, so perhaps you will consider a proposition. I would like to offer you financial remuneration to help defray the costs of your departure— Blaise would wish me to, naturally. But I will match my offer with the other tribes if you can persuade them to leave the area within the week."

It was a blatant bribe, no less, but Miklos brightened immediately.

"That's right generous of you, m'lord. I never expected such from a *gorgio*."

"Well then, shall we drink to it?"

"Aye." Miklos grinned, his teeth gleaming white in his swarthy face, and held up his glass. "To the *gorgio rye*, a *tatcho pal*—a true brother to the Rom—whose 'eart is as deep as 'is pockets."

Julian rode away, satisfied with the bargain he'd struck. He had to admit he would be greatly relieved when the Gypsies left. Their disruptive presence had caused him no little difficulty, not to mention their influence over his impressionable young wife.

Blaise wouldn't be happy about their departure, certainly. She would miss her friends keenly. But in her loneliness, she might very well turn to him.

He could think of worse consequences.

Julian shook his head, amazed at how profoundly his attitude toward his incorrigible minx of a wife had changed during the past weeks. His plan to keep Blaise at arm's length had failed miserably, he admitted. He had wanted to keep their relationship a matter of convenience. He hadn't wanted her to fall in love with him and become overly demanding. He'd wanted merely to win her respect, only that.

Yet it was no longer frightening to imagine Blaise loving him.

Julian smiled softly to himself, remembering when he'd first realized the extent of his vanquishment, remembering that entire, incredible day . . . hunting for hedgehogs, visiting the ruins that were the scene of his haunting nightmares, making love to Blaise in the open air on a glorious autumn afternoon. The Gypsy feast that evening. He and Blaise had been the guests of honor, dining on the choicest portions of hedgehog, yet afterward he couldn't have said what he'd eaten. Throughout the interminable evening he could scarcely keep his hands to himself. Seeing Blaise dance before the campfire again, her warm gaze solely for him, had set his body ablaze with need and desire.

Need and desire far more profound than carnal pleasure.

He had come to realize it that magical afternoon beside the stream. He had discovered, for the first time in his life, the difference between making love to a woman's body and loving a woman. One bewitching, irrepressible, maddeningly stubborn hoyden who was scarcely more than a girl.

His lady of fire. Blaise.

She had dared him back to life, when he'd felt almost dead inside. She had made him laugh, when nothing had made him laugh in years. She had challenged him to face his guilt, to triumph over his haunted memories. Simply being near her made him feel whole once more. Blaise filled him with a hope he had never again expected to feel, the possible hope for salvation. For four years he had driven himself relentlessly, taking insane risks, daring fate to prove him mortal. He hadn't cared whether he lived or died.

Until Blaise.

He couldn't imagine living without her now. Now he looked forward to each new day—filled with her laughter, her exuberance, her loving, her fire. His life had changed because of her. *He* had changed. Quite without meaning to, he had let her into his heart. Or she had forced her way in. He doubted now whether he could have prevented his vanquishment. Any more than he could have prevented her stubborn championship of his cause. She was determined to set him free of the past.

Julian's soft smile of remembrance faded as he recalled her outrageous scheme of two days ago, to picnic at the site of his first wife's death. Blaise had wanted to replace his nightmares with pleasant memories. At the time he had reacted with fury, yet Blaise had been right. He could only be free of the past if he forced himself to confront it.

With quiet deliberation, Julian turned his horse to ride across a stubbled field, in the direction of the Roman ruins. He had promised Blaise he would return to the meadow to face Caroline's ghost, and now was as good a time as any—high noon, when the sun shone brightly, with the pale blue sky remarkably cloudless. As different as possible from that fateful day four years ago when his life had been shattered by tragedy.

Julian could feel his stomach muscles clench with apprehension as he drew closer; his deep horror of the place had been reinforced by four years of nightmares, after all. He had no trouble envisioning the scene, no need to shut his eyes to be assaulted by vivid snatches of memories . . . the slashing rain, the gloom-filled meadow, the pile of crumbling stone walls, the crumpled body of his wife lying so unnaturally still. Unconsciously Julian slowed his mount's gait, bracing himself for what he would find.

He rounded a thick line of elms, and the grassy meadow came slowly into view. In the distance he could see the walled ruins. But the scene was not what he expected. He saw no body lying there, but a couple—a man and a woman—standing close together, their horses grazing a few yards away.

Julian blinked and brought his mount to an abrupt halt. He had never seen Caroline and Vincent together, but he had pictured them countless times, embracing, coupling on this grassy verge, their bodies melding in abandoned passion. There was no overt sign of passion now, and yet with their heads so close together, the couple managed to convey an impression of intimacy, even conspiratorial secrecy.

Suddenly Julian's gaze narrowed. The dark-haired gentleman in the distance was Vincent Foster, he was certain. But the woman dressed in a green riding habit and matching hat had ink-jet hair, not blond.

Julian felt his lungs contract as shock surged through him. *Blaise*. Blaise and Vincent Foster. The enormity of what he was seeing left him reeling in sick disbelief. He had forbidden Blaise to come here, had forbidden her to speak to Vincent. Moreover, she'd given her word that she would obey him. And here she was in intimate proximity to the man who had taken Caroline from him.

The sense of betrayal staggered him. Anguish squeezed his vitals like a cold fist, while a dozen searing questions streaked through his mind. How long? he wondered. How long had they been engaged in their secret meetings? Or perhaps their betrayal went further. Perhaps the nightmare was starting all over again. Vincent Foster seducing his wife. Blaise playing him false.

His face stiff with dread, Julian urged his mount forward. The scene about to be played out held a sickening sense of inevitability. Four years ago he would have confronted Vincent like this. Except that Caroline had died first.

A coldness seized him, settling about his heart.

The grass only partly muffled his horse's plodding hoofbeats, but the couple was so deep in conversation, they didn't immediately note his arrival, not until he was directly before them.

"So," Julian said.

Blaise started and looked up, surprise written on her features.

"So," he forced himself to say, though his throat ached, "I see how little value you place on your word, madam wife."

Guilty silence greeted his words.

"Julian . . ."

He stared at her, numb, his heart frozen. "I forbade you to see him, perhaps you remember?"

"It isn't what you think, Julian. It is all quite innocent—"

"Innocent?" Rage knotted in his belly, but he clamped his jaw shut, not trusting himself to address her in a civilized tone. He could read clearly the guilt and dismay in her expression as she took a quick step back, away from her companion.

Vincent spoke then for the first time. "How unfortunate that you should interrupt our little assignation," he said with a jeer.

"I thought," Julian responded with forced control, "I warned you to stay off my land."

"So you did, my lord, but you obviously failed to warn your lady. I am here at her invitation."

Julian's hard gaze abruptly shifted back to Blaise, who was staring at Vincent in shock.

"What troubles you, my lord?" Vincent prodded. "Are you concerned I am enjoying your lovely wife's charms? That I am cuckolding you again?"

Julian grew white about the mouth, while Blaise gasped. "That isn't true! Julian, you can't possibly believe that!"

He looked down at her, his blue eyes as cold and barren as an icecap.

"Julian, *please* . . ."

He waved her to silence, refusing to listen to her attempts at explanation. Even if he could have absolved Blaise of betrayal, he knew Vincent Foster well enough to understand his onetime friend's intentions. Vincent wouldn't scruple to seduce another man's wife for revenge. Blaise's seduction now, in exchange for Caroline's death then.

He could read that intent clearly in Vincent's bitter, mocking expression, in his smoldering dark eyes. And he knew, as Vincent stared fixedly up at him, that the time had come to settle their differences once and for all. The hatred that had been festering between them for years had finally come to a head. There was only one course open to them now.

"If you consider me to have impugned your *honor*"— Vincent made the word a sneer—"I will be pleased to give you satisfaction."

"Not half so pleased as I."

"Name your seconds, then."

"I think perhaps we can dispense with seconds. This is a private matter, after all. We've caused scandal enough, you will agree."

Suddenly comprehending what they were planning, Blaise stared in horror. "You can't possibly be thinking of fighting a duel!"

Her husband sent her a sharp glance. "I'll thank you to stay out of what doesn't concern you."

"Not concern me!"

Ignoring her exclamation, Vincent bowed from the waist. "I shall have my man of business call to arrange a time and place."

When Julian hesitated, his eyes flickering over her, Blaise guessed he would have preferred to settle the issue now, yet he also obviously didn't wish her to learn of his plans.

"Good enough," he replied.

"Pistols as the weapon of choice?"

"As you wish."

Without another glance at either of them, Julian turned his horse and rode away, leaving Blaise to stare after him in shocked disbelief. This couldn't be happening. Julian had challenged Vincent Foster to a duel—or Vincent had challenged him—and both had willingly accepted.

She turned to Vincent, distraught. "You can't fight him!"

He returned a brooding look. "Can I not? This should have taken place four years ago. I've waited that long for the opportunity to challenge him."

Blaise drew a sharp breath as she suddenly realized what could happen. A duel could very well end tragically. Dear God, Julian might very well be killed. Or he could become a killer and have to flee the country. Duels were illegal in England. That was no doubt why Julian had proposed the highly irregular course of dispensing with seconds—to maintain secrecy.

Vincent must have read the horrified thoughts racing across her features, for he smiled, a sardonic twist of his lips. "Don't be overly concerned for your husband, my lady. Julian always was a deadly shot."

Drawing her shoulders erect, Blaise looked at him with intense dislike. "Good! You deserve to be shot, after what you implied! How could you let him think I had planned an assignation with you?"

And yet she knew she would gain little by railing at Vincent or trying to persuade him to change course. She would do better to plead with Julian. In spite of his deadly coldness a moment ago, she had to try and make him see reason.

Gathering her scattered wits, Blaise ran to her horse and struggled to mount, dragging herself into the sidesaddle. They had yet to arrange the particulars of the meeting. She still had time to stop it.

She urged her mount into a swift canter, cursing herself for her idiocy. She hadn't expected her investigation of the past to have such disastrous results. Her determination to prove Julian's innocence had failed utterly. Yet she'd never invited Mr. Foster to meet her at the ruins, as he'd maliciously intimated to Julian. She'd ridden this way quite at random, finding herself drawn to this haunted place. She'd cherished the vague notion that the ruins might help her understand the tragedy that had occurred there. When she'd stumbled across Mr. Foster, though, it had seemed too good an opportunity to pass up if she hoped to learn more about Caroline's death. But she had drastically misjudged the depth of the animosity smoldering between the two men. They would accept nothing less than the shedding of blood.

Blaise reached home only moments after her husband, but even that was too late. Hedges informed her that his lordship was closeted in his study with Marsh, and had given orders not to be disturbed.

Blaise did not let that stop her. She went to the study door and tried to enter, only to find it firmly locked. Worse, Julian refused to answer her repeated knocks or her pleas to let her speak to him.

After pacing the hall for several minutes, Blaise went upstairs to pace the carpet in her bedchamber, while she tried to form a plan. The duel would have to be fought in secrecy. Otherwise they risked intervention by the legal authorities—the authorities!

She could report the impending duel to the vicar. Or better yet, Squire Ratcliff, who was a magistrate. Perhaps they would be able to stop this madness. *If* she could discover where and when it was to be held.

Just then Blaise heard movement in the next room. Thinking Julian had returned, she fairly flew to the connecting door between their bedchambers. She was half afraid it would be locked, but it opened easily beneath her hand.

She came up short, though, when instead of Julian, she found Terral. The valet was neatly laying a stack of starched, pristine white cravats in a valise.

"What are you doing?" Blaise blurted out.

He gave her a wary glance. "Packing his lordship's clothing, m'lady."

"I can see that, but *why*?"

"He's given orders to remove to London."

"London!"

She regarded Terral with anguish, but he dropped his gaze, as if to avoid seeing it.

"Do you know he means to fight a duel?" she asked, her voice shaking.

The shuttered look that had descended over the valet's face only deepened. "Aye, m'lady."

"Where is it to be held?"

"That I couldn't say."

"You can't say, or you won't?"

His silence was answer enough.

"Terral, you must help me stop him!" Blaise pleaded.

He shook his head sadly. "It isn't my place to interfere, m'lady. It could cost me my position to try."

"And you value your position more than your master's life?" Blaise asked scornfully. "I never would have suspected it of you. A duel could cost him his life!"

Terral looked up earnestly. "He's a dead shot, m'lady. He'll not lose."

"And if he kills Mr. Foster? What then? He will have to flee the country—and may never be able to return. It will finish him, coming after Lady Lynden's death. Do you think anyone would ever again believe in his innocence?"

When Terral refused to answer, Blaise clenched her fists in frustration. Finally the servant said in a low voice, "I don't know, m'lady. I don't know where the duel is to be held. It has not been settled yet."

Blaise jerked her chin up. Idiot! She had stupidly forgotten that Vincent Foster intended to send his man of business over to arrange a time and place for the duel. He could be here at this very moment. And she had foolishly abandoned the field of battle.

With a murmured exclamation to Terral, she hurried from the room and raced down the stairs. Cornering a footman in the entrance hall, she learned that Mr.

Foster's man of business had indeed arrived and was conferring with his lordship.

Without scruple, Blaise dismissed the footman and crept up to the study door, shamelessly prepared to eavesdrop. But to her dismay, she could hear nothing but the low murmur of voices.

In only a few moments, though, the voices in the study suddenly rose in volume, as if the speakers were directly on the other side of the door. Blaise jumped back as Marsh emerged from the room, followed by another man whom she didn't recognize. The man apparently knew her, for he bowed low and issued a formal greeting, introducing himself as Mr. Emmerson.

Blaise responded with polite impatience and didn't wait to see if he took his leave. Instead, she turned and entered Julian's study, shutting the door quietly behind her.

He was sitting behind his desk, writing, but neither by word nor deed did he acknowledge her presence.

Her heart sinking, Blaise glanced around the spacious chamber, remembering the first time, weeks ago, when she had confronted him here. Their argument then had ended in an explosion of passion, and begun the tenuous bonds of a new relationship, based on friendship and trust as well as carnal desire. Since then she hadn't spent a single night alone. She had shared Julian's bed, or he, hers. Not a day had gone by when they hadn't made love, or built on that fledgling trust, learning more about each other, exploring, strengthening.

But it now seemed those bonds had been sundered by her well-intentioned scheme to investigate the past. The man before her was a stranger. The bright afternoon light spilling through the long windows made his hair gleam a soft gold, but he looked untouchable, inviolate. She could almost feel the invisible barrier Julian had erected between them.

He sanded his letter and brushed off the grit, but left it unsealed before finally raising bleak, wintry eyes to her. "Were you listening at the door, sweeting?"

She didn't bother to deny it. "I wanted to know what you were planning. I would have asked you directly, but I didn't think you would tell me."

"Did you learn what you wished to know?"

"No."

"The duel is set for dawn tomorrow morning."

She blinked in surprise, wondering why he had divulged information he should have kept secret, but she could only manage a lame reply. "You can't duel tomorrow. Tomorrow is Sunday."

He gave a mirthless chuckle. "I hardly think such a minor indiscretion will tarnish my soul further."

"Where will it take place?"

"The ruins, of course. It is a fitting site, don't you think?"

The bitterness in his voice made her wince, but it also kindled her anger. "I won't let you do this to yourself, Julian," she said defiantly. "I won't let you destroy your life. I'll find a way to stop you."

"No, Blaise, you will not. I shall lock you in your room and set Terral to guard you, if I must. And have the windows boarded up so you can't slip out. Barbaric, perhaps, but in keeping with my reputation as an ogre."

Despair welled in her eyes at his coldness. "Julian, please . . . I beg you to reconsider. I couldn't bear it if you died."

His mouth twisted sardonically. "Have you so little faith in my marksmanship?"

"No, but something could go wrong . . . You could be hurt. Or you could kill Mr. Foster."

A spark of fury flared in his blue eyes. "Such concern"—his tone dripped ice—"for my dear friend Vincent."

"I am not concerned for him," Blaise declared. "Not at all. I'm worried about the consequences to you. If you have to leave England to escape murder charges, you might never be able to return." His scornful silence clearly expressed disbelief. She moved a step closer, her expression imploring. "I'm sorry I disobeyed you, but I was only acting in your best interests, I swear it."

"My interests, sweeting?" Contempt vibrated in his tone. "You meet secretly with a man who wishes me ill, you betray my trust, you flout my express orders, and you consider it to be serving *my* interests?" His nostrils flared in pent-up rage. "I could have tolerated your irresponsible behavior, even your propensity for scandal. But I draw the line at being cuckolded."

She flinched, and clasped her hands together to keep them from trembling. "What Mr. Foster implied is a lie! It wasn't an assignation. I never asked him to meet me at the ruins. I only found him there during my ride. And I thought . . . since he was there I could question him about what happened the day Caroline died. I hoped he might be able to shed more light on her death and somehow exonerate you . . . so you would stop blaming yourself. I only wanted to prove your innocence, Julian."

Julian watched her narrowly, with aching fury. She looked so wounded that he could almost believe he had wronged her. Perhaps only because he wanted so desperately to believe. Yet he couldn't dismiss her involvement with Vincent so easily, not when he could still hear the echo of Caroline's voice shrieking at him, taunting him: *I've taken a lover! Vincent adores me.*

Seeing Blaise with Vincent in the meadow had made him angry enough to strike her, but he would not take that road. He was determined not to lash out at Blaise as he once had with Caroline. He wouldn't let the nightmare begin again. He wouldn't allow his temper or his passions to rule him. The sick sensation of grief gnawed at his insides, but he locked his jaw against the emotion.

His voice was raw when he spoke; it hurt his throat. "I don't wish to hear any false explanations, sweeting. You will never convince me that Vincent intended anything so honorable as seeking my exoneration."

"Perhaps not, but that was all I intended, I swear it. Julian . . ." She took a deep breath, struggling for calm. "It is quite absurd to accuse me of infidelity. I love you."

His eyes were chilling in their dispassion. "Caroline professed to love me, yet she used Vincent against me as a weapon of revenge."

"You can't possibly think I would do such a thing! Dear God, Julian, you are my *husband*! I would never play you false."

"I once believed that of Caroline."

"I am not Caroline! I am nothing like her." Blaise glared at him, her eyes bright with the glisten of frustration. How could she prove to him that she hadn't betrayed him? "Mr. Foster and I are not lovers. We never have been. You *must* believe me! I swear it," she repeated. "I love you."

Her protestations of innocence apparently meant nothing to him, for he waved a hand in a weary gesture of dismissal. "I don't want your love. Ours was a marriage of convenience, nothing more."

"Was?"

"I think a separation is in order."

She drew a sharp breath, feeling as if he had struck her. "Terral . . . says you mean to go to London."

"Yes. Afterward, if I survive the duel. You may reach me at my town house, if an emergency arises."

"You mean to leave me here alone?"

"Marsh will see to your needs." He indicated the letter on his desk. "I have left written instructions."

"My *needs*? Marsh might be able to ensure my financial security and oversee estate matters, but he couldn't possibly satisfy my needs. What I need is a loving husband. What I need is *you*."

He heard the words, but they barely touched him; lead lay where his heart belonged. Julian shook his head as he forced himself to survey his wife with detachment. He doubted that ordering Blaise out of the room would suffice, for she would only disobey him. He could perhaps summon a footman to remove her bodily, but such an action would only create another scandal and would do nothing to quell her determination. The best course was to remove himself from her presence entirely, for good.

He rose to his feet. "There is no point in discussing this further. I don't intend to remain to see the past repeated. I am leaving Lynden Park. I mean to wash my hands of it altogether."

"And me? You're washing your hands of me, too?"

"Yes."

Blaise felt her eyes blurring with tears, her throat muscles constricting with pain.

"Don't look so wounded, sweeting. You should be gratified. I'm leaving you free to seek your pleasures outside the marriage bed. Indeed, you have my blessing."

Blindly she took another step toward him, wishing there were some way to break through Julian's icy control. How could she hope to persuade this remote stranger that she loved him when he was so intent on distancing himself from her? She moved around the desk, blocking his path. "Have the past two months meant nothing to you?"

"On the contrary. They have meant a great deal to me, sweeting. I have enjoyed your lovely body tremendously."

She stared up at him. He was deliberately trying to drive her away, she knew, but that didn't make the pain any less devastating. But she wouldn't give up without a fight. Closing the physical distance between them, she reached up and wound her arms around Julian's neck, pressing her body against him, making him feel her feminine softness. "You want me, I know it."

"My body wants you. But what you provide, I can easily obtain elsewhere."

He said it softly, with a finality that belied the relentless ache in him.

For a long, tormented moment Blaise stared at him. Yet she didn't protest when Julian pried her arms from about his neck and stepped back.

He turned abruptly on his heel then, and without another word, strode from the room.

Trembling, her legs as weak as jelly, Blaise sank into the chair he had vacated. Dear God, what had she done? Her attempts to prove Julian's innocence might have destroyed her marriage instead of gaining her what she wanted most: Julian's love. And in the end, it might very well cost him his life.

Chapter 22

Blaise never realized she'd been fooled until it was too late.

After her unsatisfactory interview with Julian, she rode straight to the Gypsy camp to consult with Miklos and Panna. She even took the time to have a groom accompany her, although she was already in such trouble that one more indiscretion would hardly matter.

Miklos lent a sympathetic ear as Blaise explained about the terrible coil she was in, but to her complete dismay, he refused to support her effort to prevent the duel.

" 'Tis not right to interfere in a blood feud," he said, shaking his head. "And a man's honor must be avenged, even *gorgio* honor."

Panna, her wise black eyes troubled, agreed, saying that fate must play out its course.

Feeling abandoned but not yet ready to give up, Blaise rode next to see Rachel Foster, hoping the woman might be able to persuade her brother to abandon the duel.

The Foster estate boasted a handsome house in the Elizabethan style, half-timbered and bold-patterned, with stepped gables and classical pediments in a rambling irregular construction.

When the front door was opened by a butler, Blaise handed him an embossed card that she'd had printed and swept into the foyer. "Lady Lynden to see Miss Foster. Please inform her I am here."

She could tell from the august servant's expression that he was not happy with her demands, but he did not dare refuse admittance to someone of her rank. "I will inquire if Miss Foster is receiving."

He showed Blaise into an attractive parlor to wait, but as he turned away, she asked with forced casualness, "Is your master at home?"

After the slightest hesitation, he answered, "No, my lady. Mr. Foster is away at present."

Relieved at least that she would not have to confront Vincent Foster, Blaise waited impatiently for several minutes for his sister to appear. Miss Foster quietly entered the room just as Blaise was about to march upstairs in search of her.

She looked more subdued than Blaise had ever seen her. Her eyes were rimmed with red, as if she'd been crying, which suggested she knew about the duel. For all her apparent distress, though, Miss Foster still retained her usual haughtiness.

"Whyever have you come here?" she demanded. "I should think you've done enough damage."

Feeling guilty for the part she had played in precipitating the crisis, Blaise didn't offer a defense. Instead she said with uncharacteristic humbleness, "I came to ask for your help."

"Mine?" Miss Foster looked taken aback.

"I hoped you would persuade your brother to withdraw from the duel."

Rachel stiffened. "You want my brother to withdraw when Julian called him out—"

"I'm not certain who called whom out—it wasn't arranged in the usual way. But I'm certain your brother was just as anxious to participate."

"What do you expect me to do? It isn't proper to interfere with a gentleman's honor."

Blaise couldn't hold back her exclamation of impatience. "What does it matter if it is proper or not when lives are at stake? Your brother could *die*, Miss Foster! My husband could die." She let that sink in before adding in a more controlled tone, "I considered going to the authorities, but I would prefer not to air our dirty linen in public. If we could convince them . . . I had hoped we could join forces and work together to prevent the duel."

"It is too late. They will be getting under way at any moment now."

"Too . . . *late*?" Blaise felt her heart stop. "What do you mean? Julian told me it was to be held at dawn tomorrow!"

Miss Foster glanced at the ormolu clock on the mantel. "I understood it was to begin at five o'clock. Vincent left a short while—"

"He *tricked* me," Blaise breathed. "Julian lied to me. Dear God, they may kill each other." Abruptly she turned toward the door, before realizing she still had no idea where to go. "Where is it to take place? Miss Foster, you must tell me!"

"The ruins."

"He told the truth about that at least." The clock showed less than a quarter hour till five. "I must go!"

"But what—"

She hurried from the room, leaving Miss Foster to gape after her. Not waiting for the butler, Blaise threw open the front door and raced down the steps, calling for her groom to help her into the saddle at once. When she was mounted, she dug in her heel and bent low over the mare's neck, demanding speed, praying she could reach the dueling field in time.

She remembered little of that mad ride. The English countryside sped by in a blur of fallow fields and green hedgerows and leafless woods. She approached the line of elms at a gallop and burst onto the meadow, terrified by what she might find.

In seconds her frantic gaze took in the scene. The meadow bathed in late-afternoon sunshine, peaceful and lovely despite the brisk breeze. Two male figures standing to one side with the horses . . . Mr. Marsh, Blaise thought, and his counterpart, Vincent Foster's man of business. A black leather case that might have contained dueling pistols lying on the low Roman wall.

But her attention was held by the two gentlemen beside

the wall—and the weapon one carried. She could see sunlight glinting off the barrel of the deadly pistol in Vincent Foster's hand.

With a cry of alarm, Blaise drove her horse across the wide expanse, not stopping until she had reached the two duelists, where she brought the mare to a plunging halt. Panting for breath, her heart beating so furiously she thought she might faint, Blaise flung herself to the ground and nearly fell in her haste. She pushed herself between the two men, holding her arms out as if to ward them off.

"I won't . . . let you . . . do this," she wheezed. "You will have to . . . shoot me first."

Both men eyed her grimly. Julian's features looked as if they had been carved from cold stone, while Vincent Foster's expression evinced brooding fury.

"I warned you not to interfere," Julian said finally, with icy calm.

"Perhaps so . . . but I never promised . . . to obey you. I couldn't stay away . . . as long as there was a chance to stop you."

"Go home, Blaise. You don't belong here."

"No, I won't go home! Not until I make you see reason. This cannot be settled with pistols."

"I agree. Indeed, Vincent and I were discussing the matter before you arrived so precipitously."

She blinked in confusion. Looking from Julian to Vincent, then back again, she finally comprehended what she had failed to see before. Julian was unarmed. He hadn't taken up the second pistol; it still lay harmlessly in its case.

Julian shifted his gaze to his opponent. "As I was saying . . . my challenge was made in the heat of anger, and I have since reconsidered."

Vincent's fierce expression only darkened. "You mean to withdraw?"

"Yes. If you feel honor must be satisfied—"

"I do! You won't escape so easily this time, damn you. I had hoped when you went off to war, the French would mete out your punishment, but they failed. After all these years you won't deny me the pleasure of attempting to put a bullet through you."

Blaise drew a sharp breath at the venom in Vincent's tone. Clearly he was not willing to cry peace.

Julian shook his head. "I won't stand against you."

"Are you such a coward then?" Vincent cried.

"No, not a coward. But what honor I have left is not worth the guilt. I am by far the better shot, so killing you could indeed be construed as murder. Besides"—his gaze flicked to Blaise—"I am not willing to shoot a man over an unfaithful wife."

Blaise didn't know whether by "unfaithful wife" he meant Caroline or herself, but before she could respond, Julian turned and walked away, toward his horse.

To her horror, she saw Vincent raise his pistol and shout, "Stop!" The tormented cry seemed torn from his soul.

Julian halted in his tracks, but Vincent drew back the hammer.

Blaise shrieked and leaped at Vincent, grasping for his arm, but he shrugged her off. From the corner of her eye, she saw Julian take an abrupt step toward her, but then he checked.

"Step aside, Blaise."

"No!" She positioned herself directly in the path of fire. "I won't let him hurt you."

Moving toward her, he took her elbow, and despite her resistance, drew her gently, inexorably, aside. Then he turned to face his foe. "Shoot me if you will."

Vincent maintained his aim, his hand shaking, his dark eyes burning with anguish.

Yet he didn't fire. After an endless moment, he gave another harsh cry, and with a violent jerk of his arm, threw the pistol away. Blaise watched it land harmlessly on the ground. Her legs went weak with relief. Blindly she reached for the wall, needing the support.

Vincent gripped his hair with his hands, and stood there, his eyes squeezed shut as if in pain. He'd had the opportunity to kill Julian, but he hadn't taken it.

"I loved Caroline," he murmured in an agonized voice. "Far more than you ever did."

"I know," Julian replied quietly.

"You killed her."

"No, she died in a fall from her horse. I accept much of the blame for driving her out in the storm, but if I am guilty, then you are as well. If she had not ridden out to meet you, her accident would never have occurred."

A low groan was Vincent's only reply.

"You were misguided in loving Caroline," Julian continued softly, relentlessly. "She only used you to strike back at me."

Vincent bowed his head, as if drained of the will to protest. "God damn your soul to hell," he whispered raggedly, his voice almost beyond sound.

"If it is any consolation, I expect my soul has already been marked for hell."

Julian turned again toward his horse, but this time no one stopped him. Blaise felt her throat close with tears as she watched him mount. The immediate crisis had been averted, and yet the trust between them had been shattered, perhaps never to be mended.

The tears slipped relentlessly down her face as Julian rode away without giving her a single backward glance.

Chapter 23

Dearest Julian . . .

Faltering, Blaise brushed the feather of her quill pen against her cheek as she deliberated the salutation to her latest missive to London. For the past two weeks, she had written Julian letter after letter, but she hadn't received a single reply. She didn't expect this one to be any different, yet if there was the slightest chance he would relent and afford her a new hearing, she had to take it.

She was swiftly losing hope, though. Despair had become her constant companion. She had never known such misery as she'd endured the past two weeks. Never known such impotence. She had driven Julian away and had no idea how to get him back. Her disastrous plan to prove his innocence had been well-intentioned but totally misunderstood. He saw her ill-conceived efforts merely as betrayal. He thought her in league with Vincent, condemning her if not for the terrible charge of adultery, then for merely associating with his longtime enemy. The worst of it was, even if she could somehow manage to convince Julian to return home, he might never again trust her.

Her heart ached for her lost love; her body ached for his touch. She lay awake at night, alone and lonely, imagining all sorts of terrors—the most terrifying that Julian had gone off to war again. In her nightmares she saw him lying wounded and in pain on some bloody battlefield in the Peninsula, with no one to aid or succor him. In less panicky moments, she pictured him receiving *too* much succor—from the beautiful Cyprians who abounded in London.

He'd admitted that he had previously kept a mistress, and Blaise could well believe he might resume such a liaison. She had only to close her eyes to envision a nameless beauty with Julian, kissing, embracing, their naked bodies locked in the writhing throes of passion.

Blaise shuddered and bent to write.

My dearest husband . . .

She had barely completed the first line begging Julian to reconsider when a quiet rap sounded on her sitting room door. She bid entrance, and looked up to find the butler, Hedges.

"You have guests waiting below, my lady," Hedges solemnly announced. "The Gypsies again. Mr. Smith and another . . . gentleman."

He hesitated over the word "gentleman" but said the word "Gypsies" with less contempt than usual, as if he knew a visit from her friends would cheer her. Surprisingly the staid Hedges had been one of her staunchest supporters during the past two unbearable weeks since Julian had abandoned her. He'd hovered protectively in the background, always at hand to anticipate her simplest request. Mrs. Hedges, too, had been invaluable, as had her abigail, Garvey. Blaise hadn't been able to confide the details of her troubled marriage to the servants, but they had guessed. And having them near, knowing she had their sympathy, somehow made her trials more bearable.

The Gypsies had proved her dearest allies. They had refused to abandon her, remaining in the district even at the risk of incurring Lynden's wrath. Miklos and Panna, of course, had been privy to the entire story; Blaise had few secrets from them. Both had advised her to be patient, to let fate take its course. Blaise did not want to wait for fickle fate to decide her future. She wanted to act now—only she had no notion of how to go about it.

With a sigh, she thanked Hedges and rose. Smoothing the skirts of her blue kerseymere morning gown, she went downstairs to the small parlor where Miklos awaited her.

He stepped forward to greet her with an uncharacteristic anxious look on his dark features. Another swarthy Rom had accompanied him, Blaise noted, as dark and tall as Miklos but more stout. He stood in the center of the room, hat in hand, as if afraid to sit down and dirty the damask upholstery.

"I 'ave some grave news, Rauniyog," Miklos said at once.

For an instant Blaise's heart leaped with panic. "What is it? Has something happened to Julian?"

"Not that I ken—I dunno anything about 'im. What I do know is you'll want to 'ear what Sandor 'as to say. You remember Sandor of the Lee tribe, what owns the monkey?"

"Oh . . . yes, of course. How do you do?" Blaise said politely, restraining her impatience.

"Well, 'e knows what 'appened to Lady Lynden all that time ago. The Lees were camped near the ruins the day her ladyship was done for. Sandor saw it all."

Blaise turned to stare at the stout Gypsy. "Is this true? You *witnessed* Lady Lynden's death?"

Sandor shuddered and looked fearfully over his shoulder. " 'Twas four years ago, m'lady," he said with obvious reluctance, "but I remember it well."

"Sandor doesn't want to talk about it," Miklos interjected. "You ken, Rauniyog, 'ow the Rom don't like to speak of the dead, even *gorgio* dead. Nor do we get involved in *gorgio* doings."

She nodded, acknowledging the Gypsy fear of ghostly spirits and unwanted attention from *gorgios*. But she wouldn't rest until she discovered exactly how Lady Caroline had died.

For the first time in two weeks, Blaise felt the faintest stirrings of hope. "I understand your misgivings, Mr. Lee, and applaud your courage in coming forward. Please, won't you sit down? I shall order refreshments for us so we may be comfortable." She walked quickly across the room and pulled the bell rope to summon Hedges. "I should like to hear every single detail about that day, no matter how small."

Bored with the evening, impatient with the aimlessness of the company at his London club, Julian pocketed his gaming winnings and rose from the faro table. With his usual charming politeness, he fended off the good-natured protests at his early departure, observing that it was well past two A.M. and that he had a pressing appointment with his tailor in the morning, to upbraid the fellow for fashioning a pair of breeches so tight they threatened to unman him.

To a chorus of ribald male chuckles, he left the elegant Subscription Room of Brooks Club and descended the stairs. After accepting his outer garments and walking stick from the majordomo, he stepped out into the chill December night and climbed into his waiting carriage, ordering his coachman to drive home.

Earlier that evening, his friend Baron Kilgore had invited him to attend a soiree at an exclusive pleasure house known for its exquisite courtesans, but Julian had declined, giving the excuse that he was now a married man.

"You can't possibly mean to remain faithful to your *wife?*" Richard exclaimed in astonishment. "She is a fetching piece, I'll allow, but it simply isn't done, old fellow."

If Richard had not been rather the worse for drink at the moment, Julian might have applied his fists to his friend's face for terming Blaise "a fetching piece." "You are speaking of my viscountess, I'll advise you to remember."

"I don't recall you having such scruples about the first Lady Lynden," Richard said petulantly. "You were as game as they come in your salad days."

"True," Julian agreed with an inward wince. "But that doesn't mean I must repeat the mistakes of my youth—or my first marriage."

Yet his reluctance to make the same mistakes he'd once made with Caroline was only part of the reason he had eschewed female companionship since coming to London, Julian reflected now as he settled back on the velvet carriage squabs. The prime reason for his stark celibacy was much more visceral. The thought of making love to any woman other than Blaise was profoundly distasteful.

Even when he had first arrived in London, numb and shattered by her betrayal, he hadn't been able to forget his violet-eyed wife. The simplest things reminded him of Blaise. A murmur of feminine laughter. A ray of sunshine. The throb of his wounded leg. Even his club, which was located on St. James Street. Blaise had been a St. James before their marriage.

He'd tried to tell himself he no longer cared, tried to divorce himself from all feeling. But the huge mansion in Berkeley Square, staffed with only a skeleton crew of servants, echoed with loneliness.

He missed Blaise. He missed her bright smile, her high spirits, her exasperating, cajoling ways. He missed her daily massages and the sensual play that always followed. He missed the wild sweetness of her body beneath him, above him, around him. He missed her. And he wanted her. *Her*, not some other nameless female who could provide him physical relief but not solace for his soul. That was why he was returning to his town house alone after an evening of pointless gaming where he'd added to a fortune already too large for him to spend in a lifetime. He wanted Blaise, with a desperate, unrelenting hunger.

And he needed her.

Julian closed his eyes and stretched his stiff right leg. He could no longer deny how excruciatingly somber and pointless his life was without Blaise. He no longer even wished to deny it. The simple truth was, he was in love with his infuriating madcap of a wife.

Yet it had taken him this long to come to his senses. He'd been terrified of history repeating itself. Caroline had cuckolded him four years ago with Vincent Foster, so why could it not happen again? Seeing Blaise with Vincent beside the ruins had brought back all those terrible memories with devastating force. It was fear that had led him to accuse Blaise unjustly of adultery. Even when she'd pleaded and tried to make him see reason, he hadn't allowed himself to believe the truth. He'd dismissed her avowals of love as merely an attempt to protect herself from his wrath.

His fear now seemed absurdly irrational. He should have known Blaise could never have acted with such duplicity. No one with her openness and forthrightness could have engaged in a secret affair with a man of Vincent Foster's brooding nature. No woman could have demonstrated her love more explicitly, for that matter. Blaise had stepped in front of a dueling pistol to protect him, for God's sake. He couldn't imagine Caroline ever doing something so reckless—or so selfless.

Julian squeezed his eyes shut in shame. He owed Blaise a humble apology for mistrusting her with such unwarranted fervor. He owed her more than an apology for his lunacy. He owed her his gratitude. Blaise had taught him to live again, brought him back to life, given him something to live for: a future. *If* he hadn't destroyed it by his blind, reactionary accusations.

He would have to beg her forgiveness, Julian decided as the carriage came to a halt. He had nothing but his thick-witted pride to preserve. Tomorrow he would give Will the order to pack. He would return home, to see if he could salvage the tattered shreds of his marriage.

He held hope for a favorable outcome, even if he didn't deserve it. Blaise's imploring letters—which he'd lacked first the interest and then the courage to answer— had been full of abject apologies and explanations for her accidental clandestine meeting with Vincent Foster, as well as promises never, *never* to disobey him again. Julian had grave doubts she could keep those rash promises. Even though the frequent reports from Marsh intimated that her ladyship was behaving with incredible sedateness in his absence, he suspected his errant wife would become embroiled in some kind of mischief before long if he weren't there to prevent it.

That thought was uppermost in Julian's mind as he stepped down from his barouche and dismissed his coachman. The rattle of carriage wheels receded, leaving a chill quiet.

He had turned to mount the front steps of his town house when a dark figure emerged from the shadows, into the moonlight. Seeing the blunderbuss trained directly at his chest, Julian gripped his cane, prepared to defend himself if possible—but then he recognized the swarthy figure.

"Miklos! Blast it, man, you gave me a turn. What the devil are you doing, lurking in the shadows?"

"Beggin' your pardon, yer lordship, but I 'ave to ask you to come with me. Quiet-like, if you don't mind."

Julian stared blankly at the weapon in the Gypsy's hand. "Come with you?"

"Aye. I'm to fetch you home. Her ladyship's orders."

"Home? Blaise?" Julian shook his head. He seemed to be having difficulty recruiting his wits. His wife's pet Gypsy was holding him at gunpoint, for some unspecified reason.

"If you'll just oblige me and 'old out yer 'ands," Miklos suggested.

"Why the devil should I?"

"Because I'll 'ave to shoot you, m'lord, if you don't. Tom, you'll relieve 'is lordship of 'is walking stick and tie 'is 'ands."

Miklos's son sprang forward obediently, if apologetically, with a length of leather harness, but was careful to keep out of range of the cane.

"Please, your stick, m'lord," Miklos prompted with a wave of his weapon. "I'm to fetch you home."

Julian gritted his teeth as he finally began to grasp the situation. He was actually about to be spirited from his London town house. "Am I to understand my wife ordered my forcible abduction?" he demanded.

"Not abduction, m'lord, never that. Only a . . . strong invitation."

"Which you give me no choice but to accept." Contemptuously, Julian eyed the wide, gaping mouth of the blunderbuss—which looked like a truncated musket with a horn muzzle—and weighed his chances of escape. Even as little as a few months ago he would have risked grave injury or death rather than yield to such coercion and threats. But recently, ever since he'd learned to live with his heavy burden of guilt, he'd developed a healthy regard for his own skin. He wouldn't chance a struggle. "Do you at least mean to tell me why you feel it necessary to engage in this absurd charade?"

"Because Rauniyog kenned you would never come without persuasion. I'm right sorry."

"Well, she was wrong. I intended to go home tomorrow in any case. Your 'persuasion' isn't at all necessary."

Miklos hesitated, looking skeptical. Then he shook his head. "I 'ave to be sure, m'lord. I promised Rauniyog to follow 'er orders exactly, so you'll come wi' us now, please. 'Old out yer 'ands."

"Blast it, man—" Cold fury welling up in him, Julian relinquished his cane and submitted to his hands being tied in front of him. "You realize, of course, that this is a singularly ill-advised action? That abduction of a peer is a hanging offense?"

"Aye, m'lord, I do," Miklos acknowledged sadly, "but I could not abandon Rauniyog in her hour o' need. If I must run afoul of the law, then so be it."

"Forget about the damned law," Julian said in a savage undertone. "Worry instead about running afoul of *me*!"

Miklos shrugged his broad shoulders and waved the gun, obviously not inviting further debate. "Please, m'lord, don't make this harder than it must be."

"Of course, how remiss of me," Julian said with sarcasm. "I do beg your pardon."

Ten minutes later, Julian found himself trussed up in a Gypsy wagon, rattling along the road north from London

in the middle of the night. He lay on a thick straw
mattress, covered with warm blankets, as comfortable
as the Gypsies could make him. Miklos had planned
well; within his reach was a wrapped cloth of bread and
cheese to assuage his hunger, a flask of ale to satisfy
his thirst, and a chamber pot to relieve himself. With a
little ingenuity he could manage, since his fingers still
had freedom of movement. But the jolts of the ill-sprung
vehicle sent vibrations of shock through his healing leg
every few moments, stiffening both his muscles and his
rancor.

Adding insult to injury had been Miklos's admission
moments ago, before he tightly secured the front canvas
flap of the wagon, effectively locking Julian inside, that
the blunderbuss wasn't loaded. "Rauniyog did not wish
to chance you gettin' hurt, m'lord, so there was never
any danger." The humiliating knowledge that he'd been
gulled enraged Julian even more than his actual abduction, which was emasculating enough.

This was all Blaise's doing, he thought with smoldering
fury. She'd meddled again, taken matters into her own
hands with total disregard for honor or convention. She had
incited her Gypsy friends to mayhem and was entirely to
blame for this outrage. Miklos was merely her lackey.

No longer even mildly amused by his minx's scandalous, high-spirited antics, Julian lay there in the dark,
clenching his teeth against the pain and contemplating his
retribution. He'd once been falsely accused of murdering
his first wife, but there would be nothing false about the
charge of murder when he finally got his hands on his
second.

Chapter 24

Blaise grimaced in self-disgust as she leveled the dueling pistol at Vincent Foster's chest. She was actually trembling; her hand shook like a willow leaf in a strong wind. Really, it was absurd that she had so little self-control. She had to remember that her drastic action was for a good cause.

Determinedly she brought her left hand up to brace her unsteady right as she met Mr. Foster's shocked gaze. Clearly she had astonished him by accosting him thus in his own drawing room. And angered him. His dark eyes flashed with animosity as he eyed the weapon in her gloved hand.

Blaise wasn't nearly as concerned about Mr. Foster's wrath, though, as by her husband's. She knew Julian would be furious at her for what she'd done, but desperate situations called for desperate measures. He had to learn the truth so he could finally be free of his terrible burden of guilt. Pleading with him to come home would never have worked, she was certain. Not when he hadn't replied to a single one of her letters. So she had sent Miklos to London to escort him home forcibly. And when she'd received word of their arrival a short while ago, she'd called on Vincent Foster to convince him at pistol-point to accompany her to the ruins.

She was risking her entire future, gambling all her hopes, on a single throw of the dice. But if it were at all possible, she intended to expose the truth and wring a confession out of the villain who truly had been responsible for Caroline's death.

"All this time you've accused Julian of murder when he was entirely innocent," Blaise declared with passion. "But I won't let your injustice continue."

Mr. Foster narrowed his gaze on her weapon, as if calculating the odds of his escaping. Suddenly he turned away, presenting his back to her.

"Stop!" Blaise exclaimed, startled by his unexpected move.

Defiantly he strode across the room toward the bell rope. "I shall ring for my butler to show you out, Lady Lynden."

She waved the pistol at him in desperation. Vincent was not acting at all according to plan. He should have meekly submitted to her threat and agreed to accompany her. Instead he reached for the rope and gave it a strong pull.

"I'll shoot!"

"Very well, shoot me if you dare. Indeed, I don't particularly care."

Blaise nearly stamped her foot in frustration. These obsessed Englishmen who didn't give a fig whether they lived or died were driving her to distraction. But she had no time now to convince Vincent Foster just how pigheaded he was being. Nor could she just shoot him in cold blood. He had probably known that when he'd called her bluff. Evidently she had badly miscalculated.

"Don't you wish to learn how Caroline died?" she asked with a frantic attempt to sway him.

Vincent had started to give the rope another tug, but his hand arrested in midair. "What do you mean?" The sharp edge to his tone told Blaise she had his full attention.

"I know how it happened. And I should think after all your years of piously proclaiming your love for her, you would want the truth to finally come out, as well."

His angry, brooding eyes bored into her like daggers.

"Julian never killed her, and I mean to prove it," she declared.

"I'm listening."

"It isn't something I can simply describe. You have to see it for yourself."

Vincent's jaw clenched, yet he remained silent, apparently debating.

The Fosters' butler appeared at the door just at that moment. "You rang, sir?"

Blaise hastened to interrupt. "My carriage is waiting below, Mr. Foster," she said, almost pleading. "An hour of your time, that's all I ask. I think you owe Julian that much."

For another long moment Vincent stared at her, while Blaise's heart beat in an unsteady rhythm. She had no idea what she would do if he refused. Her plan depended on an element of deception, and it was imperative that he be there to witness it.

"Very well, Lady Lynden. I shall accompany you . . . but without the pistol, if you please."

Blaise let out her breath in relief and returned the weapon to her reticule. The second hurdle had been cleared. The first had been getting Julian to return home. Miklos would be waiting with him at the Roman ruins. Now it remained only for her to obtain the final player in their little drama.

She turned to the butler. "Would you please tell Miss Foster that her brother and I are going out? We should return within the hour."

The august butler looked to his master for confirmation, and when Vincent gave a brief nod, bowed himself from the room.

Vincent escorted Blaise downstairs, where he commanded a footman to fetch his greatcoat and gloves. He was shrugging into the garment when his sister, Rachel, came rushing down the curving stairway, her usual haughtiness absent, her elegant forehead creased in a worried frown.

"Where are you going with her?" Rachel demanded somewhat breathlessly.

"I intend to accompany Lady Lynden to the ruins."

"The *ruins*?" Blaise saw something that looked like fear flash in the woman's eyes, but it might have been concern for her brother. "But you can't—" Rachel broke off, biting her lip, while Vincent raised a dark eyebrow.

"I cannot what?"

"Nothing. I just meant . . . you'll be late for tea. I have invited the Denbys to join us."

"The Misses Denby can manage without me for one afternoon."

He turned to go, but was forestalled by his sister's sharp "Vincent, wait!"

"Yes?"

"Whyever would you visit those horrid ruins? I thought they held unpleasant memories for you."

"Certainly they do. But Lady Lynden claims to have information regarding Caroline's death."

"Indeed? How . . . how droll. But surely you don't wish to dredge up the past."

"Not particularly. But Lady Lynden seems to think it important."

Blaise spoke then. "I can produce a witness to Caroline's death who will prove Julian's innocence."

"A witness?" The word was a soft rasp, while the color suddenly fled from Rachel's cheeks. Yet almost immediately she seemed to collect herself and forced a thin smile. "After four years? This is rather sudden, is it not?"

"I think it hardly matters how much time has passed, as long as it clears Julian's name."

Rachel turned to Vincent, who was staring at Blaise. "You can't possibly believe her. She obviously is trying to protect her husband."

Ignoring his sister's protests, he said slowly, "I want to know the truth."

"The truth? How could this brass-faced little chit have any knowledge of the truth?"

"You are welcome to accompany us, Miss Foster," Blaise said with as much casualness as she could muster.

The hatred that flared in Rachel Foster's eyes took her aback. "Well, I suppose I must," she retorted with her usual haughtiness. "If you insist on going off on this fool's errand, Vincent, then I should be there to ensure you don't get gammoned by some absurd nonsense. Let me get a wrap."

Some five minutes later Vincent handed both ladies into the Lynden carriage. It was a chill, gray December afternoon, with brooding stormclouds threatening overhead. Blaise shivered, despite the warmth of her velvet pelisse, and settled back in her seat, facing the brother and sister.

She felt a great elation at clearing another hurdle, yet she couldn't repress her trepidation that her plan might fail. So many things could go wrong. And even if they proceeded flawlessly, Julian might hate her for what she had done to him. Having one's lordly husband forcibly abducted and locked in a Gypsy wagon for the seventy-odd miles of turnpikes and country roads from London was not the ideal path to marital bliss.

The carriage ride to the ruins was accomplished in silence, as none of the occupants seemed inclined to talk. Rachel, with uncharacteristic nervousness, chewed her lip, while her brother stared broodingly out the window. Blaise generally kept her gaze fastened on the passing landscape—the barren trees and fallow fields of winter— and wished this ordeal were over. She could actually feel the tension within the swaying carriage, although she wasn't certain how much was due to her own nerves, or to those of the Fosters.

A short while later the carriage began to slow. Blaise peered anxiously out the window as the vehicle swept onto the field where the ruins stood. Her heart gave a lurch when she spied Julian. He was half sitting, half leaning against the rear of the Gypsy wagon, rubbing his wrists as if in discomfort. Blaise winced as she remembered her order to bind his hands so that he would be less likely to escape.

And his appearance . . . She had never seen her elegant
husband so unkempt, Blaise realized as the carriage came
to a halt a short distance from him. Julian looked as if
he had hardly slept. His golden hair was tousled, his
jaw stubbled with an incipient beard. He wore evening
clothes beneath his open greatcoat—a frock coat of blue
superfine and breeches of cream satin that were creased
and wrinkled beyond hope, a starched cravat and high
shirt points that had grown limp and crumpled.

But it was the way he looked at her, rather than the
way he looked, that disturbed her most. His blazing blue
eyes bored holes in her that made her want to shiver.

Her heart sank. Only once had she seen Julian look so
forbidding: the day of the duel, when he'd washed his
hands of her. He wore the same unforgiving expression
now that he'd worn then—relentless, chill, totally devoid
of human warmth. That savage countenance made his
facial scar stand out in stark contrast to the classical
masculine beauty of his features.

Unable to bear his enmity, she averted her gaze. Miklos
was there with another man: Sandor, the Gypsy who,
three days before, had confessed to seeing Lady Lynden
meet her fate. Blaise focused her attention on them as
she stepped down from the carriage. She had to forget
that her husband might very well hate her. She had taken
what she believed was the best course, and now all she
could do was see it through.

She forced a smile, mainly to reassure the Gypsies.
Sandor, in particular, appeared ill-at-ease at the proceedings. He seemed to shrink back when Miss Foster
descended from the carriage.

Rachel gave the Gypsies a disdainful glance and kept
well back, as if they might contaminate the skirts of her
fur-lined bombazine pelisse. Her brother, when he stepped
down, sent them a cursory look, but awarded Julian the
brunt of his brooding, hostile attention. Blaise could
feel the animosity between the two men. Julian's gaze
flickered over Vincent coldly, while his jaw hardened,
but he said not a word. He merely stood there leaning

against the Gypsy wagon, his arms crossed belligerently over his chest.

Apparently Vincent felt someone should take command of the conversation. He dismissed the Lynden coachman with orders to wait at the edge of the meadow, and as the carriage rattled off, turned to Blaise. "Lady Lynden, you obviously went to some trouble to stage this event. Shall we proceed?"

"Yes, shall we?" Julian seconded grimly. His normally cool disposition was in a savage state, while his leg and his pride ached fiercely. It was all he could do to restrain himself from grabbing his outrageous, disobedient wife and shaking her till her teeth rattled, an urge which was nearly as sharp as the savage desire to haul her into his arms and shower her with passion. When she'd first stepped down from the carriage and stood before him, looking so young and beautiful in a pelisse of blue velvet, her raven hair stylishly arranged beneath a matching bonnet, his heart had turned over, while his body had tightened with hunger.

Yet that hunger was tempered by cold reality. Seeing Blaise emerge from a closed carriage, followed by his longtime friend and enemy, Vincent Foster, had aroused his irrational fear all over again, and reminded Julian of why he had left in the first place. He hadn't conquered his fear, it seemed. He couldn't forget the nightmares—Caroline and Vincent together, Caroline's death—or convince himself that Blaise's relationship with Vincent was totally innocent. Nor could he dismiss her recent behavior so easily. Her obvious reluctance to meet his eyes now proclaimed her guilt in the business of his abduction from London.

At least Miklos had removed the leather straps binding his wrists. The moment he'd been set free and stood on solid ground, Julian had exhibited his skill as a Corinthian and amateur pugilist, delivering a punishing right to the Gypsy's swarthy jaw, knocking the fellow to the ground. He would have commandeered the wagon then, but a repentant Miklos had pleaded with him to stay long enough to hear what Rauniyog had to say, as she would be there any moment. It turned out to be much longer than a moment, and now he was keenly impatient for this farce to end so he could attend to his wife.

"Very well," Blaise replied with a wary glance at him from beneath her lashes. Taking a deep breath, she made the introductions. "Miss Foster, Mr. Foster, this is Miklos Smith, who was a longtime friend of my late father's. And this is Sandor Lee. He owns the monkey that performed at my ball." Rachel regarded the Gypsy with cold contempt as Blaise continued, "You see . . . Mr. Lee was present the afternoon Lady Lynden died. He witnessed the entire incident."

Julian, who had appeared somewhat bored by the discussion, gave an involuntary start. Straightening, he sent Sandor a sharp glance. "Is this true?"

"Aye, m'lord."

Rachel sniffed, while her brother eyed the Gypsy with similar skepticism. "Why have you waited all this time to come forward?" Vincent queried.

"I was afeared to speak of it, yer honor. No one listens to a poor Gypsy. But then I 'eard 'is lordship was 'eld to blame for the lady's murder, and I knew it weren't true. And 'is lordship's been good to us poor Rom—"

"Yes, yes, please continue. What happened?"

"Yes, Mr. Lee," Blaise said more gently. "Tell these people exactly what you told me about that day."

"Aye, m'lady. Well, you see . . ." Sandor peered over his shoulder. Blaise understood his reticence; he feared retribution by Caroline's spirit even more than he feared the powerful *gorgios*.

"Well, yer honors . . . it was blowing up for rain that day. I was 'ere with my wife, right over there." He pointed toward the line of bare elms. "We was looking for *hotchi*." Abruptly he glanced at Lord Lynden, as if afraid he might be charged with poaching. "We meant no 'arm, yer lordship. *Gorgios* don't want hedgehogs—"

With as little patience as Vincent had shown, Julian ignored the apology. "Go on. You said you were here that day?"

"Aye, well, there was two *raunis* 'ere also . . . a fair one and a dark one."

Rachel gave a most unladylike snort of disgust. "Must you speak in your devil tongue? What do you mean, *raw-ni?*"

"A *rauni* is a lady," Blaise replied. "Please let him continue. You said you saw Lady Lynden here?"

Sandor sent Blaise a grateful look. "Aye, m'lady, the fair one. And another lady with dark hair." Raising his hand slowly, he pointed at Rachel Foster. "I saw this lady here also."

Rachel stiffened with evident outrage. "*I?* Why, that is absurd!"

"Beware, sir," Vincent warned, leaping to his sister's defense. "I will not countenance your fabrications."

"There was two ladies," the Gypsy said stubbornly, "and they was arguing."

"Perhaps so, but you no doubt mistook my sister for someone else. You said it was raining. It must have been difficult to see clearly."

Sandor shook his black head sadly. "No, yer honor. It was 'er I saw, *before* the rain started. An' I 'eard 'er voice. I didn't ken 'oo she was until the ball when she floored my poor monkey, but I knew then it was 'er."

Julian interrupted, his voice low and commanding. "You claim to have seen my wife's death. Tell us what happened, Mr. Lee, in your own words, if you please."

"Well, like I said, I saw the two ladies argue. The fair one on a chestnut *grai* made to ride this one down—"

"A *grai* is a horse?"

"Aye, forgive me, yer lordship, a chestnut 'orse. This lady threw a stone at the 'orse, which made it rise up on its 'ind legs. The fair lady fell to the ground and 'it 'er 'ead. She never got up." Sandor sent another fearful glance over his shoulder, looking for ghosts.

"The blow crushed her skull," Julian murmured grimly. "What happened then?"

"This lady ran away. Then you came, yer lordship. And this *rye*—this gentleman—I saw 'im also. My wife an' me, we brushed off then. We didn't want no part of it."

There was a long silence.

Then Rachel tossed her head, making the ostrich feather in her bonnet quiver. "I have never heard such utter nonsense! I won't stay another minute and listen to these scurrilous lies."

As she turned away, though, her brother reached out and caught her arm. "One moment, Rachel. These are serious charges. I wish to hear what you have to say."

Shaking off his grasp, she gave him a fierce scowl. "*Say?* Say about what, pray tell? You aren't possibly suggesting I defend myself against these lies?"

"Are they lies?"

"Of course they are!"

Vincent hesitated. "Do you deny being here that day?"

"Of course I deny it!" When he remained skeptically silent, she glowered at him. "You mean to believe the word of a dirty *Gypsy* over mine?"

"What reason would he have to claim such a story?"

"How should I know? Perhaps someone put him up to it. Perhaps this common chit—" She sent Blaise a venomous look. "*You!*" she hissed. "You bribed him to make this outrageous claim."

"No," Blaise said quietly. "Sandor came to me. He had the courage to tell the truth. As should you, Miss Foster."

Rachel took a step toward Blaise, her gloved hand raised as if to strike, but Julian intervened by moving between them. "Don't even think it."

At his harsh warning, Rachel gave a sharp laugh, one tinged with an edge of hysteria. "No, no, of course not! You wouldn't want any harm to come to your precious wife! You only condone murder—"

"Rachel!" Vincent said sharply. "That is quite enough!"

She turned on her brother. "Enough? What would you know, you fool! If you hadn't gone panting after

Caroline's skirts, none of this would have happened."

"What do you mean . . . none of what would have happened?"

"Caroline's death. It was your fault as much as anyone's. My *brother*, who had no more sense than a village idiot. You were a fool, Vincent, for letting her drag you into a ruinous affair. Caroline never cared the least fig about you. She only used you."

"So you killed her?"

"I didn't kill her! Julian did! You know that!"

"I thought I did, but now . . . I'm not so certain. Perhaps you had a hand in it."

"I didn't kill her! It was an accident—" Rachel broke off with a horrified look.

"It was an *accident*?" Vincent's voice was tight, raw. "How would you know unless you saw her fall?"

She refused to reply.

"You were here that day, weren't you? You caused Caroline to fall from her horse."

"No." Wildly Rachel looked around her, at the sober faces. "No, it isn't what you think! It didn't happen that way!"

"Then how *did* it happen? Did you throw a stone at her horse, as this man says?"

"No! No—"

"Don't lie to me, Rachel."

"All right, yes! I was here, but it was an accident! I swear it!"

"Why? Dear God, *why?*" The bewildered anguish in Vincent's tone echoed loudly in the silence.

"Because—" Rachel's quivering voice broke. "I only wanted to protect you, Vincent, you must believe me." Her shrill voice turned pleading. "I thought if I confronted Caroline, I could put an end to your affair. I saw her message to you that day, asking you to meet her at the ruins. But I arrived here first. We did argue, I admit that. I was furious at Caroline for leading you on, for stealing Julian from me. But her fall was an accident, I swear it. She tried to run me down . . . The rain . . . the ground was slick and her horse reared . . . I never meant for her to *die*!" Rachel was sobbing now, tears streaming down her cheeks in ugly rivulets.

Vincent looked stunned, as if he'd taken a sudden blow between the eyes. "All this time . . . you've allowed me to accuse Julian of murder . . . you *helped* me to blacken his name . . ."

"He deserved it! I should have been Lady Lynden! I! Not that whey-faced, selfish little flirt Caroline. But he chose her instead."

Rachel was sobbing in earnest now, her gloved hands covering her face. When she sank to her knees, no one stepped forward to aid her.

The observers watched her with varying degrees of pity. Blaise offered up a silent prayer of thanks. Perhaps now Julian would finally cease blaming himself for the tragedy of Caroline's death.

When Blaise spoke, though, it was to Vincent. "All this time you blamed Julian, but you should have looked closer to home for the culprit."

Vincent shook his head, as if he still couldn't quite believe his sister's confession. Finally he met Julian's gaze. "It seems I owe you an apology. I've thought you a murderer all these years." He gave a bitter laugh. "My own sister." With obvious effort he seemed to collect himself. "I hope . . . someday you can come to forgive us."

Julian ran a weary hand over his forehead, not responding.

"What do you mean to do?" Vincent asked.

"I haven't considered yet."

"I know I have no right to ask . . . but I would be grateful if you would perhaps keep this quiet for a few days, at least until we leave the country. I think it best if I take my sister abroad for a time."

Julian nodded slowly. "I see no need to dredge up the scandal again. It would serve no purpose. My reputation is already tarnished, but I see no reason to destroy your sister's. It is enough that I know the truth."

Blaise opened her mouth to protest, but then bit her tongue. She wanted Julian's name vindicated, but now was not the time to argue with his notions of honor. She watched as he signaled the Lynden coachman, who immediately took up the reins and drove the carriage back across the field, coming to a halt before them.

"Grimes, please take Miss Foster home," Julian commanded quietly.

Vincent, looking infinitely sad, helped the sobbing Rachel to her feet and handed her inside. She seemed limp, crumpled, like a spineless rag doll.

Before climbing in after her, though, he turned back to Julian. "I've been a blind fool, I realize that now. I allowed my bitterness to destroy our friendship. And I'm sorry for that. And for suggesting an untruth." He glanced at Blaise. "I lied to you, Julian. I never so much as looked at your wife—this Lady Lynden. You're as much a fool as I if you don't realize she loves you."

With that he climbed inside and shut the door softly behind him.

As the carriage drove off, Blaise held her breath, waiting for Julian's response. But he didn't even look at her. Instead he grimly thanked Sandor Lee for coming forward with the truth and promised a reward. Then he turned a quelling eye on her Gypsy friend Miklos. "As for you, I think it is time you left. I shall deal with you later."

Miklos glanced at his wagon, the one he had used to transport Lord Lynden forcibly from London. "But m'lord, my wagon—"

"Beware, Mr. Smith, don't press me too far. I still haven't made up my mind whether to send you to Australia for an extended visit." He let that sink in. "It would serve you right to have to forfeit your wagon, but I'll consider the matter later. Just now I wish to be alone with my wife."

Blaise's heart suddenly began an erratic pounding, while her stomach clenched. Afraid to be left alone with her grim-faced husband, she cast a pleading glance at

Miklos. But both Gypsies were climbing up on Sandor's horse. And in all too short a time they had departed, riding across the field to disappear behind the elms, leaving her alone with Julian.

She gave him a fearful glance. He was leaning once more against the back of the Gypsy wagon, his arms folded over his chest, his jaw hard and set.

"Come here, Blaise," he commanded silkily, his voice resonating with menace.

Blaise eyed him warily—and remained exactly where she was. "Julian, please, you don't want to do anything rash—"

"I won't tell you again, sweeting. Come here. We have a few crucial issues to settle, wouldn't you say?"

Chapter 25

Hiding her hands behind her back like a guilty child,
Blaise glanced helplessly across the field, where
Miklos had disappeared.

"Don't bother calling for aid," Julian warned. "Your
cohorts in crime won't save you."

Blaise swallowed hard. "Are you very angry with
me?"

"What do you think?"

"I'm sorry for what I did Julian, but you see—"

"*Blaise* . . ." He trailed the word out threateningly.

"You . . . won't do anything violent?"

"I might. I will, if you don't come here this instant."

She forced her feet to move. Step by slow step, she
closed the distance between them, till she stood a scant
yard away.

"Closer." His voice had lowered slightly. Had it also
softened? she wondered hopefully.

She took the final steps, halting directly before Julian.
The disreputable stubble on his jaw did nothing to lessen
his air of menace, and she found herself nervously
clenching her gloved hands together as she looked up at
him warily. Something predatory showed in the narrowed
blue eyes, in the curved sensual line of his mouth. His
gaze was hard and penetrating—yet at the same time
intently searched her face, as if drinking her in.

Then he reached for her.

Blaise flinched involuntarily, but instead of wrapping
his fingers around her throat as she expected, Julian
twined them in the ribbons of her bonnet and tugged.

Her eyes widened as he drew the bonnet from her head
and tossed it carelessly on the ground. Then he began to
remove the pins from her stylish coiffure.

"What are you *doing*?" Blaise asked with a measure
of alarm.

"I'm punishing you."

His cryptic answer did nothing to reassure her, or
clarify why he needed to take down her hair in order
to punish her.

"Julian, please . . . I can explain . . ."

"I'm not interested in your explanations."

He tossed away the final pins and let the ebony cas-
cade fall down her back. His piercing gaze held hers as
he captured her face in his hands, his palms framing her
jawline.

"You have every right to be angry with me, Julian,
but you see, I was *desperate*—"

"Shut up, you infuriating brat . . ."

His mouth descended on hers then. Hard and compelling, he kissed her, his lips rough, urgent, punishing.
Ruthlessly his mouth parted her lips, his thrusting tongue
forcing its way inside. His hands clenched in her hair,
holding her prisoner.

Yet to her startlement and immense relief, his fierce
plundering was more hungry than vengeful. Her body
leaped in response, and Blaise shuddered with longing. After Julian's long weeks of absence, she was
just as hungry for him. The sharp, relentless ache of
desire flared inside her, feeding the memory of other
intense moments of passion they had once shared.
Blaise let out a soft moan as she clutched at his
shoulders.

Abruptly Julian drew back. His eyes smoldered, not
with anger but with heat—a heat that had somehow trans-
ferred itself to her.

Without a word, Julian grasped her by the elbow and
propelled her around to the front of the wagon, where
he shoved aside the canvas flap behind the peacefully grazing horses. Then, in a single swift motion, he

bent and caught Blaise up in his arms and lifted her inside.

The interior was dim except for the light from a high, small window. Julian allowed no time for her eyes to adjust, though, but climbed in after her and lowered the canvas flap, shutting them inside. His greatcoat slid from his shoulders as he pushed Blaise to the straw mattress and turned her onto her back.

She gasped in surprise, yet before she could recover her wits, he had followed her down, his lithe body covering her. She could feel distinctly the hard, full pressure of his arousal through their clothing.

His elbows planted on either side of her shoulders, Julian dug his fingers into her hair. His chiseled face was hard and impassive, but his eyes were alive with burning emotion.

"I lay here," he muttered, his voice low and thick, "for twelve hours, planning exactly what I would do to you when I got my hands on you. And now I have you."

He intended to take her right there, right then, Blaise realized with shocked comprehension. Her mouth went dry, while excitement pounded in the pit of her stomach, tightening every muscle in her body.

Then he kissed her again. His mouth, wild and rough, sank into hers, filling her with the hot, searching stab of his tongue that followed the motion of his hips. The stubble on his jaw scraped her soft skin, but she didn't care. He showed her no tenderness, but she wanted none. She simply wanted him. If this was to be her punishment, then she would gladly, gladly suffer it. She wanted him, wanted this . . .

She uttered not a single moan of protest when he shoved her skirts to her waist and bared her naked loins; instead she helped him shamelessly. She felt his hand rake the curve of her hip, the flat plane of her belly, then move to the silkiness of her crotch. With a whimper of delight, Blaise let her hips arch wildly against his probing fingers.

Almost as if he wanted to torment her, Julian suddenly broke off his kiss and raised his head. His eyes glittered with barely controlled passion as he moved his fingers between her legs, raking the ebony pelt there, probing the feminine cleft, finding the hot, aching bud hidden by her velvety folds.

Breathing hard, his face taut, he watched her start and shiver under his touch. He stroked her roughly, deliberately arousing. And at each rough brush of his fingers against her silky skin, she shuddered.

Unable to wait any longer, he shifted his hand to the thick bulge at his groin. Feverishly he unbuttoned the front flaps of his breeches and smallclothes to free his rigid manhood, which jutted from a nest of downy, dark gold hair. Then his hands positioned her legs apart, ready for him.

"I want to be inside you." His tone was hard, uncompromising, while his eyes had darkened to a midnight shade.

Blaise felt the surging, hard, silky flesh brush her inner thigh and made a soft whimpering sound of need. "Yes . . . please . . ." She reached for him, almost sobbing with longing. Her flesh clamored for release, throbbed with heat.

Spreading her thighs farther apart, Julian lowered himself onto her and thrust heavily inside her. She was fully, slickly ready for him. Gritting his teeth against the ache in his leg, he sank deeper, deeper into her, going as deep as he could with a single powerful thrust. "Take me . . . all of me . . ."

Blaise gasped as she fully absorbed his hard length. The sudden assault of his maleness on her senses took her breath away; the hard stretching pressure of his invasion was a shock so intensely pleasurable that she nearly screamed with it. She could feel him huge and hard inside her, filling up every inch of her, possessive and commanding.

And then he seemed to lose all control. With a rough sound of passion, Julian exploded against her, his thrusts driving deep and hard, carrying him into her to the hilt, his groin grinding against hers. There was nothing gentlemanly about him now, only the need to take her, to sate himself after the long bleak days of separation.

Yet Blaise responded with equal passion; her body wanted him wildly, savagely. She sank her nails into his back and clung to him as he pounded into her, meeting the driving need of his body without restraint.

Their breaths came in harsh gasps as they strained together in frenzied pleasure, their coupling raw, primitive, carnal. In only a moment she cried out in shattering release. An instant later his hips jerked in the spasms of completion, his surging climax pumping hotly into her.

When it was over, they lay there, still joined, still vibrating with powerful aftershocks. Blaise closed her eyes in ecstasy. Her whole body quivered with sated warmth. She heard Julian draw a long ragged breath, felt him bury his face in the hot flushed skin of her throat. She cradled him gladly, her fingers tangling in the soft golden curls of his hair, holding him close.

His voice, when he spoke, was raw and husky. "I've been going mad, wanting you."

Her mouth curved in an uncertain smile. "I was afraid you hated me."

"I should, you little wretch."

"Julian . . . I'm sorry, truly—"

"Don't try to cozen me, minx," he muttered dryly in her ear. "You're preening over the success of your scheme, admit it."

"Well, I think I deserve to preen just a little. It *did* turn out just as I had hoped."

Julian tried to repress a reluctant chuckle, but Blaise heard it, and her hopes soared. Perhaps she hadn't destroyed her marriage after all.

"I suppose you orchestrated Rachel's confession?" Her husband sounded more resigned than disapproving.

"Yes, but it wasn't easy, let me tell you. Mr. Foster nearly overset all my plans. He wouldn't accompany me, even when I threatened to shoot him. And he *had* to come. Otherwise, Miss Foster might have continued to deny her involvement in Caroline's accident."

"You threatened to shoot Vincent Foster?" Julian's choked laughter teased her ear as he buried his face in her raven tresses.

"I had no choice. But it didn't succeed—he's even more stubborn than you are. But I was quite determined. And in the end, he proved no match for me."

Julian eased his body off her and settled beside her, saying unsteadily, "No, Vincent is certainly not up to your weight."

The air was chilly inside the wagon. Solicitously Julian pushed down the hem of Blaise's skirts to cover her slender bare thighs and drew a blanket over them both. Quite naturally, she nestled her head in the curve of his shoulder.

"I only did it for your sake, Julian. Even if you hated me forever, you had to know the truth about Caroline— so you would stop blaming yourself."

He heaved a sigh as he toyed with a black lock of her hair. He couldn't absolve himself totally of his first wife's death, yet the burden of guilt that had weighed him down for so long had lifted. It was one more thing for which he owed Blaise his gratitude. Yet to admit it would only encourage her. He compromised. "It pains me to say it, minx, but your scheme worked."

With a contented murmur, Blaise snuggled closer to him.

"There is, however, still the minor matter of my forcible removal from London to be dealt with."

"Yes, well . . ." Blaise said meekly. "Really, Julian, I think you might be grateful to me."

"*Grateful?*" Julian lifted his head to fix her with a baleful eye. "I spend the past dozen hours trussed up like a Christmas goose, in this godforsaken rattletrap, with perhaps two hours' sleep, while my thigh tightens up like wet rawhide, and you expect me to be *grateful*?"

"But I already apologized for that. And I am truly sorry about your leg," she said fervently. "I never meant for it to be hurt. Indeed, I told Miklos to ensure your every comfort. But I simply *had* to take drastic action. You wouldn't reply to any of my letters, and I had no idea when, or even if, you would ever come home—"

"I planned to set out today."

"You did? You really meant to return home?" She stared at him blankly. "Well, I didn't know that. And I was *desperate*."

"You are always desperate. But that doesn't excuse your disobedience. As memory serves, you swore to me that you would behave. Threatening to shoot my neighbors does not precisely fall under the category of 'propriety and decorum.' "

Blaise looked repentant. "I didn't think you read any of my letters."

"I did, fool that I am. I should have consigned them all to the fire."

"I'll massage your leg, if you wish."

"Perhaps later. Just now I want to make certain you heed my warning. The next time you dare even *think* of concocting one of your schemes, sweeting, I'll afford you the punishment my father was fond of when I was in short coats—a sturdy birch rod. You won't be able to sit down for a week, I promise you."

"But, Julian, my intentions were good. What if—"

"No! I don't give a bloody damn how good your intentions are, I won't countenance any more of your machinations, do you understand me?"

"Yes, of course, Julian."

Her meek tone didn't fool him for a moment. Julian eyed Blaise narrowly, torn between exasperation and the fierce desire to kiss her breathless. "Why do I have the distinct feeling you haven't fathomed a word I've said?"

"But I have, Julian, and you have my promise, I swear it! I'll never, *never* disobey you again."

"Until the next time I refuse to grant you your way," he said dryly.

"Do you think . . . will you ever forgive me?"

"I expect so . . . *if* in the future you will attempt to confine your scandalous behavior to our bedroom."

"Then . . ." She hesitated, giving him an uncertain glance. "You mean to give me another chance?" she asked in a small voice. "You won't send me away?"

Something twisted in his chest, making it difficult for him to breathe. His blue eyes turned entirely serious as he took care answering. "Yes, if you'll allow *me* another chance, Blaise. I owe you an apology, as well. I behaved abominably, jumping to conclusions and accusing you of adultery."

"You *did* misunderstand. How could you possibly think I would take up with Vincent Foster? I *love* you. I would never be unfaithful to you."

"I realize that."

"I tried to tell you that before you left, but you wouldn't believe me."

"I know, and I was wrong."

"I am not *Caroline*," Blaise said indignantly.

He smiled at her tone, but managed to say soothingly, "I know, sweeting. You are nothing at all alike. Caroline would never have placed herself in the path of a bullet meant for me."

"I didn't want you to be shot. I love you, Julian, you should know that by now. I just wish . . ."

"Wish what?"

"That you could love me in return."

Julian lay back, staring up at the canvas roof. If he had been at all unsure of his feelings for Blaise, the long separation had convinced him where his heart lay. He couldn't imagine facing the future without her. She had filled up all the dark and empty places in his soul. "I do love you, minx."

Abruptly she raised herself up on one elbow, peering at him in the dim light. "You really mean it? You love me?"

"To distraction." His lips curved ruefully. "Can't you tell? I assure you, I wouldn't suffer such affliction from anyone else."

Her radiant smile made it seem as if the sun had suddenly begun to shine within the small wagon. Tenderly, he drew her down against him, holding her close, but Blaise apparently needed verbal as well as physical reassurance.

"You truly don't regret being forced to marry me?"

"Regret it?" Thoughtfully he pressed his lips to her forehead. "No. Perhaps at first I did. I resented you for making me feel. Certainly I didn't want to love you. I fought it at every turn. But I discovered I couldn't help myself."

Inordinately pleased, Blaise rubbed her face into the hollow of his throat, seeking his warm, heady male scent. "I didn't want to love you, either. I thought you were a cold-fish Englishman like my stepfather."

Julian winced.

"And I didn't want a marriage of convenience. I think they're horrid."

"We don't have a marriage of convenience. We have a marriage of *inconvenience*."

"Do you really mean that?"

The hurt in her voice jolted him. Tightening his arms around her, he squeezed threateningly. "Yes, I mean that, you enchanting little torment—and I wouldn't change it for the world—even if I could, which I doubt is possible. I expect Panna would say you and I are fated to be together."

"You don't have to be stuck with me," she said hollowly. "I could always go live with my Aunt Agnes—"

"Hush, idiot. I love you, Blaise, and I'm not letting you go. Never. I'd sooner cut out my heart." He held her away and smiled. "Which would be foolish, considering that I just got it back." His voice softened. "These past fours years, I've felt as if my soul were missing. You helped me find it again. You brought me back from the dead."

Blaise shuddered as she realized how close she had come to losing Julian. "I just wanted you to stop blaming yourself."

"I have . . . I will. That's all in the past now. In fact . . . what do you say we begin anew, sweeting? From this day onward, we start fresh."

"Oh, Julian . . ." Her violet eyes sparkled with happiness. "I would like that above all things." She fell silent a moment. "I know! I have a splendid idea—we can repeat our vows in the Gypsy fashion. I'm certain Miklos wouldn't object. Gypsies love a celebration."

Julian didn't find much to favor in the suggestion, but he didn't reject it outright. "We'll see."

Lazily he glanced up at the small window, gauging the remaining daylight. "I suppose I should send a message to Will Terral in London. He'll be concerned that I never returned home last night. When I was wounded, Will appointed himself chief mother hen, and he only relinquished his duties to you—and you weren't there. He didn't approve of my abandoning you, by the by. His scowling face these past weeks was enough to drive me to drink."

"He is only worried about you."

"I know. It wouldn't surprise me to learn he's called out the Bow Street Runners at my disappearance." Julian gave a shuddering laugh at the thought. "Faith, I hope this story doesn't get bruited about town. I'll never live it down. No one would understand how a war hero came to be abducted by his wife and her Gypsy henchman."

"You wouldn't really have Miklos transported, would you?"

"I haven't made up my mind."

"Julian, *please?* He only did what I asked."

"He should have known better than to listen to you." Beneath the blanket, Julian flexed the knuckles of his right hand in satisfaction. "I must say I took great pleasure in planting him a facer."

"You didn't! That was rather poor-spirited of you."

Her husband made a sound much like a grunt. "He deserved far worse. As do you. I still haven't settled on a fitting punishment."

"I think I like this one."

"Indeed?" Julian turned onto his side, facing her. "Then by all means we should continue." Purposefully he tugged off her pelisse and her gloves. Then slowly he began the delicate task of unfastening the hooks and tapes of her clothing, as usual turning her disrobing into an exercise in sensual pleasure.

Prevented from helping, Blaise spoke as he worked. "I should like to go to London with you some day, if you wouldn't mind."

"I might risk it. I suppose I should give them fair warning first—take out advertisements in all the papers perhaps, announcing your arrival. I doubt you would be there two minutes before you set London on its ear."

"Well, at least I would be where I could compete with your London mistress."

He caught the uncertain, probing note in her voice. "I don't have a London mistress, Blaise. I don't have any kind of mistress, and I don't want one."

"You don't?"

"Absolutely not. I haven't so much as *thought* of another woman since I met you. Why would I, when I have you?"

"Truly?"

"Truly."

She smiled in fervent relief. Then her eyes suddenly widened as she recalled his earlier words. "You really meant to return home today? To *me*?"

"Yes, sweeting. Only to you. No one else."

By now he had bared her breasts. His hungry gaze moved over her, lingering on the pale sweet mounds with the rosy areolae and budded nipples. He reached out to stroke her. His palm barely brushed her nipple and she arched her back in ecstasy.

His lips curved in a sensual smile at Blaise's reaction. Her breathing had changed, going more shallow, while a delicate flush warmed her skin.

"Julian . . ."

He ignored her plea. His fingers toying with her, he fondled her breasts, caressing them with both hands.

"You have a perfect genius for causing trouble."

A breathless moan was her response. "I try, Julian . . . truly I do, but you must know by now it is hopeless."

He knew that was true. Extracting promises of good behavior from Blaise was one thing, but expecting her to keep them was entirely another. Like trying to capture fairy dust, it simply wasn't possible.

He shook his head sadly. "What am I to do with you?"

Her violet eyes misted as she pulled his head down, seeking his lips. "Just love me . . ."

Julian felt his loins tighten and swell. He wanted her slender legs clasping him, her body sheathing him, the wild sweetness of her body beneath him—or above him, it mattered not. He simply wanted her.

Suddenly his body throbbed. He couldn't bear to be separated from her even for the time it required to finish removing her gown. Swiftly he moved over her, spreading her thighs to mount her.

"Julian, your leg . . ."

"My leg be damned. I want you."

He watched the way her face changed as he slowly eased into her, watched the radiance that lit her features as her body softened and warmed around him.

"Oh . . . Julian . . ." Her voice was breathless, reverent, adoring.

"My lady of fire . . . I love you . . ."

Blaise sighed, feeling her heart soar with hope and contentment at his tender expression. She had never seen Julian's eyes so intensely blue, so full of love, so entirely at peace. Her beautiful, scarred nobleman had at last conquered the ghosts of his past. And he would find joy in his future, if she had anything at all to say in the matter.

Epilogue

With enraptured eyes, he watched the raven-haired beauty dance in the firelight, his carnal hunger heightened by the joyful knowledge that she belonged solely to him. Blaise was his wife now, in heart and spirit, as well as in name.

Julian, Lord Lynden rested against an oak log, captivated by the sight. She was radiant, glowing with energy, her fair skin luminous in the red-gold light of the Gypsy campfire.

She danced only for him, her violet eyes flashing, her lips parted in breathless exertion, her gaze turned to him as if only the two of them existed in the world. She whirled and leaped and spun to the cadence of the violins and tambourines, arms stretched overhead, feet stamping rhythmically to the wild music, slender hips swaying, colorful skirts flaring.

His maddening, bewitching Gypsy wench. His love. His lady of fire.

Because of his healing thigh, he had managed to avoid the dancing, but Julian was content to watch, breathing in the chill, smoke-scented night air, sipping mulled wine, savoring the simple pleasures of Gypsy life. His senses hummed and throbbed to the alternately haunting, then frenzied strains of a Gypsy love song. He felt incredibly alive—and incredibly fortunate to have found Blaise. How barren his life would have been had he never stumbled across her in the posting inn in Ware, never pursued her along the byways of the English countryside, never been compelled to wed her. Even her outrageous misdeeds had no power to diminish his love for her.

He had taken his revenge for his abduction by imprisoning Blaise naked in his bedchamber for three entire delicious days. It had been a time of sensual exploration and carnal satisfaction. They'd scarcely left the bed, indulging their heated passions till they were temporarily sated, slipping into exhausted slumber, and waking to make love again.

This was their wedding celebration. At a repentant Miklos's invitation, they had repeated their wedding vows a short while ago, this time in true Gypsy fashion.

According to custom, Blaise had spent the previous night in Panna's tent, and Julian had been unable to see her until the wedding. When it came time to collect his bride, he had to pretend to capture her, with the entire tribe looking on, laughing and shouting encouragements.

Miklos, as chief, acted as priest, but there was no formal ceremony. The bridal pair had merely to pledge their troth and step over a broom, and the thing was done. Panna had consecrated the marriage then by sprinkling a handful of salt over the broken halves of a bread loaf. Bride and groom exchanged the halves with each other, ate a few bites, and washed them down with wine. Afterward they received wishes of luck, and then the dancing and feasting and noise began.

For the Gypsies, a wedding was a great social occasion that often lasted for several days, although in this instance, since Lord and Lady Lynden were merely honorary Rom, the affair would end tomorrow. The Gypsies had stewed a whole sheep, however, and there was plenty of wine and ale to go around, courtesy of the Lynden cellars. Later that evening the couple would consummate their marriage in a bridal tent. The night was cold enough to frost the breath, but Julian intended their passion to keep them warm.

He was contemplating that pleasurable event with

anticipation when Miklos came to sit beside him on the log.

" 'Tis a fine night for love, m'lord."

Julian's lips curved in agreement, but he made no reply, feeling no need to restate the obvious.

"I 'ope . . . that you've forgiven me for my little transgression of the other day."

Looking up, Julian eyed him narrowly. "Forgiven, but not forgotten."

"Aye, not forgotten." The Gypsy gingerly rubbed his sore jaw and the tender bruise where Julian had floored him. "You've a mean right, m'lord."

"You'll do well to remember it."

"Indeed I will. And for sure, you won't 'ave to worry about us outstaying our welcome. We'll take our leave by the end of the week, you have me word. We poor Rom know when we're not wanted."

Julian's mouth twisted wryly at Miklos's unconvincing imitation of humility. "Doing it too brown, my friend. You're welcome to return in due time, as you well know . . . Preferably next spring. Perhaps by then Blaise will have shed some of your rascally influence."

"And mayhap there'll be a fine son on the way."

Julian grinned appreciatively at the thought.

"I've no fear leaving 'er in your 'ands. Ye'll be good to our Rauniyog."

Panna shuffled up to them then and slowly lowered herself onto the log, settling on Julian's other side. Her white teeth flashing, she peered at him with her sharp black eyes. "Shall I read yer fortune, me fine lord? Would you care to know whether yer firstborn will be a son or a daughter?"

"If you don't mind, I prefer that you allow me the pleasure of guessing."

Glancing toward the campfire where Blaise danced, Panna grinned in satisfaction. "It doesn't take the cards to ken where yer 'appiness lies."

"No," he murmured, his expression softening with love. "There's no doubt at all."

"Not that your future will be all rosy. She'll lead you on a merry chase, mark my words. You'll no longer even be master in your own home."

"Allow me my illusions, Mother, I beg you," Julian said dryly.

Panna threw back her kerchiefed head and cackled, a raucous sound that carried in the relative silence since the music had just ended.

Blaise, still breathless from the dancing, joined their circle. "What are you laughing about?"

Rising to his feet, Julian caught her around the waist and drew her tenderly into his arms. "You, minx. Panna predicts that you will be the bane of my existence, but says that I should resign myself to my fate."

Blaise looked up into Julian's warm, dazzlingly blue eyes—and smiled. "You shouldn't find it too burdensome, as long as you love me."

"I'll always love you, minx."

Her heart full, her eyes glowing with happiness, Blaise reached up to stroke her husband's scarred cheek. She felt his avowal of love more binding than either of the oaths, *gorgio* or Gypsy, that had made them husband and wife. And Julian's love was all and more than she would ever want.